FINDING PEDDIE
IN A STATE OF GRACE

FINDING PEDDIE IN A STATE OF GRACE

A Novel

EAMON KOLARITY

iUniverse, Inc.
New York Lincoln Shanghai

FINDING PEDDIE IN A STATE OF GRACE

iUniverse books may be ordered through booksellers or by contacting:

iUniverse
2021 Pine Lake Road, Suite 100
Lincoln, NE 68512
www.iuniverse.com
1-800-Authors (1-800-288-4677)

This is a work of fiction. All of the characters, names, incidents, organizations and dialogue in this novel are either the products of the author's imagination or are used fictitiously.

ISBN-13: 978-0-595-39462-3 (pbk)
ISBN-13: 978-0-595-67711-5 (cloth)
ISBN-13: 978-0-595-83860-8 (ebk)
ISBN-10: 0-595-39462-0 (pbk)
ISBN-10: 0-595-67711-8 (cloth)
ISBN-10: 0-595-83860-X (ebk)

Printed in the United States of America

For Lauren (aka Lolly & Little Lou)
who put up with the hours

CHAPTER 1

▼

Boys will be boys. Too bad the same can't be said of men. Naturally it takes all kinds to make a village. There's the town drunk, the village idiot, and maybe more than one garden variety of pervert. I am cultivating the garden, making a pest of myself. But the good people of Santa Fe don't know the real me yet, that I'm here, in their own backyard. I'm not sure when to announce myself.

The teachers during recess think they know me. I am respectable enough and welcomed often in genteel circles. The girls and boys swirl in innocent delirium around the adults, though I can remember the heartless cruelty of childhood. Child's play releases raw energy but that can go either way, a good thing or bad. Cruel, as I say. I'm given to pay more attention to the boys. Reckless boys, with more true emotions at play. Girls show more feelings in repose, just chatting away. I find boys choke up over words. They want to pound flesh. I look upon the boys playing with abandon and wonder which one.

*   *   *   *

Preach to one person at a time, the priest had learned. Make the faithful feel the homily is a personal God bending their ear. But even people of faith have changed with the times. If a preacher rip-roars today a cautionary tale of mortal sin and eternal despair, the stern words are discounted as the rantings of a punishing God. Hell has morphed from open sores and everlasting moans into a lonely place of opportunities lost and love denied.

Father Andy Leary suppressed a smile as he deliberately, in solemn ceremony and fine vestments, rose to deliver the Palm Sunday homily in Santa Fe, New Mexico. He usually opened with a mild witticism, to loosen up the flock, but today's topic was no laughing matter. One of their own was missing. A boy, Pedro Martinez, gone now four days and counting. Ten years old, seemingly too young to runaway that long. Father Andy knew Peddie (as the boy was called) in passing, a beautiful child amongst so many in the parish. On certain Sundays the young children gathered around the altar, angelic faces upturned, to be asked gentle questions by their spiritual father. Peddie always raised his hand, waving it with unbridled enthusiasm. I have the answer, Father Andy, call upon me, me!

Public safety workers and community volunteers have been combing the parched arroyos and pinon scrub lands in the vicinity of the last sighting. No sign of Peddie. Registered pedophiles in supposed remission were being questioned. Family members held a tearful press conference begging for Peddie's return, that whoever has him could drop off the boy no questions asked if no harm done. The congregation expected the Church to respond. Father's Andy's sermon this Palm Sunday in the year of the Lord 2002 could only provide a partial answer to the faithful's prayers.

Father Andy looked out at his flock and wished he could command the stage through force of personality alone. Without my vestments I am nothing. Am I as good a man in secular cloth? Many priests were going out into society without the Roman collar or a monk's robe. Certainly most nuns, except for the cloistered orders, were going about the Lord's work anonymously, in plain clothes, looking like Amish women. The only things missing from the picture were the buggy and bearded man. Father Andy never left the rectory without his uniform. Being a Franciscan friar, he wore a humble brown robe. He wanted to be recognized near and far as a man of God.

Andy was a short man, 5 feet 7 inches, fast closing on forty, showing the signs of middle-aged belt-loosening that the loose robe helped to disguise. He had a full head of reddish brown hair and a neatly trimmed beard lightly peppered with gray. The priest grew the beard to hide a double chin. He had a face given to blushing for no reason. It was his Irish heritage, he assumed, the fair skin and sour shame rising so easily to the surface.

The priest paused as always before preaching. He looked up at the large stained glass window that faced east towards the rising sun. The rainbow light streamed down, casting sacred hues onto God's messenger. Andy liked to bask in the reflection of Mary's agonized countenance as she embraced her Son's broken body at the foot of the Cross. The priest had heard that there was a contentious debate many years ago whether the new church should feature a depiction of Christ's Ascension instead. The parish council—heavily Hispanic—voted for the morbid image and the pastor concurred. Consecrated gore found favor in Spanish worship.

Father Andy moved out from under the rainbow of grief. It was time to call the faithful to the colors:

> My brothers and sisters in Christ, our community of faith has been tested by one of our own, one of our precious children, missing from his home. I know Peddie, many of you know Peddie Martinez, a wonderful boy full of the joyous spirit and spontaneous energy that we adults envy in our children. We pray for the boy's return but we must do more than that—we must do everything possible to return him to the warm embrace of his family.

Andy paused again and gazed at Peddie's mother and sister sitting in the front pew. Mrs. Martinez was always involved in decorating the sanctuary for the liturgical seasons, her specialty being flower arrangements. Amelia came across as a subdued woman with an aura of sadness even during the best of times. Now she looked in her mourning clothes…well, like death warmed over. But the promise of joyful reunion was there too, a sprig of yellow flower, pinned on her black dress. Many others had similar flowers or ribbons of solidarity and hope.

The priest had to look away before his eyes misted over. As much as he desired ethereal control, this moment threatened to overwhelm him. But Andy wasn't certain if the feeling was rooted in real concern, or was it simply show time. He so wanted his feelings to be pure. As he scanned the faithful in the pews, the faces reflected appropriate anxiety. This was no time to preach doom and gloom. There was no evidence that the boy was dead or even in dire distress. Peddie was just gone, period, somewhere or other. A priest must offer eternal hope, not pile on terminal despair.

The phrase, preaching to the choir, suddenly leaped to mind and almost made him laugh. An absurd impulse given the occasion; silly season in the face of fear. What kind of man am I? Why do I want to smile on the outside while crying on the inside?

But then the friar's self-absorption was brought up short by a grinning face in the crowd. In the back, someone he recognized, Ray, yes, Ray, that's the name, right, not sure of the last name, pencil thin, very tall mustached Hispanic fellow with slick black hair. Ray was active in the parish, a parochial school mentor, tutoring children with academic deficiencies. He and the priest had crossed paths on occasion over the years at the Little Flower parish, Santo Thérèse las Pequeño Flor.

The priest wanted to wipe the smile off the man's face. How dare Ray grin, showing such mocking disrespect to a dreading mother? What words would bring this raggedy man back to his senses?

> We live in troubling times. Our children are not safe. Many of us remember an age when everybody knew everybody else, and doors were left open to those in need. Our children could play outside without a care in the world. Truly, just as palms were laid on the path of Christ entering Jerusalem, so too our children's path through life should be cushioned by the loving care of adults. Sadly, now, even the most trusted caregivers have fallen prey to base desire. We pray to God, we appeal to the Holy Trinity, that we return to a state of grace, a state of compassion, a state of being that will keep the wolf at the door and the Lamb in our hearts.

Ray nodded at the friar's reflections but still his expression bothered Andy deeply. There was something there grossly out of place. The priest shivered suddenly with a horrid intuition. It couldn't be, no, no way—but anything's possible! The priest had read enough crime fiction to know that detectives went to funerals because the killer may be there to pay his last, well, respects is not the right word. The police scanned crowds at crime scenes in hopes that the bad guy would be revisiting. But the santuario was not a crime scene and this Mass wasn't funereal. Surely rank evil wouldn't be lurking in this sacred place. Pray God that Peddie didn't fall victim to a respected member of the parish. But most child abductions are not perpetuated by strangers in the night, but rather by the nice man next door whose true nature we never knew.

Father Andy shook himself to clear his head. His eyes focused on Ray again but then looked beyond to seek divine inspiration in the rays of light filtering through the sacred stain.

> We as a community of faith cannot go about our business or sit idly by as long as Peddie is missing. The police need our help and I bless each and everyone who give of themselves. Let us now have a moment of silent prayer for the boy and his family, and then let's get out there and find the child. Go out to love and serve the Lord. By finding Peddie!

Brothers and sisters in Christ, a few moments of quiet prayer and reflection.

The priest returned to his chair and bowed his head. But his mind raced rather than reflected. God expected action from His priest. What was God's will and how do I abide by it?

*   *   *   *

A few minutes later, at communion, passing out the Eucharist to the faithful in line, the priest stole a glance to the back pew where Ray lurked. He was half expecting the silly man to be sitting or kneeling with head bowed while those without mortal sin received the Body and Blood of Christ. That self-denial would be playing by the rules of the Catholic game. Andy remembered from his youth that the poor souls who abstained were targets of idle speculation: what great sin did they commit? Mere venial sins—lust, for example, confined to the mind and not spreading to other organs—wouldn't be cause for denying yourself communion with God. But Ray wasn't there anymore; he must have snuck out. The priest's attention came back front and center to the remaining parishioners in line. And there was Ray at the very end! The priest exclaimed, "Sweet Jesus!" instead of the pro forma murmur, "Body of Christ," that the woman before him was expecting. The woman gave him a curious look as the priest placed the quivering wafer on her upturned hand. These days the Eucharist was received by all but a few hold outs this way, and then they put the consecrated wafer in their own mouth. More sanitary that way and sacred a wash. Only a few elderly parishioners nostalgic for the Latin Mass stick out their hoary tongues anymore. The pious woman whispered the expected "Amen" and turned to swallow the Body whole or chew it up as she pleases.

Moments later it was Ray's turn to partake. The man's manner now was subdued, pious even, but his eyes were wide open and beseeching. The priest reached into the silver bowl and brought the wafer out. Ray opened his mouth and stuck his tongue out. Something in his manner, tongue rolling up to lick his upper lip, struck the priest as obscene.

"The Body of Christ," the priest whispered, trying to conceal the quaver in his voice. He placed the Host on Ray's tongue and jerked his hand back as though shocked by static electricity.

"Amen to life, Father," Ray said quietly. He turned on his heel in almost a military drill move and returned to his seat.

CHAPTER 2

▼

After the procession out of the sanctuary, Father Andy stood at the main door to say a few parting words to the faithful. He always struggled to marry names with faces. Everybody knew the priest but the dozens pressing his palm, expecting recognition of every tyke in tow—well, they were all brothers and sisters in Christ but damn if His priest could know each and every one as family. Amelia Martinez and her teenage daughter Gabriela passed by and the priest gave some unsolicited advice. Trust in God and pray hard; don't shy away from cameras; media attention and beseeching God makes all the difference in the world.

Not everyone sought their padre's attention. People in a rush to beat it out of the crowded lot walked briskly out side exits. Ray was one of these, Father Andy catching a glimpse of his back. The priest had a sudden impulse to tackle him on the spot or track him back to his lair. A spy in the sky, a predator for Christ! But then the priest was brought down to earth by, "Father, Father, are you going to be there?"

He focused on the man shaking his hand, Mr. Sanchez, yes, this was one parishioner whose first name was a mystery but saying "Mr." triggered "Sanchez" without hesitation. The old man had sandpaper hands that spoke of a lifetime of hard labor.

"Be where, Mr. Sanchez?" the priest said.

"At the ski area parking lot at 1, Father, a bunch of us are going up the trails to see if the boy is there."

Now the priest remembered and cursed himself for not announcing it at Mass. The county sheriff had put out a call for volunteers to follow up on a vague sighting report of a familiar looking boy and strange looking man hiking up in the basin.

"Yes, I'll be there. Are you bringing your dogs?"

"Most everybody are bringing their dogs." The old man looked out the church's glass doors at the bright sunshine. "The weather is cooperating at least, no. Later, Father!"

The last of the worshipers streamed past the priest with their memento palms in hand, in remembrance of the palms joyously laid in the path of Jesus on a donkey entering Jerusalem. Father Andy went to the changing room to shed the High Mass vestments and don his everyday friar's robe. He left the church on a mission but would have to think long and hard about the first steps. Join the community this afternoon for the search for sure. But how was he to act in light of his sixth sense about Ray?

Andy wondered if he was being foolish and paranoid. Inappropriate behavior in holy places happened; human beings couldn't all be harmonious members of a heavenly choir. Parishioners left their cell phones on. Infants cried (okay & charming in its place) but a couple little devils seemed to save a week's discontent for Sunday service. Fidgeting children popped gum, poked each other, rolled their eyes. The Easter parade now included hip-hugger jeans and Harley-Davidson T-shirts.

The priest decided he couldn't report a feeling to the police. Feelings are not facts. Only the fact of crime could condemn a man. What hard evidence could the priest offer? Off-putting grins in church (venial sin); answering "Amen to life, Father" instead of the routine "Amen" (bad form but nothing mortal)—even a devoutly Catholic cop couldn't arrest a man over ritual faux pas. Casting suspicion on an innocent man would prey on the priest's conscience.

The priest decided to launch his own quiet investigation. The first step was to call Mrs. Alarid, the vice principal who coordinated the volunteer mentors. Is there any connection between Peddie and Ray? What manner of man is he? Is he a family man? Father Andy recalled seeing Ray frequently at Mass but he never seemed to be with anyone. Worship at Santo Thérèse las Pequeño Flor was so much an extended family affair that black sheep and lone wolves stood out.

The rectory was a modest house in a nearby track development called Nava Adé. Every residence and commercial building in Santa Fe was adobe by ordinance as the city fathers wanted to maintain an old Spanish Southwest façade for the tourists. Mud and straw were the traditional building materials but most of modern Santa Fe was fake adobe: dry wall stucco painted in earth tones. Rich Texans escaping the heat of the Lone Star summer or wanting to ski in winter were choosing 7000 ft high and cool Santa Fe for a second home and eventual retirement. New Yorkers weary of metropolitan life and wary of terrorism were also moving west. Hollywood figures such as Shirley MacLaine, Gene Hackman, Val Kilmer and Ali MacGraw had large homes and ranches up remote roads on the outskirts. Santa Fe was christened 'Holy Faith' by its first colonial governor and fancied itself in modern times as the City Different. People of means wanting to escape the same old same old were rushing to the land of enchantment. They wanted to gallop into the sunset and wave their cowboy hat; they desired to go into the sweat lodge and feel the flutter of eagle's wings.

Artists since Georgia O'Keefe's heyday had been attracted to northern New Mexico. Wide open spaces under the best sunrises and sunsets to be found anywhere drew visual artists in particular. Raised in the sprawling suburbs of Chicago, Andy remembered some spectacular sunsets but learned in school that pollution helped color the sky. In New Mexico, the days still began and ended with nature calling the shots.

There was something very magical about the night skies too. The priest had traveled some, relocated often enough, but nowhere else had the night skies seemed so alive. One late night returning to Santa Fe after saying Mass in Taos in the northern mountains, a bright light seemed to follow the car, paralleling the highway and closing fast. Andy decided not to outrace the star but instead, courageously, stopped on the shoulder and got out to see if the tracking UFO was an optical illusion or something really sinister. The light continued to move erratically but no shaft of light zeroed in.

Andy remembered a parish party where he met the military son of a Santo Thérèse family. Antonio Rael told the priest something that shed light on the mysterious sighting. Antonio was a Black Hawk helicopter pilot operating out of Kirkland. Father Andy, always curious about conspiracy theories, asked the airman about Internet chatter of black helicopters on secret U.N. operations over the good old U.S. of A. Rael said that the U.N. had no secret ops going on as far as he knew. But he explained how mysterious night lights can be misunderstood. His outfit participated in night exercises throughout the state. They practiced precision night landings on open range land and high mesas. No town hall meetings were held before or after so ranchers and passersby were left in the dark. 911 panic calls came in that UFO's had landed and shadowy figures were spreading out. Were we being invaded by Martians or One World types? Was it a drug dealing rendezvous? Antonio filled the priest in on the mundane truth. After the long jumpy ride the crew members fanned out to stretch their legs and seek privacy for a piss in the wind.

Father Andy called Mrs. Alarid's home but found that she and her husband were out, having brunch before joining the search at the ski basin. The priest hung up and checked his watch. Just enough time for a fast happy hour.

Andy went to his bedroom and changed into his sweats. His dog Pope knew what was coming, began tearing around the room, jumping up on the bed. Pope was a spoiled shepherd mix who has been with the priest for over four years now. Most days the Pope had a couple long unleashed runs. His doggie buddies—mostly yard dogs—waited in slobbering anticipation along the fence line. The priest took great pride in giving his dog the run of the rectory as well as wild and wooly times.

The priest and his dog loved their time together. About two miles of exercise, Andy power walking, Pope agitating the yard dogs, chasing jack rabbits and road runners—without the dog to take care of, the priest would have only himself and could easily surrender to the recliner. Today they jogged the homeward leg to make sure they could get to the ski basin in time. Back at the rectory Andy took a short stinging shower as Pope panted on the bed. Usually Andy dallied in the shower, a sinful indulgence in drought-ridden New Mexico. The rectory yard, after all, was xeriscaped in harmony with the high desert, mostly a stone garden with scattered native plants and trees, watered wisely through drip. The only spot that received a daily drenching was a small patch of grass preserved for Pope to lie on.

After a vigorous towel drying, the priest put on a terry cloth robe and padded over to the dresser where he kept his Irish whiskey. Sipping Jameson's after the doggie run was the capstone of happy hour. He drank it neat, saving water that way too. The fine stuff was another personal indulgence that the priest could easily justify. The vow of celibacy alone entitled a man to take a liberty or two. Jameson's was certainly not the drink of a poor monk who had taken a vow of poverty at ordination. But surely God didn't intend His priest to make the rounds smelling of Wild Irish Rose.

Andy sat back in his recliner, read a passage or two from his holy books, and mused about his life as a man of the cloth. He felt the familiar warmth spread in his belly as the whiskey took its effect. After show time—the saying of Mass, the pressure of delivering an inspiring sermon, the parting small talk—Father Andy sought a private audience with his Pope. The priest laughed uproariously, no longer needing to keep himself composed. A role model I ain't, the priest proclaimed, and if I want to dance a jig at a funeral, by god (maybe one of the libertine Greek gods), I will!

The priest's rocking recliner was on a swivel and after checking Pope's plopping place (still on the bed), Andy spun around several times. He put his foot down to stop the spin and Pope took the cue, bouncing off the bed and onto his master's lap. Squirming with unconditional love, the dog licked the priest's hands and face, demanding (a condition perhaps) undivided attention in return. Andy talked over life with his pet. Pope had the most expressive eyes and rich body language that the priest alone understood completely.

"What do I do about this Ray, boy?" the Franciscan wondered. "God hasn't given me an easy nut to crack."

The dog mulled this over and responded, "The Pope says don't jump to conclusions. The Pope says take things one step at a time."

The priest realized this canine-human dialogue would sound wacky to non-dog lovers. But Pope was a useful sounding board. Peddie's disappearance and the intuition that Ray was involved presented Andy with a dilemma for the ages. The boy was one of his own. Ray was a valued member of the parish. The priest felt the heavy responsibility to do right by both.

Will God give me His blessing to find this boy safe and sound? Are secular authorities similarly blessed to do everything humanly possible? Do they get down on their hands and knees after all else fails to beg for divine intercession? But here I am—reclining like an indolent heathen, mulling over man, beast and boy. The priest didn't have a great amount of faith in temporal action. As a young man away from home and in the clutches of the monks at the seminary, Andy flirted with political activism as the answer to the world's woes. He attended a primary election rally at a union hall just outside Chicago's Loop. Teddy Kennedy was on a campaign swing lambasting the Reagan reactionaries and wooing the progressive crowd. As the Senator paused to relish the applause, he pointed at his dear friends in the near and far reaches of the hall. Once the finger descended upon the seminarian and young Andy Leary felt blessed by the Kennedy, any Kennedy would do. Afterwards, Andy realized that Teddy didn't know him from Adam, that the recognition was generic rather than glorious. Kennedy loved them all but no one in particular.

No, no, politics is no life for the soul. My Pope simplifies life and teaches me all that I need to know. Why stress out about what hasn't happened yet? Why feel guilt over what's dead and gone? Be here now, my hound from heaven counsels. Curl up and sleep like a baby, run with the wind and bark with your buddies. Life is good if you don't think about it. The priest said the Serenity Prayer as happy hour came to a close:

God, grant me the serenity
to accept the things
I cannot change,
the courage to change
the things I can,
and the wisdom
to know the difference.

The priest often saw himself as lacking everything the prayer embraced—acceptance, courage, wisdom. Just for now though, clean as a hound's tooth, sipping his Irish neat, life was a great game played masterfully by the Lord's disciple. A little booze helped. Enough to change his consciousness; not enough to blot it out. The priest knew full well that too much alcohol made you as stupid as, well, his beloved, besotted father. Andy's late father was rarely mean when he drank. He just made less and less sense.

The memory took its toll. Andy rarely spoke of his father but thought of him often, too often. Gone eleven years now, cirrhosis of the liver, a lousy way to die, withering away with yellow skin and a terrible thirst water alone could never satisfy. Over the years the priest had witnessed many deaths. Some passings had been sudden: called to an accident scene or to the hospital E/R. A few murder victims even. People dead, dead, cold with death but for the sake of family given God's blessing and undying forgiveness. Most of the terminally ill lingered for months in hospices or at home and the priest got to know them well. Some still had their wits about them; others stared blankly into that good night. Those who could talk shared precious memories with their priest. They remembered joys and losses, children doing well, grandchildren full of mischief, vacation pictures yellow with age, month and year scribbled on the back.

The priest tended to his dad over the last few months in the hospice. He wasn't alone; one of his sisters was there day and night. Their mother, drained of love and affection by the years of binge drinking, came once for a strained visit but couldn't bear to come back. Andy's older brother and younger sister, estranged from the old man, stayed away. Penelope did send a get well card.

Andy and Circe didn't want their dad to die alone. The hospice staff was compassionate but they were still strangers. They said all the right things but without the history of living together, we know nothing of each other and our feelings are disconnected. The priest knew his father very well indeed. As a kid he spent endless hours with the old man in his attic sanctuary. There dad escaped the downstairs nagging and was able to smoke his cigars in peace, study his Daily Racing Forms, and gulp his Jameson's. There were no deals cut in the smoke. Father and son just sat together and mulled over the racing history of ponies. They also rambled through every other topic known to man. The son was taught how to ruminate and smoke. But dad kept the Irish whiskey near and dear and hid the bottles in a nook the son never found.

The cigar smoking ended when the boy went off to seminary and betting on the ponies never became an obsession. It helped that the Santa Fe race track was closed as Indian casinos sopped up the gambling dollars. The priest occasionally went to the casinos but in his friar's robe drew too many curious stares to feel comfortable at the slots. He left win or lose after popping in a roll of quarters. Without smoking or gambling as a Cross to bear, Father Andy viewed the Jameson indulgence as a daily toast to his father's memory. But the priest only sipped the devil's brew as he feared family history repeating itself.

Andy remembered a line from a song faintly echoing from childhood: "It begins with the family and later comes round to your soul." His family was a rich mix of the sacred and the secular. The baby boy had been named after Ayn Rand, the American philosopher of self-made humanhood idolized by his mother. Mother loved robust philosophy and called her life a great leap into tangible truth. As an ardent feminist, she cheerfully referred to God as a She. God exists as always, mother affirmed, but He just went through a sex change with more enlightened times.

"She forever after, Ayn," mother asserted.

"You just want me in your amen corner," the teenage son countered. "Sex doesn't matter when it comes to God, mother."

"So you say, young man. Sex always counts and you'll find that out in your own time!" mother replied in a taunting tone.

It's hard to win an argument with your mother. The boy wanted pure and simple maternal love served up with home baked pie á la mode. But mother was an indifferent cook and avid coupon clipper so day old pie and thin ice milk for dessert and serve yourself thank you very much. Her self reliant stance and nagging logic didn't win over her son; just provoked a conflicted Ayn to fire a potshot before retreating in disarray to his bedroom to touch his privates impurely.

The teenage son in open rebellion embraced the Holy Roman Catholic Church, his father's faith, in a reaction against the moral relativism that mother expressed in no uncertain terms. Ayn sought rock solid truth and old time religion. Perhaps beyond that he sought to escape the sting of growing up with a girl's name. With his father's blessing he began calling himself Andy. His classmates still needled him with "Ayn, Ayn, the girlie man," and the boy's macho identity only came to fruition when he went off to the Franciscan seminary. He was the only one in his high school circle to answer the Calling. Away from home he became quite a cut-up after the long sullen adolescence. Roughhousing was frowned upon at the seminary but Andy was forgiven his erring ways. The Church was finding fewer and fewer willing to follow Christ into holy orders. Enough young men left of their own accord that those remaining were safe from dismissal. Seriously flawed characters passed cursory muster.

Happy hour was over. It was high time to find the missing boy.

CHAPTER 3

▼

They come to you if you have something to offer. No, not candy, silly, candy belongs to a more innocent age. Now it's more likely pot but hard liquor still works like a charm. Kids grow up so fast these days. In my time it took months or years for racy thoughts to fester before dirty deeds materialized. Now it's lickety-split from thought to action. I find myself reverting to youth, but not to my own youth, rather to the pubescence of modern times. Boys have a hard edge these days. Once you break through the crust, though, they have a sweetness that lingers on the tongue all night.

*   *   *   *

March was indeed going out like a lamb. The priest and Pope loved the first hint of spring in high country. Cactus flowers on the yucca, prickly pears, delicate wildflowers—columbines, pennyroyals—weren't yet blooming but wouldn't be long coming. Hyde Park Road climbed through a wooded landscape, with stumpy pinon pines and juniper giving way to majestic ponderosa pines and aspens. Their final destination—the ski basin—was above 10,000 feet. The priest whizzed past overlooks with tourists lingering without a care in the world. Historic Santa Fe spread below. City fathers strove to preserve the illusion of frontier days by zoning out tall buildings. But water was the true leveler. New Mexico's growth was constrained by, as the Riders in the Sky sang so sweetly, "water, cool, clear water." The land of enchantment wasn't blessed with plenty wet. Mother Nature didn't find room in the moving vans for rain water.

Father Andy pulled his Camry into the parking lot. Some fifty or so vehicles (including several squad cars) were already there and a crowd was milling about. The Santa Fe County sheriff was being interviewed by a TV reporter with a mini-cam rolling. The Franciscan friar let Pope out of the car with his collar on but off leash. Pope liked people and was surprisingly meek around other dogs. The priest was always amused by Pope's provocative scamper along the fence line, barking and leaping, a let me at 'em pose, only to shy away when one of the dogs managed to scramble over the fence. Pope was fixed so that took the testosterone edge off any confrontation. The priest spotted Mr. Sanchez and his three dogs: two Labs and a bull terrier, the terrier running rings around the Labs. Other dogs were there too, some leashed, some free, fidgeting by their owners. A few sat without a twitch at parade rest. The Franciscan blessed all creatures but scoffed at owners demanding best in show demeanor when out in nature.

Pope was a short legged shepherd mix, a shelter dog found abandoned in the Jemez Mountains. There was a bit of the coyote in his eyes and lean body, and certainly feral dogs roamed the back country. Late one night in his car Andy even spotted a pack of wild dogs prowling the streets down near the dry riverbed. They looked hungry and horny and the priest pitied any saucy cat or bitch in heat they ran across.

Father Andy joined the crowd at the trailhead. Several of his parishioners came up to chat as they awaited their marching orders. Many in the crowd still carried the palms they received at the Catholic services across town. The three nuns of Santo Thérèse were there and gathered around their priest. They were very different women indeed. One—Sister Claire—was the stern and ever serene 'lay facilitator' in charge of the choirs (adult and children's) as well as coordinating the laity committees. She wore the practical clothes now favored by her order. For the search she had on jeans and a heavy sweater to ward off the afternoon chill. Father Andy admired her no-nonsense manner but always felt awkward in her presence. A couple formidable nuns from his youth came to mind. Perhaps he was reminded of his mother too. Sometimes it was all the priest could do to restrain himself from tossing the nun's hair into an unholy mess.

Another nun of the parish was Santa Fe born-and-bred Sister Munificent, a throwback to bygone fashion, still wearing the white habit. The priest had never seen a wisp of her hair. Sister 'Muni' had been at the parish school for ages, transforming generations of hellions into children of God. Her memory was erratic, sometimes calling the grandson by the grandfather's name, and her temperament volatile, transforming a simple phonics lesson into a rant against a favorite target, the godless Jerry Springer. The priest often wondered if the good sister drove her

3rd graders away from trailer trash TV or to tune in out of curiosity. She was a great fan of Pat Boone and played Boone spirituals on the boom box in the classroom. She had the kids sing along.

The last nun of the parish—Sister Maria Anne—was someone very special to Father Andy. How special she must never know. Sister Maria was principal of the parochial school, a good administrator, cheerful and capable. She was a lanky woman in her late thirties with an unusual personal path to her vocation. Growing up Catholic in St. Louis, Maria was devout but showed an early and enthusiastic interest in boys. That interest peaked when she wed a week after graduation from the University of Missouri. Six months later her husband Jody was dead, killed in a bar brawl at a bachelor party. The argument started over who was the better country fiddler, Roy Acuff or Erol Scruggs.

Jody's sudden, stupid demise led to a crisis of faith for Maria. She plunged into intense prayer and meditation to keep her sanity and find solace. Within a year she entered the Sisters of Saint Claire as a novitiate. Now, some sixteen years later, she had matured into a woman of substance, and lovely besides: a creamy complexion, strawberry blonde hair in, as she humorously put it, "a Joan of Arc cut", and clear blue-gray eyes behind wire-rims. She also was blessed with a figure that led to randy speculation even in a pious mind. Father Andy often caught himself watching her walk away with his eyes tattooed to her swishing ass. She deserved better than that, but there you have it.

Sister Maria was wearing hiking clothes, her "lumberjack chic" as she put it, stone wash jeans, untucked plaid wool shirt, a warm Gore-Tex jacket, Doc Marten's boots, St. Louis Cardinals baseball hat. She had binoculars around her neck and a small backpack with a couple water bottles sticking out. She had flipper sunglasses attached to her wire rims. Andy had suggested prescription sunglasses but she dismissed the switch as vain indulgence rather than real need.

"Trail mix, Father?" Sister Maria asked.

"With pleasure, Maria," the priest responded.

The priest was hungry as his routine with Pope and now this hike to find Peddie had left no time for lunch. Andy didn't like missing meals. This Palm Sunday morning, as with most all Sunday mornings, the priest had prepared a large Denver omelet for Pastor Gurule and himself. It was the one meal they shared without fail so they could discuss parish business.

The two priests had to fend for themselves for breakfast and lunch but had a widow woman from Mexico come in to tidy up and cook dinner. Señora Alvarez spoke little English and cooked little American. Tacos, burritos, menudo, red snapper or chicken Vera Cruz on special occasions, refried beans and Spanish rice, fried ice cream during summer—she pleased Father Andy more than Pastor Gurule with her spicy concoctions. Andy had been raised on a bland diet and responded well to the green or red chili in almost everything she prepared. Gurule told his assistant that Andy was blessed with a young stomach while his own was ruined by a lifetime of hot chili. Señora Alvarez couldn't do blah, so the pastor offered up a sour expression to the Lord.

Sister Maria turned her back so the priest could dig into her pack. Andy took out a water bottle and found the zip lock bag with the trail mix. He took a long squirt of water and gobbled a couple handfuls of mix. He squatted down and gave Pope a long squirt. He got up and returned the bottle and bag to the pack. Andy was trying to figure out a roundabout way of bringing up Ray. He spotted Mrs. Alarid across the way; the vice principal in charge of vetting school mentors. She was accompanied by her husband and two of their teenage sons. They were an old-fashioned Catholic family, eight children so far and leaving it up to the Lord on whether they would be blessed with more. Good kids by all accounts, both parents with active careers—Father Andy was amazed that they still found time for each other. The priest had recently run across the couple at a fancy restaurant and saw their fingers entwined, noticed they found things to talk about from soup to nuts.

He needed to find out more without starting a witch hunt. If he discovered a connection, a mentoring relationship, the priest would bring this fact and his suspicions to the police and wash his hands of the consequences. Father Andy knew the police had visited the school taking statements so perhaps Ray had already been questioned and cleared. But even so Ray's behavior at the Mass was disturbing. The priest felt strongly that the man was trying to tell him something. Life can mean many things; a pervert has his own take on it. Ultimately, the boy was the key, the boy's life. The priest would start with the boy and work the man in as an aside.

The crowd turned to the sound of a vehicle squealing into the lot. It was a heavy truck, a Ford 250 extend cab. The phrase, get me to the search on time, popped into Andy's head and he wanted to share the quip with Maria, impress her with his quick wit, but all her attention was on the truck. Raul Martinez, Peddie's father, and the boy's brother Freddie piled out of the cab and came over to the searchers. Seeing the friar in his robe, they veered over his way. Father Andy reached out his hand but Mr. Martinez wasn't having any of it.

"Mr. Martinez, I'm so sorry about all this. Your son has been in our prayers."

"Mucho gracias, Padre, but I don't believe in no fucking prayer," Raul responded, his hand in the air, waving off divine intervention. His eyes were bloodshot and the priest caught a strong whiff of beer. The father was feeling no pain or, perhaps, too much pain. The priest glanced at Peddie's older brother Freddie. The young man's eyes were downcast and his mouth pouty.

"Prayers can't hurt, Mr. Martinez, but God needs our help. That's why we're all here," the priest replied, motioning towards the searchers edging closer to hear the tense confrontation.

Martinez seemed to be revving up for another blasphemous salvo. The priest didn't know how to fend it off but Sister Maria came to the rescue.

"Freddie Martinez, dear me, I remember you!" Maria exclaimed, reaching out and grabbing him in a hug and then drawing back to look the young fella over. "My, you're a grown man now, and here to find your brother too. Good for you! Is that your honkin' truck? What a beauty!"

The nun steered Freddie over to the F250, a slick work horse for sure. Raul's bleary eyes followed Sister Maria and his son as they chatted by the truck. He also took in friends, neighbors, the cops, the TV reporter with the camera rolling—all looking at him, all there to find his boy. Raul must realize he didn't look good, beer gut spilling over his belt, unkempt hair barely contained by a cap that read BUG OUT. Martinez was an exterminator by trade.

"Mea culpa, Padre, that's what we use to say, no!" he blurted out, his eyes watering. "Mea maxima culpa. You see, Padre, I was an altar boy once. I prayed like a son of a bitch back then. I remember those days."

The priest figured it must have been long ago. This was the first time he had the pleasure of meeting Mr. Martinez. The mother and the children were the churchgoers with the father occupied elsewhere. Father Andy only recognized him from the initial tearful family TV appearance after Peddie disappeared on Wednesday last.

Martinez looked out upon the crowd and addressed them in a loud, slurry voice. "Amigos, pardon my sorrow. I'm not feeling good. Mucho gracias for coming here. I will shut my trap now."

He turned back to the truck. At first the priest thought he was going to drive off but he just sat there. Then he reached down and fiddled, brought up a can of beer, and took a swig. Oh boy, in full view of the police, with the camera rolling.

The priest hurried over to the TV reporter, Sam Fujema, broadcasting on Channel 4 out of Albuquerque. That was the channel he watched for local news and Sam was on the air all the time with Santa Fe features. Father Andy had first met him when Santo Thérèse sponsored a benefit for a parish family stricken with AIDS. The drug-addled husband likely caught it from a dirty needle, passed it along to his wife, and their youngest child was born with it. The family clung to each other with the compassion of the doomed, surviving with the help of expensive HIV drug 'cocktails', though they were susceptible to every bug making the rounds. Sam handled their story with sensitivity, allowing the husband and wife to talk longer than a sound bite, actually interested in what they had to say off camera.

Along with many in the crowd, Sam was staring at the bent out of shape patriarch chugging his beer.

"Sam, good to see you again," the priest said, startling the reporter and snapping his microphone to attention. The priest wondered if all reporters on duty had that impulse when surprised, cock your microphone, be ready to fire a question.

"Oh hello, Father," Sam said, shaking the Franciscan's hand. "You know, I didn't expect anything like this," motioning to the truck. "That's why they call it news, I guess."

"Sam, every parent has a different breaking point. We don't want to add to that family's sorrow, do we?"

The reporter looked at the priest and nodded his head impulsively. Father Andy was confused by the body language, whether the reporter was or wasn't willing to put aside the public's right to know that a parent of a missing child can fall apart in public in the most embarrassing way. Sam was the youngest son of a Japanese immigrant family relocated from San Francisco after Pearl Harbor to a New Mexico internment camp. At war's end they returned to California to discover that their restaurant had been sold for back taxes and their home heavily vandalized. The Fujema family moved to Albuquerque seeking a fresh start. Sam was the postwar baby of the family, coming as an unexpected gift from the kami.

Sam finally turned the noncommittal shake into a decisive nod. "Okay, Father, okay, okay! The drama of the missing boy trumps the news value of a drunken father. Dysfunctional family—so what else is new? I have enough footage to update our viewers on the search. No reason to destroy sympathy. Sheriff Baca gave me some good quotes. I do want a shot, Father, of you leading your people up the trail. I've come up with an interesting angle on that."

The priest thanked Sam and, excusing himself, moved on to the sheriff. Pope tagged along and Baca instinctively reached down to pet the dog. Andy first met the long serving sheriff years ago at an interfaith meeting about social justice and juvenile delinquency. The priest thought the sheriff's little speech was stating the obvious in a rather charming way, emphasizing the pivotal role of faith communities in providing healthy youth activities. From all the priest had read and heard of crime fighting in the far-flung county, the sheriff seemed to be doing the job.

"You have a real hound dog here, Father. The bad guys better watch out with this bad boy on their trail," the sheriff said, patting Pope's back and then gently giving his paw a shake.

"Well, I don't know about that, Sheriff," the priest responded. "He has problems catching anything alive but maybe he'll be of help. But it looks like you brought along the pros," motioning to a couple leashed police dogs with their deputy minders.

"They're trained more for crowd control than for tracking," Baca said. "Cujo over there has a nose for drugs though. But they need the exercise and sometimes it helps them to mix off leash with other dogs, civilians like. All these dogs here will make a racket along the trail. If the boy is lost or can break free, maybe he'll come to the sound of the barking."

The priest motioned over to Martinez drinking in his truck.

"I want to ask you for some forbearance with Mr. Martinez there. He's in no shape to drive or hike for that matter. But I just don't think he needs legal trouble right now."

The sheriff shrugged his shoulders. "Oh, I know that jerk over there. I went to school with his brother Manny. Wait here. I'll take care of it."

Baca went over to the truck and leaned into the open window. He spoke quietly to Martinez. The priest wondered if he was going to get the man to pour out his beer and confiscate any Coors tall boys left over. Separating an alcoholic from his booze is fraught with danger. The sheriff reached in and his hand emerged with the truck keys. He said a few more words to Martinez, patted the back of the man's head, and came back to the priest. Freddie and Sister Maria accompanied him.

"The guy will sleep it off and Freddie here will drive him home later," Baca said, turning the keys over. "Mixing a mountain road and booze, a bad mix, no! Let's get on with it, Father."

The sheriff turned to the crowd and raised his voice.

"Folks, folks, lend me your ears here! You all know why we've come together, and I appreciate your help. Freddie Martinez represents the family and will be walking along with us. Father Leary from Santo Thérèse is here too and maybe we'll find the boy today with prayers and good luck. As you all know, we may have a runaway or maybe somebody up to no good took the boy. All we know for sure is that he never came home after school on Wednesday. We're up here because we received a tip that a boy looking like Peddie was seen with a man yesterday. Nothing strange about a father and son hiking but the witness said they were arguing instead of enjoying the scenery. So let's take a look around. Not a bad place to spend a Sunday afternoon."

Baca motioned to his two deputies holding their shepherd dogs.

"Let me introduce Deputy Lanner and Deputy Rivera here with their highly trained dogs. We're breaking up into three groups to cover the Winsor Trail and the Baldy Trail and that area over at the ski runs. I will go with the Winsor group; Deputy Lanner, Pete here, will go to Baldy; Manny Rivera will cover the ski trails. We have about six hours of sunlight but let's shoot for meeting back here at, say, 5:30 or so. If we find the boy, the deputies or myself will shoot our pistols. But I don't want any shooting if one of your dogs starts chasing after something. It could be an innocent squirrel or coyote or deer. Unless it's something human that don't belong here, don't fire into the air for that brings people running. I see a couple hunting rifles out there and maybe some guns I don't see. Let the deputies lead the way, gentlemen. We're not out here for sport. Call yourself a posse if you want, but let's not have an accident. Okay, buckaroos? Are you with me on this?"

The sheriff looked out and saw many nods and heard a number of yeahs.

"Good, good, thanks again for coming. Now, who goes where? Why don't we do as we did in school, remember those nuns in the school yard, folks! Let's count off 1, 2, 3. Let's start with the good padre here."

Father Andy said "1" and that started a ragged round of people saying a number. It was ragged because people weren't lined up in a row. The crowd was in family and friend packets, so individuals hesitated saying a number and some said the same number simultaneously. But finally it got done and the sheriff rallied the 'one' group over to Winsor Trailhead. Andy's hope of asking Mrs. Alarid about Peddie and Ray was dashed by her being part of the Baldy group. On the plus side Sister Maria was going along with him and may offer some insight with sly questioning. The priest also registered that Ms. Stenholm, Peddie's 4th grade teacher, was there and going up Winsor too. Laurie would know Peddie well and any outside adults hanging around at school.

Sheriff Baca took a well-worn pair of Nike athletic shoes and a T-shirt out of two plastic bags and went over to each of the dogs going with the group. He asked Andy to control Pope long enough for him to get a good sniff. Pope heeled on command and the priest beamed. Four of the other dogs were still leashed so obedience was no problem. A couple owners gave their dogs treats after they got a whiff of Peddie. The sixth civilian dog—a cocker—was off leash and very agitated. The sheriff, muttering in frustration, went over to the priest and displayed a nipped hand.

"Damn dog! He drew first blood before we even start. Too many damn dogs, Father. But it's amazing how many victims are found by a man walking his dog. Here, of course, we pray that the boy is amongst the living. Now I have to bandage up my yowlie before we start. Thank God I have my tetanus shots up to date."

Baca walked over to his squad and opened the first aid kit that the priest figured was standard equipment for a police vehicle. He returned quickly with a bandaged finger and dramatically pointed it up the trail past the waiting volunteers. The Channel Four camera was rolling as the crowd parted, allowing the priest and sheriff to lead the way. Father Andy knew his clerical garb would play well, projecting a positive image for a Church desperately needing good news. Andy knew the archbishop would be watching. But then Sam's 'angle' on the shot became apparent. The numerous Catholics in the crowd still carrying palms laid them down in the priest's path. Oh how great the sacrilege! A false idol for the evening news; all I need now is an ass to ride on.

The unleashed dogs took point, literally bounding with exuberance up the rising trail. A toy dog—a Shih Tzu with a wool body vest—stayed on leash and was gathered up by her owner whenever the pesky cocker came near. The searchers were climbing to where the trail broadened along the ridgeline. Here the conifers occasionally gave way to alpine meadows and offered vistas of the twisting road far below and the mountains across the way. It was a glorious day for a hike but the nature of the beast could be revealed around the next bend.

The priest and sheriff began talking.

"So, Sheriff, where's the city police today?"

"Well, it's county up here you know. I coordinated it with Andrews and she'll be working her guys hard again tomorrow. Unless we find the boy today, God willing."

Solidly Democrat and on the liberal side, Santa Fe had a woman police chief, Sheri Andrews. She had worked her way up through the ranks and knew the capitol city well. Santa Fe had its fair share of crime and social tensions: gang bangers, friction between the growing gay community and homophobes, resentment of the locals over both the rich and poor moving in from out of state or country, the traditional American conflict between cowboys and Indians, mostly over water rights and casino revenues. Of course domestic squabbles still spilled over into the public square.

"So how's the investigation going? Any leads?"

"It's a real mystery, Father. No one has come forward to say they saw the boy snatched off the road after school. So what happened on that mile walk home?

His mom was waiting and waiting and is still waiting. Just to be straight with you, Father, and this is not for publication, we have no leads except for that anonymous sighting report up here. Anyhoo, we're stumped."

"Hire a psychic yet?" the priest enquired with a slight smile. Santa Fe had plenty to choose from, mystic folks seeking enlightenment on the high sagebrush plains. They avoided old line churches such as Santo Thérèse, and were worshiping their own potential in their own way.

The sheriff's breathing became labored soon into the steep climb in thin air. The priest noticed a pack of cigarettes in the top breast pocket of his uniform shirt. The sheriff was a big man gone to tar and nicotine.

"No, no, I don't believe in that head shit. I believe in legwork and phone calls. Routine police procedures will solve this case. You know, Father, I can't imagine he ran away even given that old drunk he has for a father. I mean, where would a ten year old go? How far could he get? Somebody would have noticed a hitch-hiking boy, no! We checked with Greyhound and no little boy broke open his piggy bank to buy a ticket. We called on his buddies and their families. No little boy hiding under the bed. We checked every tree house and tepee in town and out. No Peddie to be found!"

The priest was pleased that he had the sheriff sharing. Maybe he could find out about the investigation at the school.

"So, Sheriff, Father Gurule and I were wondering about our school and anything you found out there. He is one of our boys after all. Anything we should know about?"

"Nothing looks phooey, I can tell you that. The boy was seen leaving with his book bag. That's his teacher back there, isn't it? I've read all the reports by my guys. Andrews and I can handle this better than outsiders. We want to keep the damn state investigators out of it. And the FBI?—Yi, yi, yi! We can take care of our own."

So far so good—school personnel and volunteers are not implicated. The priest figured the next step should be to find out more about the Martinez family. He was acquainted with Amelia but she was so withdrawn that he didn't know her well at all. Gabriela, her fourteen year old, was just another bored face at the school and at Sunday Mass. Freddie, about to graduate from high school, had attended the parish school but the priest didn't remember him.

"What about the family? Any insights there?" the priest asked.

Baca paused before responding. He finally turned towards the priest, both still walking briskly, and spoke in a hushed voice.

"Just imagine. Padre, we are in the confessional now. This is only for God, you and me, that's all. Are you with me on this?"

Father Andy resisted the temptation to say, "Yes, my son, go on," as the sheriff had at least 15 years on the priest. He just nodded and murmured, "You bet."

"When you eliminate the unlikely, Father, you're left with the likely. The likely is either a stranger snatch or family involvement. Now Peddie could have been taken by a stranger and be hundreds of miles away. Or six feet under around here, and we all go home to cry. His picture has been sent to law enforcement agencies throughout the region. We even contacted that <u>America's Most Wanted</u> show. That Walsh guy said he would try to air a short notice but it increases audience appeal if you have a suspect too. Or, what do we call it now, person of interest. In this case, though, we find everybody interesting."

The sheriff glanced behind him to check how close the other searchers were. He looked reassured when he saw Sister Maria and Laurie Stenholm engrossed in conversation.

"Now it's no secret that family has problems, serious ones, no! That bastard we left drunk as a skunk has multiple DUI's on his record and wouldn't have a license at all if I had my way. His brother told me that Raul can't be reasoned with, that the cursing comes quick if cutting back comes up. I like to take a drink myself; we all do."

The sheriff glanced at the priest and Andy wondered if the happy hour shot of whiskey was still on his breath. The priest used breath mints but knew that hard liquor can leak through the skin.

"But there's drinking and then there's drinking," the sheriff continued. "So we've been talking to the family, you betcha. Trying to get a sense of what it's like to grow up in that family, with that father. Can't be easy street at all. Maybe something terrible happened after school that day. Maybe Raul was beating on his wife in a blackout, the boy comes home and jumps on his back, the father throws him off and the boy hits his head. I could see that. An accident sorta, no intention to kill the boy, but why ruin your life because of an accident. The man wakes up with a killer hangover and a dead kid. A few crocodile tears, a couple shots and a beer to settle his nerves, then he goes out and buries the boy in a shallow grave somewhere. Amelia, more wife than mother, raises a false alarm. She didn't call the city cops until 11 that night. Most mothers would call us an hour after her child is late, ten years old for god's sake, Father, ten years old!"

"What was her explanation?" the priest asked.

"She cried first, but then mumbled some nonsense about not knowing what to do. We verified that she did call a couple of Peddie's friends, talked to the mothers. No luck but then she said she wanted to wait for Raul to get home. But of course they tell us he didn't get home until late. He stopped at a bar after work but he never tells his wife what bar, he didn't want her pestering. But nobody saw him working that afternoon; he had a couple morning appointments and his last customers remember him leaving their house around 1. Jorge over at Tiny's said he was plopped on a barstool for awhile but cut him off around 3 or so, and Raul stormed out. That's what Jorge said at least, covering his ass for all I know. Don't sic the lawyers after me, Mister Lawman, I cut the drunk off before he kills anybody. Don't sic the MADD mothers after me, Mister Lawman!"

The sheriff laughed but then realized the occasion was not a joking time. He wiped the grin off his face and ruefully shook his head. He spoke again in confidence.

"So Raul told us he drove up here to cool out after Tiny's. Nobody was with him of course; nobody saw him. He may have come here; he may have gone home to raise hell. We can only suppose but that's another reason we're up here searching. Murderers let things slip; most of them are not smart people. They're dumb as shit. Pardon my French, Father, but they're dumb fucks. Thank God they're dumb. Maybe he dumped the boy up here."

The torrent of morbid speculation and their brisk pace uphill was taking its toll. Wheezing a bit now, Baca turned towards the straggling group and announced loudly, "Take ten, amigos!" They had only been on the trail for less than an hour but it was the most difficult stretch, the climb to the ridgeline. The priest shepherded the priest over to a fallen log. He wasn't through dumping yet. Sister Maria and Laurie headed for the same resting place but the sheriff waved them off. The women gave him a dirty look as the priest shrugged, mouthing a heartfelt, "Sorry, Sister," for he really wanted a break from the voluble sheriff. Pope ran over and plopped at the priest's feet, panting from his exertions. Andy wanted to cop some water again for the dog from the nun's backpack but figured digging for clues came first. Baca took out his pack of Camels and offered one to Andy. The priest demurred. Outside of puffing on cigars with his father years ago, Andy had abstained from tobacco. He wasn't going to start now, on this sad and beautiful day.

The sheriff lit up and took a long drag. They sat silent for a couple minutes. The priest found the revelation of "nothing phooey" at the school a great relief. Maybe his sixth sense about Ray shouldn't be taken as gospel. Pastor Gurule will be pleased as there were serious liability issues at stake.

The priest turned and asked gently, "Any other ideas, Sheriff?"

Baca threw his spent cigarette down and ground it out. He lit another before responding.

"What I've told you, Father, is just my mouth shooting blanks. I've got nothing to take to the D.A. What we have is a missing boy and a father who drinks like a pig. The poor mother gave us permission to search the house, their yard, and their vehicles. Raul was royally pissed but didn't interfere. No blood traces, no signs of violence, no disturbed ground, nothing."

The sheriff took a drag on his Camel before summing up. "So we search blindly up alleys and hope to catch a break. Somebody knows what happened to the boy and that somebody knows somebody else. People like to talk, no!"

People liked to talk, yes, the priest well knew. Penitents liked to share their dirty little secrets. Andy had been a priest for some sixteen years and was getting tired of secrets. If the truth be told, in his younger years, he derived a voyeuristic pleasure from hearing sins of a sexual nature, particularly from the mouths of humbled women. He could offer the forgiveness of Christ; send them back to the pews to say their penance of Our Father's, Hail Mary's, and Glory Be's. But to go out and sin no more is a pipe dream, the priest realized, for people are bent that way.

The friar wanted to offer the sheriff some consolation. The standard phrase that came to mind, God's will be done, always seemed to have a calming effect. People of faith found comfort in the familiar.

"God's will be done, Sheriff. Thy will, not mine, be done," the priest said, cuffing Baca gently on the shoulder. The sheriff looked up and instinctively made the sign of the Cross.

The many tall trees sheltered the resting searchers from the relentless sun of New Mexico. The heat of the day was usually dry in the southwest. But vigorous exercise still drained the hikers even if less sweat was involved. Such a warm day for the last of March, the priest mused, Indian winter perhaps. The snow pack was starting to melt. The watersheds could always use the water, and for awhile the Rio Grande would churn for the rafters and kayakers.

The sheriff ground out his second butt and heaved himself upright. The priest stood up and the rest began stirring. Pope sat up on his front paws and gave the priest the look. Feed me and how about a drink, buddy, the look demanded. Andy cursed himself for not coming better prepared. His happy hour always left him in dreamland. God provides, God provides, look at the lilies of the field, they neither reap nor sow; a few barley loaves and fishes multiplied to feed the masses—the New Testament gave the impression that pure faith in God leads to a free lunch and getting by on your looks alone.

The priest went over to the nun.

"Maria, I was wondering if I could impose upon you again for some water. It's for the dog."

The nun looked hugely amused and reached down to fondle the dog. "How can we deny the Pope? I'm not sure if dogs understand how a squirt bottle works. The old cupped hands method works best. Do you want to be the cupper or squirter, Andy?"

The priest paused, feeling a bit pixilated, before he replied, "I prefer squirter."

Maria squatted down and Andy squirted some water into her cupped hands. Pope slurped and slurped some more. Physically they were so different: Andy short and pudgy, Maria tall and lissome. He wanted to assume the mantle of authority that the Church bestowed upon him. Priests stood higher on the peaking order than nuns. Nuns fancied themselves brides of Christ but priests were His good buddies. The men had the awesome privilege and responsibility to hold the wafer and wine aloft as they are transformed into the Body and Blood of Christ. Priests baptized babies, confirmed children into the age of reason, forgave sins of all nature. Nuns traditionally nurtured the minds and souls of the young with a Christian education as well as tending to the sick and dying. Essential service to be sure, but the weighty decisions of the parish and the performance of sacred ritual were left up to the men.

Andy always felt expectant in Maria's presence. But what he was pining for was impossible. Lust was at the heart of it. He prayed, prayed hard, to be relieved of the bondage of self. Sometimes desire went into remission but then, with a laugh or a wink, or the woman lightly touching his arm to emphasize a point, the cancer came back to eat at his soul. She unknowingly stripped him of his clerical cover, exposing the naked man underneath.

In many ways Sister Maria deviated from the stereotypical image of a nun. When amused, she belly laughed: when greeting, she favored bear hugs or hearty handshakes; when animated, she liked to touch flesh. When angry, she sometimes cursed—though she substituted "by gum!" for any derogatory reference to God. She played soccer with demonic energy. She ran a good school and kept her underpaid staff happy by trusting her people and backing them to the hilt. The Catholic tradition of learning by rote was still the core of the curriculum but fun learning games helped engage the juvenile mind. The strict discipline that older Catholics either fondly recalled, or bitterly remembered, was also maintained. Principal Maria built in plenty of recess periods to let her young charges exhaust themselves into a teachable condition.

The good sister was utterly captivating and the priest was hopelessly charmed. They had worked together for some seven years now. Andy effectively ran the parish as Pastor Gurule, a figurehead beloved by all, was too doddering to handle day-to-day decisions. Maria and Andy pored over the school's budget, always tight because many families were poor enough to qualify for a sliding tuition scale down to zero. The school building was cursed with the common weakness of Santa Fe structures: a flat roof. Flat tar roofs took a beating from the elements—the incessant sun as much as the intermittent moisture—and patches were frequent. This summer the roof's replacement couldn't be put off any longer: $ 77,000 and that from a devout Catholic contractor.

The priest looked over at the sheriff and saw that he was bending the ears of a couple. Now what would he be talking about, the priest wondered. Was Baca taking them into his confidence too? But one can't assume the mystery of Peddie was on everybody's lips. People meander into small talk to fill the void.

The priest wanted to stay focused on the boy. The child was one of his charges yet so little about him was known. The sheriff, still engaged in spirited discourse, started up the trail that was now mostly level along the ridge. Father Andy was now free to talk with the two women. As the boy's educators, they knew him as a student and growing child. The priest often observed that women paid close attention to a child as he is today while men looked years ahead at who the child could become.

"I was wondering, ladies, how Peddie seemed to you on Wednesday. Was he nervous, afraid, just average? I mean, how was he really?"

The two women looked at each other before the principal responded. "Well, Andy, it just so happens I really noticed the boy that day. It was during mid-morning recess. Nothing stands out more than a child moping about, off by himself. I went over to Peddie and asked what's up, buddy? The boy wouldn't look me in the eye, just kinda mumbled, 'Not feeling good.' I told him to go see the nurse and he went shuffling off. I made a note to ask the nurse later how the poor kid was faring but got distracted by other matters, by other children tugging at me. Knowing what I know now, nothing was more important than following-up on that boy."

Laurie reached out to pat the nun on her back. "Maria, you didn't know and I didn't know. The boy was quiet and withdrawn that day but all the children have their moods. I see a frown on a face and I try to involve the child. Lob him a question that he can hit out of the park. Usually that works though sometimes I take the child aside later. Find out what the real problem is. Often it's coming from the home. None of my business really unless there are signs of real abuse. At the end of the day I was going to talk with him and whoever picked him up. I think what threw me off was that no one was there to pick him up. The child hurried off before I could grab him."

Laurie Stenholm was a young teacher in her second year at Santo Thérèse parochial. A transplant from Minnesota, she moved here with her boyfriend after their graduation from college. She was visibly pregnant with her first child. A sensible planned pregnancy for a teacher, wanting to deliver during the long summer off. The priest doubted that the planning was based on Catholic doctrine, the hit-or-miss rhythm method. Andy knew from experience that it was nearly hopeless to expect Catholic mother don't wannabes or hadenoughs to tow the line. She and her boyfriend, now her fiancé, had no date set to make it legal. It would likely be one of those shameless weddings where the bride wears off white and hands her new born to the maid of honor. Laurie needed to work during her final trimester, as her fiancé had found his calling as a sculptor but was yet to be discovered by art patrons.

"Was that unusual? No one there to pick him up?" the priest asked.

"Sometimes the mother was there, sometimes his brother was," Laurie answered. "I admit I never saw his father pick him up once. Thank God, the way he is! I only met Mr. Martinez on parent's night and I wasn't impressed then either. The boy talked mostly about his brother. A little hero worship going on there I think."

"Freddie and Peddie—I'm not surprised they are close," the priest said with a smile.

Sister Maria laughed. "Freddie, Peddie, say that ten times fast. The family that rhymes together, stays together. And Gabriela they call Gabby. I love it! But seriously, Andy, Freddie was a good student when he was with us and I understand he's an honor student at St. Mike's. He's planning to go to UNM next year. He says he wants to become a scientist and work at Los Alamos. I'm sure he's pretty broken up by his brother's disappearance."

"Does he have any idea about what happened?" Andy asked.

"I don't think so but we didn't get into educated guesses. I did broach the subject of Peddie running away but he didn't think so. The boy would have told him if he was thinking of that. Freddie apologized for his dad's appearance, said the man is sitting around watching TV all day, drinking beer. He's not even watching the news, just watching the Sci-Fi channel. When Freddie told him he was coming up here to help out, Raul insisted on coming along and driving too. It's lucky we don't have another family tragedy to deal with."

These insights into Freddie's close relationship with his baby brother were all well and good though a direct conversation would be better. The young man was off searching with the Baldy group. The priest had always been intrigued by puzzles. He enjoyed reading mysteries and here he was at the center of a real life one. A priest as sleuth, Andy smiled at the thought. He remembered Sean Connerly as a Franciscan friar investigator of murders in a medieval monastery in the movie Name of the Rose. Yes, the role model should be James Bond as a plot-busting monk, combining vespers with bon mots, the power of prayer with high tech gadgets. Perhaps he could lasso the evil one with rosary beads that explode when fingered. Bond was taller and more rugged but Father Andy could be just as dogged. He suddenly realized that his destiny was to find Peddie, come hell or high water. And in New Mexico high water was unlikely.

The priest wondered what part of the sheriff's 'confession' he could ethically divulge to the women. One revelation was okay to mention and could lead to the subject of interest to the priest—Ray.

"I was talking to the sheriff and he assured me that so far school personnel have been cleared."

Sister Maria visibly bristled at the 'so far.' "I know my people, Andy, and there's not a bad apple among them. You know our background checks are extensive and I look each in the eye before I hire them. I can spot evil a mile away!"

"I know that, Maria, I know," said the priest in his most placating tone. He didn't mean to criticize Maria's managerial style or question her farsightedness. But after all, surely child molesters passed all sorts of background checks. He just had to plow ahead, even at the risk of pissing off a woman he cared for—deeply. "Baca and Andrews have to investigate all the possibilities, you know that, Maria. You can imagine how relieved I was that our staff has been given a clean bill of health. But that brings us to our volunteers—our mentors, for example. How much do we really know about them?"

The nun turned on the priest and Andy could imagine her eyes flaring behind her tinted flippers.

"What did that sheriff tell you, Andy? We saw you guys whispering so we couldn't hear, waving us away. Come on, my man, give it up! Let us silly little women in on the secret."

The priest wished that he was wearing his own sunglasses so he could hide his lying eyes. He felt himself blushing; his beard hid most of that, thank God. Why should I be ashamed? My heart is filled with good intentions.

"Well, Sister, it just so happens that the sheriff did confide in me. I can tell you that we're on the road to finding Peddie but there's no light at the end of the tunnel yet. It's always darkest before the dawn, I guess."

Such blather, the priest realized, wasn't likely to ease the women's suspicions. In truth he, and apparently the sheriff, didn't know anything that anybody with half a brain wouldn't suspect. To pretend to hold the key to the mystery would be as false as it is irritating. But the priest did have Ray's odd behavior at Mass to ponder. The friar desperately needed to sort out what was real, what was fancied.

The priest felt suddenly overwhelmed. He didn't know anything about anybody. He certainly didn't know Sister Maria in the biblical sense. The priest was confused by the conflict between body and soul. Unlike Sister Maria, he wasn't confident he could spot evil a mile away. Or up close either—in the mirror.

Andy knew to bring up Ray's name directly now would cast premature suspicion on the man. If the priest mentioned the background, he was worried less about being misguided and more about appearing alarmist in Maria's eyes.

"The sheriff did tell me that he thought it unlikely that Peddie was a runaway. The logistics of a ten year old disappearing on his own for this long is daunting. Baca did ask for our help with finding out more about the volunteers. So humor me for a minute, Maria. You ladies know more about the mentors than I do. Anything you can tell me would be appreciated."

The priest was trying to subtly pull rank. There was a missing boy here and no time for nonsense about citizens above suspicion.

Sister Maria shrugged her shoulders and spoke less stridently. "I'm sorry, Andy, I know people can hide who they really are. Look good on the outside and be rotten to the core. I'd hate to think any of our dedicated volunteers could be involved. I can see what you're after, Father. You want to know who worked with Peddie or seemed to have a relationship. Actually, Laurie would know better than I."

Laurie took the cue. "Peddie is a special ed. kid but we were mainstreaming him for socialization, I guess, so we delay the stigma. Academically, he had a real blind spot for math so I took advantage of the mentor program to get him some help. Mrs. Pilar is his tutor and he seems to be making progress. I always thought the boy was smart enough but the bad home environment was clogging the brain cells up. He didn't really talk much about his family. But I do remember one day when he blurted out in class that his dad was a drunk. I did talk with him that day, talked with his mother after school. But you can see that that situation hasn't improved. As his teacher I can't solve all the problems in a kid's world."

"I know that, Laurie," the priest said soothingly. "I think I know Mrs. Pilar, don't I? She's the one with the limp, right?"

"No, Father, no," Sister Maria replied, "that's Ruta Gonzales who mentors a third grader, Joey Armijo I think. Mrs. Pilar wears purple all the time; her nickname around the school is the Purple Lady."

"Oh yeah, I've noticed her. What's with the purple? Wearing Lent for all seasons?" the priest asked, referring to the purple vestments and altar cloths that symbolized the most somber liturgical season.

Laurie answered him. "I'm not sure why. So many women wear dark colors to hide the pounds. But Ruta's no chubby so it must be a fashion statement of some sort. I'll ask her when school starts up again next week."

"Not a big deal, Laurie. Mrs. Pilar certainly seems like a nice person. It's funny how we assume that a bad guy has to be a guy, you know, that sexual violence against a child has to be committed by a man. Old news, a pedophile being a man. When we think of a woman, we think of nurturing, protecting. Given the family situation, do you think Mrs. Pilar took Peddie to a safe place? A sanctuary so to speak?"

"I seriously doubt Mrs. Pilar would do something crazy like that," Sister Maria asserted. "I know the police interviewed her and, like, she has a houseful of kids so it's hard to imagine Peddie fitting in. She told me that the police asked her about Peddie's mood during the tutoring session that day. She told them it went fine, he was fine. Okay, okay, okay! was how she put it to me. She seemed very upset. She's probably the type of person innocent in every way who would fail a lie detector test."

"Ah, lie detector tests," Andy said. "I wonder if the cops have used them yet."

The two women shrugged their shoulders and the three searchers fell quiet. The hiking was easier now along the ridgeline. The priest was pleased that he still felt strong and hardly winded despite his pudgy frame. All the long walks with Pope were paying off now. Now if he could only eat less, perhaps jog more to compliment the walking, the love handles would melt away and the priest would emerge more a fit disciple of almighty God. He had certainly tried over the years, joining health clubs, taking aerobic classes, playing racquetball, lifting weights. He would feel wonderful for awhile and then slack off. Heredity always plays its part. You see it every day—roly-poly parents with chubby kids in tow, the long and lanky marrying and soon string bean offspring are produced. In genetics Andy got the short of it. His father was short and stout, eating hearty while drinking plenty; his mother was tall and slender, one of those freaks of nature who can eat and drink anything and everything and not put on a pound. Andy's three siblings took after their mother. God gave the old man one child to bend and shape as nature and nurture wilt.

The priest looked over at the visibly pregnant teacher. Laurie was a sturdily built young blonde, blue-eyed woman from Scandinavian stock. The priest wasn't even sure if she was a practicing Catholic. He and the pastor didn't dictate to Sister Maria whom she could hire. There was no openly gay teacher at the school but people had their suspicions. One of the seventh grade teachers was spied giving her partner a passionate kiss while being dropped off one morning. The incident led to a formal complaint. Andy wasn't up to transom peeping so referred the matter to Sister Maria to investigate, interrogate, or bury. The principal dismissed the matter in short order, telling the parent to her face that Suzanne was a great teacher and her personal life was her own, case closed.

"Laurie, are you getting tired at all?" the priest asked. 'I'm sure we could find someone to walk back with you."

"No, I'll go on. Peddie is my student, my responsibility. I keep on wondering if any of this would have happened if I would have made a simple phone call to the mother. I could be home now with my honey."

Laurie's voice was breaking down with her last few words. Sister Maria reached over and they walked arm in arm for awhile. Father Andy admired that about Maria. When trying to comfort the sick and dying, the priest said all the right things, anointed the eyes and lips, maybe even felt the right feelings, but rarely hugged the person in pain or facing death. He knew he could train himself to be more tactile but it sure wouldn't come natural.

Andy looked at his watch and noted that it was getting on to 3 o'clock. The searchers would be turning back in awhile. There had been no gunshots in the air. Outside of several squirrels and the birds of course, the hikers hadn't even seen wild things. The true back country lay miles ahead, up more obscure trails. Except for the murmur of conversation, there was a quiet in nature that was comforting to the priest. The dogs weren't tearing about anymore. The wind was kicking up and tops of the spruces were swaying gently.

CHAPTER 4

▼

The priest returned to the rectory that evening and found a scribbled note—
Eat!—from Señora Alvarez on the fridge. It was secured by a magnetized Irish
Blessing that was an ordination gift from his father many years ago. His parents
combined to give him an expensive silver chalice but Andy treasured his father's
afterthought more. The Blessing was an ancient and universal wish:

May the road
Rise to meet you,

May the winds be always
At your back,

May the sun shine warm
Upon your face,

The rains fall soft
Upon your fields,

And until we meet again—
May God hold you
In the hollow of His hand.

The priest wondered if God was holding Peddie now. Would the boy be
allowed to grow up to begat children, to be blessed in that profound way? All
hope of lasting peace was dependent upon having children to inherit the earth.

But then Andy pondered the terrible thought of the sins of the father being visited upon the son. The priest remembered the scene he had just left at the ski basin parking lot, the end of today's search to discover true sin.

*　　　*　　　*　　　*

The three groups of searchers gathered back at the lot exhausted and disappointed. A bushed Sheriff Baca gave a brief address that owed much to Churchill's defiant rhetoric in the face of long odds. Turning over every rock, beating every bush, a clarion call to never give up hope. Baca asked the priest to say a few words. The priest knew enough not to go on for long:

> Peddie has already been discovered by
> God, blessed by Christ, innocent and pure.
> It's by the grace of God that we will find the
> boy and return him to his shattered family.
> St. Francis of Assisi, the guiding light of
> our city's founding, and St. Thérèse of
> Lisieux, the Little Flower, who
> provided the spiritual cornerstone
> of our parish, these saints and any other
> inspirations of your choosing can shed
> light so we can find lost souls. Let us
> have faith and bow our heads in
> meditative prayer.

Father Andy hoped that "any inspirations of your choosing" would placate any atheists who joined the search for reasons of humanity alone. Most everybody bowed their heads; some closed their eyes and held hands upraised. Many used the prayers of their youth—the Lord's Prayer, the Hail Mary—while a few crafted a prayer for the occasion. After a couple minutes people began peeking around and wondering if it was kosher to leave. Creature comforts awaited—hot shower, a late Sunday dinner, a warm bed—temptations overwhelming the nagging desire to show solidarity with the pious. People began to stream to their vehicles, leaving the priest to wait out the die hard faithful.

But when the priest saw Freddie breakaway to go to his truck, he felt compelled to catch up to the young man. He needed to find out more about that family. The priest had called the Martinez home on Thursday when the news broke about Peddie's disappearance. He talked with the mother briefly and was

about to invite himself over when she cut him off with "Pray for us, Father"—
click! Prayer alone doesn't cut it. A man of the cloth wants to dry the tears.

The priest came up behind just as Freddie reached his truck. There was no
sign of Raul. Did the man stumblebum into the woods? Freddie jerked open the
driver's door and saw his dad slumped over on the seat, beer cans tipped over on
his lap. Freddie looked around with furious eyes and was startled by the priest's
close presence.

"Freddie, let me help you get your dad out from behind the wheel."

Freddie shrugged his shoulders, eyes downcast, and pushed blindly past the
priest to go around to the passenger side door. He jerked it open, reached over,
and flung two Coors cans onto the ground. The friar then pushed the dead
weight while Freddie pulled. Raul stirred and mumbled as the two men heaved
him to the passenger side. Freddie slammed the passenger door and came back to
the driver's side. He jumped in and slammed that door too. The priest grabbed
his arm before he tore out of the lot.

"Freddie, hey, listen, will you! I really want to help. Can I come over to the
house tomorrow, anytime, really?"

The boy licked his lips several times before responding in a strained voice.
"That's cool with me, Father. It's fine with him too," motioning to his wasted old
man. "Come out about 4. I'll clear it with Mom. Okay?"

The priest nodded and let go of the arm. Andy went over to his car where the
hungry Pope was waiting impatiently.

*   *   *   *

Father Gurule tottered into the kitchen. The pastor told his associate that the
search made the TV news. Andy winced, remembering the ludicrous laying down
of palms, orchestrated by that TV reporter. Gurule didn't mentioned palms so
perhaps the sacrilege hadn't made the cut. Andy gave the pastor a sanitized version of the search, leaving out Raul drowning his sorrows as well as the sheriff's
confidential suspicions. He did tell Gurule that he was going over to counsel the
family tomorrow afternoon. Pastoral counseling is very good, the old priest
agreed. Should I go along? "Better not," Andy replied in as gentle a tone as possible. He didn't want to hurt the pastor's feelings but found it best to be direct.
Andy couldn't tell the real reason for excluding the pastor. That the visit was less
pastoral and more inquisitorial.

As Father Gurule left the kitchen he murmured, "Palms, oh palms," and
chuckled. Andy now knew that the incident had made the news. The archbishop

in Albuquerque and many diocesan priests probably watched as Peddie's disappearance was the lead story out of Santa Fe. The Catholic school connection had been noted and Archbishop Beckworth himself had called Thursday to find out more. The spectre of the ongoing pedophilia scandal amongst Catholic clergy haunted their conversation. Back in 1993 priest misconduct with boys and girls led to the forced resignation of the archbishop and mucho dollars in settlements. The new archbishop—Beckworth—came in to clean house and was determined to prevent the moral rot returning. He asked Andy to call him with regular updates until the boy's fate is known. The priest knew tomorrow he would have to make such a call to the diocesan office and talk to the boss. "Palms, oh palms," echoed in his head more than "Peddie, oh Peddie."

American Catholicism was still reeling from revelations of pedophilia by trusted servants. The practice of quietly transferring suspect priests from diocese to diocese by complicit bishops had come to light in Boston and other troubled sees. The Vatican was scrambling to calm the faithful and keep the collection baskets full. Recovering Catholics—bitter from the ruler rapping by rabid nuns—wondered now if there had been an element of sadomasochism in the strict discipline. Some poor souls were haunted by memories of violation. Lawyers were seeing gold in them thar spires and were seeking if not absolute truth, at least fair settlement.

Spokesmen for gay organizations asserted that pedophilia was a disorder that crossed sexual orientation boundaries. Nothing in the nature of homosexuality led to the dark side. The Church debated excluding gays from the priesthood. To practice celibacy was difficult in the most innocent of times; in our modern age we drown in a sea of sexual titillation over the Internet or on cable 24/7 if so desired. You can wake up to porn or cap your night with sleaze. Even the best of men fall prey. The Pope asserted in an encyclical that homosexuality is an objective disorder. But so far the Church deigned it permissible for priests to be gay provided they didn't practice what they felt. Do ask, do tell, don't do.

*   *   *   *

The rest of the evening was quiet at the rectory. Father Gurule had an old cat that finally came to a territorial understanding with Pope after several years of growling and screeching. During most daylight hours Pope had the run of the yard while the cat sauntered freely around the house. The cat retired early to her old master's bedroom and the dog knew instinctively not to cross the threshold. The pets slept with their priests. Andy remembered the eyebrow raising by the mattress salesman when he said he wanted a queen size bed. The implied question—why would a celibate priest need a big bed?—was left unanswered as Andy decided to let their tongues wag. Gurule read a tell-all biography of Mohandas Gandhi and found out that Gandhi in his dotage slept with two young women on a regular basis. The biographer didn't claim sex occurred but left the impression to the lewd imagination. Gurule told Andy that what was good for the pacifist icon should be good for a humble parish pastor. Andy couldn't tell if the old priest was joking or not.

On Monday morning Pope woke up the priest at 5 o'clock as always. The dog's biological clock was as reliable as any alarm clock. The dog day's greeting was less jarring than your typical buzzer. Pope just crawled over from his side of the bed and nuzzled the priest's neck, and then began licking his face thoroughly. Andy had to jump out of bed to escape the sloppy love. The priest's morning routine was to take his dog out for a long pre-dawn walk come rain or shine though that early there was mostly moonshine. This time of year there was a very slight brightening on the east horizon while a canopy of stars and the crescent moon lingered. The priest treasured this walk straddling day and night; no one was bothering him yet.

Once his dog was taken care of, the priest made a pot of coffee for himself and his pastor. Gurule had morning Mass duty, the daily 7 a.m. service. Andy could faintly hear the old man stirring in the master bedroom with the big bathroom. Soon he would emerge to eat his oatmeal. It was a bland way to start the day but best for the pastor's delicate digestion. It allowed recovery from Señora Alvarez's fiery dinner. Andy usually had wheat toast slathered with jam and a big bowl of cold cereal with sliced fruit. He ate it in his bedroom, wanting to read the morning newspaper in peace.

There was brief mention but thankfully no picture of the Palm Sunday search in the New Mexican. The county sheriff and city police chief released a joint statement thanking the community and said promising leads were being followed up. The priest assumed, given the pessimistic picture that Baca privately painted, that the authorities wanted to reassure rather than demoralize the general public and worried family. Father Andy relaxed in his recliner sipping his coffee, eating his cereal, munching on his toast, with the newspaper spread on his lap. He ate carefully, watching the crumbs. Andy liked clean and neat. He loved dust-free surfaces, made his bed every morning, vacuumed frequently, kept his basin and bowl spotless. The only signs of disorder were the dog's chew toys scattered about.

He had no overt religious symbols in his room. Father Gurule had a big crucifix over his headboard but Andy decided to display subtler affirmations of faith.
The priest during his happy hour would gaze upon and wring spiritual solace
from Monet's *Water Lilies, Giverny* and Gauguin's *The Vision After the Sermon
(Jacob Wrestling with an Angel)*. Look at the lilies in the pond; they float effort-
lessly, worshiping God simply by their beautiful nature rather than by an inspired
decision. And after the priest preaches at Mass, he often wonders if the faithful
wrestle as much with their angels as with the devil.

The two priests split the weekday Mass schedule. A couple dozen or so of the
faithful attended the simple morning service. Since this was Holy Week, stretching from Palm Sunday through Easter, both priests had to do double duty with
nightly prayer and worship services. There were always the sick at home and in
care facilities to be visited with the sacraments. Routine parish administrative and
financial affairs couldn't be forgotten either. But Holy Week rituals trumped the
everyday, as they celebrated the high points of the Christian drama: Jesus' trium-
phant arrival in Jerusalem, the Last Supper, Judas' betraying kiss in Gethsemane
gardens, Pontius Pilate washing his hands, the Crucifixion on Golgotha, the glorious Resurrection.

The most significant and arduous ritual was the 33 mile walk that Andy led,
the Good Friday pilgrimage from Santo Thérèse to El Santuario de Chimayó.
The march actually started late Thursday night so the priest and the hardiest of
the pilgrims could arrive by noon. It was from noon to three that Jesus hung on
the cross till his temporary demise. El Santuario was a shrine whose dirt was
believed to contain miraculous healing properties. On Good Friday some 30,000
pilgrims descended on Chimayó to somberly pray and cross themselves with a
sacred smudge.

The priest had never witnessed a miracle at the shrine. That lack of a 'Walk,
by God!' moment didn't prevent the sick and crippled from coming year after
year. Father Andy felt terribly moved by their struggle. Many were forced to give
up before the dawn. Though the accompanying vans were ready to give a lift the
rest of the way, some said no and were driven home in abject despair. The priest
tried to console these poor souls, buck up their spirits, by telling them that the
soul was the only true thing, the body so fleeting.

Father Gurule got his morning news from the small TV in the kitchen. As
Andy went back into the kitchen to pour himself another cup of coffee, he heard
the voice of Sam Fujema reporting from the ski basin. Sure enough, the clip
shown included the palms being laid before the leaders of the Winsor Trail

search, a stern expression on the sheriff's face, a stricken one on the priest's. Andy wondered how viewers would interpret the pain on his face.

Father Gurule offered what comfort he could. "Look, Andy, don't worry about that nonsense. If you live as long as me you laugh at the banana peels. You slip and laugh and pick yourself up and go on. What really matters is our spiritual side and our feelings towards each other. You know, amen to life, my boy!"

Andy felt a shiver run through his body at the phrase, "amen to life." Father Gurule was echoing what Ray said at communion. What kind of amen corner is this, the two men singing out of the same hymnal? The priest believed in spiritual serendipity, divinely inspired coincidence. But what message is God whispering in my ear?

"Father, you're right of course," Andy said. "I'm taking this too much to heart. It's just that the archbishop wants an update and we know so little. The sheriff, by the way, gave the school a clean bill of health. Sorry—should have told you that last night. It appears the boy left the school safely. They seem to be look-ing at the family."

"Yes, I know that family well," the pastor responded. "I baptized and con-firmed all three Martinez children. I remember that Raul as a young family man used to come around the church, attending Mass. But the drink took him, Andy. He lost his faith though he doesn't appear to interfere with his wife's worship or his kids' Catholic education. It's funny how some parents say the hell with you, you mother church, but rush their newborns in to be baptized."

The two priests both burst out laughing at the disconnect between what peo-ple say, what people do. The pastor and his associate rarely laughed together. One memorable night they watched a rented movie together, <u>Going My Way</u>, the classic Catholic fable about two Depression era priests in the same position in New York. Bing Crosby played the easy-going, crooning priest assigned to replace Barry Fitzgerald, the bemused, weathered Irish pastor. Andy loved the movie and he and Gurule laughed at the humor and the humanity. They even sang along with Father O'Malley and the ragamuffin children's choir on the "I'd rather be a pig" or bird or fish song. The next day, as the no-nonsense Sister Claire drilled the Little Flower children's choir, the two priests came in like mis-chievous sprites to suggest the children sing the back to nature song. Claire shooed them away with later, later but later never came.

After breakfast the priest went over to the parish office. He dealt with routine paperwork till 9 a.m. He decided then to get the dreaded call to the archbishop over with. He anticipated a short and pointed conversation. Though the arch-bishop's homilies and pastoral letters were far from the soul of brevity, his dealings with his religious and lay staffs were notoriously curt. Father Andy often wondered how Beckworth responded to a vacillating sinner in the confessional. Could he resist saying, "Oh, get on with it, pray tell!"

The archbishop's secretary put him through.

Archbishop: "Here."

Priest: "This is Leary of Santa Fe. I want to update you on the boy."

Archbishop: "Still missing."

Priest: "Yes, despite trying."

Archbishop: "What was that business with the palms?"

Priest: "I was blindsided by the TV reporter. He got a few to lay down palms and then the rest followed."

Archbishop: "Like sheep, huh?"

Priest: "Something like that."

Archbishop: "Go on."

Priest: "I had a long talk with our sheriff and so far no solid leads. Just some suspicion about the family."

Archbishop: "Just so. Anything else?"

Priest: "Just that the school staff has been questioned and cleared. So far sitting pretty."

Archbishop: "Good to hear. How's Gurule holding up?"

Priest: "Like a rock."

Archbishop: "Say hello for me."

Priest: "Will do."

Archbishop: "God bless you both."

Priest: "Ditto."

Archbishop: "Call me in two days or sooner if anything comes up. And Leary, the truth now—nothing funny going on up there?"

Priest: "No, Father, no funny business."

Archbishop: "Keep it that way, my son. Later!"

Father Andy hung up and breathed a sigh of relief. Andy realized that holding back that funny business with Ray at Mass was denying the archbishop absolute 'truth' but was not lying about what was proven to date. Intuition is real enough but drawing conclusions requires facts on the ground. The archbishop had no need to know about first impressions.

The priest spent the rest of the morning working out the logistics of the ecumenical service that the Catholic and Protestant ministers traditionally co-sponsored Wednesday night of Holy Week. As de facto head of Santo Thérèse, Father Andy handled liaison with his fellow Christian ministers. With the defeat of godless Communism, swelling self-absorption and materialism run riot represented the greatest dangers to the soul. Despite differences in dogma and practice, the clergy worked together to encourage people to dwell on their spiritual side and worship as they please, but please worship. Pastor Gurule wasn't having any of it. The old priest believed that the Holy Roman Catholic Church was the only true one, with a direct historical link with Jesus Christ. Gurule particularly scoffed at the Episcopalians. He said it was a bogus religion with its Anglican roots planted in perfidy by Henry the Eighth. A pseudo church created so the king could wed at will and divorce by offing their pretty heads without papal intervention. The Episcopalian's unofficial motto, "high on ritual, low on guilt," was mocked by the pastor as "it's okay to sin as long as you look good doing it."

But the pastor was out of step with the modern Church. Gentle persuasion has replaced harangues as proselytizing approaches to unbelievers. Catholics didn't cold-call for Christ anymore. Father Andy was of two minds about the change. The attraction, not promotion technique may mean fewer converts but perhaps they stick around longer without coercion from the get-go. But Andy admired true believers. He occasionally saw the young, clean-cut Mormon missionaries pounding the pavement in Santa Fe. Their faith was surely tested by slammed doors. In the graveyard hours of the pilgrimage, whenever the footsore priest prayed for a second wind, he thought of the Mormon kids. Perhaps that is the essence of ecumenicalism: a Catholic priest drawing inspiration from Mormon practice. After all, even the parochial Gurule looked to Gandhi for life lessons.

His phone conversations with the participating Protestant ministers went smoothly as plans for the Wednesday evening's ecumenical service were reviewed and finalized. It was a big deal for the priest; the archbishop himself would be coming up from Albuquerque to take part. Because Santa Fe was traditionally and still nominally a Roman Catholic town, a Catholic parish always was included while the Protestants had to rotate. This year it was the Episcopalians and Presbyterians turn. Observant Jews did their own thing, with Passover at sunset Wednesday also. Jews and Christians had quite a history together, some of it bloody, with pogroms against the Jews winked at by Christian potentates. Pope John Paul had already offered the Church's belated apology for stoking anti-Semitism over the centuries. Father Andy did his part at the local level by befriending young Rabbi Bernstein. One monthly activity was for the priest and the rabbi to take their dogs up to the national forest for a long afternoon.

Before lunch Father Andy drove over to St. Vincent's Hospital to visit the sick with the sacraments. St. Vincent's was Santa Fe's only hospital and was nick-named St. Victim's by local wags. Andy usually handled the hospital outreach while lay volunteers did home visits Sunday afternoon with communion wafers. Father Gurule didn't get out much anymore. The state had rescinded his driving privileges due to fading eyesight and diabetes-numbed feet. The pastor still visited with a few favorite shut-ins. Sister Muni drove him in her old Volkswagen beetle. Both of small stature and further stooped by age, they literally disappeared in their seats. Tailgaters probably wondered if the VW was being operated by remote control.

Andy spent a couple hours almost daily at the hospital hearing confessions, distributing communion, offering whatever comfort he could. Some patients would never go home again. Many brought the havoc upon themselves, through a sick mix of self-abuse: smoking, drinking, binge eating, drug overdose, unprotected sex. The priest wondered if God was as harsh as man in judging. People wanted to add insult to injury. If cancer ever cuts me down, the priest concluded, let it be a blameless one like bone.

After the hospital visit Andy took lunch at the rectory. Since his normal happy hour would be spent at the abnormal, unhappy Martinez compound, he decided to devout some time to his dog and exercise. The priest reluctantly stayed away from a shot of Jameson's because he figured alcohol on his breath would distract from his moral message to the family. On his fast unleashed walk with the Pope, they carried on a spirited conversation. It was a bit one-sided but useful in reaching clarity on what to do next. Later today or tomorrow at the latest he needed to call Mrs. Alarid and find out more about Ray's mentoring. Given what the sheriff said, perhaps Ray was simply a red herring. But Andy wanted to leave nothing to chance.

Then Father Andy remembered that the parochial school keeps written records on its volunteers. These records were kept in a locked file cabinet in Sister Maria's office. Andy didn't have a key but knew where the principal stashed hers. With the school closed for Easter break, it was unlikely Maria or her office staff would be there today. The priest could take a peek with no one the wiser.

Father Andy stopped at the school on his way back to the office. The parking lot was indeed empty but for one pick-up, probably the head janitor's. The school had no alarm system to disarm. A few years ago in the wake of the Columbine massacre an expensive alarm system was installed but soon produced too many false alarms. When it reached the point of fines, the school administrators and board agreed to disable the system permanently. Andy was secretly relieved as he had too many PINS and passwords to memorize already.

The priest saw the janitor polishing the floor at the end of the corridor. He waved at the man but Diego's eyes were glued to his task. So be it, Andy decided, he could be in-and-out without encouraging idle curiosity. The priest ducked into Maria's office and retrieved the cabinet key from the back of her desk drawer. He opened the cabinet and found the mentor files. He didn't know Ray's last name so spent a minute or two fingering through the last names. Luckily snapshots were stapled to the basic info form so the priest found the person of interest without too much trouble. Ray's last name was Yazzie.

Andy sat at Sister Maria's desk to examine the file. The first thing that cried out was marital status—single—and the second was his birth date—May 16th, 1951. That made the man just past fifty and still single. The form also contained a divorced box to check and it was blank. Single, single. Maybe the form should be updated with a gay box. Is that at all relevant in evaluating the man's worthiness to mentor? The priest liked to say no; certainly nurturing wasn't the province of heterosexuals alone. The priest knew the all-embracing Maria wouldn't preclude a gay man from being around her children. But in the light of Andy's intuition, Ray's lifestyle became pertinent indeed.

To become a mentor at Santo Thérèse required a felony background check. Ray came up clean. Three non-family members of the community vouched for his respectability with phrases like "dedicated", "hard working", and "cares about people". He listed his occupation as retired. Under reason(s) for wanting to become a mentor, Ray wrote succinctly, "To give back". His address was listed as on a street in Nava Adé, in the same neighborhood as the rectory. It was close to the church, close to the school.

According to the file Ray was in his third year as a mentor. The file listed the teachers and grades he worked with but, alas, not the individual students. He worked the last two years with Mrs. CdeBaca's third graders. That would coincide with Peddie's grade last school year. But the school had three third grade classes and the priest didn't know which one Peddie had been in. His student file would reveal that but those records had been completely computerized. The priest didn't have a password. He never had occasion to access files behind Maria's back before.

The priest returned Ray's files to the cabinet and locked it up. He returned the key to the little box in the back of her desk drawer. Out of curiosity he opened the drawer beneath. In this one Sister Maria stashed her personal hygiene and touch up aids: hair brush, toothbrush and paste, mouthwash, lip stick, blush, lip balm, and Tampex. Andy muttered, "Oh gee," as he looked down on the nun's make-up as a woman. He was most curious about the lipstick as the nun rarely wore lipstick, at least out in public. The priest would have noticed. He picked up the lipstick and turned the bottom so the tip emerged. Ruby red! A bold color even for a streetwalker; an absurd one for a nun. The priest figured she must have confiscated it from a schoolgirl growing up too fast. He turned the bottom so the tip disappeared, turned it so the red tip came out again, back in, back out, finally in for good. He put the lipstick carefully back in the drawer, placing it in the same spot, same angle—maybe. He turned to the hair brush and gazed at the strands of strawberry blonde hair. So fine, so lovely, so impossible. The priest impulsively extracted several strands of her hair. He looked around, saw a stack of envelopes near the printer, grabbed one and placed the strands inside. He licked the flap, sealed it, and stuffed it into his pants pocket under the robe. Andy placed the hairbrush back into the drawer, less concerned now about perfect placement as who the hell remembers such trivial as angles of personal items in a drawer. He left the office and looked down the hallway at Diego changing polishing pads on the machine. The janitor looked up when the priest closed the door to the main office. They waved at each other but the keyed up priest decided to leave it at that. Diego may wonder at the sudden appearance but wouldn't question the associate pastor's right to be there. Father Andy hurried out of the school, feeling soiled yet strangely elated.

The priest fully realized that he had just committed a sin. The critical question was—venial or mortal? His snooping around was certainly motivated by good intentions. God wanted him to pursue all leads. But no higher power wanted a priest to chase after a nun. Andy's lust for Maria was unseemly at the very least, over the top at times. The friar surreptitiously ogling her figure was certainly not winked at by God. And stealing away with memento strands was unconscionable. This was sin!—and must be confessed to save his soul.

This was the absolute worst time for a priest to wander off the reservation. The Church during Holy Week needed each and every one of its religious on duty without distraction. His obsession with Maria has gone on for years but he had never allowed it before to interfere with their professional partnership. Seven long years of courtesy and respect—now this blatant violation of her privacy. Thank God there was no panty for him to sniff!

It was a sin against his better nature. But in the eyes of God was it mortal? Unforgiven mortal sin would prevent him from presiding at Mass. He could feign illness to get Father Gurule to fill in tomorrow morning but that would compound lust with a lie. The priest was raised with the conviction that impure thoughts were venial in nature. A cheating heart alone doesn't put you in harm's way. Real cleavage from God requires hard core actions.

But what actions lead one to rejection at heaven's gate? Touching yourself while envisioning the wellspring of desire—was that mortal? Undressing her with prying eyes—was that beyond the pale? Touching her without permission was certainly so, and a crime besides. Over the years the priest had touched the nun in casual conversation as people do, to emphasize a point or show empathy. That went both ways; Maria was a serial toucher. Innocent on the surface but the priest knew better, and felt terrible and titillated at the same time. Given Sister Maria's straightforward, expansive nature, there was more than an occasional hug. Looking into her eyes, Andy realized that she felt nothing more than mild affection. It was so unfair that the surge of anarchic emotion was all coming from his side.

Father Andy cast a professional eye on his misbehavior. He decided to give himself a pass. For one, he didn't steal anything but a few strands of her hair; certainly far from a scalping. Secondly, he had proven over many years that he could exercise self-control and not jump her bones. The sin was therefore venial and could be confessed at his leisure.

Andy went to confession every three months whether he needed it or not. But it wasn't as though he had to imagine sins to make the experience more real; there was always something askew that be construed as sin. The priest usually sat face to face with Gurule as using the privacy screen between colleagues would be pointless. There would be a frank discussion of human failings that ended with a mild penance of meditative prayer on your knees. The priest bemused that he wasn't found out again. If he felt truly ashamed of his sins, Andy traveled up to Jemez Springs to confess to Father Ansalmo. Ansalmo was rector of a retreat facility for troubled clergy. For forgiveness of truly mortal sin, Jemez was the destination of choice.

Andy loved Ansalmo. Over their many years of friendship, Andy would look into the old man's crinkled face and shimmering eyes and take to heart the taunting: tell me one I haven't heard before, shock me with the unforgivable. Every dirty deed had been forgiven to date; the old man would gently shrug his shoulders as he said go out and sin no more.

The modern Church recommended confession face to face for the laity too. The theory was that though our sins weigh us down as we enter the church, a friendly face and absolving words would put the spring back into our step. The traditional confessional booth was still available at Santo Thérèse but two simple chairs, out in the open, were set-up so you could spill your guts knock-knee with your priest. This evening, from 6 p.m. to 8:30, the penitential service would take place, the first of overtime nights for both priests during this holiest of liturgical weeks.

Father Andy had no more time to dwell on sin and forgiveness. He needed to be over at the Martinez home by 4. Along with offering transparent spiritual consolation, he must be crafty in his probing of the boy's disappearance. The priest had an ace in the hole that a police detective couldn't play. Father Andy could offer the ultimate winning hand: divine forgiveness. He didn't know if confession was in the offing but at least the priest would gain insight into the workings of the family.

He started up his car in the school lot. Andy looked at his watch—3:50. The Martinez compound was just minutes away by car from the school, about a fifteen minute walk. It was over that short distance that Peddie fell off the map. He may have walked along the road or taken a short cut through the scrub land and shallow arroyo. Andy was acquainted with the arroyo as it was part of Pope's running loop. There were several blind spots where a vagrant up to no good could have grabbed the boy. If he walked along the road, a stranger could have lured him into a car. But there were many cars on that road right after school. No one reported anything suspicious. Of course if Peddie freely jumped into the car of a trusted adult, no passerby was likely to think twice.

CHAPTER 5

▼

'Spiriting the child away,' I love the phrase, as though we are shepherding a lost boy into the realm of the gods. Instead we plunge head first into the down and dirty landscape of the human body. They don't say deflower when it comes to a boy; the language is so much kinder, decorous even, towards the fairer sex. I've always stayed out of the ladies room but I suspect an experience there far different from the gents. Chamber music, soft wipes, heart-shaped soaps—no wonder they always want to bring a girlfriend along. Such ambiance for one of those necessary but off-putting bodily functions. We never look good doing it. Making love is a different affair; there's fluidity to it, a certain beauty. Love calls for a mirror. I don't want to say "the fuck you say" unless I have to. Ha! The language of boys is so crude these days. Just ask any teacher. Does the child babble of things yet to be experienced? It seems if I want true innocence I have to rob the cradle. But that's not my m.o. I'm willing to risk the desired one not being as good as he appears.

*   *   *   *

The priest pulled into the Martinez compound, located just outside the modern Nava Adé development. Andy wondered if the Nava developer had made an offer to the family, as their 4-5 acres had great value on the growing south side. The Martinez home was a traditional adobe structure, timeworn with many visible cracks. Their grounds had the flavor of rural New Mexico, with a couple rusted out, stripped down old trucks on one side of the house and a dented Ford sedan on the other. Old porcelain fixtures—several bathtubs and basins, kitchen sinks—were piled into one of the beds. Several working trucks including Freddie's F250 were parked next to an outbuilding that served as office and storage for Bug Out, Raul's business. There was a chicken coop next to the truck carcasses, the roosters and chickens clucking and bobbing at seed scattered about. A coyote fence of rough cut cedar sheltered the back and sides of the coop but left the front open to all predatory comers.

The grounds had no xeriscaping, no stone gardens. There were several apple trees and patches of buffalo grass surrounding the house. A child's swing and slide set—one of those metal ones in bright red—sat close to the abandoned trucks. Father Andy tried to imagine young Peddie playing there. At ten years old, he had probably outgrown the set. It was weathering slowly in the high desert, waiting for grandkids to discover the simple pleasures. The priest had trouble seeing Raul as he is today—drunk, belligerent—pushing a deliriously happy child on the swing or catching him off the slide.

The priest was surprised that there were no beds of desert flowers or a vegetable garden. Amelia's specialty, after all, in her church work was the floral arrangements for the liturgical seasons. It appeared that she had little time or energy left over to dress up her own property—at least outdoors.

Andy got out of his car and was immediately confronted by three barking dogs appearing out of nowhere. One was a pit bull and the other two of dubious parentage. The pit bull looked to be most dangerous, baring his teeth, coming terrifying close to the priest, perhaps catching a whiff of Pope. The priest didn't move, just leaned against his car door, trying to appear unruffled. The dogs barked; the fowl clucked and crowed; his heart raced. Out of long standing habit, he carried rosary beads and a couple dog biscuits in his pocket for Pope. The Franciscan didn't know if fingering the beads would help more than offering the biscuits. He had two biscuits; there were three dogs. He would have to count his fingers if he tried that. Certainly St. Francis of Assisi had the gift to talk angry dogs down but his modern disciple was no mimic. Andy looked to the house for salvation. Several windows were open.

The door flew open and Freddie came rushing out. The mixed breeds immediately turned tail and retreated to one of the abandoned trucks, their fortress. The pit bull remained steadfast at the foot of the intruder and received a sharp kick in the side from Freddie for his trouble. The dog scurried away, whimpering.

"Sorry, Father, about the dogs. They bark like crazy but haven't bit a priest in years," Freddie said in a tremulous tone.

The priest glanced over at the dogs now resting in the sun. The pit bull was busily licking its side. Andy wondered if the dog was just bruised or really hurt. The priest, feeling both grateful and disgusted, focused again on his rescuer.

The Franciscan showed Freddie his biscuits. "I always carry these around for my dog. I was willing to share but that one over there wasn't having any of it. I don't mean to lecture, Freddie, but what about a fenced doggie run? And a Beware of Dog sign? People sue these days over dog bites."

Freddie shrugged. "Actually, Father, we do have a sign posted, over near the front door." The young man motioned to the small sign with bold letters, PROTECTED BY PIT BULL SECURITY. "Does that protect us against lawsuits, Father? Wouldn't want the Church suing us! But seriously, Father, my dad likes the dogs to be unleashed and they don't seem to wander far. The chickens seem to like them loose. They keep the coyotes away. But come in, Father, we need comforting more than the dogs."

They went to the still opened front door with Amelia Martinez watching the commotion. The woman looked none too happy. But the priest had never known the woman to smile, at least in public; can glummest be a lifestyle choice? Of course, given that her youngest was missing, the priest didn't expect her to be beaming.

"Come in, Padre, to my house of sorrows. Do you bring any news of my boy?"

"No news, Amelia, just the good hopes and prayers of our community. And if I know anything at all, God is certainly on our side."

The priest resisted a humoring wink. Also, as is his way, he didn't squeeze her arm or hug her.

The Franciscan passed by Mrs. Martinez through the small foyer into the living room. The living room space was dominated by a long and large caramel-colored leather sectional. One side of the L-shape had a built-in recliner and it was there that Raul resided. He didn't jump up to greet the priest. Raul had a beer in his lap and another cool one waiting on the pull-down drink holder/armrest. A big projection TV was on with the sound turned up rather than muted out of respect for a pastoral visit. Andy glanced at the screen and saw an old black and white movie playing. Raul looked up at the priest and then beyond to his wife wringing her hands. He shrugged, muted the sound, but kept the flick going.

"Want a beer?" Raul asked.

"No, Mr. Martinez, I'll take a rain check on that."

Amelia went over to a cushion chair facing the sectional and motioned for the priest to sit there. The mother sat down in the wedge seat and her son sat on the far end opposite his father. The priest looked at the three of them and they looked back at them. Andy knew from reading mysteries that clues can hide in plain sight. He looked briefly around. Religious art predominated. Several retablos occupied nichos in the walls. A large painting of the Virgin of Guadalupe loomed over Freddie's head. In the corner of the room was a shrine but not to God in heaven. On a pedestal was an alien creature, the kind you blow up for your kids. There was a framed sign posted above the creature: **ROSWELL HAPPENED/LIVE WITH IT.**

Raul motioned to the TV. "Have you seen it, Padre? It's a great one," he said in a slurry voice. Though beer drunk, Raul made a stab at cleaning up for the visit. His wet hair was slicked back; he had shaved off Sunday's grizzle. A small bandage covered a razor cut on his chin. His clothes were clean and presentable: khaki shirt, denim jeans. He wasn't wearing shoes though; just white socks with a hole in one exposing the tip of his big toe. It was hard for the priest to concentrate on the man's bloodshot eyes.

Andy looked away to the great movie. The scene jogged his memory; he had seen this flick many years ago. Given what Freddie said about the science fiction channel on day and night, the priest assumed the b&w movie must be classic sci-fi. On the screen cars came to a sudden stop and baffled drivers jumped out. An actor came on, the priest recognized him, an English actor, Michael Rennie, that's who.

"Yes, Mr. Martinez, I seem to remember this. Can't recall the name though."

"The Day The Earth Stood Still is the title, Padre. They don't make 'em like this anymore," Raul said. "How it goes, see, this space saucer lands in Washington and everybody goes ballistic. The army is called out and they surround the craft with tanks and artillery. Jets circle overhead. All popguns when confronted by the power of the universe. The twist, see, is that the space creature is here for good only, to warn us earthlings about the error of our ways. People went fucking crazy with fear for no reason. No fucking reason at all!"

The priest heard a gasp coming from Amelia at the 'fucking' slip. The Franciscan had been around vulgar characters in his life and tried hard not to judge them harshly. He tried to find the good in people, even profane ones. Raul took a long swig of his beer and the priest felt a terrible thirst. He would have loved a beer but out of respect for the mother would stay far, far away from sidling up to drunken alienation.

Raul's bleary eyes returned to the movie. The phrase he used—'people went crazy with fear for no reason'—resonated in the priest's mind as he saw the obvious fear in Mrs. Martinez's eyes. A mother's eyes missing her child, not knowing if her baby was facing another night alone or in bad company. Her first born showed no fear though. Freddie's eyes reflected clear-eyed resolution. Freddie, a high school senior, struck the priest as the man of the family. By all accounts he was the true father figure for his kid brother. Father Andy could see Freddie pushing the boy on a swing at the heavens, catching Peddie as he slid giggling down the slide.

The priest pretended to watch as his mind drifted away. In 1997 his sister Circe and her kids visited from Chicago so they could all make the pilgrimage to Roswell, New Mexico for the 50th anniversary celebrations of the alien crash. The initial press release in 1947 stated that the wreckage was from a UFO before the military's overnight retraction. A concerned citizenry was informed in the revised version that it was a weather balloon brought down by bad weather. The alien on Raul's pedestal came from the description that the local funeral director gave of the autopsied creatures. Whatever the truth behind the crash, mysterious sightings in the blue sky and black nights of the west happened all the time. The common theories were that they either came from outer space or from rumored and real military bases such as Area 51.

The Roswell celebration was a hoot. The children had an alien look-alike contest. There were several abduction seminars. One memorable testimonial was by a Native American who spoke movingly to a hushed audience of his visit to his tribe in outer space. The tour of the actual crash site at the MacBrazil ranch was most interesting. The guide asked Andy, as always dressed in his friar's robe, if the possibility of extraterrestrial life was compatible with Christian belief. The priest scored some points for his side by responding: "Well, God is rumored to be out somewhere, we believe that, and what form His angels come to us is beyond our knowing."

Back in the here and now, the priest wondered what to say. He didn't have the leisure to watch the end of the movie, the happy ending. He had confessions to hear. If Sheriff Baca was right in his speculations, the priest was looking at a killer. Raul looked more pathetic than dangerous. But Father Andy wondered if that was the way it was in real life, that a child killer didn't have telltale signs of evil on the make: nostrils that flared, throbbing veins in his forehead, eyes inflamed with rage and lust. But Raul's eyes were indeed bloodshot, fed by the poison of soddened days and nights.

"They come in all sizes, Padre. Do you see that?"

Andy shook his head instinctively not because he believed that one size fits all but rather to shake off his dreaminess. A priest inquisitor needed to achieve a cold intellectual state, a dispassionate mind, if the mystery was to be solved, evil confronted and destroyed.

"I'm sorry, Mr. Martinez, I don't quite understand. What comes in all sizes?"

Raul motioned to the TV. "Monsters from outer space—what do you think?! I really shouldn't say monsters because some come down to do good. You see, Padre, Hollywood usually goes the other way, like in that <u>Independence Day</u> movie. Did you see that one?"

"No, no, I didn't, sir."

"Well, that was a good one too, special effects like wow! Pow! When the President took to the jet to battle the monoliths, I cheered like fucking crazy and you would have cheered too. But it had nothing to do with reality, you know what I mean?"

The priest looked at Amelia Martinez who was preternaturally pale and at her son whose brown skin seemed to grow darker. He turned his attention back to the man in the recliner. The priest felt his own fair skin flush with anger and frustration.

"And what is reality, Mr. Martinez?" The priest found his voice rising, his mind overwhelmed with passion. "I'll tell you what reality is! Your boy is missing and you sit here watching a silly movie. And you weren't in any shape to look for him yesterday either. Man, pull yourself together! Your boy needs you; your family needs you. What the hell are you doing?"

The obscenity slipped out but God would just have to give him a pass. Father Andy was pissed off at the world as we have it. He wanted something better and cleaner for innocent life such as Peddie's.

An aroused Raul pointed at the Roswell alien in the corner. "But you don't know what's going on, Padre. Maybe my boy was taken by a higher form of life. I believe it was for research only. After they examine the boy, he'll be returned to us." He looked over at his wife. "Amelia baby, he'll come back to us. He'll be older and wiser. You'll see, baby."

"Oh, Raul," his wife cried, her hand rising to cover her mouth. With an agonized groan Freddie jumped off the sectional and rushed out the front door, slamming it behind him.

Raul looked at the door and muttered, "Like wow! Like pow!" He picked up the remote and switched off the TV. He clicked the reclining footrest into place and got to his feet unsteadily. He lurched over to the seated priest, leaned over, grabbing the arms of the chair for support. The two fathers were in each others' face. Andy could almost taste the stale beer. He wanted to look away, hold his breath.

"You tell me, Padre, what I should do! You want me to come over to the church and light a candle for my boy? You want me to say 'mea culpa, mea culpa, mea maxima culpa'? Wipe my ass and save my fucking soul? Give a poor sinner a break, Padre, tell me what to do! I want my boy back. I want Peddie to come home. Tell me, you—"

The priest pushed Raul back forcefully enough that he fell hard on the tile floor. His wife rushed to her husband's side and knelt down. Andy got up and looked down at the shaken man on the floor. Raul looked as though he was emerging from a black hole and amazed to be back on planet earth. The priest heard the door open and looked over his shoulder, fearing it was the incensed son. It wasn't Freddie; it was the other sibling, Gabby. The girl walked in to find their parish priest looming over her father down for the count. The teenager didn't look shocked or even surprised.

"Mom, what's happening now?" she said in a monotone. "Is there news about Peddie?"

"No, honey, there isn't," Amelia responded, getting up to her feet. "Father Andy came by to visit and your father slipped, that's all. I'm going to get him to bed. Keep our guest company, Gabby. Maybe give him some of those cookies I baked for Peddie. See if he wants something to drink. Okay, honey?"

"Sure, Mom. Where's Freddie?"

"He went out somewhere. He'll be back."

The priest bent down to help Amelia who was struggling with her subdued but dead weight husband. With both of them lifting and heaving, they managed to get him up. They let him loose for a second and then thought better of it. Raul was still swaying as though adrift on a rough sea.

"I'll help you get him to the bedroom, Mrs. Martinez."

"No, Father, no! He's mine to get to bed. Stay with Gabby while I care for my husband. He hasn't been well. Go on now. Gabby will take care of you."

The priest let go and the husband and wife shuffled their way towards the bedroom. Father Andy turned towards the girl. Gabby was carrying a gym bag and was dressed in shorts and a St. Michael's T-shirt. Her skin had the healthy flush that comes after exercise. She shrugged her shoulders.

"Welcome to our happy home, Father! Dad doesn't fall asleep like normies do; he just passes out. Quicker that way. Coffee or tea, Father? I have a stash of herbal teas if you'd like."

The priest glanced at his watch before answering. "Coffee, please, black and a cookie sounds great." It was 4:55 and the priest needed to be at the church to hear confessions at 6 p.m. Though the sacrament was somewhat out of fashion, both priests were needed for the Holy Week rush. Sometimes Father Andy thought that they could move things along by posting a sign above one confessional for express forgiveness of 10 sins or less, and the other reserved for serial sinners stocking up.

The priest sat down again and waited for Gabby to return from the kitchen. In detective fiction tossing the victim's or suspect's bedroom often revealed clues and insights into the person's character and lifestyle. The friar couldn't figure any pretext for visiting the master bedroom—I mean, bless the prostrate drunk? hear his sorted confession?—but thought of a way to ask for entry into Peddie's room.

The priest hoped that the caffeine would give him the lift to see the day through. Rising before dawn led to a late afternoon droop. What normally rejuvenated the priest was his happy hour with Pope and a libation or two. Then a little later having a good dinner with wine before relaxing with a book or watching some TV. But Holy Week offered no rest for the weary clergy. Andy said silently a fast prayer that God would allow him to do justice both to sacred ritual as well as the missing boy.

Gabby came back with coffee and a small plate of cookies.

"You said black, Father, but I didn't know whether that meant sugar or not."

"No, Gabby, black is black to me." Even as he said it, what echoed in the priest's mind was a fragment of a song: "Black is black; I want my baby back. It's gray; it's gray, since you went away." So many songs listened to so often, the priest mused, maybe our life could be like a grand opera, the everyday sung in perfect key, leaving the soap out for that only brings tears.

Andy noticed that the cookies were chocolate chip with some sort of nuts. His favorite, and Peddie's apparently too. The coffee was strong and he thanked the Lord for that. Then he realized he should be a gentleman. He offered his server a cookie.

"No thanks, I'm trying to watch the carbs. I was over at a friend's house jumping around to a Richard Simmons video. He looks like a geek but he used to be really gross. I mean really gross! Supersized! So jumping around for him really worked. He's probably sushi man now too. I need to watch myself. Don't you think, Father?"

Gabby brought her hand up to the side of her head and tilted it in a provocative pose and wiggled her hips.

The priest smiled and sought to reassure. "You're hardly fat, my girl."

She gave Father Andy a 'tell me another one' look. In truth, Gabby was petite like her mother but her stomach showed some pooching signs of her father's genes. Andy knew that around puberty, girls often have a distorted view of their bodies as though seriously scrutinizing themselves in a fun house mirror. Kids can be so cruel in the locker room. In some ways Gabby would fit in with the cutting edge of cool, sporting a small gold nose ring, tattoos on both arms, and spiked purple hair. But teenagers can find flaws in the Virgin Mary.

Gabby went over to the sectional and sat on the reclining side so recently vacated by her father. She reached down, untied her athletic shoes, and kicked them off. She pulled the recliner arm and stretched out. She gave the priest a long stare over her bare legs and anklets. The priest glanced at the legs before quickly returning to her eyes. Andy felt suddenly exposed and awkward, holding the coffee in one hand while balancing the cookie plate in his lap. There was no end table relief. The priest had already wolfed down two cookies and wondered if a third would appear gluttonous. He hated eating when the person sitting across wasn't.

"You know, Gabby, when I was your age I thought I was fat too and I stopped looking in the mirror. Now I look in the mirror all the time and it cracks too. But seriously, you'll become more comfortable with yourself as you grow up. I get my exercise by taking my dog out for long walks and we go out to the woods often. Believe me, fall in love with nature and you'll fall in love with yourself. At least that's my experience."

Gabby opened her mouth as though to reply but then looked away from nature boy. Her eyes seemed to be misting over. Andy sensed the girl's vulnerability beyond the hard edge, facing the volatile changes of teenage years while coping with an alcoholic father and missing brother. She tried to appear blasé about Peddie's plight but her question about breaking news revealed her true colors. She cared for her baby brother.

The priest realized he was lying through his teeth—about himself. He still avoided mirrors. Fat staring back, too many chins (who was he fooling with the beard!) Maybe at some halcyon age all will be right with the universe and in the mirror. But not today and probably not tomorrow. Nature hikes didn't keep the priest from sensing the decay of time.

Father Andy shook his head to clear it of self absorption and focus again on this girl in need. "You know, Gabby, we have to do the best with what we have. I know this must be a difficult time for you. I just want to tell…"

"Where's Freddie?" Gabby interrupted in a strident tone. "What happened to my brother?"

"Freddie's just gone for awhile, honey." It was her mother responding, finally leaving her husband to sleep it off.

Amelia joined her daughter and sat in the wedge seat again. She looked over at her visitor. "How were the cookies, Father?"

"They were great, Amelia. I'll take a couple with me if I may. I'll enjoy them after the penitential service tonight. I wanted to ask, though, if I may see Peddie's room, just to get a sense of the boy. It might help me personalize, you know, my prayers."

The priest wondered if she would buy his flimsy pretext. He certainly didn't want to raise false hope or real fears based on his premonition about Ray. He couldn't very well share the sheriff's suspicions of family involvement. The Martinez's expected spiritual comfort and potent prayer from their priest. They didn't need loose lips. But a visit to the boy's bedroom wasn't really necessary for prayer to have its impact. I mean, it wasn't like, save Peddie, dear Lord, You know him, the Santa Fe kid who likes chocolate chip cookies with nuts and is a Broncos fan. The Franciscan wondered if to focus on one child was shortsighted. God save all children in harm's way, a blanket appeal, across the whole wide world.

"Of course, Father. Gabby will get that doggie bag together and I'll show you my boy's room."

Gabby clicked the recliner down and came over to relieve the priest of his cookie plate and empty coffee cup. Andy got up and followed Amelia down the hall.

"When Peddie was born we decided to build upon the house, giving us his bedroom."

It was a small room with a poster on the door that warned: KEEP OUT—AREA 51—THOSE WHO TRESPASS WILL BE TRANSPORTED. Inside the room the motif wasn't alien chic but more contemporary American boy. There was a poster of the rapper Enimen on the wall. An M-1 tank and Stealth fighter models stood sentinel on the small dresser. There was a small trophy with a silver baseball bat between the fighting machines. Peddie slept on a captain's bed with storage drawers underneath.

With the boy's mother watching and sleuthing time running out, Andy couldn't scour the room for clues. The priest sighed, realizing that he was no Sherlock, able to discern foul play from disturbed dust on the mantle. He assumed the police had already checked for forensic evidence. According to Baca, nothing was found and certainly nothing appeared out of place to his amateur eye.

"You can see, Father, that my Peddie is a normal boy, a good boy. He wouldn't of run off and he'd put up a loud fight if a bad man tried to drag him away. Promise me he'll come back. You're a man of God. You know more than me. Promise me, Father!"

The priest had never heard Mrs. Martinez raise her voice before but her last words were nearly screamed. She also grabbed the sleeve of his robe. The clichéd and fatalistic "God's will be done" wouldn't do. Saying what is true would be too cruel. He had to promise a happy ending.

"I promise, Amelia, that your boy will come back to you safe and sound."

The Old West wanted posters flashed in his mind: DEAD OR ALIVE. The priest wished the woman a fond farewell and half-expected a stirring "God's speed" in return. But she just nodded and stepped back to allow the priest to leave Area 51. Gabby gave him a zip lock bag full of cookies on the way out.

CHAPTER 6

▼

It's always best to get to know them first: the whole person, inside and out. The experts say that might actually inhibit 'abuse' as it wouldn't allow you to objectify the 'victim.' Nonsense, I say. It's the whole child I want to seduce; I want the boy to want it as bad as me. It's not really hard as sex even consumes the minds of babes. Proper people want to think differently, that we're better than that, but centuries of rape and pillage suggest otherwise. Lust has nothing to do with civilization but everything to do with reality. The way things go down. Okay, okay, I know most of us suppress lust for the sake of appearances. But I want to be a natural man. Skin is more compelling than clothes. Be honest now.

*   *   *   *

The priest was tired and bored—hungry too, as there was no time to eat after the wrenching visit to the Martinez family. He took a quick bite out of one of Amelia's cookies. He had finished three so far, one after each confession. None of the sins perked his interest. They were mere specks in the eyes of God, hardly high crimes or dastardly deeds. One poor man agonized over chronic lust for his wife's sister. The priest wasn't moved or aroused by his plight. Andy had heard the same confession from the same man ad nauseam over five, six years. To hear him tell it, it was his only sin; his soul spotless otherwise. Father Andy didn't have anything left to offer but grudging forgiveness. He had suggested psychiatric therapy to no avail. The Franciscan counseled a move to another state, or at least another parish.

Most penitents recited their sins great or small in a droning voice. The priest often sensed that they were hiding something, not graver sins necessarily, but rather cause and effect, the why of sin and its emotional impact. The men in particular didn't flagellate themselves over their failings. The female sinner was not as different as one would imagine. Sniffling was rare; no need to get out the handkerchiefs. Whatever pain or shame the penitent felt was shared with someone other than the father confessor. Andy often wondered if people really believed in the eternal consequences of sin. I mean, I forgive them with God's grace and save them from an ugly afterlife; why don't they jump with joy as they leave the church?

In parochial school Andy remembered fast and frequent confessions with 'Our Father's' and 'Hail Mary's' mumbled as penance. As a school kid he probably said a thousand of those prayers. It wasn't that he was a bad boy; the rote prayers were prescribed regardless of the nature and number of sins confessed. It was almost mathematical—every minute in the confessional translated into three minutes praying on your knees. Average length of a juvenile confession: 4 minutes. Out of there to seventh heaven in no time flat.

The sacrament was now officially called penance and reconciliation. The modern Church tried to soften the hard edges of the ancient rite, moving away from fire and brimstone if you hold anything back to a fuzzier recognition that sin alienates us not only from God but also from our fellows. A funny thing happened though on the way to enlightened spiritual healing; adult confessions became few and far between. Most parishioners went to be reconciled once a year at best. Yet fewer and fewer Catholics sat crestfallen during communion, denying themselves because of unforgiven mortal sin. Either modern Catholics were better actors in their time or what constitutes mortal sin in their minds has been whittled down to capital crimes. Perhaps people settled for forgiving themselves and left God out of it.

The priest suspected that the on-going pedophilia scandals were also to blame. The effect was to knock Catholic clergy off their moral pedestal as the taint of pederasty replaced hero worship. The image of a priest as a gently humorous man such as Bing Crosby in <u>Going My Way</u> was replaced by the horny-handed cleric hiding his face from the camera. And the Church's authority was further undermined by the tepid response of American bishops, transferring offenders to another diocese far away, hoping for a geographic cure short of heaven or hell.

Andy spent the first hour or so of the service in the alcove dedicated to face to face reconciliations. Father Gurule was in the traditional privacy booth. The old priest preferred being there, ensconced in the comfy chair, though he would grudgingly trade places with his associate for the final hour. Just before the switch, Father Andy had his first interesting confession. The fella was new to the parish and would be welcomed back to confession anytime. What perked Andy's curiosity was not juicy sin. Rather, the man dealt with the minutiae of failings in his everyday conduct with his wife and children. To the priest they didn't seem like sins at all but more the rough and tumble of human beings living together. What impressed Father Andy was that the man cared enough to examine his most intimate relationships in the light of his Christian faith.

The church was empty as the two father confessors approached each other for the switch. Gurule complained that his butt hurt and his back ached. In the old days, he said, the church would be filled with waiting penitents and he wouldn't have time to feel sorry for himself. Maybe my diabetes will progress so I won't feel my butt next year. Andy suggested that the pastor take off early for the rectory. Father Gurule agreed after a mock protest. Andy called Sister Muni on his cell to drive her VW bug over to the church and take the old priest home.

A little later Sister Muni and an elderly parishioner came into the church together. Andy ducked into the confessional to hear the woman out. The old lady spoke mostly Spanish and Andy struggled to understand her sins. In the end the priest was clueless but forgave her anyway. He sent her off with, "Rezar por favor, Señora, ¡adiós!" The lady asked, "Qué rezo, Padre? ¿Cuantos?" baffled by what prayers the padre wanted, how many. Andy repeated, "Rezar, Señora!" The woman left the booth muttering. The Anglo priest pledged again to learn more Spanish, as his labored pronunciation and limited vocabulary shrunk the range of his pastoral service.

Father Andy was about to peek out to see if the old lady was still kneeling when he heard the penitent's door open and close. The priest waited for another boring litany of sin. Hopefully a litany in English.

"Bless me, Father, for I have sinned. My last confession was 25 years ago."

The priest inwardly groaned as a quarter century was an awful long time for sins to pile up. This wasn't going to be a ten minute job if the man was thorough and honest. How was the priest going to prevent overtime? Andy told himself to be patient and trust the Lord. God would soon enough provided manna in the form of Señora Alvarez's leftovers.

The friar was shaken out of his selfish concerns by the silence in the booth. The quarter century man wasn't proceeding as expected. The traditional opening of "Bless me, Father..." was supposed to be followed by "I have sinned..." this way and that, every which way known to man. Just silence. Perhaps he had forgotten the format or was too choked up to speak? But the man's voice initially sounded matter of fact, just like most of the faithful Father Andy forgave over the years. The by the numbers start usually meant a laundry list of sins would follow without passion. The voice sounded vaguely familiar and the priest tried to place it. Then the shock of recognition set in, sending a shiver through the priest. He remembered Ray saying, "Amen to life" and now knew he had the man incarnate in the box. A willing participant in a sacred rite demanding truthfulness, as well as confidentiality. The priest sensed a trap being sprung. Did Ray have sins of the flesh to confess? Sins the priest was duty bound to forgive but cannot share with civil authorities for meting out corporeal punishment.

"I have sinned, Father, but not in the way you think."

"What way do I think, Ray? It is you, isn't it?"

"Come on—you think I'm doing harm to Peddie. He's a dear boy and I don't get my jollies from harming children. I want you to believe that, Father; I <u>need</u> you to believe that! You caught me smiling at Mass because I know the boy is safe, out of danger. Returning him to that family would be the sin, the worst sin in the world."

Ray paused and the priest wondered what to say next. His sixth sense at Mass was correct after all. Ray Yazzie—single, single—had the boy everybody was looking for. But Ray was claiming that he created a personal sanctuary for the boy. Andy had observed the family up close and had a feel for the terrible problems. He needed to hear more but out in the wide open spaces, not in this confidential spot.

"Ray, what if we talk about this outside the church? I believe you when you say the boy is okay. I saw Peddie's father today and it wasn't pretty. Let's go outside. I'm sure we can work things out man-to-man."

"No, Father, absolutely not! None of this man-to-man sh—stuff. It sounds like you want to whip my butt or set up a duel or something. No, no! I come to you as a priest. I want you to hear my confession. I want your forgiveness, Father."

The priest had nowhere else to go but to carry through the sacrament. He could only hope that Ray was playing it straight. If the truth be told and the boy is safe, a happy ending could be worked out. Something else was jelling in the priest's mind. Ray's manner of speaking, clear enunciation in a lilting tone, suggested that the man was indeed gay. The priest knew that mannerisms alone don't tell the whole story but he had rarely been wrong in gay-spotting.

"That's why I'm here, Ray. Of course I'll hear your confession."

"Thank you, Father, I knew I could depend upon you. I realize that people are praying for the boy but they don't know him like I do. I tutored him for one full year but he needed more than reading and arithmetic. It took most of the year for Peddie to tell me about his father. Damn drunk! You know what that man does for a living?"

"Sure do—he's an exterminator. Runs that company with the great name, Bug Out."

"Yeah, noble profession, exterminator. Listen, Father, I don't mean to run anyone down. I like to see vermin gone as much as the next man. A few years ago he apparently had busy crews and actually met a payroll. Now he's a one man show. I guess Freddie helps out on weekends but that's it. The man's a lost cause; you know that and I know that."

The Franciscan almost blurted out that Raul was still the boy's father despite his addiction. But the priest realized that cajoling rather than arguing was probably the strategy to follow.

"Granted that the man is a falling down drunk. I don't condone that. Tell me more of what I don't know."

"You must understand, Father Andy, that I didn't seek Peddie out that day. The poor boy came knocking at my door after school all upset. Crying like a baby! I took him into the kitchen and gave him some milk and cookies. Once he calmed down he told what was going on. The dirty thing that happened!"

Ray paused for a breath and the priest waited him out. The dirty thing that happened? What leapt to mind was sex and not the loving kind.

"You see, dear old dad is screwing his own daughter. Peddie peeked at them the night before, Tuesday night, and he didn't know what to do and who to tell. He knew what they were doing. These days kids at 10 know more about sex than my generation knew at 20. Innocence is lost at too young an age. But in that family no one is innocent."

The priest wasn't as shocked as he wished to be. He had personally run across a number of incest stories over the years. A few times he had to swallow his disgust and offer forgiveness to the remorseful molester in confession. But he was lucky that these fallen men (they always seem to be men) had already been found out by the proper authorities. Often booze or drugs loosened the inhibitions that kept family affection from turning carnal. The priest had also been called upon to counsel incest victims. It was always a terrible situation and the healing process long and difficult.

"Did the dad, did Raul," the priest asked, wanting to sound clinical but failing as aftershock disrupted his composure. "Did that man see the boy looking at—the act in question?"

The priest wondered what Ray's expression was behind the screen. Was he grinning as at Palm Sunday Mass? Andy had an impulse to leave the booth, open Ray's door to confront him, look him in the eye. Wipe that mocking smile off his damn face! Before the spirit moved him, Ray spoke again.

"The poor kid didn't know if either saw him. He was at the crack of the door in the shadows as one lit candle illuminated their bodies. He ran back to bed and pretended to sleep. He said he wondered if it was all a nightmare but then realized he was wide-awake. He was scared stiff because he couldn't remember if he closed the door completely. Raul doesn't believe in sparing the rod. So Peddie planned on running away but didn't know where to go. We read a story together once about a kid from New York who ran away to the forest and built a cool tree house and made friends with the animals. But he told me he didn't know where the Adirondacks were. It was so funny the way he tried to pronounce Adirondacks. But remembering the runaway story brought him to me after school. I promised that I would help build him that tree house."

"But why didn't you take him to the police, Ray? Raul needs to be locked up. This family needs to be helped, not put through hell."

"I don't trust the police," Ray responded adamantly. "Social workers, foster care, what a joke! You know the whole system is a travesty, Father! Peddie needs love and support right now. He needs a time out."

"But this can't last, Ray! The boy has to come back eventually. If you want justice, let's call the police. I was walking with Sheriff Baca yesterday; he's a decent man. I can personally vouch for the sheriff. Let's bring this mess to him. Think of Gabby; what she's going through! She's a victim too. Have pity on her."

"I can only help one child at a time," Ray said with resignation. "Maybe you should help the girl. Besides praying for her soul, I mean."

The priest had appealed to Ray's sense of compassion and that had come up short. Andy didn't mind the challenge to get involved; indeed, since the Mass he had been walking the talk. But his sacred vows to respect the confidentiality of the sacrament prevented direct intervention. He had to get the man's acquiescence. Perhaps fear-mongering would work.

"You could use a prayer or two yourself, my man. Everybody is looking for the boy and when they find him, they find you. I believe you are well-intended but the cops may lack sympathy. I hate to disillusion you but you won't be a hero in the eyes of society. I'm not sure in the eyes of God either. You're going to be charged with something and probably get convicted too. It doesn't have to go down that way, Ray. Give the boy up now! I'll back you all the way. Let's go get Peddie and stop this nonsense."

The priest might see himself as the soul of reason but sounded as though at wit's end. He had no clear idea if the man was telling the truth or spinning a fairy tale. But why would a person come to a church to lie? He had the whole wide world to lie in. Did Ray believe professions of innocence would protect him from disclosure? If instead he gave a harrowing recitation of abduction and abuse, killing even, did he figure that the priest would not only withhold forgiveness but also turn him in? Or was Ray simply nuts, not holding the boy safe or otherwise? From Andy's reading of police procedurals, he knew there are some very disturbed people out there who were ready to drop a dime on their bad selves anytime and confess to the crime, the gorier the better. But Ray didn't sound crazy. He was telling a credible story.

As a matter of Church policy the father confessor gave the benefit of the doubt to the penitent. He never had occasion to say: "I don't forgive you in the name of the Father and the Son and the Holy Spirit because you're so full of shit." No, trust was the bottom line, not trusting in human nature, no, but trusting in the universal desire to save one's soul by coming clean. But the truth didn't set the father confessor free; Father Andy was imprisoned by his vows. Ray called all the shots. Peddie's fate, and Gabby's good night or worst nightmare, was in his hands. Also in God's hands, but He works in mysterious ways.

"I know, Father, that this can't last. I have sympathy for his mother and have no death wish, believe me. I apologize for the position I'm putting you in. I wish you no ill will though the religion you front for is a pisser. You see, Father, I have one of those love-hate relationships with Catholicism. It's a long story, another time maybe. It's getting late. Don't you want to hear my real sins? I have come to confess to my priest. Are you ready to hear my confession, Father?"

The taunting again made the priest angry but he knew he couldn't deny Ray the sacrament. Perhaps the prospect of forgiveness would set up a sense of obligation. He knew it couldn't be horse-trading, like I give you a ticket to heaven and you give me the boy! His seminary education never contemplated haggling in the confessional.

"That's what I'm here for, my son. Go on."

"Thank you, Father, for I have sinned. Wait a minute; I already said that, ages ago. Well, back in 1978, I sinned—just kidding—I know you don't want a year-by-year accounting. Let's begin and end with shame. I have lived a life of toxic shame and am paying a price for it. I want to make a clean breast of it."

"I'm listening."

"I know that you are and I appreciate it, Father. I've already told you that I fell into this thing with Peddie and there is no shame in it. Indeed, it might turn out to be the shining moment in my life. I haven't had a lot of those. I have been a selfish man in my own world. 'An island upon himself.' Isn't that the quote?"

"Yes, I know that quotation," the priest responded. "John Donne. I ran across it awhile ago. 'No man is an island entire of himself.' I remember one guy, a married guy, improved upon it by saying to me, claiming he told his wife, 'No woman is a continent either.' You have to laugh. Donne also wrote, 'Ask not for whom the bell tolls, it tolls for thee.' Sad thought that."

"Yeah, I saw the movie, Gary Cooper, Ingrid Bergman, such tragic love!" Ray said wistfully. "I've had love like that. Something classic like that. I've done the noble death scene. You know what, Father; they do it better in the movies. Know what I mean?"

The priest yearned to see every pore of Ray's face; instead he had to settle for a faint shadow. The man's voice had lost some of its arch tone and was breaking up with feeling. Andy wondered if it was play-acting. But the priest figured he had to play along even with mock pathos for Peddie's sake.

"I saw the movie and read Hemingway's book too, as a teenager. But back to the toxic shame you were talking about, Ray."

"Oh yeah, the down and dirty, mercy me. You see, my good Father, I'm gay; you might have figured that out already. I never asked to be born gay or Catholic for that matter. Don't get me wrong! I'm not saying being gay alone is a cause of shame or sin. I'm just saying it hasn't led to heaven on earth for me."

To be gay and Roman Catholic was indeed not the happiest of unions. The Church viewed active homosexuality as a grave sin, an "objective disorder" as the Pope characterized it. Along with other fundamentalist religions, Catholicism stigmatized gays as descendents of the bad actors of Sodom and Gomorrah. Funny thing is, many priests are gay in orientation, deep in the closet, the Church praying that they keep their cocks in their cassocks. Father Andy had developed friendships over the years with a number of gay priests. Sometimes over drinks they would have heart-to-heart talks about the conflicting demands of sexuality and the spirit.

Ray continued. "The shame stems from lust. I wanted love forever and settled for lust in the meantime. Maybe true love required too much work. I won't go into the titillating details but let's just say that I've been out there. Now I'm dying from HIV/AIDS. Let's just say I didn't catch it from a blood transfusion. Don't get me wrong though! I've always had willing partners, no forced sex or anything like that. And I know you're wondering about young boys. No underage sex unless you count the dating when both of us were underage. But that was with the girls anyway back in the days of pretending. Maybe my Catholic upbringing steered me clear of that man-boy perversion. I really don't know anything for sure! But one thing is pretty certain; Peddie's safe with me. He's a beautiful child and I wouldn't harm a hair on his head."

"But what does the boy want?" the priest interjected. "He's close to his brother and must miss him badly. His mom is broken up by this and wants her little boy home. Peddie must miss his sister and maybe those dogs too. The father's abuse must be stopped, Ray! That shame must be stopped! Don't you see that?"

Ray did not immediately respond. The priest suddenly felt faint-headed from too much emotion and not enough comfort food. He looked down at his lap to the three cookies remaining in the bag. He resisted the temptation to munch on one; these were for Peddie after all. Andy was second-guessing himself like crazy; was he too emotional, not nearly logical enough? Can a priest use in good conscience strong-arm tactics?

"I know I've laid a burden on your doorstep, Father. I had to talk about it with someone, okay? I chose you, okay? Rather than trust a broken down old queer, why don't you ask Peddie for yourself? Let the boy tell you the truth. Let the boy tell you what he wants. How about it? That's what you want, isn't it?"

The priest let out a great sigh of relief. He had a news flash of yours truly, the priest-hero returning with Peddie to a homecoming that Raul would watch on the jailhouse TV.

"That's more like it. Let's go!"

"Hold on a minute, partner! Peddie is safe but he's not staying over at my house. I'll tell you where we can meet but it can't be tonight. Let's meet, say, around 9 tomorrow morning at McCauley Hot Springs in the Jemez. Sorry about the delay and the distance but both of us have to give a little. Do you know the Jemez?"

Here the priest's outdoor experience came in handy. "I do, yes. I've hiked up to the springs a number of times with my dog. I can find it in the dark. Seriously, Ray, why don't we go now? Get it done."

"No, no, that won't work! If you want to see the boy, it's my call. Okay?"

The priest gave up the push for closure tonight. He had the passing notion that he could follow Ray surreptitiously up to the Jemez Mountains or wherever he has Peddie stashed. But that would be dangerous with chances of discovery great and likelihood of recovery slim. Father Andy couldn't see himself freeing the boy by force.

"Okay, Ray, you've got a deal. I'll be up there tomorrow morning. Anything else?"

"Yes, Father, don't forget forgiveness. I have committed other sins over the years but have made my peace with God about them. I have confessed to a harmful sex drive and want to make my peace with that. I want to go to heaven and see what closet the gays are kept in. Please forgive my sarcasm, Father, I'm only human. I just want to die in peace."

The priest didn't know who made it to heaven and which conflicted souls were shut out at the pearly gates. Saints were shoo-ins but the issue was in doubt for the rest of us. Father Andy was invested with power though, the power to forgive in the name of Christ. Eternal outcomes were for a higher power to decide.

"Ray, it's been many years since you've heard these words. Please listen carefully. For penance I want you to get on your knees and say five 'Our Fathers', that's it. But tonight I want you to make a living amends too. I trust you mean well by the boy. Make preserving Peddie's innocence your shining moment that represents your triumph over the sins of the flesh. Now I forgive you in the name of the Father and the Son and the Holy Spirit. Go in peace and sin no more."

"Thank you, Father!" Ray sounded choked-up. "See you tomorrow."

The priest heard the booth's door open and Ray's shadow disappear. If the man did the prescribed penance, he would be in the pew for a few minutes. Andy looked at his watch: 8:35. The official Holy Week penitential service was over. The priest's mind wasn't at peace. He had never confronted such a dilemma in his priestly life. Not even close. If the boy was truly alive and well, that's one thing. If the boy was alive but Ray's shining moment is cut short by the dark side, and the priest rendezvoused with an abused child or even a dead one at the springs, then Father Andy wasn't sure how he could live as a man or a friar with the guilt. If Ray was just seeking forgiveness before hauling his sorry ass out of town with the beautiful boy, then the bonds of confidentiality would keep the priest from telling. And what happens if the police arrest the wrong man? Could the priest undertake a desperate sabbatical to track down the true abductor?

The priest realized that he could do nothing tonight to prepare for worst case scenarios. He would go home to the rectory and consult with the dog. Take Pope out for a walk in the moonlight. The priest left the confessional to find Ray gone. Andy went to the electric main box and switched off the lights of the sanctuary. The nightlight in the church was a spotlight imaginatively focused on the altar and the life size crucifix beyond. The priest said a fast prayer as he gazed at Jesus on the cross. Prior to his disappearance Peddie Martinez was just another precious child amongst so many. The priest didn't really know the child. Now the priest knew who had him. Tomorrow the priest would confront the face of good or evil. Or the death of innocence. It would a long night.

CHAPTER 7

▼

The priest took Pope along on the ride up to the Jemez. It was a glorious red sunrise in the Land of Enchantment. If Andy was driven by faith rather than fear, his spirit couldn't help but be enriched by the feast that God and Mother Nature provided the senses. But the priest was out on a limb and not out on a lark. His religious career was at stake. The public disgrace would be devastating if word got around that a priest put sterile vows (however sacred) ahead of the welfare of a living, breathing child. Though it would be difficult to defrock a priest for following canon law, exile to some spiritual wasteland was likely. A fixer-upper church in an ugly place. He would no longer find sanctuary in beautiful Santa Fe.

If things blew up in his face, Father Andy wasn't even sure if family would stand by him. His mother, no fan of the Catholic Church, might say the hell with Rome; you are now and will always be my self-made son. But mother's maternal instincts could be overwhelmed by the public impression that Andy provided aid and comfort to a child molester. Of his siblings Andy could only be sure of his sister Circe's unconditional love.

But the Franciscan was most concerned about Sister Maria's reaction. Having her hold him in high esteem was critical to Andy's manhood as well as his clerical position. If he fell out of grace in her eyes, no amount of puppy love from Pope would compensate. Her love of children would work against understanding and sympathy for the friar's dilemma. She would just see a ruined boy and a live priest together, in scandalous embrace.

In the long history of the Roman Catholic Church priests have gone to the stake standing up for confessor confidentiality. Dish the dirt or meet your Maker;

the cuckolded prince must know the sins of the princess. Legal and political pressure in a democracy can be just as overwhelming with the tabloids sensationalizing the issues. These sad days the fed up laity wasn't in a forgiving mood.

Andy prayed hard on the hour and a half drive up to the mountains. The simplest prayer was the best: "God's will, not mine, be done." Man proposes, God deposes. While the priest fervently believed that, he realized that God doesn't pump gas or do the legwork in finding a lost boy. The Serenity Prayer also suggested a road map on how to live a Christian life. Acceptance of the inevitable, courage to act when the opportunity arose, and wisdom in choosing either decisive action or calm submission. But the priest knew the temptation of using prayer and meditation as an excuse to not act at all. If Ray doesn't give up the boy voluntarily, was the priest ready to come to blows. Andy's last fistfight was in grammar school. And he had lost that one.

The priest didn't feel on top of his game. For one thing he was hung-over. After the penitential service he sought to calm his nerves with several shots of Jameson's. He was hungry yet couldn't eat. The hard booze did cut short foreboding. Andy jerked awake on his recliner, startled, fearing he had overslept. Then he looked at the clock—2:48 a.m.—and the panic subsided, replaced by irritation that he had hours to wile away before dawn. Andy was too keyed up to fall back into blessed sleep.

He went to the fridge and found a platter of Señora Alvarez's left-over soft shell tacos—shredded beef and black beans—Andy's favorite. He sprinkled some grated cheese and green chili on top and micro-waved one after another, gobbling each in gauche haste. After six tacos the priest belched and farted. He wasn't at all pleased. But it was certainly easier to look and smell heroic when somebody's fawning eyes were upon you. If Sister Maria was there to see him through the night, he would act with more grace under pressure. Gird for the games with a gentle lady's silk scarf tied to his jousting lance. Instead he was alone, bloated, breaking wind, losing faith in himself alone and not trusting God.

An Alka-Seltzer helped settle his stomach; a long hot and cold shower gave his pallid skin some color. A long walk with Pope before dawn also revived his spirits. He left a note for the still sleeping pastor to cover for him at morning Mass. He didn't explain the reason as he wanted to leave no lies. Andy drove away from the rectory as always attired in his brown monk's robe. He had his silver cross around his neck and his rosary and Swiss Army knife in his sleeve pocket. Practical concessions to a hike in nature included wearing Rockport walkers, carrying a thick sweatshirt in his backpack, and bringing along 45 sun block to beat off the relentless high altitude sun. He also filled his backpack with goodies for Peddie:

several candy bars, the last of his mother's chocolate chip and nut cookies, and a large bag of trail mix. He packed extra biscuits for the dog. He left room in the pack for water bottles he would buy along the way. He put in a small first aid kit. A compass and ready dog biscuits he would carry in his other sleeve pocket; his seldom used cell phone attached to his belt. As a final morale booster he put on his lucky Chicago Bears cap. He prayed that a helmet wouldn't be needed.

The McCauley Hot Springs were located along a well-marked trail in national forest land in the Jemez Mountains. It wasn't really back country; the compass and Swiss Army knife though could come in handy if fleeing with the boy became necessary. The priest doubted that Ray would go off on him. The man was a regular churchgoer after all. Though he was a wise ass during much of the confession, he had almost begged for forgiveness at the end. If he didn't believe in the Franciscan's spiritual authority, he wouldn't have asked for the friar's blessing.

After a fast stop at a convenience store for bottled water, the priest sped north to the mountains. The landscape was coming alive with the spring run-off; the rolling red hills dotted with green pinon and juniper. In the distance were the mountains—to the northwest the Jemez still cloaked in darkness, to the northeast the sun peaking over the Sangre de Cristo's, the Blood of Christ. The city-owned water company was also called Sangre de Cristo, giving some of the pious pause as they drank tap water.

Andy reached the Pojoaque Pueblo's Cities of Gold complex where he turned west to the hot springs trailhead. He was dismayed by the number of vehicles in the casino parking lot. Perhaps the early birds were there for the cheap buffet breakfast, not to try their dumb luck at dawn. Once past the pueblo reservation land, the road climbed the hill to Los Alamos where the atomic bomb was born in WWII's crash Manhattan project. The priest thought that weapons of mass destruction should be bastard born in a dirty backwater rather than the heavily wooded, scenic Los Alamos area. Most people of the cloth were pacifists and certainly the Vatican hadn't given its blessing to a war since the Crusades. During his ministry in Santa Fe the priest had met several nuclear physicists from the national labs. They were gentle, distracted souls, as far from warrior-like as one would imagine.

After passing through Los Alamos the priest reached the stretch of road overlooking the Valles Caldera National Preserve. Of all the beautiful places in New Mexico the Valles Caldera gave the priest the greatest pause. A massive volcano erupted eons ago, leaving behind a vast depression, mostly meadow land where cows, horses, sheep and elks grazed in peace. Often the priest stopped to gaze in awe and wonder. Today he sped past with a sideways glance.

Andy reached the Jemez Falls campground parking area. There were several RV's parked there and tents up but no one was out and about. Andy let Pope out of the car and put on his backpack. He checked his watch—7:20—no time to tarry as he faced three miles of strenuous hiking and a 9 a.m. deadline.

As always when off leash outdoors Pope was joyous and intensely alive. He ran and sniffed at every scent and scat of prey or predator. A squirrel crossed their path and scurried up a tree to escape the racing dog. With his tags on his collar jingling it was hard for Pope to surprise wild things. So healthy rabbits, squirrels, cats, and birds had nothing to fear. The priest said a short prayer that his dog wouldn't corner any creature sick or wounded.

The last time Father Andy and the Pope came to the springs, last summer, they were accompanied by Rabbi Bernstein and his dog Taffy. It was a pleasant hike in great weather. At the springs the rabbi stripped down without hesitation to join several people in the hot water. A couple had suits on; the rest were skinny-dipping. The Franciscan stayed clothed in his friar's get-up, ridiculous looking in this natural setting, drawing more stares than the buck-ass naked. Andy, hardly a prude, sat on a fallen tree next to one of the pools and continued his conversation with the rabbi. Both men saw innocence rather than corruption. The nudity left the priest cold.

The rabbi and the priest were discussing an odd topic for a pristine setting. The Israeli-Palestinian conflict—the priest was wondering which side God was on. Bernstein knew the history better than Leary. Leon saw the feud as being more about land than religion or blood and the issues could be resolved by artful compromise and mutual respect. The cycle of suicide bombing/Israeli overkill would eventually play itself out. After all, the most passionate Palestinians were not living to fight another day. As for God picking sides, the rabbi suggested that people of good will on both sides had His ear.

The priest wondered what God's will was concerning Peddie. Sheriff Baca said that God couldn't be so cruel as to allow the boy to die before his time. But wander through an old cemetery sometime and notice all the small headstones. In this modern age, with many childhood diseases eradicated or isolated, in societies with good health care, the odds of children surviving into adulthood have increased so much as to seem a birthright. Child victims of violence become big news on cable, unless they get beaten up and die in the ghetto. God's plan for Peddie could be benign if the priest did everything humanly possible to save him.

But he was winging it without support; the cavalry wasn't going to arrive in the nick of time. Unless the Commander issued the marching orders.

But will what will be will be? Regardless of how strong the Franciscan was, how persuasive, how inspired, was Peddie's fate already sealed by God's unfathomable agenda? And what kind of morality play was it—for adults only, or child's play? And did the motivation of the players make a tittle of difference in the end? The priest wanted to be purely driven by concern for the boy rather than his career advancement or how Sister Maria would judge him. In the spirit of St. Francis of Assisi, the friar wanted to be an instrument of the Lord's peace. As he hurried along the trail, sweating from the physical exertion as well as the physic pressure, the priest took comfort from the conviction that it is in dying that we are born to eternal life.

The sweat dried and he felt suddenly a peace that surpasseth understanding. He paused to drink some water at the Jemez River Falls. The refreshing waters of spring reassured the priest that new life was replacing the dead of winter. Even if the boy dies, what awaits him, the promise, is a rose garden. To argue for a long life till the broke down body gives up the ghost is to recognize as much value in human struggle as in sitting pretty. Part of the equation was simple jealousy: the boy should have to earn his way into heaven rather than be given an early out.

Andy looked at his watch and saw that he was running early. He slowed his pace for the final stretch. Taking time out to smell the flowers—Andy was humored by the thought. The wild flowers weren't blooming yet but he could easily imagine smelling them. He was in the mood to imagine sweet things.

The Franciscan paused again on the trail as he approached the final bend. Was he ready? As ready as a priest could be—a cross around his neck, rosary beads in his fingers. If a vampire awaited, the cross may come in handy. Of course the Swiss Army knife lay in reserve. Switzerland hasn't experienced an invasion in centuries so the weapons in their arsenal must be respected. The priest smiled at the thought of Hitler's panzers faced down at the border by many pronged knives.

The priest took out a biscuit and gave it to his dog. Pope would instinctively protect his master but wasn't by nature or training an attack dog. Pope certainly was eager, taking off up the trail, out of sight. The priest knew the dog would come back shortly, tail and tongue wagging, urging Andy to come on, come on, there's nothing to be afraid of. Come on, don't be shy, there's adventure ahead!

Sure enough, Pope returned and leaped up at the priest in his excitement. Come on! The priest resolutely pointed ahead and the dog raced off again. Andy took a deep breath and followed. Around the bend the springs were visible about a hundred yards ahead. There were two figures visible in one of the pools. The priest recognized the larger as Ray; he assumed the smaller was the boy. Andy thanked the Lord; Peddie was alive! That fact established—now the boy's liberation was the next step. No one else was around, so it would be Ray versus Andy, mano á mano. The dog was already at the pool's edge and he wasn't barking. Ray was chest deep in the water; Peddie was up to his neck. Ray and the boy looked at the priest approaching.

"Hello, Father, hello!" Ray said in a cheery tone though his smile seemed strained to the priest. "Glad you could come."

The priest looked from Ray to Peddie. The boy soaked motionless in the shallow springs, staring wide-eyed up at his parish priest. He was a beautiful boy indeed, dark-haired, brown eyes, looking none the worst for wear. His lips were parted as though he had something to say. Andy waited a few moments but finally had to break the silence.

"Peddie Martinez, I presume. How's it going, kiddo?"

The boy looked away and said, "Okey dokey, Father. They've been looking for me, haven't they?"

The priest almost laughed. He managed to keep his face straight.

"Well, yeah, everybody in God's creation has been out looking for you. Your family is really sad and wants you to come home. Miss Stenholm wants you back at school next week."

"What about Freddie? Has Freddie been looking for me?"

"Freddie's been out there. I just saw him yesterday. He wants you to come home. Your mom doesn't know what to do with herself with you gone. I've come to take you home, Peddie."

The priest decided to be direct as not only a way to get a reading on Peddie's feelings but also to smoke out Ray's true intentions. Father Andy figured a good Catholic boy would respond instinctively to priestly directives. If Ray's heart was in the right place, he would stay quiet now and keep hands off. The priest looked down at the murky water as both the man and boy's arms were hidden from view. There didn't seem any funny business going on. They were close but not touching.

Peddie looked at Ray before responding. "Did you tell him what I saw? Father Andy knows, doesn't he?"

Ray nodded and his hand surfaced to brush the boy lightly on his cheek. "I did, I had to, my dear boy. Father Andy had to know why I have you out here."

The priest now fully accepted as true what Ray revealed during confession. Peddie came to his mentor/friend after the trauma of witnessing incest. Why the boy didn't rush to his mother, brother, teacher, police, or even his priest remained to be discovered. A matter of fear and trust obviously. The priest knew now that he would have to deal with the taboo of incest. How do you paint the picture of a happy homecoming when such a horrific crime occurred within its confines?

"What happened between your father and sister was wrong, terribly wrong, a mortal sin, Peddie. Your father is a very sick man and badly needs help. You can help him and Gabby by coming back and telling the truth. No one will yell at you; no harm will come your way. Your dad will go away and get the help he needs. How about it?"

The priest didn't mention that they would probably lock Raul up and throw away the key. He wasn't quite sure what feelings the boy had for his father. Andy knew he shouldn't assume hate; at one time there must have been love. A drunkard for a dad—well, the priest had been there. But he loved his own dad despite his addiction. In the Leary household there had been no incest as far as Andy knew. That made all the difference in the world. It was hard to see how a family could stay together after such a trespass? And what effect on the emotional life of Gabby, all of fourteen years old? Many 14 year olds these days have more than a nodding acquaintance with sex but precious few are involved incestuously. From his pastoral counseling over the years the priest heard the stories and witnessed tragic consequences. One young girl committed suicide. Another case ended in a late term abortion, with the girl being institutionalized afterwards. Sometimes you have to wait for tragedy to strike. The Franciscan remembered one middle-age woman's seemingly happy life suddenly turn morose, as the beast of remembrance was released after years of gnawing at her skin.

The priest needed to bring Peddie back to give Gabby a chance to heal while still young enough to forget. Father Andy needed the boy to bear witness. It was a tremendous burden for a ten year old but there you have it. Peddie started crying and leaned into Ray for support. Ray's expression turned downright maternal as he cradled the boy. The priest knew that Ray was by far the stronger influence. Father Andy was a looming figure in a friar's robe, standing in for God in a way. Ray was with the boy in warm water, naked, as though taking Peddie back to the womb. Between the human touch and divine authority, there is no contest.

Ray looked up at the priest. His eyes were tearing as he held the boy. The man's face went from evidence of sadness to flashes of elation. The priest wondered what inducement could he offer Peddie to return to real life. Real life meant a painful accusation against his father. Real life meant a broken family. Real life meant cruel teasing at school. Real life couldn't come slow enough.

The priest took off his backpack and zipped it open to give Pope a squirt of water. He looked with resigned amusement at the treats he brought for Peddie. The candy bars were mushy; his mother's cookies crumbly. Pathetic lures for the boy! The boy looked well-nourished but children always seem to respond to treats. The boy didn't appear to be wanting materially. His clothes and sneakers, piled neatly on a rock, looked clean and presentable. Andy doubted that Peddie was sleeping rough. Ray must have a cabin up here or perhaps one of the campers back at the trailhead was his.

Ray didn't look all that healthy up close. He was all skin and bones, with his exposed shoulders showing a few telltale blotches. In confession Ray said HIV/AIDS were the wages of sin. The communicability of HIV made it imperative that Ray was keeping his hands to himself.

"Do you guys want some water?" Andy asked.

"Sure, Father, absolutely," Ray responded. "This water in here is drinkable in a pinch but has a lot more sulfur and mineral stuff than I can handle. Who knows if any radium from Los Alamos is leeching into it too."

He gently unwrapped the distraught boy and stood up in the shallow pool. He waded the few feet over to the bank. The priest glanced at his penis, registering that it was flaccid. Ray noticed the once-over.

"Look but don't touch, Father," he said and gave the priest a goofy grin. Ray reached out and offered his hand to the priest. Andy shook the wet hand in a manly fashion. Normally Andy avoided handshakes, feeling the gesture spread more germs than warm feelings. He wished he could get by with a simple nod of the head.

Andy gave one of the water bottles to Ray who took a long swig. He told the boy still in the water to open up his mouth. He squirted the water from several feet away and the boy giggled as he tried to catch the stream. The last of the water was squeezed out with a rude noise, causing all the guys to laugh. The priest reached into his backpack for the second of the three bottles he brought along. He called Pope over and squirted some more water directly into the dog's mouth. Then he drank the water himself.

"Peddie, I've got some goodies for you. Your mom baked some chocolate chip cookies for you and I have a couple candy bars. They didn't travel well but still may hit the spot. Have one?"

The boy smiled and waded over to the priest. He said, "Cookie, please," and Andy gave him the biggest intact chunk in the baggie.

Ray plopped down into the soothing waters again and turned positively expansive. "We did have a hearty breakfast, the boy and I. My cabin has a small kitchen and we're not lacking for food. It's not like we have to go out hunting for game or digging up roots every morning."

Peddie laughed again. Pope, responding viscerally to the sound, began tearing around the pool with his characteristic leaps of yapping joy. The dog suddenly plunged into the pool. Peddie whooped with delight as he grabbed the paddling dog. Pope began licking the boy's face. The boy's blues begone.

The priest felt the odd man out. He wanted to share in the giddiness but felt too heavy the weight of responsibility. Get Peddie home safe, have Raul taken away, and shepherd Gabby into therapy. Father Andy had to be the catalyst, keeping his wits about him. Rational results, God's plan, the priest was certain.

If Ray and Peddie were having, say, a gay old time in the woods, could the boy be persuaded to come back? The boy only mentioned his brother by name; by all accounts he and Freddie were close. The priest assumed that he loved his mother and sister as well. And hated his father? Peddie wasn't himself that day at school, lethargic, depressed, out of it. He came to Ray scared shitless. The ten year old apparently knew what he witnessed was beyond the pale. He feared punishment from his drunken father.

The Franciscan knew that children were growing up too fast into the complicated world of sex. Andy didn't see a computer in Peddie's bedroom so at least surfing for a cyber peep show or a little dirty chat wasn't an after-school activity. But maybe he had buddies and those buddies had their parent's passwords. Back in Andy's day sex education was left to the imagination. He didn't remember incest, homosexuality, birth control or abortion being mentioned in class. The most explicit sex education occurred on an eighth grade field trip to the Hinsdale Health Museum outside Chicago. The nuns shepherded the newly minted teens into the small auditorium where Olga, the transparent woman of the world, held sway. The electronic manikin with her internal organs visible lit up each and gave a short lecture on form and function. When the mammary glands started glowing, the boys hooted. When the organs of the groin explained their reason for being, it brought down the house. The nuns were beside themselves to quiet the boys.

These days, at St. Michael's High School, the priest knew that there was a conscientious effort to help bewildered teens with the complicated nature of sex and to make the inevitable as safe as possible. Condoms were not provided by the Catholic school nurse of course but at least the body's development was part of the curriculum rather than just a field trip. But even the liberal-minded Sister Maria didn't suggest sex education for 4th graders. She left it up to the parents. Unfortunately, courtesy of his father, Peddie's initiation was the crudest possible.

"Your sister needs help, Peddie. Gabby is hurting and you can save her. Come back with me. Ray will come along, won't you, Ray?"

Peddie looked at Ray and the man gave him an encouraging nod. It looked as though the priest was winning. But then Ray spoke up before the boy could respond positively.

"Father, you know that I won't stand in the way of Peddie going back. But humor me by coming back to my cabin first. I have my reasons; I have some questions of faith. I'll give you and the boy a ride later over to your car. Let's have a drink together and shoot the shit."

The priest sensed a trap. Ray was promising to let the boy go easy but may have a hidden agenda. Would the boy veto the delay and make a bee line home? Looking at the boy's obvious comfort from spending time with his friend, Andy despaired that he had a chance of winning the boy over. But he had to give it his best shot. He vaguely wondered what adult beverage Ray had at his cabin.

"So what do you say, Peddie? I could have you home with your mother and brother in a few hours. You heard Ray; he says it's okay. Come with me now, my son."

The boy pointed at Pope out of the water now, shaking and spattering spring water. Peddie smiled and said, "I like your dog, Father; he's cool. Let me play with him while you guys talk. That's what I want to do. What's his name again, Father Andy? I forgot."

The priest knew he had lost the fight for a quick resolution and he best surrender with grace.

"The boy's name is Pope and he's not to be confused with the Holy Father. He loves to play around. Have you seen any wild animals up here?"

The boy nodded with glee. "Oh yeah, some deer woke me up yesterday morning. I ran out but Ray said to leave them alone. He said the woods are not a petting zoo. Maybe I'll see a bear before I go back to school."

Ray laughed. "Just wait a minute, Daniel Boone, I never promised you a bear in the woods. I have seen black bears maybe a dozen times, but that's over a zillion years of coming up here. And what have I told you to do if we run across a bear?"

"Sing a song!"

"And what song works the best?"

"*Time to Say Goodbye.*"

"That's right, my boy," Ray replied in a prim, proud tone. "You've heard that one, the song, haven't you, Father?"

"That's Sarah Brightman, isn't it, and Bocelli, the blind tenor, sure. I have the CD. Didn't know that bears would be scared off by Sarah!"

"Not scared off, Father, beguiled, beguiled." Ray gave the priest the goofy grin again. "The beauty of her voice beguiles wild things. Lulled into a teddy bear."

The priest couldn't help to be amused—beguiled even. "Oh yeah, I'm sure! I listen to the music and I do love it, but I'm far from being a bear."

Peddie pointed at the priest's cap and Ray commented, "No, you're not a teddy bear either, Father. The boy and I can both see that."

They were making fun of Andy's hometown Bears, the football kind. The priest felt more like a bad news bear than close to cuddly. He was addressed as 'Father' out of knee-jerk respect but he was a father in name only. A father with no sons. Here he was, deep in the heart of nature, dressed and ready to go monastic. Somehow in this setting, clothes didn't make the man. Ray and the boy seemed freer than the friar, looser, embracing the here and now. Andy was mired in the past, his legacy as a priest, and the future, grim if this encounter turns out to be a gross misadventure.

Ray grabbed Peddie's ear and gave it a playful tug. "Time to say goodbye to the springs, my boy. Let's get out so we can go play."

The man and boy emerged from the pool and went over to their clothes and towels. They started to dry off. The priest looked away from their bodies and went over to a mossy rock to sit down. Pope came over for attention. Andy gave him another biscuit and some stroking behind his wet ears. The priest was always unabashedly physical with his dog. He was a shedder so the priest brushed him daily. Oral hygiene was emphasized by the vet so Andy awkwardly brushed the dog's teeth too. Pope still had doggie breath but the priest could live with that. Though the dog hated it, Andy washed him with flea and tick shampoo outside on warm days; in the tub in the cold of winter. Cleaning up after was a chore. When the wet dog smell departed, revealing a shiny coat, the Pope forgave his priest by licking his face. Sloppy, simple love. The human kind seemed impossibly complicated by comparison.

The priest felt a human presence and looked up to see Ray and Peddie ready to go. Peddie didn't have his bland brown pants, tan shirt parochial school uniform on; he was wearing jeans and a Hawaii shirt that Ray must have bought for him. The boy put on a Colorado Rockies cap. Ray looked positively jaunty in safari shorts, khaki shirt, and pith helmet. He wore sunglasses and hung a Sony Walkman around his neck. He strapped on a fanny pack.

Andy got up and shrugged on his backpack. He put his own sunglasses on. The weary priest wondered how far it was to Ray's cabin. Ray must have been reading his mind.

"It's about three miles to the cabin. Off that way," pointing in a direction without an obvious trail. "And I promised Peddie that we would practice our Sarah in case we run into a grizzly bear. So let's take it slow and sing *Time to Say Goodbye*. I do a great Sarah."

He punched the Walkman button and the voice of Sarah came on crystal clear and loud. Ray led the way into the underbrush. For the priest it was like entering undiscovered territory. But it wasn't as though there were tangled vines to hack through. The path was just indistinct and probably missed by all but the most adventurous hiker. In the shade of the tall trees it was cool enough but the priest felt mugginess in the air. Andy recalled the red sky at dawn and wondered if the 'sailors be warned' admonition applied this far inland. Glimpses of sun peeked through increasing cloud cover.

The soaring beauty of Sarah's voice echoed nature's munificence. The group was walking through a forest of many spruces and aspens. The path through the trees occasionally gave way to alpine meadows with soft grasses waving in the freshening breezes. Pope rolled over and over in the grass and Peddie ran around and around the rolling dog. Andy and Ray paused to catch their breath and observe with envy their apparent endless energy. The priest noticed that Ray looked more than a little winded. Andy could just imagine how a terminal illness can take the wind out of your sails. He took a long swig of water, wondering again what Ray had to drink at the cabin. It was while resting in the meadow that the *Time to Say Goodbye* cut came on for the first time. Ray indeed had Sarah's lines down pat:

> When I'm alone
> I dream of the horizon
> And words fail me
> There is no light
> In a room where there is no sun
> And there is no sun if you're not here
> With me, with me—
> From every window
> Unfurl my heart
> The heart that you have won
> Into me you've poured the light
> The light that you found

By the side of the road.

Time to say goodbye
Places that I've never seen or
Experienced with you—
Now I shall
I'll sail with you
Upon ships across the seas
Seas that exist no more
I'll revive them with you.

Ray's singing voice had a thin beauty, falsetto, with expressive heartbreak. The priest now understood how a siren song can mellow animal instincts. Ray fell silent as Andreas Bocelli took over from Sarah. Tears began rolling down his cheeks. Peddie stopped playing with the dog and came over to hold the man's hand. The man and the boy stood together till the end of the song. The priest wondered if they would all join in for the refrain but that didn't happen. After Sarah moved on to the next song, Peddie released Ray's hand and came over to the priest. He tugged at the friar's sleeve and Andy bent over. Peddie whispered, "He gets like that all the time."

Ray turned off the Walkman and wiped his eyes dry with his sleeve. He started walking resolutely again towards the next stand of trees. They continued their journey to the cabin in silence. After another hour of navigating through thick woods they ran across a more established path next to a glorified creek, the east fork of the Jemez River. The spring run-off gave it transitory energy but it was hardly raging. The priest knew that much of the rest of the year the river subsided into an uninspired flow down to a dribble in drought years. They hiked along the river trail for awhile. After another mile of easy going Ray plunged again into the trees. Very soon they came upon a rutted road and followed it to a log cabin in the middle of a small meadow. There was an SUV, a Ford Explorer, parked next to it.

Ray turned to the flagging priest. "And now for that drink, Father, we've both earned it today. I think the boy wants to stay outside for awhile with the dog. Right, Peddie?"

Peddie nodded enthusiastically. "Does he do any tricks, you know, stupid pet tricks like on TV?"

The priest pretended to take offense. "Stupid is not the word I would use. Pope is the smartest dog this side of Rome. I taught him everything he knows. He hunts, he fishes, plays baseball."

Ray laughed and then started to cough, a hacking cough. Peddie went over to him and held his hand until the cough subsided. The boy then went over to the priest and tugged at his sleeve again to whisper in his ear.

"Ray gave up smoking last year but it's probably too late. I smoked a cigarette with him once and got sick. He said, 'See!' So I decided to give up cigarettes before it was too late."

The priest patted the boy on the back. Andy remembered the cigars he and his dad smoked in the attic sanctuary. Clouds of pungent smoke, a rich stream of consciousness. One evening dad told him that when courting Andy's mother, and for some years after, husband and wife used to talk like that, like there was only today and no tomorrow. The priest suddenly shivered with a profound sadness. He realized that he had been one of those forlorn kids who had never witnessed tangible love between his parents. They gave life to their children but lost their life together.

A pale Ray said, "I guess I laugh till it hurts. These days it hurts like hell. I can't even remember what I thought was funny."

He paused but the priest couldn't help him out. He couldn't remember what was funny either.

CHAPTER 8

▼

I don't take lovers; I take hostages. Go figure—the ransom! Ha-ha! It's the seduction of the caught by the captor, the victim becoming compliant, even embracing their bondage. I'm reminded of Patty Hearst as a kidnap victim turned bank robbing revolutionary. It's sorta like converts to a faith becoming more rabid than those born into religion. Maybe part of it is our desire to ride the wave rather than make waves. I am an educated man and have studied the phenomena of persuasion. I am not a brute and shy away from violence. I want willing accomplices and am as patient as can be. After all, the fun is as much in the hunt as in the capture.

*   *   *   *

The priest was waiting for his drink to be served. Ray didn't have any Irish whiskey but Tennessee sour mash wasn't bad in a pinch. Ray brought over the Jack Daniels served neat per request. Andy was grateful but wary. Having one drink together might ease the tension but more may release petulant feelings. Ray had matters of faith to sort through so the priest would listen. Trust comes if someone really listens, unhurried, without judgment. Given the unusual circumstances Father Andy didn't really expect that love would strike the men silly and an epiphany descend upon this cabin in the piney woods.

Ray was drinking beer out of a tall, ornate stein, the kind you buy on a whim during October Fest. He seemed in no hurry to spill his guts. The two men were sitting across from each other, the priest on a mission style sofa and Ray in a

Morris chair. Andy looked around the room, a combined kitchen/living room open space. Everything was neat and in place. Lacy curtains clashed with the rustic feel of pine. Father Andy had heard that gay men were fastidiously tidy and wore natty clothes while lesbians dressed down and loved the lived-in look. Straights could go either way. As the first sip of bourbon suffused his being, the priest's nervousness disappeared and confidence bloomed.

The door was open and the priest could hear yelps of delight coming from the boy and dog outside. Andy admired the boundless energy of youth. He certainly felt his age after the long hike. A long soak in a hot tub or at least a fast shower would make him feel human again. He had an absurd impulse to take off his hiking shoes and sweaty socks and rub his dirty dogs. He sat stiffly, the weight of his shoes locking his crossed legs in place. He took another sip.

The silence became uncomfortable. Andy cleared his throat and spoke up. "Your home away from home?"

"Yeah, it's been our retreat for ages. I came up here a lot as a kid. Back in those days the river had more cutthroat than stocked rainbow or brook. Used to catch as many as we wanted. I guess dad got some kind of permit but I don't remember it limiting our catch."

Ray took a long draw on his beer as the priest responded. "I remember fishing in Salt Creek as a kid, outside Chicago. I don't know why they call it Salt because it's fresh water. Fresh water then at least; now it's a sewer. As a kid we caught snapping turtles and cat fish. My mother refused to cook the fish; she called them bottom feeders. Okay then, we found the right place for them—snuck the dirty fish into the mail box of the witch up the street. Got a wicked rush from that."

"So you were a bad boy, Father, shame, shame!" Ray said playfully, wagging his finger. "And did the wicked witch receive a snapping turtle special delivery too?"

"No, no, couldn't be that cruel—to the turtle! I already had enough sins to confess."

"We ate every bit of the fish we caught but there's no catfish in the Jemez. Now they tell us since the Cerro Grande fire that we have to watch radium seepage from the labs. I still eat the fricking fish. What's it gonna do—kill me before my time? What a cosmic joke!"

The priest had water still on his mind. "I was raised on well water, community wells. The water, I guess, tasted alright and we kids didn't think twice about it. But years later my parents received a notice from some environmental agency that the water had naturally occurring radium in it. Dad sent me a copy of the notice. The language was so murky that I couldn't figure out if the radium was a curse or a benefit, like atoms for peace maybe. After all, I suppose you could say that the Black Death was naturally occurring too."

Andy paused out of courtesy in case Ray wanted to comment on the Black Death. The man tilted the beer stein, licked his lips as he swallowed, and smiled off in the distance. The priest related another memory from a sheltered childhood.

"I remember how every summer the mosquito truck came around. We kids loved playing in the clouds of smoke, riding our bikes recklessly, whizzing through the clouds. Back in those days the spray was DDT and neither the kids nor the parents knew there was any danger. It was just stinky stuff. Do you remember, Ray, that crazy scientist who came on TV to gobble DDT pellets to prove how harmless they were? Never heard if the sucker lived a long life bug-free or not. Years later, you know, I was determined to independently investigate the truth of the matter. I called the Illinois state government and managed to reach a microbiologist who framed the issue as they say. He said that the mosquitoes spread St. Louis encephalitis and what would I rather have. I told him a perfect world, and he got a kick out of that. Said there are probably pests in paradise too."

Ray grinned and raised his stein in a wavy motion that reminded the friar of a drinking song in an old German movie.

"And in heaven there is no beer!" Ray exclaimed. "I love my beer, Father, and will sorely miss it. Perhaps the place below has hops and barley and you can ferment your own. But in the meantime, I'll drink my fill in this mortal coil." He drank deeply and wiped the foam off with his sleeve. "Mortal coil indeed! My, I'm turning poetic here. Sylvia Plath comes to the Jemez."

The priest saw nothing wrong with poetic; he tried to incorporate rhyme and reason into his sermons. Andy was humored by Ray moving from doing a great Sarah to mimicking the doomed Sylvia. The man certainly seemed to gravitate to female role models. Could he relate to Mother Theresa of Calcutta or Thérèse of Lisieux? Perhaps Sister Maria, more emphatic and a softer presence than the priest, would gain Ray's trust in a second rather than having to pose as a drinking buddy all bloody afternoon. The Franciscan glanced at his watch—just past one. Raul probably waits for the fall of darkness to molest his daughter.

Ray finished his beer and got up to get more from the small fridge. As he returned to his chair he said, "When I was a kid everything I did seemed sinful. I knew I was different right off and being gay, knowing that I was gay, came around the same age that straight kids got acquainted with their private parts. Being a maricón in my culture colored my world and everything I touched seemed tainted by who I was. Who I couldn't escape from, after all, Father. I'd get down on my hands and knees and pray to be relieved of my perversions. But I couldn't stop thinking of sex because for the longest time I couldn't talk about it, desire as I felt it. Who was I going to talk to back in those days? Most everybody of my persuasion were deep in the closet."

Andy nodded. "And your parish priest wasn't much help?"

Ray cackled but his face turned grim. "The last person I was going to confide in was Father Rodriguez. I figured my penance would be a zillion Our Fathers and the word would leak out. I heard enough trash talk from my bros already without them knowing for sure. I began to fight and became skilled enough to win most. Few blades in those days, no Saturday night specials, just our fists and maybe a baseball bat on special occasions. The odds were always stacked against me. It's funny how bullies need an audience, and often bystanders want to take sides. I know from experience that they rarely back the underdog."

"But what about your parents? Your mother?"

"Well, that was an early version of don't ask, don't tell, that game. My father was a meek man who seemed pleased that I was fighting a lot. He never asked what for, just told mom, 'Boys always go after each other.' I'm convinced mom knew early on that her son was a different kind of cat. She told me years later that in kindergarten during playtime I liked to rock in the small rocker they had, rock with two dolls in my arms while the rest of the boys roughhoused. I don't remember that but I can just imagine her panic. She hung out at church a lot, praying for my soul, praying years later that her teenage son show more cojones for the girls. She wasn't a lewd lady, far from it; neither of my parents would use words like that, but that's what they hoped for. The straight missionary position just as the good Lord intended."

"But surely they loved you regardless," Andy said with a forcefulness that was more spontaneous than calculated. Parents make mistakes all the time, give mixed messages, but at heart mean well for their kids. The priest noticed tears welling up again in Ray's eyes.

The priest repeated, more softly, "Surely they love you."

Ray took another gulp from his stein. A little beer foam was left on his mustache. The priest reflexively motioned to his own upper lip but Ray didn't catch the hint.

"They did love me, Father, but far from unconditionally. Mom was more accepting but she's gone now. Dad is still in stubborn denial. The question I always ask myself—is it love if you reject the real person you profess to love? Being homosexual, Father, is not a character defect or physical flaw that you can work on, like starting a crash diet or promising not to lie anymore. I am gay in my gut and that must come from God. My parents never accepted that when I was growing up. It was sorta like the emperor with no clothes. I was their emperor, their only son, their only hope for the Yazzie name living on. But at least mom doesn't have to witness her only son wasting away. Listening to her blame leukemia or cancer would have been a hoot."

Ray jumped out of his chair and reached out for the priest's glass. "I'll freshen your glass, Father, and I've got to take a pee. Don't worry—I'll be sure to wash my hands."

Andy knew he should just say no. His tolerance built up over the years would permit him to stay functional after a couple more but he faced a long drive back to Santa Fe. It wouldn't do to have a glassy stare and liquored-up breath as he squealed into the police lot with the found boy.

"It looks like a storm!" It was the boy, standing in the doorway and pointing at the sky. "The sky is turning black."

Pope was at the boy's feet, tail wagging, looking up at his newfound buddy. The priest got up from the sofa and joined them at the door. Indeed the heavens were threatening to open up, the wind kicking up dramatically.

"It's time to batten down the hatches, me hearties!" the priest said in his best ancient mariner drawl. "Up to the main mast with you, take in sail and don't fall into the roiling sea. An extra portion of rum if we survive this one."

"Oh, Father Andy, we're in the forest, not the ocean! You can't fool me."

"That's the wonder of it all, boy, our bodies anchored in one place while our minds travel to the ends of the world. You don't always have to be where you're at."

Peddie looked up at the sky and the rain started to fall. A few drops became a pelting. "But I want to be here! This is fun. Storms are great. I've never been afraid of them. Mom would come in to hold me when I was a little kid. She thought I was scared but I wasn't. Really! I pretended and she was happy."

The priest tried to remember if he was scared of storms when he was growing up in Illinois. He couldn't recall his mother coming in to calm his jitters. She and dad must have done that. What parent turns a cold shoulder to a crying child? But mother was made of stern stuff and wanted her children to face down irrational fears.

Peddie leaped off the stoop into the rain. The dog leaped after him. The friar knew that with the crackle and crash of lightning all around, the boy and dog should stay under shelter. But Andy didn't have the heart to cut short such ecstasy from defying nature. People do get fried by thunderbolts but the priest doubted that the cabin was safe either from an act of God.

The priest was suddenly spooked out of his musings as he felt a hand on his shoulder. It was Ray with the freshened whiskey glass in the other hand. He said, "Sorry about the scare," as he handed Andy the glass. Both men looked out at the rain dance.

"One time in Chicago," the priest remembered, "I was over at a minister friend's house, a Lutheran, for a genteel garden party. Jim's new wife was a Methodist minister so it was a mixed marriage of sorts. I didn't know her well, only met her at their wedding in the Rockefeller Chapel on the University of Chicago campus. At any rate, there were several people over and we were enjoying ourselves but it wasn't the liveliest party on record. The high point was playing badminton. I was a young guy and would have preferred a knockdown game of volleyball or touch football. Oh well, Jim and Babs, I swear, that was her name, Reverend Babs, got to choose the game."

The priest took a sip of the sour mash and continued after a loud thunderclap. "This has to do with extreme weather, believe me, Ray; you'll see the connection. It was mostly sunshine at the start of the garden party, a perfect day, but as the badminton game got heated, a front came rolling in from the north. Black clouds, strong winds—the rain suddenly came down in sheets. It was funny though; none of us ran inside. We responded like Peddie out there, dancing around, jumping with joy, rolling around with their collie, loving every moment. All us church people acting like holy rollers, daring God to strike us down. We finally went in soaking wet and as we were toweling off in their mud room Reverend Babs summed it up for all of us. She said, now listen to this one: 'I haven't felt like this in years' is what she said. Since she was still a newlywed, I had the naughty thought of wondering how thrilling their honeymoon was. But I know what she meant—nature letting loose, and our defiance in the face of it, was like a fountain of youth for all of us."

Ray nodded and went in to get his stein. He returned to the porch and both men gently clicked their vessels together and drank.

"Thanks, Ray, I have a terrible thirst for my mother's milk. That's what my dad always used to say."

"Your father was a drinker?"

"Yes, you could say that. Dad was an alcoholic really—a sweet man but he died of cirrhosis. He managed to keep it together for years, provide for his family, but the drinking got really bad towards the end. It's sad because the man never reached his full potential."

"Full potential? Now there's a concept!" Ray exclaimed. "Did your old man have unrealized talent?"

"He wrote poetry is what he did. I considered it good poetry. On our birthdays dad would read a special poem before the candles got blown out. My brother always thought it was hokey but I appreciated the sentiment. My sisters got all teary-eyed too. He was never published and never tried as far as I know. You can't raise a family on poetry. He made his living as a building contractor."

"Are you following in your father's footsteps—Father?" Ray asked to the accompaniment of tree branches creaking and the crack of thunder all around now.

"What? You mean the poetry or the drinking perhaps. Well, I put as much poetry into my homilies as heaven allows. And I count every drink and will not cross the line like my father. You know, a drink or two brings me closer to God. No, really, I mean that sincerely. It makes me want to talk to God. I have some pretty profound thoughts."

"Right on!" Ray exclaimed again. "Sometimes I feel that way too. Before I was diagnosed I wasn't much of a drinker. Now every moment alive deserves a toast. I also smoke pot to help with the nausea and give me an appetite. Gotta eat to live, you know?"

"Are you taking the drugs available, the HIV drugs? I've heard there have been tremendous advances."

"Sure thing, Father, I take them—off and on. I'm not the greatest patient in the world. I'm always wondering what there is to live for. First my mother died, then my partner Pete, even my dog died, run over by a fucking car. I'm sorry, Father. I'm a little short on faith these days. That's the heart of the matter."

The question of faith should be right up my alley, the priest thought. He should be able to spit out a glib answer. But what is required for a leap of faith? All the inspired logic in the world won't convince you if you're not in the mood. The emotions must be there in spades; a sense of foxhole desperation helps too. Does a terminal illness like AIDS drive you to make peace with your Maker? Or do you go down denying God the satisfaction?

"Peddie, my boy, it's time to come in!" Ray shouted to the boy still running around with Pope in the driving rain. Peddie looked over with the universal juvenile glare of disdain at an adult spoilsport. The angry sky reminded the priest that adults weigh risk differently than a heedless child. A grown-up errs on the side of caution.

"The boy's welfare is a reason to live, Father," Ray said quietly, "but he's not mine."

Peddie and the dog joined the two men on the porch. The four stood where the slanting rain couldn't reach them. Pope started his drying out by shaking vigorously, spraying drops every which way. Ray looked as though he was going to suffer a heart attack and rushed into his pristine cabin for towels. The priest understood and held his dog at the doorstep. Ray came back and handed a bath towel to Andy.

"Your dog has muddy paws and is very, very wet. Please clean him up. I haven't the time to mop up after him. I'll tend to the boy."

Peddie giggled and threw off his shirt. Ray started to dry him vigorously as the giggles escalated. The priest concentrated on his dog who laid flat on his back, displaying the muddy paws and nether regions.

The almost dry Peddie broke free and ran into the back bedroom. He emerged wrapped in a terry cloth robe many sizes too big. Ray had taken the boy's wet clothes and draped them over one of the wood chairs in the kitchen. Then he fussed and lifted them off the chair and put the remaining dry towel on the back. He carefully placed the pants, shirt, and underwear on the towel so the drips would be absorbed by cotton. The priest had noticed no washer/dryer so Ray must have to haul dirty clothes back to his house in Nava Adé. The old cabin did have indoor plumbing and electricity from a generator. There was no TV or radio. There was a tall bookcase filled with novels and non-fiction. Besides books to read, the man and the boy had CD's for the Walkman.

Peddie settled himself on the floor and called the dog over to him. Still panting from his exertions, Pope laid down with his head in the boy's lap. Ray smiled at the fast and easy bonding.

'Your dog looks like he gets plenty of exercise. He's got great endurance."

"Yes, he does. I take him off leash around Nava Adé all the time. Do you have any pets at home, Ray?"

Ray looked away towards a window. The rain was still beating on the glass. His expression turned somber as the priest cursed himself for not remembering the dead dog comment.

"No, nothing could replace that dog in my heart. Harvey could have survived but the vet said he would have to amputate one of his legs and he would never be the same. I couldn't see doing that to an active dog. So I okayed that he be put to sleep. I couldn't sleep myself for days after."

"I know where you're coming from," the priest said. "I don't know what I would do without my Pope."

"Your Pope indeed! And if he passes, I suppose, people will know a successor is named by white smoke coming from your chimney."

"Very funny. But I admit the name has been controversial. One parishioner accused me of sacrilege. I threw him off by saying that the dog's full name is Alexander Pope. The poet, not the Holy Father."

"Quick thinking, Father. I named Harvey after the Jimmy Stewart movie, about the big rabbit that only Stewart saw and talked to. I loved that movie. My dog was just a mutt from the shelter that I figured had only been yelled at before I adopted him. Only I saw the great heart in the dog, the loving heart, only I saw that. He was with me for eight years."

"Maybe you could find another like him, Ray. The shelter has a lot of Harvey types."

Ray's face turned sour and dismissive. "I haven't got the time or energy for another dog. I left my heart with Harvey."

In another time and place the priest may have laughed at such mawkish sentiment. But he knew full well how a good dog can steal a man's heart. It was like having an affectionate child, a child who never grows up.

Ray motioned to the door that still stood open. The porch overhang kept the downpour out. A cool breeze was coming in.

"Usually the hot springs have several bathers this time of year. I was worried that Peddie would have to hide out in the trees. But I guess the soakers paid attention to the forecast and stayed home."

The priest took another sip of bourbon. "You seem to be isolated from the world. Don't you have a radio or phone? I don't see a TV either."

"You got that right!" Ray responded with a slap on his thigh. "By design I am not bothered by bad news up here. I do have a cell phone but reception is in and out. I flirted with the idea of getting a dish but finally figured that I didn't need 100 channels of noise. I want peace and quiet above all. I have my CD player so I can sing along with Sarah and Celine and Cecilia whenever I want. I talk enough back in town. I used to sell life insurance for a living and that required talk, talk, talk! I made a professional pest of myself. The pitch had some meaning I suppose but now seems so pointless. I want a place of no comment and no need to know and I find it up here."

A place of no comment or need to know? Perhaps heaven is like that; no back-biting and ignorance is truly bliss. The priest was also tired of mingling with nosy and noisy fellow sinners. Andy never felt guileless in his human interactions. There were always hidden agendas and unspoken feelings. Both deep affection and visceral loathing were left unconsummated as people stayed oh so polite. The priest thought again of his nun. On some days all seemed a playful tease, innocent flirting; on others his mood was down and dirty. His confused feelings were buried in the shallow grave of fond regard.

Father Andy took a long sip, draining his glass. One thing though, today with Ray and Peddie, the priest tried to be transparent. Come back, little Peddie, come back to save your sister. But deep in his conscience he knew his motives were a mixed bag: a desire to save bodies and souls, a wish to strike a heroic pose. The friar wanted to be born again into a state of grace. Perhaps with enough prayer and meditation that immaculate time would come.

Andy focused again on the boy. "What do you think, kiddo? No TV, no Play Station, you must miss it. No Enimen CD's either I bet."

Peddie continued stroking the dog's fur as he responded. "Yeah, I miss the TV a little bit but I like listening to the lady singers. But I enjoy the woods and we even caught some fish the other day. That was so cool! I like swimming in the river too. It's cold but I can stand it. It's okay after I get in."

With the heavy rain added to the snow melt, the Jemez River was likely to become a torrent for awhile. Flash floods in the high desert occasionally happened down dry washes now that most historic wild rivers have been tamed to satisfy never-ending human thirst. The priest silently blessed the rain as the arid Southwest needed every drop. Andy tried to stay away from beseeching God for rain as he figured Mother Nature kept her own counsel. Let the Indians do their rain dance for the tourists; let Padre Gurule curry favor by praying for the heavens to open up. Father Andy preferred that people live in harmony with nature rather than dam it in accordance with their rapacious will. The priest liked white water. This spring he was considering asking Maria to come along on his annual rafting trip. He had yet to confide in anybody but old Father Ansalmo about his impossible desire. His friend and father confessor advised the conflicted friar that he treat Maria as a child of God, and cut the thing off if he can't leave it alone. Father Andy always left the Jemez retreat with a bemused heart. Lust had finally been put into perspective. The only problem is that that perspective was still front and center in Andy's consciousness.

The Franciscan was beat. Adrenaline can only carry you so far. He needed to take his rest—badly. When in New Mexico, take a siesta. Go to the fiestas and powwows, but take time out for a siesta. Andy preached that to the weary faithful: lay your body down when you can. Let the wicked have no rest. The priest looked down and noticed his whiskey glass was empty. He didn't remember downing it. The sofa was comfortable enough but the priest would have preferred his own bed. Any old port in a storm.

CHAPTER 9

▼

The priest awoke disoriented. For a few moments he was confused about where he was, why slumped over on a strange sofa, not in his warm bed. Then he remembered where and why, and was comforted by the sight of his dog sleeping on the floor below the sofa. The priest looked around the room to get his bearings. Where were Ray and Peddie? Out and about after the storm? Sunlight filtered through the parted lacy curtains. The priest checked his watch: a little after 4 o'clock. He didn't really feel rested though the siesta lasted several hours. The day was waning and the priest was running late.

The priest sat up and twisted to get the kinks out. He expected an achy neck or irritated back from slump sleeping but someone—Ray he supposed—had placed a soft pillow under his head.

The dog awoke and leaped without hesitation onto the sofa. The priest allowed him to get in a few licks before starting the dialogue that characterized their days together.

"Where are they, buddy? Where'd they go?"

Pope sensed what the priest wanted, jumped off the sofa and bounded towards the door, not the door out but the bedroom door. He scratched the closed door once and whined as he looked back at his master. Andy got up and padded over. He felt a sudden chill. Maybe this cabin was not a sanctuary after all. He wondered if the door was locked; should he knock? The priest bent over and put his ear up against the keyhole. A faint sound of snoring. It was an old fashioned key hole and Andy decided to peek. He saw the foot of the bed, and bare soles on the bed, different sizes. The priest stood up in welling anger, wondering how he could be such a fool. An aging, sick gay guy and a fawning boy—come on! The priest had not given twisted human nature its due.

Father Andy was about to break down the door when he realized he should try the knob first. It turned and he pushed the door open. Ray and the boy were still asleep with a sheet partially covering them. All the priest saw was skin, too much skin. Ray's arm was draped over Peddie's body. The man was the one snoring. Angry beyond belief, the priest rushed over to the bed and whipped the sheet off the two. Both jerked awake and stared up at the glowering friar. With a shock of recognition, Ray shook his head adamantly.

"It's not what you think, Father. It's not like that. This boy offers me comfort but it's not carnal in nature. Believe me, Father, dig up a Bible and I will swear on it. I have one in that bookcase out there. Let me put on some clothes and I will swear on it. I don't really care what you think anyway! The boy helps me sleep. That hike wore me out, okay?. I feel sorry for myself sometimes, okay? I don't want to die alone. Nothing bad is going on out here. Ask the boy! Ask Peddie, come on, ask the boy!"

The priest looked at the frightened boy and wondered how to phrase intimate questions. Both the man and boy had their underpants on. But he had to verify that the nap he so rudely interrupted was innocent rest, not corruption of the flesh.

"Peddie, look, kiddo, I'm sorry about going off like this," the priest pleaded, "but I need to know if anything sinful is happening to you. Is Ray touching you in a private place, in a bad way?"

The boy's eyes were wide open, seemingly blinkless. Peddie looked at Ray for guidance and the man whispered, "Tell the truth and nothing but," and gently squeezed the boy's forearm. Peddie looked back at the priest and then at the dog sitting in a squirm on the floor. As if on cue, Pope leaped onto the bed and nuzzled and licked the boy. The bed was filled to capacity with two human bodies and an affectionate canine. The boy started giggling under the love assault. The tension was broken but the priest still waited for an answer. Andy didn't like the vision of dragging the boy away from the adulterated bed. The priest was no expert on HIV/AIDS and its germination. He wondered if there was a grace period, as with pumping a stomach after a drug overdose or sucking the venom out of a snake bite. Maybe medieval blood-letting and then transfusion of clean, fresh blood.

Peddie held the dog still for a few moments and smiled at the priest. Tousled black hair, shiny brown eyes, bronze skin—the boy was at a wonderful stage of life, running through a stark land of emotional extremes: indescribable delight, inexplicable sadness. The complex issues of adulthood didn't yet affect a boy of ten. But then the priest realized that the boy was a witness to alcoholism, incest and AIDS. Gazing at his grinning face, the Franciscan wondered if a kind God blesses children with short memories.

"Ray is a good guy, Father Andy! He's not being bad. He's sick though and I want him to get well. He tells me that he'll never be well again. That makes me sad."

The grin disappeared and the boy started to cry. Ray put his arms out to cradle the boy. With the dog between them the gesture was a stretch. The priest had the sudden urge to spit out, "Give me my damn dog back!" Ray loved Peddie and vice versa; Andy and the dog loved each other—let my dog go, go to comfort the one who feeds him and needs him more. The thought of food made the priest realize how hungry he was. Father Andy hadn't had a proper sit-down meal for over a day. But it was awkward to ask Ray to share his food after jumping to dirty assumptions and impersonating the wrath of God. Should I believe Peddie? Should I grab the Bible from the shelf and look Ray in the eye as he swears his innocence? The boy obviously believed that nothing bad was happening in the cabin and knew nothing good was happening at home. The priest could leave but the boy was in no hurry. Andy wasn't even sure if his dog wanted to go home with him. The priest decided to try and relax and hope for the best, or at least for a decent meal.

Ray sensed the priest's decision and rolled out of bed. "It's time to eat hearty, my scalawags. The doggie needs to eat too. Let's shake and bake."

Peddie jumped off the bed and Pope dutifully followed. The friar wondered what food Ray had for man, boy, and beast. He was willing to help rustle it up. But first Andy needed to relieve himself and clean up. Ray had earlier pointed out the small bathroom. No shower but at least hot water to splash his face and wash his hands.

"I guess I'll use your facilities," the priest announced, "if nobody needs it."

Ray smiled at the deference. Even grown-up Catholic schoolboys have a tendency to raise their hand for permission to go. "Be our guest, Father. Don't worry—Peddie and I can pee off the porch. I have to smoke a doobie before eating anyway. It helps me get in the mood."

It had been years since the priest had smoked a reefer. Seminary days, with his buddy Eddie. They both realized it was a sin, illegal besides, but at the time seemed innocent enough. Young Andy Leary inhaled, inhaled bent over to increase the effect, and soon experienced a vague, dreamy sense of well-being and languor. A serious case of munchies drove them to the local Jewel where they did wheelies with the cart in the aisles. The next morning their dorm room was strewn with open bags of potato chips and Little Debbies.

The Franciscan went into the bathroom. Andy took off his brown robe, revealing denim jeans and a plaid wool shirt. He doffed them too, down to a ripe T-shirt and underpants. He peeled those off and took a long piss into the bowl. He then washed his hands and face and paid particular attention to his arm pits and genitals. After drying off he felt human again and less like an animal in the dank woods. He rolled his T-shirt and underpants into a ball and wondered if they were worth hauling out. Andy threw them into the small trash can and unrolled some toilet paper to cover them up. He put on his jeans and shirt and robe over the top.

Ray and Peddie were puttering about in the small kitchen. The priest noticed that Pope was already chomping through a meal, beef chili (no beans thank god!), spicier fare than his usual kibble. He seemed to be enjoying the change. At least he didn't have to hunt for his dinner; his predatory instincts were so dulled that he'd be out all night and probably turn vegetarian by dawn. The priest smiled fondly at his dog. Being off in the woods made the priest wonder about his own survival skills. Foraging for nuts and berries, stalking quarry, rubbing sticks together to spark a fire—the priest had been a decent boy scout and hiked the back country occasionally as an adult. He knew how to tie a secure knot. He could pitch a tent and secure food from scavengers. He could read a compass. But he had never been in a do-or-die fix. Living rough would surely test his faith in himself as well as divine providence.

This was hardly a hardtack existence in the Jemez. The cabin didn't have the bells and whistles of modern life but had all the essentials. People can entertain each other after all. Singing together with the glorious voices of the divas in the background, sweet music with the murmur of cool, clear water, the nectar of the gods, human beings just happy to be alive.

It was chili mac for the boys. Ray was the chef, pouring several cans of chili into a pan on the stove. On the second burner a large pot of water came to a boil. Ray poured a couple boxes of Kraft Macaroni and Cheese into the water. The smell of the chili heating up commingled with the smell of marijuana. Ray turned away from the stove to offer the priest a toke. Andy demurred. Their parish priest getting a buzz would set a terrible example for the boy. The priest settled for a beer.

Peddie was drinking a Coke and the dog joined him on the sofa. Pope was a shedder and the first sign of spring in the rectory was dog hair galore. The priest wondered if Ray would suffer a seizure. But the man was mellow and preoccupied with his pots. Andy went over and sat in the Morris chair. A platter of crackers with sliced cheese was on the small pine cocktail table. The ravenous priest gobbled one up, then another with more decorum. He took a long chug of the Cerveza.

The meal was served on the round wood table off the kitchen space. Ray brought over a second unbidden bottle of beer for the priest and pop for the boy. He left the butt of his reefer in the ashtray and placed his foaming beer stein in front of his plate. He brought over the chili mac and ladled generous portions onto the plates. He returned the large pot to the stove and came back with two extra packets of processed cheese. He tore open the top of one and sprinkled a heap of yellow powder onto his steaming chili mac. Then Ray passed the remains of the packet to Peddie and the second packet over to the priest. Andy liked cheese well enough but preferred the kind that looked real. Nevertheless he sprinkled a little onto his food and stirred it in till the yellow disappeared.

"As you can see, Father, we don't stand on ceremony here," Ray said before he dug in. "Haute cuisine is for my city life. We kinda eat out of box and can here. Did have a couple nice fish dinners though, cutthroat we caught ourselves, right, Peddie?"

"I like it all! The fish was good and I didn't mind having the eyes looking up at me. Ray told me that's the way to eat it, head on."

"Actually my boy, I'd expand on that maxim," Ray said enthusiastically. "A true hunter must stare down his prey in life and in death. I don't believe in trophy fish and moose heads on the wall. Eat what you catch. Don't fish with grenades or hunt with an Uzi. A great philosophy for the sporting life!"

The conversation diverted the priest from taking the first mouthful. The piping hot food could stand a little cooling anyway. He was reminded of his childhood.

"We used to eat fish every Friday of course. I remember the canned tuna and fish sticks. Never had a whole fish on my plate until I left home for good. But I certainly agree with the eat what you catch mindset. But you practice catch and release with the young ones, right?"

Ray nodded his head and by silent assent, the three shut up and began wolfing the food down. The already sated Pope settled under the table and let out a contented sigh. The priest felt reassured by the feel of his dog against his stocking feet. A pet knows who brung him to the party; Pope's instinct would be to follow the priest to hell and back. The phrase—home away from home—flashed in his mind as he realized how relaxed he felt in present company.

The priest noticed that Peddie was chewing with his mouth open. Given the uncouth household he was being raised in, Father Andy wasn't surprised. If he had a kid, he would teach him manners. Andy felt suddenly deflated, knowing that Catholic priests won't be allowed to wed and raise a family while this Pope is alive. And to hope that Mother Church would change with John Paul's passing, well, hope springs eternal but the traditions of the Holy Roman Catholic Church die hard. Andy often felt in his counseling with families that he was faking it. Offering advice to harried parents without the essential experience of the ups and downs of raising a child. Empty words based on book learning and vicarious experience. He remembered sitting down with one set of concerned parents with two teenagers acting out in ways attracting the attention of the juvenile justice system. The forty something father and mother, just off work, dressed for success, shaking their heads in unison. The man saying ruefully: "You know, Father, I used to be very judgmental of my parents, all the mistakes they made. Then I became a parent myself."

Apparently the pot smoking worked as Ray scarfed up every morsel. Then he looked up, smiled briefly before his face soured. He excused himself and rushed into the bathroom with his hand cupped over his mouth. The sound of retching made the priest drop his fork.

Peddie glanced at the closed bathroom door and then back at the priest. "He eats too fast, Father. Ray has eyes bigger than his stomach. I remember around Christmas, he smoked his pot in the car and there was enough smoke for me to get stoned. We went to the Wendy's window and ordered everything super-sized. That was a big mistake. We ended up pulling over and he threw up with his head hanging out the window. A couple cars beeped their horns. I was so embarrassed. I ducked down under the seat."

The priest wondered again about corruption. "Not a pretty sight I bet. Does Ray share his marijuana with you?"

"No, Father Andy, no! But I can smell it," Peddie said as the priest heard his dog sigh again. "He's told me that I have to grow up first. But I didn't tell him," glancing over at the bathroom, "that I already smoked pot with Freddie. A couple times after school too, one of my bros had one and we went down to the arroyo to smoke it. But I can take it or leave it."

So Freddie introduced his kid brother to marijuana. When the priest was growing up, illegal drugs weren't part of the Catholic grammar school experience. Andy did have his first beer with his father in the attic room but that wasn't till he was fifteen. Or was it fourteen? Andy had to help himself to hard liquor, a couple years later, as the old man held dear his whiskey.

Take it or leave it, Peddie said. Given such a stark choice, most people take it. The priest's formative years were in the 1970's, a narcissistic era by all accounts. The mission was to achieve a higher state of consciousness as fast and painlessly as possible. It was so difficult for parents with a wastrel past to lecture their children on the pitfalls of drugs and drinking. How do you know how much is too much until you've experienced more than enough? How do you keep your kids from tasting the fruit of the tree of good and evil? And is that tree planted and nurtured by you, or society, or God the demented Gardener?

The priest shook his head at the image of a drunk, lost in space Raul sitting down for a rite of passage talk with Peddie. Calmly explaining the difference between a good buzz and a bad trip, guiding his son through the haunt of the birds and the bees—the bad dad led by foul example and had his own notion on what scenic was. Peddie was more likely to trust his brother. The priest was disturbed to hear about the pot smoking. While Andy viewed cannabis as a benign drug, he did believe that the age of reason should take root before silly season comes calling.

"When I was your age, Peddie, pot was around but I had far better things to do. I can't remember feeling deprived. Drugs can make you crazy and do things you regret the next day. That's why they'll illegal."

"But Ray doesn't turn crazy," Peddie responded. "He just eats too fast but he's not hungry without the pot. He says his doctor told him to eat or his pills won't help him. So that's what happening."

"I know, I know, nothing wrong with drugs that help us. That's why doctors tell us what to take and what not to take. They have years of schooling and know what will help us stay well or get better."

Peddie absorbed this for a few moments before responding. "So if I want drugs, I go to a doctor."

"Well, you only go to a doctor if you're really sick. Like Ray and marijuana—he's sick and needs medicine. Pot helps with his appetite but, like you said, he has to take the time to chew—with his mouth closed. If you're healthy you don't need a doctor so you don't need drugs. Have you ever heard of a natural high, kiddo?"

"You mean like winning a baseball game?"

"That's right! You know, like winning at sports or climbing a tree or catching the biggest fish. You don't need drugs after doing those things, after winning fair and square," the priest said. Of course he doubted that Ray's doctor would suggest pot as a palliative. He did prescribe the wonder drugs which held off—for awhile—the onslaught of the virus. But from what Ray said, the patient wasn't taking the meds religiously.

Peddie reached down to pat the dog who gave out another sigh. Still looking under the table, the boy asked, "But what if the other team cheats? Then it's okay to use drugs?"

Robbed of victory, let's break out the bong? The priest didn't see the sense of preaching about the value of moral victories or keeping a stiff upper lip. A ten year old wouldn't understand. Andy had the impulse to spit out, "Be true to yourself!" figuring that would sound good and wise to impressionable youth. But the priest wasn't sure how fully formed in character and temperament a child is. If he's incorrigible today, wait until tomorrow, he'll be the cat's meow. Perhaps the priest should tell the boy: "Be true to worthy role models." The boy loved Ray. Also, Freddie and the boy were close. Both men serve as father figures, filling in for the biological father otherwise engaged.

But the priest wasn't sure if Ray was the best role model. Andy's concern wasn't only that Ray was HIV-positive and even confessed to lust being a chronic failing. It was the man's spirit rather than his sexuality that gave the most pause. His fatalistic attitude didn't represent a moral victory over impending death. Ray had no apparent faith. He wasn't taking his medicine. His life was going up in smoke.

It was Holy Week. The rituals center on the passion of Jesus Christ's last few days on earth getting His affairs in order and showing the Romans and the rabbis how hard it is to kill a true God. His Resurrection from the dead and Ascension later body and soul gave hope to all us sinners that we too would rise without blemish upon the Second Coming. The priest remembered the blemishes on Ray's skin at the hot springs. In his case mortal sin disfigured more than the soul. The light of the day was fading fast; the priest had pressing business back at the parish. His note to Father Gurule only suggested an absence till late afternoon. He wondered if his cell phone would work in these jagged mountains.

A backup plan of staying overnight was forming in the priest's mind. The next Holy Week event that he absolutely had to attend was the interfaith service on the plaza tomorrow night, Wednesday night. Alarms would sound if he didn't show. A missing priest posted next to a lost boy's photo—people will talk and connect the pixels. So the absolute deadline to return to the parish was tomorrow afternoon. By staying the night, he could watch over the boy. Perhaps by morning the boy could be cajoled or guilt-tripped into coming back voluntarily.

Father Andy looked at his watch—6:15—and figured the pastor would be back at the rectory after the 5 p.m. short version weekday Mass. He had to try to reach Gurule to allay his curiosity and concern about his associate's mysterious absence. Also, he had to ask the old pastor to possibly cover for him through part of Wednesday.

Ray finally emerged from the washroom and muttered, "Sorry, my stomach went south on me," and pushed his plate away. After a token "Hope you're feeling better," Andy asked Ray to step outside, just the two of them. The friar looked below the table and told his dog to keep the boy company. Pope was still pooped, and barely fluttered an eyelid.

Andy and Ray walked a short distance from the cabin. The priest wanted to try his cell out in the open but also needed to feel out his host about staying overnight. About intentions too, about the adults combining their efforts to influence the boy to go home to face the music. Music scratchy and discordant as what goes around, comes around.

The sky was cloudy again and darkness had fallen. The priest wondered if more rain was on the way. Another downpour could make the muddy road out impassable. He stopped and turned to face Ray.

"I'm truly sorry you're sick, Ray, but I need to figure this thing out. I need your help with the boy. Peddie seems content here but we're the adults and he's the child. What we say goes. Wouldn't you agree? Peddie goes back one way or another. You're the one who clued me in on that drunk's violation of his daughter. We have the responsibility to stop that. What do you say, man?"

The priest wondered if he was pulling it off, the righteous call for concerted action to save the innocent. God's mouthpiece?—In the olden, golden days of Christendom the Franciscan's robe automatically commanded respect and obedience was assumed. These profane days, well, it was a crapshoot. Andy didn't particularly feel in sync with the divine. Usually the achy muscles after vigorous hiking were soothed by a hot bath. Endorphins released, the priest would feel like a god at rest, a minor god but one at peace with the universe. Today the hiking, junk food, hard liquor, and a restless siesta combined to make Andy feel as common as dirt.

Ray paused to think before responding. "Well, Father, here's the way I see it. Peddie's the one child I know and love. I do feel sorry for his sister but I owe my allegiance to the boy and his welfare. If Peddie really wanted to go back, you wouldn't hear a peep out of me. It doesn't matter what happens to my sorry ass. I'm on my way out anyway. But my boy doesn't want to go, not yet at least. I worry about what happens when he goes back. Will the police believe his story? They certainly will if the girl backs him up. Is his sister going to tell the truth too, Father? I know nothing of incest but I can imagine that bastard might have her intimidated to say nothing, to tell no one. If Gabby says it didn't happen, where does that leave my boy? Do you really think Peddie would find safe haven back in that family? He'd probably disappear again, only this time for good."

The priest hadn't really considered the possibility that Gabby wouldn't confirm the incest. In his mind everything would be routine when they returned to Santa Fe, routine and tragic. The bad father would be charged and convicted; the remains of the family would stick together somehow. Maybe Freddie would take over the family business. Gabby would go into intensive counseling to deal with the anger and shame. In God's time healing would take place. But if Gabby dissembled or kept her mouth shut, all bets were off. Perhaps the incest would stop as the mother would now be vigilant. Maybe she would leave Raul based on her son's accusation alone. Maybe she's heard things in the night. But if the entire family hangs together, no telling what a drunk, resentful man would do to his spoilsport son. Ray was right on about the danger. At the very least Peddie may be ostracized during the formative years when nurturing is so necessary.

Perhaps Peddie's testimony could remain confidential with the priest the conduit. Since the boy talked directly to the priest, the bonds of confession no longer applied. No prosecution was likely on hearsay alone but a probing investigation could scare sober and chasten the abuser. No corporeal punishment was likely except for whatever whipping his conscience laid on. The Franciscan trusted that a higher power would eventually mete out retribution.

Gabby's cooperation was essential for more down to earth punishment. The priest could see the girl confiding to the right person, perhaps a trusted father figure such as…me! Father Andy made her acquaintance yesterday but didn't really know her. The priest recalled seeing her at Sunday services with her mother over the years. Maybe Andy can be the catalyst. Perhaps the girl will confess her father's sins. Perhaps and maybes begged for resolution.

"Okay, Ray, okay! I can see where you're coming from. Let me go back alone and talk to the girl. But I want it understood that regardless of what she is willing to attest to, the boy comes back tomorrow or by Thursday at the latest, kicking and screaming if necessary. I want your word, Ray. I promise to do all I can to make the police understand your good intentions."

"You have my word, Father. Shall I swear on the Bible? Just kidding. Listen!— I know I can't keep Peddie forever. No need to plead my case to the cops though. I've made my peace with God last night, right, Padre? The boy has school next week. I assume we can get this Gabby thing resolved by then. I just want you to give it your best shot with the girl. Maybe I'm wrong; maybe she's primed to spill her guts to the right person. Believe me, Father, I don't mean to make light of the girl's ordeal. I've experienced enough pain in this life to not wish it upon the innocent."

The priest looked into the man's eyes in the faint light and saw sincerity. As with any person, the priest has to trust his instincts. All the facts in creation can't replace instinct. In any legal contract who reads the fine print anyway. What really happens is you look across the table and you either trust the person or feel the willies.

"All righty then!" the priest exclaimed, relieved that a course of action was agreed upon. "Ray, believe me when I say prayer can be a comfort in your time of trial. A lot of people aren't aware that St. Thérèse of Lisieux is the patron saint of AIDS sufferers. Pray to her, Ray, it can't hurt!"

The man didn't throw himself prostrate on the ground but did bow his head at the mention of the Little Flower. Andy wondered if the man meant to drive him immediately over to his car at the trailhead or offer shelter overnight. He was about to ask which when Ray offered shelter.

"I'll tell you what, Father. It's late already and the road out is tough after a heavy rain. Why don't you stay the night and I'll get you over to your car bright and early in the morning? We can kick back and relax tonight. I can offer you an air mattress that ain't too bad for one night and beats the sofa anytime. Peddie and I usually go down to the river to bathe. Why don't you join us? The water's freezing but you feel like a million bucks afterwards. At this time of evening sometimes we run across critters down there for happy hour."

The priest chuckled. 'Sounds good, Ray. Can't do anything about Gabby tonight anyway. How's cell reception by the way? I need to reach Father Gurule to tell him what's up, a sanitized version at least. I left him kinda in a lurch."

"Good luck with a call out, Father. I haven't had much occasion to use mine. I'll collect the boy and your dog; towels and a flashlight too. Back in a jiffy."

Ray walked back to the cabin while the priest dialed the rectory. Gurule, hobbled by his diabetes, answered after nine, ten rings. His hello sounded as though coming from the bowels of the earth.

"Hello, Father, can you hear me?" Andy spoke loudly, ready to shout if necessary.

"Is that you, Andy?"

"It's me all right!"

"Good, good, wondered where'd you gotten too. Where'd you gotten to anyway?"

"Pope and I are out and about. We're staying overnight up in the Jemez with a sick friend. Sorry about…"

The dreaded static of bad cell reception in the mountains interrupted the call. Andy heard faintly Gurule's voice, "Didn't catch…" and Andy shouted, "Be back tomorrow!" More static and then click, dial tone. At least the bad connection kept him from telling whoppers. Tomorrow, face to face, he may have to resort to subterfuge. Though he could ethically tell his pastor about Peddie, Gabby and the family situation, Andy wanted to handle the approach to the girl on his own. The old man would just get in the way. How was Andy going to call the girl out and get her alone? He'd worry about that tomorrow.

"Ready if you are, Father?"

Ray's voice, coming out of the shadows, made the priest jump.

"Sorry about startling you. Did you get through?" Ray asked.

"More or less, mostly less. Static took over."

"Atmospherics, Father. You know, the first time I heard that word was in one of those Pearl Harbor movies, Tora, Tora, Tora! Did you see that one?"

"Yeah, I did, years ago. That was the one with Jason Robards as the admiral in charge. What was his name again?"

"Kimmel," Ray replied. "But it was Martin Balsam who played the admiral and Robards played General Short. Remember, in Washington, just before the attack, the admiral there wanted to send an imminent war warning to Kimmel. The communications officer said that the 'atmospherics' were bad that day. Someone said, 'Why don't you use the army's signal service?' The navy com guy replied drolly, 'What makes you think their atmospherics are any better?' It's the only laugh in the entire movie."

Peddie piped in. "I saw that movie! I like war movies. The Japs and Nazis always lose."

Ray motioned to the panoply of nature cloaked in darkness. "What I like is how you say it in Mass. 'Peace be with you. Peace I leave with you.' A peace that surpasseth understanding. Right, Father? War is easier to comprehend but I want peace now."

Ray turned for the short trek to the river. The priest asked along the way why his family didn't build on the banks. Ray explained that river front property, even in the middle of nowhere, was prohibitively expensive back in the 1930's when his grandfather scraped together some money. Lucky thing too, as the federal government used eminent domain to acquire streamside private property for the benefit of wildlife and outdoor lovers.

They could find the swollen Jemez River by the rushing sound alone. At least one wild thing was drinking its fill as Pope ran ahead and barking started. They heard major rustling through the underbrush. The priest feared for his dog but

Pope stood safe and alone on the riverbank. He still had his fur ruffled and was sniffing the wind for trouble. Whatever trouble he found was going rather than coming. It appeared safe to go to the water's edge.

The priest could see the roiling white water. He wondered how deep it was, how swift, how cold. Ray must have sensed his fear.

"Don't concern yourself, Father; the swimming hole is downstream a bit. The river pools there nicely and only the very middle is over Peddie's head. Pope will keep peepers away."

The allusion to Peeping Toms made the priest realize that he had no bathing suit or underwear for that matter. The priest hadn't skinny-dipped since teenage years. Here he was with an unabashed gay man and the boy every cop in the state is looking for, and he was going for a dip sans his friar's habit. Strange day, but life offers a few strange days to go along with the same old same old.

Peddie rushed ahead with the dog at his side and both were already in the water as the lagging men reached the swimming hole. Ray immediately shed his clothes and plunged in with an overly theatrical "Bur-r-r!" Father Andy, uncertain if a brief prayer before disrobing was appropriate, shucked his robe, jeans and wool shirt and folded all neatly on a dry rock. He flirted with the idea of waving his hand in the water, dipping his toes, but then decided to be brave. He wasn't an old maid after all. Andy gingerly walked into the water and felt the shock of the snow melt on his skin. The freeze reached his thighs and the priest hesitated. The tender groin is always the hardest to overcome. There was no easy way out, so the priest dived and surfaced with an excruciating, ecstatic yelp.

Ray and Peddie laughed and splashed some water the priest's way. Pope paddled over to Andy and the priest held his dog for awhile. The river bottom was a bit rocky so the wader's feet gently touched down, pushed off, while their arms treaded water. Finally, after a long day that started dry and turned to mud, the priest felt human again. He asked Ray about soap and Ray left the water to retrieve a bar from his backpack. He told the priest that it was a special cleansing bar supposedly harmless to nature. The priest nodded at the 'supposedly' and just rubbed his armpits with it briefly, before handing it over to the boy. Without using it, Peddie passed the bar to Ray who returned it to his pack.

Rock formations bordered the large pool fed by the rushing water. The priest was happy about the bare rock, so as not to leave the water clean only to get muddy feet ashore. Andy felt great after the initial shock of immersion. It was quite dark now but his companions were still visible floating, quiet now, arms swaying on the surface of the water.

The rain began to fall but it was a light drizzle. No lightning streaks, no sound of thunder—it was still safe to be in the water. Pope had enough and plopped on the stone bank waiting for the human being to come to their senses. The priest floated on his back, enjoying the feel of the gentle warm rain. In the moment he felt freer than he had for years. Any flaws of flesh and character were accepted as a consequence of being born into a world of willfulness and whimsy. The priest didn't feel as though he had to struggle anymore with his devils.

CHAPTER 10

▼

They were in no mood to rush back to the cabin despite the drizzle and darkness. Their skin tingled with the afterglow from the cold dip. With the clothes and towels soaked on the stone bank, they couldn't dry themselves properly. The priest slipped his friar's robe over his head and decided to carry his jeans and shirt. Ray and Peddie put on their jeans, wrapped their shirts around their waists, and stuffed the other wet things into the backpack. The drizzle stopped and the drifting clouds parted enough to allow glimpses of the moon and stars. Everything in the woods smelled fresh as the infrequent rains in the American Southwest didn't foster the verdant decay of tropical rain forests.

Ray the pathfinder knew the way home in the dark. He gave the flashlight to the priest to allow him to illuminate his footfall. The swimming hole was less than a mile away from the cabin. Andy had lost track of time but knew it was getting late. In his occasional walkabouts in the wild the priest would be hunkered down by now around a small campfire. It was spook time when beastly apparitions circled closer and closer, just beyond the flickering light. Rabbi Bernstein, often along on these treks, liked to start his scary stories with "There was a man once who…" or "Once upon a time there was a boy consumed by curiosity…" The clergy never swapped stories about damsels in distress. Andy never asked Joel about this. Perhaps it was a Jewish thing, or maybe two men of the cloth, one celibate by vow, were shy about spinning fantasies about women beset by demons.

Father Andy and his companions walked in comfortable silence. Small talk would detract from the magical mood. The priest's mind was empty of fear and worry, of grim scenarios and worst cases. Whatever will be, will be, que sera, sera!

They broke free of the trees and saw the light on the porch across the meadow. The night air at attitude was turning downright chilly. Pope ran ahead and they found him panting at the door.

After drying off and changing into terry cloth robes, Ray piled some logs and kindling in the hearth and soon a fire was roaring. Ray suggested a game of poker to close out the night. Ray had a rack of colored chips and distributed an equal bank to each. He didn't ask the priest to dip into his wallet so the chips really represented funny money. Beers for the men, a Coke for the boy, three bowls with mixed nuts—the players were stoked. A large bag of potato chips was ripped open and passed around. Andy took a handful of chips and tried to stack them neatly on top of the nuts. Several tumbled off onto the table. Seeing the priest's vain effort, Peddie pointed at his own larger stack of potato chips precariously perched on his nut bowl. Artistry of sorts—not a single chip on the table. Andy was reminded of the petty humiliation of years ago when he was giving downhill skiing a try. Awkward and embarrassed on the bunny hill, he struggled to stay upright on the gentle slope. All around him, kids barely out of the womb passed him laughing and fearless, without ski poles for god's sake. The seminarian fought the urge to run them over out of spite.

The priest asked Peddie, "Do you know how to play poker, my son?"

The boy looked down with a shy smile. "Sure, Father, Freddy and Gabby and me play all the time. Strip poker."

Ray looked from the boy to the startled priest. "He's joking of course, Father. Our Peddie is quite the jokester."

The Franciscan remembered adolescent strip poker and it wasn't much of a joke. During Catholic high school days, he and his older brother would camp out with three or four other boys in a large tent in the Leary backyard. By the dim light of kerosene, with flashlights as a complement, the teens played strip poker, told dirty jokes, and ripped some outrageous farts. The loser of the last stitch of clothing game had to leave the tent and dance naked in the moonlight. The pale white bodies were illuminated not only by the moon and the stars but also by crisscrossing flashlight beams. Having no memory of which cards played, and lacking a poker face, Andy lost early and often and had to dance alone more than once. The flashlights played on his baby fat. A couple times his dick became wicked to the vast amusement of the boys. Over the years whenever he watched a war movie featuring Nazi searchlights targeting flak on the belly of the bomber, the priest would shudder with the memory of the pseudo-erotic dance.

Altar boys by day, devil in the flesh worshipers by night—the boy were lucky they didn't live in Puritan times. There was no demonic touching though one night a weird wrestling match broke out between two near naked boys. The argument arose over cheating at cards. Both boys wanted to lose the last hand. The fight ended abruptly when the neighborhood dogs began to bark and back porch lights came on.

Father Andy considered what the boy said. "Actually, kiddo, I prefer straight poker."

Ray laughed and started to shuffle. "Okay, boys, it's a draw! Let's stop the b.s. and play some serious poker. 7-card draw, deuces wild."

The host played astutely and was lucky to boot. The ten year old did indeed know how to play poker, when to hold them and when to fold them. The priest hadn't played in years but the rules of the games came back to him. As happened in the tent long over, Andy lost more than he won.

Father Andy piled on the potato chips as his poker chips disappeared. Though only funny money was at stake, the priest wanted to win! The deep serenity felt earlier dissipated as he went mano á mano ý boyo.

The hands continued. The men were on their third beer when stupid jokes started to be told. But then Ray told a very odd ghost story:

> It all started with a boy, pale as a ghost, a boy whose body hated sunshine, and loved to roam around at night. I know you're thinking vampires, blood suckers, stakes through the heart—but it wasn't like that with him. He was a lily white boy with a peculiar skin condition. His skin wouldn't tan. He could lie out for hours and still be as white as pork. Just imagine that you're a self-conscious kid, on a beach with sun-worshipers, and you're lying there like a beached whale, with everybody pointing and staring. But whales in distress receive loads of help, animal lovers pushing, pulling the beast out to sea. Nobody lifted a finger to help the poor boy. It made him want to be buried in the sand.
>
> So the boy concluded it was better to embrace the night. In the dark he found something really weird. He could lie out under the stars, lay down in a swimming suit is what I'm saying, and his skin would tan to a golden tan. For a few hours he was the king of the hill, the toast of the town. The denizens of the night were impressed. But then a problem cropped up. When dawn broke, the tan disappeared and the boy was back to his sorry white ass. A miracle by night reverted to a freak of nature by day. What curse prevented his perfect tan surviving the light of day?

He went to his parish priest for counseling. The kind padre heard him out and suggested he confess his sins, clean his slate. The boy couldn't think of any sins to confess. He wondered if he should imagine, pleasing the priest and saving himself. The boy was quite confused about what God wanted him to do. But then suddenly he got it; he had to be bad first, act out, lie, cheat and steal, before he could be saved. A blameless life is not worth living, and won't buy you a place in the sun.

An amazing transformation happened then. The boy went home feeling completely different. One positive result was he was able to sleep at night, sleep like a baby. Another big thing was that he was able to go down to the beach, lay out his towel and feel his skin warm up gloriously. He laid there like everybody else, soaking up the rays, and the boy finally felt a part of, not like a fish out of water. He was so grateful that he lost track of time, turned red as a beet, and went home to be berated by his mother even as she applied cool crème to his burning skin. She grounded him for days. But the boy felt liberated regardless. Next foray to the beach he took along sun block. He started to work seriously on the perfect tan.

The card playing had been suspended for the duration of the ghost story. The priest was mesmerized by its unconventional nature. He wondered what the only boy in the cabin took away from it. Peddie's skin was naturally brown and didn't need the sun to make it perfect. As for the boy's immortal soul, the priest could only dabble in it. The priest in the story advised confession as telling the truth about lies frees you up to burn in the sun rather than in hell. Andy always felt that way after confession, a lightness of being, a certainty of salvation.

The Catholic Church seemed to acknowledge that a loss of innocence was the prerequisite for heavenly peace. The death of an unbaptized infant was a tragedy in many ways, for the grieving parents in particular, but also for the baby whose only fault is original sin. The immature soul is shuttled off to limbo. Now limbo is a nice neighborhood but lacks the trappings of heaven. The theologians of the Church, after many years of deep reflection, also decided that our beloved pets pass on into limbo too. A consolation prize, so to speak, for the babies denied heaven. Father Andy could just imagine Pope's reaction to being denied entrance with his master at the pearly gates. He'd find the nearest fire hydrant.

The games began again but soon petered out. The priest knew it was bedtime when he started to nod off with a rare winning hand. Ray brought out the air mattress and blew it up. He gave the priest a blanket and pillow and tossed a couple logs on the fire to keep the room pleasantly warm. There was only room for one on the mattress. The groggy priest told his dog, "I'll flip you for it," and flipped a poker chip, caught it and slapped it on his wrist. "You lose, Popey." The dog sighed and jumped up on the sofa and curled into a ball. It had been a long day of intoxicating smells. The next day promised new adventures. Pope wouldn't have to think twice about keeping his nose to the ground.

CHAPTER 11

▼

The priest slept soundly through the night and was awakened by Pope's licking. The priest protested that a little more sleep would be nice but the dog said absolutely not, take care of me first, sleepy head. God may have given man dominion over the beasts and creeping things in the beginning, but most modern day pet owners have ceded control back to the beast. Father Andy rolled off the air mattress, onto his knees, and said a fast prayer.

He got up, grabbed the terry cloth robe, and tied the strap loosely. He went to the front door and let the dog out. Pope leaped off the small porch and sniffed around a bit. He soon found a tree stump to stake his claim on. The priest also felt the need to go. He looked back into the cabin, considered the small bathroom and then shrugged. When in nature...but find your own tree slump.

It was a glorious dawn. The sun hadn't yet risen above the eastern mountains but its light was chasing the stars away to the still dark west. The priest noted no reds in the sky; the interfaith service tonight would hopefully be blessed with good weather. The morning dew made the meadow grass glisten but the dirt road out—what was visible—appeared to be negotiable. The priest had a full day ahead and couldn't wait for perfect conditions on the ground.

Father Andy left his dog to frolic awhile longer in the wet grass. He went into the kitchen to fix breakfast for the dog. There was left-over chili mac but the priest figured that would be too spicy. Instead he found cans of corn and Chunky Soup. He opened both cans and drained the excess water from the corn. He ladled half the corn into a large bowl and added the sirloin chunks and potato bits from the soup. The final concoction looked better than his usual kibble with a little wet food mixed in. The priest filled another bowl with water and took both bowls out to the porch. The dog took a nanosecond to discover the food.

The priest wondered if he could have his regular private breakfast in such a setting. There was no morning paper to read and no room to retreat to. Improvisation was dependent upon Peddie and Ray sleeping in. But there was a stir from that quarter as Ray ducked into the bathroom. The priest figured it would be a gracious gesture for the guest to prepare breakfast for all. He found coffee, eggs, milk, butter and jam, and a hunk of cheddar cheese in the fridge. Bread was in the cupboard; roughing it for breakfast meant no toaster. Cheddar cheese omelets and whole wheat bread slathered with butter and jam wasn't bad under the circumstances.

Ray came out of the bathroom and, noticing the priest puttering about in the kitchen, smiled and said good morning and thanks for fixing breakfast. Peddie emerged from the bedroom stretching and rubbing his eyes. He went into the bathroom. Ray ducked back into the bedroom and soon came out fully clothed and hungry for bear. But not hungry enough, as he went over to the covered bowl on the cocktail table where his stash was. He methodically rolled a big doobie and lit up. Stretching out on the sofa, he looked over at the priest slaving at the stove.

"Make mine a three egger, Father. I don't have to worry about cholesterol at this stage in my life."

Ray took a long drag and the priest, his back to the sofa, sensed the man's eyes on his ass. Red eyes from the marijuana smoke. Red eyes at dawn, sailors be warned. Buggering to come in the forecastle. The Franciscan wondered where that provocative imagery came from. Sodomy on the high seas where international law prevails. The language of love is international; lust too knows no boundaries. Father Andy tried to concentrate on the sizzling omelet instead of unsettling thoughts. What is it like to feel a cock up my ass? Is it alien invasion, an aberration of nature? Or does God give us our head to find our own innate expression of love? The priest had scant experience with physical love since he entered seminary right out of high school. He wasn't exactly chaste during school days but he was very awkward and scared of consequences to body and soul. Sometimes the Franciscan wondered if a cultivated spirituality was a poor substitute for the immediate, intense pleasure of making love. Some of the female saints, depicted in paintings on bended knees, looked utterly carried away by prayer. To the laymen's eyes, they looked as though the most passionate orgasm was being experienced. Thérèse of Lisieux, the Little Flower, was a sterling example; every fiber of her being fused to God. Father Andy fell far short in his many bouts with prayer. The priest wondered why he couldn't experience more impure joy in his yearning for God.

Peddie came out of the bathroom and asked where the dog was. The priest told him outside. The boy went to open the door and the dog was right there, leaping up on the boy. Peddie held the Pope upright, asking him how's he doing, telling the dog that he loved him too. The boy looked over at the priest.

"I smelled something good all the way in the bathroom."

"Yes, kiddo, it's good and done. The doggies had his grub already; now it's time for the men to eat. Get the plates out, Peddie, and the silverware. I have the coffee brewed. Do you want a cup, boy? Great! Ray too, right? Fine! Three mugs."

So they sat down to eat. The priest wanted to make it crystal clear to the boy the why and wherefore of going back without him today. Andy certainly wasn't going to scare the bejesus out of Peddie with the possibility that he would have to go it alone with his accusation. The boy needed to be reassured. Also, the priest wanted to convey the message that the responsible adults on the scene were on the same page.

"Pope and I are going back to Santa Fe after breakfast, Peddie," the priest said, noticing the boy's sad glance at the dog under the table. "I want you to know why you're staying with Ray a bit longer. I'll be back tomorrow, certainly within a couple days. Ray and I agree on that; you have to go back. We have to stop this business between your dad and Gabby. It's a sin and a crime, you understand that, don't you, my son?"

Peddie looked up and said, "What?"

"Just what I said!" the peeved priest exclaimed. Here he was talking mortal sin, and Peddie and Pope only had eyes for each other. "Your dad is sick and needs help. Your sister is a victim and we have to stop the abuse. I know you want to do your part and I will do my duty. Then I will come back for you, Peddie."

The boy's eyes suddenly widened with recognition. "You're going to tell Gabby what I saw! She's going to hate me! Are you going to tell my dad?"

Father Andy felt calm and resolute in the face of the boy's terror. "No, no, my boy, I doubt if I'll be talking with your dad. The first priority is Gabby. She's not going to hate you! You'll be her hero. You'll be her special brother."

Peddie shook his head vigorously and cried through his tears. "No one will like me anymore! Mommy doesn't understand. No one understands!"

The boy was obviously terrified. Raul Martinez was a burly drunk, a freak of nature. Cops with big guns and nightsticks may be needed to take him down. A bloody confrontation was in the offing. It was also possible that Ray would take the fall. Good intentions may not prevent legal liability. Gay man, runaway boy—the authorities would assume the worst. Ray already was condemned to whither away by a decaying immune system. A prison term would be double jeopardy. As a convicted child molester, he would be short eyes behind bars and that may entitle him to early release to his Maker.

The friar gazed across the table at the man whose knowing grin started it all. Nothing happened since as Andy expected. Here he was, a man of God breaking bread with fugitive kind. Father Andy hadn't a clue what fate had in store for all of them. He looked down at his dog for comfort and advice. Pope wasn't paying much attention to the human drama; the dog was lying contentedly, licking his paws and nether regions. Of course the priest was a responsible pet owner so the Pope's private parts didn't work as nature intended.

Did Andy really care what happens to Ray? Did he trust the man? The answers were yes on both counts, the sixth sense driving his initial suspicions on Sunday being metamorphosed into a certain love. The Franciscan was suddenly jolted by the recognition of love however conditional. It was a feeling grounded in compassion for a terminal man. It wasn't physical at all, for his desire from early on and always was for the girls, the mysterious, just beyond his grasp girls. Platonic love was all to the good and less messy besides. The priest's solemn vows precluded romance anyways. But unlike his dog, if Andy's balls are licked, no telling where crude sensation will send his lonely heart.

Ray reached across the table to touch the boy's shaking hand.

"I can't predict what will happen, Peddie," the priest said in a quavering voice. "Lord knows I will do everything I can to make things right for you at home. God loves you, kiddo. Remember that through all time you are a child of God. And Ray and I are here to make sure no harm comes to you."

The boy stopped crying and brought his arm up to his eyes to soak up the tears with his T-shirt sleeve. Ray withdrew his hand and a sour expression came over him. He rushed into the bathroom. Peddie made the old finger down the throat gesture.

"Oh my, is this the way every meal ends?" the priest asked.

"When nothing is happening, he's usually okay," Peddie said, looking over at the door. "Since you came, Father, a lot has been happening. I know you're going to help me. I'm not really afraid."

The boy turned to look directly into the eyes of his priest. A steady, brave stare from a boy who had seen too much in his young life. The priest again felt the weight of responsibility for fragile lives. He must pray for strength. He must pray to God. That should come natural for a preacher.

The priest found his own eyes watering. He looked away and brought his hand up to rub his chin. He stroked his short beard, the hair hiding his weak chin and jowls that cried for a turtleneck. Andy felt one of his bouts with inferiority coming on. The litany was always the same. My flesh is so lame. I'm not as smart as I think I am. My character leaves a lot to be desired too. The priest knew that tearing himself down wasn't going to help the situation. Andy had to trust that God wouldn't give him more than he could handle. A priest had to trust God.

"You'll be just fine, Peddie. Everyone will be all right," the priest said faintly, not really believing his words. Sure, absolutely a lead-pipe cinch, and Santa Claus and Peter Pan will come along for the ride. The tooth fairy will ride shotgun. The priest smiled despite himself at the image of a fanciful stagecoach racing through hostile Indian territory. When he was Peddie's age, Andy started the transition from blind faith to the knee jerk skepticism of teenage years. He tried to remember if he still believed in Santa and fairies after his Catholic confirmation into the age of reason. His young head certainly was swelled with myth, waiting to be pricked by disillusion. But God was always there. Without belief in God Andy would truly lose his way.

A pale-faced Ray rejoined the two at the table. Andy thought he could detect the faint odor of vomit.

"How are you doing, Ray?" the priest asked.

"How do you think I'm doing?" Ray responded, his voice dripping with sarcasm. "I'm dying here, and there's nothing to be done. I'm sorry about being a kill-joy, but that's the way it goes."

"But surely a cure is in the works, and medicines in the meantime. Look at Magic Johnson, all the good years he's had since announcing he has AIDS. You might live longer than you think. You might find yourself waking up ten years from now still bitching about your fate. Come on, Ray, count your blessings!"

"Yeah, years of vomiting up my guts. Oh Father, I know I should be more positive! I do take my meds most days and my doctor tweaks the mix every now and then. There are advances I know; smart people are working hard for a cure. I told Doctor Garduno about the pot and he made no comment. What do the lawyers say—silence implies consent? But doc did say to cut back the booze. Alcohol doesn't help? Little does he know."

"There you go, Ray," the priest said enthusiastically. "Maybe a change of diet will help too. Less spicy foods; give up the junk. There's always a way!"

"Look, Father, I'm trying every day to find reasons to live, ways to fight back. This boy here gives me a reason to live. Now I have to give him up. Just as I've had to give sex. To do no harm anymore."

"But that doesn't mean you have to give up love," the priest asserted. "Isn't that the core of living, to love somebody, with all our heart and soul? Isn't that the answer to pain?"

"Perhaps the cause of pain too. I experienced such a love once, a great love, my first love. You see, there was a boy once. Don't worry, Father, I call him a boy but he was old enough. Gary and I met early on in college. Gary was something else those days, full of fire like the saints with a halo. He was such a precious boy. But then he changed, or I changed, or life changed us some fucking way. He ended up leaving me with a post it note. Three words: I can't breathe. He couldn't breathe? I thought our love was making us free."

The priest shook his head at the notion that love interfered with living. All consuming love indeed, swooning through the night. But then you wake up and smell each other.

"But that's ancient history." Ray had tears rolling down his cheeks. The boy gazed steadily at him while the priest looked away. "Then is then and now is now, right? I'm just feeling sorry for myself; don't mind me. You see, Gary was my first, my first man. Many years later I found a better match, Pete was his name, Peter Werke; you may remember him, Father, the columnist for the New Mexican. I don't know if Pete and I had a great love but it was very real and very touching. But then my man died from this disease, caught it from me, damnit. I've been alone ever since."

Peddie changed the subject out of the blue. "What are we going to do today, Ray? Can we go down to the river again?"

Ray took up his napkin to mope up his tears. "Sure, my dear boy, we'll go to the river today. But first let's see the good Father on his way."

*   *   *   *

On the hour and a half drive back the priest decided to game plan his approach to Gabby. Given his tense visit on Monday, he figured that calling her direct could raise alarms if Raul found out. The priest couldn't see himself staking out the compound, waiting for the girl to emerge alone. At fourteen years of age Gabby wouldn't have a license so may walk over to the nearby bus stop. But these days middle-class kids always seemed to have someone in their circle with a license and the keys to daddy's car. Any approach involving others would be awkward to carry off.

But then a way came to him, a person he could ask for help without revealing all. He could ask Sister Maria to call the girl. As her former principal, the nun knew Gabby. Maria was very popular with her kids. They came when called. But how much to share with his friend and colleague? What does Maria need to know? Father Andy wondered again about the constrictions of confession. A long day and night had passed and much conversation had taken place. Was that all a continuation of the confidences started in the booth? The priest didn't think so but didn't know so. One priest-professor during seminary stated flatly that the sacrament required total secrecy, no exceptions allowed. Andy raised his hand to ask if some clear and present danger to life and limb would require some bobbing and weaving around dogma. The professor said absolutely not and shut off further discussion. Now real life confronted rarified dogma. The priest was willing to bet the ranch on real life winning.

Sister Maria would help if the priest asked, even if the reason wasn't revealed. But would that be fair to his fair lady? The priest smiled at his train of thought, marrying a little Rex Harrison–Audrey Hepburn remembrance with his cold calculations. If the truth be told, the priest was aching to share the burden of his secret knowledge. He glanced over at Pope in the passenger seat. You can only expect so much from your dog. Yes, yes, he would share with the good sister the real reason for the call. He wondered what her reaction would be. His greatest fear was that Maria would second-guess his strategy. The nun would certainly question leaving a defenseless boy in the care of an HIV-positive male. There wasn't a homophobic bone in her body but she was certainly aware of NAMBLA, the organization widely loathed for promoting man-boy love. She needed to know the whole story. After all, she didn't get to hear in person Ray's strong denials of abuse. She wasn't there when the boy said everything was okay. At least the priest did not have to reveal Ray's confession to interminable lust. That history was sealed.

The nun would probably urge immediate notification of the proper authorities. Ray and Andy's logic may escape her. Who knows if Raul would slip into Gabby's room tonight? What if that abomination happened last night as the priest swam like a carefree kid and played poker after? But the priest knew that the burden of proof beyond a reasonable doubt lay with the girl. Gabby was underage; would the mother give permission for her to be medically examined? And if evidence of sexual contact and loss of virginity was discovered, so what? These days most teens were sexually active. Without Gabby telling all, the police would be faced with an unsubstantiated claim by a ten year old with a runaway imagination.

Yes, yes, my Maria could be persuaded to go along with the plan. Perhaps she would be a better candidate to sit down with the girl. A woman to woman sharing rather than revisiting the Inquisition. He could be gentle when he was of a mind to be but nothing like Maria. Would the aura of a friar elicit the truth better than a sisterly embrace? The priest could offer the blameless girl God's blessing and blanket forgiveness. The nun could offer a shoulder to cry on. Perhaps he and Maria could play good cop/bad cop. Father Andy would sternly demand the truth; Maria would offer tea and sympathy. Yes, that dual approach may work.

The priest sped back to Santa Fe with his dog hanging out the window, taking in the sights and sounds, smells too. Andy drove with blinders on, his eyes on the race to the finish.

CHAPTER 12

▼

Nothing went according to plan the rest of the day. After a fast hot shower and a change of underclothes, the priest drove over to the parish to check in and call Sister Maria. Both Father Gurule and Mrs. Mondragon, the church secretary, were in. The secretary said hello with emphasis but made no direct comment on his absence, just pointing at his stuffed message/mail box. The priest noted that one of the messages from yesterday was from Archbishop Beckworth. That was one call he would have to return promptly. The priest didn't know how far to go in filling in the boss. He dare not lie but could legitimately hide the truth behind the dictates of the sacrament. Even the Holy Father in Rome couldn't press a priest to discuss what was first revealed in the confessional.

The Franciscan went into his office and was about to close the door to make his phone calls in privacy when Gurule tottered out of his office.

"Father Leary, my boy, glad to see you back. I only caught part of what you were saying yesterday. Damn cell phones, no!"

"You're right about the cell phone, Father," Andy said, scrambling to tell a little without saying a lot. "I was up Jemez way visiting a sick friend."

"Is that the good Father Ansalmo? He's not doing well?"

"No, no, it wasn't Ansalmo," the priest replied. Good guess on the pastor's part, as he knew of their friendship. Andy wanted to change the subject. "I see the archbishop called. Did he talk to you?"

"Yes, he did, Andy. We didn't talk long; he just wanted an update on the investigation. I told him what I read in the New Mexican. He did ask where you were. I told him you were out visiting the sick. Turns out I was right. The archbishop says he's looking forward to the service this evening and has decided to accept our invitation to stay the night."

So Gurule gracefully covered for him. Even though the archbishop was visiting and staying the night, a token call to the Albuquerque diocesan office may be in order. If everything goes like clockwork today, perhaps tonight at the interfaith service he could break the news of Peddie's safe return. Better yet, let the archbishop announce the good news. It wouldn't do to upstage the boss.

Andy briefly reviewed with the pastor the timing of the candlelight service on the Plaza. It started at 6:30 and should be a wrap by 8 or so. Gurule wanted to discuss their other Holy Week obligations but Andy put him off with later over lunch.

The first glitch came when he couldn't reach Sister Maria by phone. First he tried her cell; no luck. A call to the convent was answered by Sister Muni, who said Maria was out, not sure where. The priest tried the school office in vain. No answer except a recorded message from an enthusiastic Maria reminding callers that school's back in session next Monday. Sighing, Andy called Maria's cell again, leaving a message to call him ASAP.

Andy busied himself with meaningless paperwork but found it hard to concentrate. Siesta time came when the office closed between noon and 2 p.m. Before he left the office, he made two calls. One was to the nun's cell again; still no answer. The priest left another message, in a more urgent tone. If he had to call again, desperation may seep in. He said a fast prayer that God grant him patience. Que sera, sera! Feeling calmer now, he made the call to Beckworth. Thankfully, the archbishop was busy in a meeting and the priest left a message with his secretary. With the archbishop coming in person tonight, Andy doubted there would be a call-back.

Over lunch the pastor didn't dig further into the identity of Andy's mysterious Jemez friend. They talked at length about who would handle what the rest of Holy Week. Gurule had filled in for Andy at yesterday's morning Mass and they agreed that the associate would be the early bird tomorrow. Because of the interfaith service tonight there was no 5 p.m. Mass to cover. On Holy Thursday night there was a high Mass at 7 p.m. with the ritual washing of feet and the transfer of the Blessed Sacrament to the Altar of Repose. Both parish priests traditionally presided at that service. A mini-Passion Play was performed by a high school troupe directed by the exacting Sister Claire.

Immediately after that special Mass Father Andy led the Santo Thérèse contingent on the arduous all-night pilgrimage to El Santuario in Chimayó. This most devout group—usually 30 to 50 marchers depending upon weather—

cheated a bit by busing it to north Santa Fe to start the walking at the large veteran's cemetery. A solemn, short service of peace and remembrance of the ultimate sacrifice preceded the first step out of the cemetery. Then the humbling walk through the night and morning with only a breakfast stop along the way; pacing themselves to arrive a little before noon on Good Friday. Thousands of pilgrims from all points on the compass gathered there to honor Christ's suffering on the Cross. The dirt at the shrine was said to contain miraculous healing properties. Proof of miracles rested in old wooden crutches left by pilgrims walking away free in bygone days. There wasn't a single motorized scooter put into mothballs there and the priest had never witnessed a miracle in modern times.

On Holy Saturday evening there was a celebration of the Easter Vigil Mass with the Sacrament of Baptism for adult converts. Of course Easter Sunday was jam-packed with choir performances, extended services with long communion lines, even an Easter egg hunt. Both priests were already worn out just reviewing their schedule. Of course Peddie's rescue and Gabby's liberation from fear had to be squeezed in too.

Father Gurule was hobbled by old age and diabetes and Father Andy was bogged down by his divinely inspired mission. Andy didn't see how he could ask the poor pastor to take on more. That's why the meeting with Gabby must happen today, with Peddie's return tomorrow morning or very early afternoon at the latest. So, frankly, the priest could take a nap before his all-nighter. But the day was waning and no call-back from Maria. The Franciscan was tempted to go with Plan B but there was one problem. There was no Plan B.

After the lengthy business lunch Andy didn't have much time to rest or let Pope run before returning to the office. He settled for a short walk with the dog and a single shot of Jameson's back in his room. He read a short passage from his divine office, the little black book of daily prayers and meditations for Catholic clergy. The priest went back to work still feeling overwhelmed but more trusting.

He avoided the temptation to pester the nun again. Instead he worked on the details of the interfaith service to ensure smooth sailing with the archbishop there. Beckworth would deliver the Catholic take on the Christian message. Andy was sure all the ministers would find common ground in the fight against aimless disbelief. Finally around 4 Sister Maria returned his calls. She apologized, explaining that she had her cell phone off during an impromptu trip to Albuquerque to call on the diocesan literacy program specialist. Afterwards she went shopping at the Cottonwood mall.

Andy didn't want to explain anything over the phone. He just asked for a prompt meeting. A curious Maria said sure, come on over to the convent. He said he'd be right over. Ten minutes later a concerned Maria answered the door.

"Andy, what's going on? What's happened? Come on in here."

The nun stepped back, giving the priest room to slip past. As always, the agitated priest took a sly moment to look her over. She was wearing jeans and a simple cotton blouse. Typically she wore casual when off-duty. On school days Maria generally wore a plain black skirt and white blouse, with a gold cross around her neck. The priest often wondered if the traditionally bi-colors of the Catholic religious reflected the world view of their religion. No shades of gray allowed here, and peacock colors would be a sure sign of the pride that goeth before the fall. Of course the monastic orders were allowed some latitude. Franciscan friars wore brown, humble brown; the Dominicans favored white robes, symbolizing purity, but more easily showing stains.

"I'll tell you all about it, Maria. It's a private matter though. Is anybody else home?"

"Well, Muni is in her room, watching TV, Springer time you know. But seriously, Andy, what's the big deal?"

"A private place, Sister, please!"

"Clare is out and about. She's the one you're worried about, right? I know she'd pester me to tell all if she came in and we shut up all of a sudden. Okay, Andy, let's go for a walk. Let me go slip on my new shoes."

Maria turned to go to her room. The priest noticed her bare feet and admired her backside. Maria's hair, never covered by a habit, was strawberry blonde in a pageboy cut. The priest wished that she'd let it grow out. He fantasized running his fingers through her locks and then dropping down and below to strawberry fields forever. But then he would run askew of her gold cross. He shook his head, chastising himself that now was not the time, as if there was ever a time for a priest to carry a torch for anyone but the Virgin Mary. Andy often wondered if Maria felt his eyes follow her whenever she walked away. The nun never turned to glare or wink. She never stiffened her gait or paused to check the tuck of her blouse. If she knew, she let it go.

Maria returned wearing a neat new pair of athletic shoes. She briefly kicked up her heels to display her purchase, saying the salesman told her that these were appropriate for tennis, racquetball or ping-pong. She asked him if they were okay for walking. After a pause, he conceded walking would work though he had better shoes for that. The nun was about to burst out laughing but then sensed the sales guy was dead serious. Maria laughed now, trying to get a rise out of Andy, who managed a strained smile.

The convent was out on SR 14, the Turquoise Trail, with lots of open space for short hikes. The sagebrush high plains always gave the priest pause; the stark beauty, God's handiwork. Desert critters were occasionally about: scurrying quail and roadrunners, jack rabbits and cottontails rousted out of their dens, elusive coyotes crying at night, shying away by day, prairie dogs peeking out of their holes, slithering snakes too though the priest had never run across the legendary rattler. In a sense the priest and nun were out on a nature walk, a human nature walk.

The priest decided to start with the good news. "Maria, there's nothing impossibly wrong and I've actually got a bombshell announcement. Peddie Martinez is alive and well. I know where he is, and he's in safe hands."

The nun took a quick step in front of Andy, turned, and looked him in the eye. "What do you mean, Andy, safe hands? I had the car radio on the drive back and there was no report of the boy being found. Where's he at?"

Andy gestured that they should continue to walk and Maria relented, turning forward again.

"The short answer is that he's holed up in a cabin up in the Jemez. Ray Yazzie is with him; it's Ray's property. You know Ray."

"Ray? Of course I know Ray. But how did he end up with the boy? You're sure he's okay, right?"

"The boy is fine, Maria. That's where I was yesterday, this morning too. Peddie's in good shape. Ray is taking care of him."

"But why didn't you bring him back? His mother is worried sick."

"That's where it gets complicated, Maria, and the operative word is sick. That family is dysfunctional to the max and Peddie ran away under duress. Let me explain…"

So the priest did, explained as much as he understood. The incest, the little witness running away, Ray contacting the priest (without specifying the medium of contact—confession), his trip up to the hot springs and fears for the boy thankfully unrealized, a long day and night confirming that the boy was there of his own accord. His sister the one now in harm's way.

Maria asked the obvious: why not bring in the police posthaste? Let the proper authorities deal with the incest. Andy conceded her point but explained Ray's fear that the girl wouldn't corroborate the boy's story, leaving him to suffer retribution from the enraged father. If they could just approach Gabby, get her to acknowledge the sexual abuse, then Raul would be banished from the home, likely arrested with no bail, or the kids at least placed in protective custody. With Raul out of the picture, the family could start to put the nightmare behind them.

The priest could tell by the nun's tentative nod that he was winning her over. She asked what if, what if the girl does deny it?

Andy reassured her that in that case they would go up to the cabin without delay to get the boy. Given the justified paranoia about child abuse, it was likely that even without Gabby's confirmation the suspect father would be grilled by the police. Perhaps Raul would confess under the pressure cops can apply. The priest could also see Ray being charged but Peddie's testimony would hopefully get his mentor off the hook. If not innocent of child endangerment, perhaps a suspended sentence. The case would be over. The priest could leave sleuthing behind and return to the spiritual stuff.

The nun responded with adamance. "But we have to think, Father, about what's best for the children? Ray must know that there's a price to be paid. Look at all the fuss and fear he's put the community through; the parents wondering if there's a child snatcher prowling about. And look at how the poor mother has suffered. I know Ray is a good guy but he is homosexual, that's an open secret over at the school. Are you sure nothing is happening between he and the boy? Are you absolutely sure?"

The priest hesitated before responding. He remembered the closeness between man and boy, the touching closeness. As with any man, the priest had to trust his instincts, go with his impressions. His impression was that Ray and Peddie's relationship was one of a loving father and son. But Andy realized that Raul was the father of record, and how perverted that love turned out to be.

"Maria, Maria, I have prayed hard since all this came down. As God is my witness, I saw nothing between the two that raised a red flag. Unless I'm blind, the boy trusts Ray. I trust Ray too. He has the boy's best interest at heart. Maybe we can second-guess his actions since the boy showed up at his doorstep. Ray said he felt the boy needed a time out to calm down. You know the value of time outs, Sister."

The principal looked at her priest a long moment before saying simply, with conviction: "I believe you, Andy. What can I do to help?"

Andy was thrilled with winning her trust. He felt himself grow in stature in her eyes. By silent consent, the two turned around to walk back to the convent. The priest glanced at his watch—4:38 p.m. The day was passing without resolution. There was precious little time to arrange a meeting with Gabby before the interfaith service that he must attend.

With the convent in sight, Sister Maria looked again for guidance. "So what do you want me to do exactly, Father?"

Andy decided to be direct and decisive. "Call her, call Gabby, and have the girl come over to the school to meet with you. Realistically the meeting should take place tomorrow morning, the earlier the better. I have to say Mass tomorrow but should be free from 8:30 on. We need to work out a pretext for the meeting but that shouldn't be too hard. If the girl confirms her father's advances, we drive up to the cabin with her to pick up Peddie and bring both children to the sheriff. If Gabby denies everything, we let her go home or go hide but still we go up to the Jemez to pick up the boy. We take him to Baca and let him handle the fall-out. That's exactly what I want you to do, Maria."

"I understand, Andy, now I understand. What are we going to tell the arch-bishop?"

"As little as possible until we get the children to the police. I don't want to try to explain this mess to him after the service tonight. I don't see how he could help with the meeting with Gabby."

Maria grabbed the priest's arm and turned him towards her. Her eyes were grave and her voice, normally buoyant, was reduced to a raspy whisper.

"You realize, Andy, the consequences if this blows up in our face. If the boy gets hurt somehow, if the girl comes to a bad end, if Mr. Martinez turns violent, no one will understand our delay and people will be looking for someone to blame. That would be you and me, Andy."

The priest had the absurd impulse to cry out with biblical force: "Oh ye, of lit-tle faith! Trust the Lord, thy God almighty!" He knew that it would come across as comic and wasn't likely to strengthen faith or stiffen backbones. Biblical farce may relieve the tension though. It's funny how people play off each other's mood. Andy shows up agitated at the nun's doorstep and she responds with that comical bit with the athletic shoes. The suddenly fearful nun, wondering if they would drown crossing the Rubicon, grabs the priest and he goes into a Charlton Heston as Moses impersonation. And her trembling hand on his arm, meant to emphasize foreboding, sent a sexual shiver through him. Two people communi-cating, but never on the same page.

The priest decided to surrender their fate to the tender mercies of the divine. "God's will be done, not ours, Sister," he said with only a slight quaver in his voice.

Back at the convent she asked him to come to her room. The house did have a land line in the kitchen that Sister Muni used but both Claire and Maria depended upon wireless. The friar had never been in Maria's bedroom or any nun's private quarters for that matter. The sister's room was a holy mess, with clothes tossed here and there and the full bed unmade. Andy was surprised as her public habits were clean and orderly, her professional life a model of efficiency. Was this personal disorder just for today, or a daily response to the pressure of being a religious role model? Whatever the reality of her private life, the nun didn't apologize and the priest wasn't in any position to wag his finger.

Maria asked if he had the phone number of the Martinez home. Sorry, Andy said, left it back at the office. The nun sighed and said she'd look it up in the phone book in the kitchen. Left alone, the priest had a choice of seating as Maria left him standing. The edge of the bed was unseemly. Her comfy chair with a pharmacy floor lamp for reading was possible but Andy figured she may want to make the call from there. The priest settled on the small backless bench in front of a vanity. He looked critically in the mirror and imagined Maria making herself pretty. Whatever make-up she used was subtle as the priest rarely noticed it. A light blush lipstick, some color on her cheeks—yet the vanity table top had a number of crèmes and lotions and an ornamental box that the priest suspected contained something other than relics.

Then the priest focused on the real Maria in the mirror, looking curiously over at him. "Primping, Father, during Holy Week no less? I guess you want to look your best for Beckworth."

She laughed and Andy spun around on the bench, lifting his legs to clear the edge. He was pleased with his grace as he took the kidding in stride.

"Thanks for inviting me to your inner sanctum, Maria," the priest said with a broad smile. "I feel privileged getting to know you beyond the veil," motioning around the room.

It was then that the framed photographs in a corner curio registered. Maria noticed where Andy's eyes had gone, to her people behind glass, protected from dust and grime.

"Those are the people I've talked about. Do you want to meet them face to face?"

"I'd be honored, Maria." He bounced off the vanity bench and joined the nun in front of the curio. The nun squatted down to start at the bottom. The priest bent over her to focus on the first framed photo.

"That's my Uncle Remo and his Libby Ann. I remember unc always liked to dress up when visiting, in suit and bow tie, you can see his favorite bow tie there. Unc had a nasty habit of chewing tobacco. I remember that he would be sitting in our living room dressed in his Sunday's best, with just a pinch between the cheek and gum, and lean over to spit the juice into the spittoon. It was a gold spittoon that he carried with him everywhere. When he died, they laid him out in that suit, and put the spittoon in the coffin with him."

"His wife is still with us?" the priest asked.

"Yeah, Libby Ann is still with us but it's hard to keep track of her. Since Remo died, she shuttles around the country, living with each of her kid's families for exactly six months at a time. Since she had eight children, all grown up now, she hasn't made full circle yet. She's on number 5 in Fresno, California. She just returned from six months in Costa Rico with number 4, Trudy. I wonder if she'll skip number 7, that's Lucia. They had a falling out."

"Happens in the best of families," the priest observed.

"Sure does, sad case though," the nun mused. She motioned to the next shelf up. "Moving up the family tree we come to my brother Peter and my sister Carrie. These shots are a bit dated, what, by ten years or so, but they don't really look that much different. Pete's married, has two children with another in the oven. He's a high school teacher by the way. Education seems to be in our blood lines."

"I met them two, three years ago, remember? When they all came to visit, remember? They were a lot of fun, a loving family. So what about Carrie? Is she teaching too?"

"She actually gave it a try out of college, poor thing, but went inner city high school, East St. Louis, and the kids ate her up. It's so hard out of college when you're only a few years older than your seniors who sense blood in the water. Carrie's up the river in Rock Island now, doing accounting."

"Married with children?"

"No, never married. She's chosen a different path; lives with her long time girlfriend. They adopted two babies from Romania."

"Oh, Romania," the priest said.

"Sweet gal, my sister," Maria said, looking with a thousand mile stare, back to St. Louey, Louey, having the big old Mississippi banks to play along. The priest only had the creek up the street but still imagined river pirates and boogie men. Andy was jealous of Maria's milieu growing up; what ghosts and sprites emerged from the great river fog to thrill the imagination of the young girl. Now they were so grown up, often too busy, too distracted to gaze in awe at a glorious sunset or to play for hours with no profit or loss in mind.

The nun shook her head slightly. She smiled wistfully at the priest. They were quite close, still leaning over to look closely at the photos.

"Don't mind me, Andy, I'm just remembering, that's all. Maybe we better make that call."

"No, Maria, no rush. I want to know a little something about your other people. These are your parents, aren't they?" The priest pointed at two formal photographs, one a wedding shot and the other of the elderly couple holding each other just as close.

"Yes, that's Mom and Dad. This was taken at their fiftieth wedding anniversary. They were married just before dad went off to war, World War II. That's why he's wearing his air force uniform. He was a pilot in the South Pacific. Mom told me he wrote some very sweet letters and once sent for Christmas a grass skirt woven by the island ladies. These were war years and it wasn't like they had Fed Ex around. Weeks later the grass skirt showed up, a mess of wet slop. Dad suggested in the soggy note that she wear it to a dance at our church as a novelty but only dance with the ladies, not some draft-dodging guy. Instead she gave it a decent burial in one of the holes the dog was constantly digging in the back yard. She wrote back to Dad that the skirt made quite a splash at a church social and afterwards gave it to the priest to auction it off to raise money for war orphans. A little white lie for love I guess."

Andy smiled, enchanted by Maria's recollections. On the very top shelf there was a single photograph, a larger framed photo than the others. The priest knew who this was and wished he could skip the fond recollections to come. It was of a young man outdoors, handsome, with wind-tossed hair. The guy had a great smile going. This was Jody, Maria's late husband; the nun had shown Andy once a snapshot of the same enlargement. Maria gazed quietly at the boy she married. She didn't bubble over with humorous anecdotes. For the first time in her bedroom the priest felt like an intruder, a gutless voyeur. He wanted desperately to offer physical comfort but didn't know how without turning it into a sexual intrusion. He wanted to whisper a few eloquent words that would ease the pain of loss. But in the presence of this woman, this lure for all my feeling, I don't have the emotional distance for any eloquence to flow. I straightened up and stepped back, feeling a bit dizzy. I just can't compete with a dead lover and a crucified God. Just a simple caress and I will shed my friar's disguise and fall naked into her arms.

Maria kept her eyes glued to Jody's photograph and started to whisper so faintly that the priest had to lean back down to hear.

"I don't think I ever told you about Jody and our first date. We agreed to meet at the campus activities center and go from there. I dressed up for it; it's telling that I did because almost always I was in jeans, you know, you wouldn't catch me dead in a dress. But that day I wore my best dress. I guess I smelled good too. I remember that it had just rained, a hard rain, and everything smelled fresh as I hurried over. So there he was, waiting outside the center and I don't know what came over me but I rushed across the street. And, surprise, surprise, I slipped on the wet leaves and fell flat on my back, soiling my pretty dress. Jody rushed over to help me up. He reached over to brush the leaves off but then—it was so cute— he realized brushing off my backside was a bit premature. It was our first date, Andy, I told you that."

The priest whispered, "Yes," and didn't know what else to say.

"You know what he told me later, what my Jody told me months later. He told me that when I fell, was when he fell in love with me. He said he was always a sucker for fallen angels."

It was all Andy could do not to fall on his angel a mere whisper away. But his Catholic conscience quieted his passion. The priest had sacred promises to keep. So I didn't leap on her bones. I just waited without comment as I needed to know no more, hoping dear Maria would come to her senses, to leave the dead and tend to the living. Maria turned away from the curio and went over to her bed, taking up the cell phone on the nightstand, looking at the slip of paper with the Martinez number.

The priest sat down again at the vanity, the mystical mood broken, miffed that Maria didn't want to brainstorm a pretext for calling Gabby out.

"Hello, is Gabby there?...This is Sister Maria over at Santo Thérèse. Hi, Mrs. Martinez, how are you doing?...We're all praying for your son's return. Anything new?...He'll be found safe, Emelia, for everybody is watching out for him, praying, God too. Is Gabby there? I need to talk to her. Okay, sure thing...Gabby girl, how are you?...We're all hanging in there, honey. I know how you miss your brother.... Well, girl, I need to talk with you in person. Something's come up. Can you come over to the school tomorrow morning, say around 9 o'clock? Can you do that for me?...No, nothing heavy, but it's been ages since I've seen you. How are things going over at St. Michael's?...Math, huh. I remember math was never your strong suit. You were better at English; I know you like reading.... Social studies too, huh. Well, we can't ace everything in life, can we? Just do your best, honey, you're a smart girl.... So tomorrow at 9?...Good! The front door will be open and just come to my office. We'll have a great talk.... No, no, I'll give you a ride home.... Okay, Gabby?...See you then. Bye for now."

Maria folded up the cell phone and put it and the scrap of paper down on the night stand. She looked over at Andy. "She'll be there. Less said the better when you're trying to pull a fast one. You know, Andy, I've run across that Raul several times over the years, parent-teacher nights, events like that. He always seemed to have liquor on his breath. Drunken parents are real memorable. I never realized that he was more than a drunk. That he's a monster."

The priest wondered if now was the right time to strategize. Andy's frame of reference was almost completely fictional, from TV shows such as <u>Law</u> <u>and</u> <u>Order</u>, cops and robbers movies, and the police procedurals he loved to read. The interrogators sat in the same sterile room as, in this case, the possibly reticent victim. If the whole story, nothing but the truth, is not forthcoming, then the bad cop turns nasty and dismissive, storms out of the room to cool off. The good cop takes over with soft drinks and sweet reason.

Andy fully realized that Gabby was not some accessory after the fact. She deserved to be treated with kid gloves. As much as the priest wanted to stage-manage tomorrow's meeting, he realized that there was no substitute for human empathy and a generous dose of sympathy. Sister Maria would be better at that, particularly with a young girl involved.

"So, Maria, thanks for making the call. Do you feel like talking about tomorrow?" Andy asked, glancing at his watch. It was just after 5; barely time to eat a decent meal before the service at the plaza. Given the time squeeze, he wanted the nun to say no and she obliged. They agreed to rendezvous at her office at 8:30 in the morning so they could prepare for the girl's arrival.

He got up to go. Maria shooed him out with a playful push on the back. The priest got into his car for the short ride over to the rectory. As he came to the end of the long driveway, Sister Claire's jeep turned in and the nun gave Andy a tentative wave and curious look. So much for escaping without leaving behind wagging tongues. He could imagine Maria casually dissembling—with as few words as possible. But even white lies are big deals to church people. Andy felt sudden regret that he put his beloved Maria in such a compromising position. But he didn't know what else to do.

CHAPTER 13

▼

The interfaith service was well attended by Christians of every stripe. It was a cliché among the clergy that many nominal members only surfaced on Easter and Christmas. The churches were standing room only on these high holy days. Donations tended to be generous as guilt over missing ordinary Sundays made the suddenly faithful dig deep. Certainly the ministers did their best to inspire and entertain. The choirs were in fine voice; the altars never saw so many flowers. Though some fundamentalist preachers still summoned images of fire and brimstone if you turn lazy on Sunday and crazy the rest of the week, such admonitions were no longer the norm. Gentle persuasion and a folksy manner were employed instead. It always helped if you could deliver a homily laced with good humor and thoughtful life lessons. Father Andy tried to milk his personal experiences to bring his flock closer to God. This experience with Peddie's disappearance and the rot in the Martinez home, properly sanitized for all ages, would provide manna from heaven for a month of Sundays.

The priest smiled at the archbishop and his fellow ministers there to preside over the outdoor candlelight service. The Catholic prelate looked very high church, wearing finely woven vestments that outshone the simple purple cassock that Andy wore. Beckworth was a tall man in his late fifties, trim and vigorous, with thinning silver hair, wearing designer wire-rims. The Lutheran minister wore a simple gray dress with a large silver cross around her neck. The Episcopalian cleric, disciple of a religion so close to Catholicism in ritual though far from accepting the Pope's authority, wore a vestment as fine as Beckworth's. Father Andy worked closely with these Protestant ministers, as well as others around town. He made a point of attending their church social events if at all possible. By contrast Father Gurule was attending this ecumenical service under protest, just to please the archbishop, for the old line priest didn't cotton to the homogenizing movement in Christendom. Gurule believed his traditional faith was the one true one that had stood the test of time. The rest were a bunch of heretics. He didn't go so far as saying to hell with them, for God gets to decide that. The Roman Catholic God gets to decide.

This public demonstration of Christian unity had been going on for several years now. The Protestants rotated ministers in, two each year, while the Catholics, the predominant religion in Santa Fe in terms of numbers, had a different sponsoring parish each year. The evening's mild weather was a godsend and the historic plaza packed. Volunteers circulated through the crowd passing out small candles to be lit a little later. There was no hat passing so the folks would leave the plaza with a lightness of being but no lighter in the wallet. Save your donations for Easter Sunday was the unspoken message.

The service was impressive and a beautiful expression of their commonly held yet extraordinary Christian faith. The choirs from all three sponsoring congregations were there to perform. Each group sang their two favorite hymns, and then all three combined for a moving rendition of the climatic exclamation of faith of Handel's *Messiah*. Between the individual choir performances, each minister spoke briefly to the crowd. Father Andy spoke a few words but simply to introduce the archbishop. Beckworth, as wordy in his sermons as pithy in private discourse, exercised admirable restraint, recognizing that the ecumenical nature of the event required equal time rather than a filibuster for your faith. He did mention Peddie, asking for a poignant moment of silent prayer and that the candles be lit to help the boy find his way home. After the archbishop spoke the *Messiah* chorus was sung, with the choir directors urging everybody to join in. The hallelujahs wafted over old Santa Fe. Under a starry night the yearning for communion with God flickered with hundreds of candles held by mortal beings wishing for more.

As the faithful broke up to go home in peace, the priest reflected again on the benefits of organized religion. In a country that worshiped the individual, where Sinatra's old tune *I Did It My Way* was the mantra for so many, it was gratifying to see people of faith come together to worship one God. Andy didn't believe in a designer God, divine inspiration coming inside out rather than outside in. His mother was like that, following Ayn Rand's philosophy of rugged individualism, creating your own reality while laying claim to your own expansive space. The son considered that way of living an isolating and dangerous one, leading to delusions of grandeur. The priest did concede that he was a child of God but asserted no genetic relationship. Father Andy was convinced of one thing, <u>God</u> <u>is</u> <u>out</u> <u>there</u>, and a worthy life is seeking faith in a higher power, not a close encounter with the false idol within.

The priest said his goodbyes and accompanied a muttering Father Gurule to their car. The archbishop and his assistant drove up together from Albuquerque and would caravan over to the rectory. Beckworth was staying the night in the small guest bedroom while Father Alire slept at St. Francis Cathedral's rectory. Early next morning, the visiting priest would come over to pick up the boss.

It was just past 9 o'clock when Andy and Father Gurule sat down with the archbishop for a nightcap. Gurule had a glass of red wine and Beckworth a scotch and soda. Andy drank his Irish whiskey straight as always, a finger full, for he needed to keep his wits about him. Andy felt a need to say a few hopeful words about Peddie.

"My sense of it is that the authorities are about to make a breakthrough in finding the boy," the priest said, choosing his words carefully. "There's definitely a mood of optimism. I don't think the boy has come to a bad end."

The bishop took a sip of his drink. "Glad to hear that! What do the police think happened? That he's a runaway?"

"Yes, that's the prevailing theory. That someone he trusts took him in. There's no evidence of a stranger abduction or a sex thing."

"And he ran away, what, for the usual reasons?"

A yawning Gurule spoke up. "I've known that family for years. The mother's piadoso and is a great help around the parish. As a matter of fact, Andy, we had to scramble for a fill-in on flower arrangements for Sunday. I remembered that Mrs. Oliso works over at Fred's Flowers. She's going to do it."

The pastor turned to Beckworth. "But Peddie's father is another matter entirely. The man's a lush, no. He provides for his family but he raises hell after hours. If Andy's sources are right, I'm not surprised that the boy ran away."

Andy had nothing to add to Gurule's overview of the sacred and profane aspects of the family. He resisted the urge to blurt out: "The bastard's not only a drunk; he violates his own daughter!" Now was not the time. The Franciscan was glad that the fading fast pastor was offering his insights. Andy had already hinted at secret knowledge and he hoped the archbishop wouldn't pick up the scent. Beckworth had come to New Mexico in the early 90's after sex scandals rocked the diocese. The previous archbishop resigned in disgrace after it was discovered that he was not only negligent in oversight but years previous had compromising encounters with teenage girls. Jonathan Beckworth came in to clean house and he

was decisive in dismissing tainted priests and approving a multimillion dollar settlement with abuse victims. Andy was assigned to Santo Thérèse around that
time as part of the influx of priests from out of state to replace the shamed. The
archbishop was justifiably paranoid that the rot would return. The current round
of pedophile scandals and cover-ups was causing many American Catholics to
question their faith. The laity's response was initially patient, denying what their
eyes revealed, an emperor with no clothes type of tale. Until a child pointed out
the ugly truth. Now Catholics saw naked priests everywhere, and bums the word.

Beckworth dipped a finger into his drink and stirred. Then he took his finger
out and licked it. He looked at his priests and mused, "Alcoholism is a terrible
thing, terrible, the toll it takes on families. A lot of the problems in our brother-
hood start with the booze too. I'm gratified to hear that the Church is blameless
in this affair. We can't afford another priest going off the reservation. Don't you
agree, Father Leary?"

"Absolutely, sir," Andy said quickly. "No doubt about it."

Beckworth gazed at him a few moments before continuing. "You've done a
credible job here, Leary. You built on the strong foundation that Gurule here,"
motioning to the old padre now softly snoring, head tilted back, "labored so long
and hard to establish." The bishop's voice softened now to keep from waking the
pastor. "He's a weary warrior for the Lord who's fought the good fight. He and
that good sister, Munificent, started something good here years ago and have nurtured its growth since. You are my pick, Andy, for carrying on the tradition. You
and the nuns you're blessed with, your good deacons too, your strong parish
council. But you have to keep your nose clean, remember that."

"Yes, Father, I know," Andy responded, trying not to jump with joy. He was
being anointed heir apparent of a mature parish in a charming community. The
Franciscan always assumed his good work would be recognized someday but this
was the first time the archbishop was so explicit.

Beckworth motioned to the old priest and Andy understood. They both went
over to nudge Gurule awake and help him to bed. Luckily, the pastor had finished most of his wine before nodding off. The spilled dribble disappeared on his
black pants. The priest's dog got up from his slumber too, stretched, and joined
the three men shuffling towards the pastor's bedroom. Pope followed at their
heels but was stopped at the threshold by Gurule's snarling cat. Pope ruffled his
fur, stood his ground, but wisely decided not to trespass. The dog had plenty of
space to roam unchallenged day and night. The cat was on her last legs just like
her master. Gurule confided in his pet just as Andy confided in his. Being a dog

lover, Andy thought his Pope was a better listener. Dogs attach themselves to people; cats to places. And a good dog is always willing to share his licks.

CHAPTER 14

▼

The priest had problems falling asleep that night. His mind was crowing with the good news from the archbishop. But there was a possible sour note: the uncertain outcome of the impending morning meeting with the girl. He and Maria had never worked together before on such a thorny problem. It was hard to imagine a meeting with incest at the top of the agenda going swimmingly. Would the resolution bring him and the nun closer together or alienate each from the other forever?

Andy stayed under the covers and managed to get some sleep. Pope woke him at 5 a.m., their regular time. The priest had morning Mass duty as well as needing to prepare breakfast for his esteemed guest. He let the dog out into the back yard instead of going on their predawn walk. He brewed some coffee and took a fast shower to free up his bathroom for the archbishop. He got out the fixings for Denver omelettes and toast for three. As requested, he woke Beckworth at 5:30 and tried to wake Gurule. The pastor rolled over, pulled the covers over his head, and grumbled that he was still digesting last night's fiery dinner from Señora Alvarez. Let me sleep, he begged.

So Father Andy and the archbishop sat down together for breakfast. The morning paper had several stories about the war on terrorism and the drumbeat to follow the Afghanistan easy conquest with an invasion of Iraq. Beckworth told Andy that he saw analogies between this period and the era of the Crusades in the Middle Ages. Onward, Christian soldiers! Only this time it wasn't marching to Jerusalem; rather, it was humveeing to Baghdad to depose of the tinpot dictator Saddam and protect Israel from his weapons of mass destruction. The archbishop, a history buff, reminded his priest that the Crusaders were initially successful against Islam, but ultimately Saladin marshaled his jihadists and kicked the Christians back to fortress Europe. Would history repeat itself? Certainly the modern Vatican didn't have any divisions to defend Christendom; the Swiss guards barely kept the tourists in line. But the Pope and the Church still exercised great moral persuasion. The American war machine, flush with more dollars than sense, was determined to prevent a future Pearl Harbor or 9/11. But the greatest tanks and jets have quite a time of it stopping an inspired suicide bomber.

There was one story about Peddie's disappearance and the archbishop perused it. Without comment, he passed the paper over to Andy. The story contained nothing new; County Sheriff Baca and City Chief Andrews were quoted as saying all leads were being followed up. Beckworth said to the priest: "I guess you know this Baca and, what's her name, this Andrews lady." The priest responded: "I know Baca better than Sheri. She's new to her job while Baca's been around forever it seems. I walked by his side on the Palm Sunday search." Andy didn't elaborate and, thankfully, had to ask the archbishop's leave to go say the morning Mass. Gurule emerged from his bedroom to keep Beckworth company while the prelate waited for his assistant to show up.

The weekday morning Mass, lightly attended during ordinary time, had a decent turnout for Holy Thursday. The priest could sleepwalk through the ritual but took pride in delivering even short homilies that weren't off-the-rack. Father Andy had a professional's knowledge of the Bible and could craft a cautionary tale or inspiring take out of the rich material anytime. Catholic theologians favored the New Testament, seeing it as less reactionary and closer to the core of Catholic doctrine. The Old Testament, while inspired by God and a rousing rendition of Judaic history, was infused with the prejudices of clannish minds. Homosexuals in particular took it on the chin. Sodom and Gomorrah contained a nest of them, though the straights there weren't choirboys either. In the New Testament the life and teachings of Jesus was one of tolerance and inclusion. Jesus made the point over and over that we were all sinners and needed forgiveness for trampling over others in pursuit of selfish pleasure. Though Christ was without sin Himself, the better half of His nature easily winning out, no doubt he smelled like a man, stumbled like a man. He had His winning ways, by all accounts.

The priest decided to sermonize on prayer today, feeling the spirit of the message may carry over to his meeting with Gabby. He used as a starting point the definition of prayer by the parish's namesake—St. Thérèse of Lisieux, the Little Flower.

'For me, prayer is a surge of the heart; it is a simple look turned towards heaven, it is a cry of recognition and of love, embracing both trial and joy.'

My brothers and sisters in Christ, these few words from the Little Flower remind us not to overcomplicate our faith. She didn't weave a fancy quilt of the proper form of prayer, the proper time to pray. She called prayer a 'surge of the heart', 'a simple look towards heaven', 'a cry of love'. To our dear Thérèse, prayer was an emotional leap of faith, not a sterile exercise of intellect. The words didn't count for much; the feeling was everything. I can imagine her in her chambers, on her knees, her face ecstatic with the shock of recognition that God is everywhere, that God is everything, that He will be there for you in plague times as long as your heart is in the right place. As long as your heart hasn't gone cold.

But notice that the Little Flower embraces both sorrow and joy, both a world of hurt as well as, if I may slip into heresy here, heaven on earth. She wasn't one to be glum; a life of faith should fill us with wonder and joy. Remember the world she lived in the late 1800's in France lacked the trappings of modern life: cable TV, cell phones, on-line shopping, microwaves, miracle drugs. She might have been happier for missing all that but she did die very young at age 25 from tuberculosis. Life could be brutal and short in those days. If blessed with children now, they have every opportunity to grow up, marry, and give us grandchildren. Has anybody here looked up their family tree? Let's have a show of hands. Come on, folks, don't be shy now!

A handful of parishioners raised their hands as a titter swept the faithful. Father Andy liked to involve his flock any way he could. Often the audience was amused; sometimes it woke a few of them up. Andy had no illusions that he was a spellbinding speaker. But it was his mission in life to preach the Gospel and touch the human heart and soul.

The modern Church was making every attempt to involve the laity in ritual and even the governance of the local parish. So at Mass there was the sign of peace: hugs and a peck on the cheek for loved ones, a clammy handshake with the strangers in the next pew. There was often kumbaya-type songs that encouraged clapping and thumb clicking. The Franciscan always felt that the typical Catholic crowd was still inhibited in expressing joy, that their feelings were suppressed by the setting. Given his ecumenical bent, Father Andy had attended services in black Baptist churches as well as other evangelical congregations. These worshipers let go with full-throated singing, emotions over the top, lamentations so heartfelt that the sorrow and pity were infectious. The priest was attracted to this raw spirituality. He had the soul of a charismatic.

> Well, my brothers and sisters, it was quite an education for me to see my mother's family tree. The Cohan's came over from Ireland to settle in Canada, around Toronto, in the early 1800's. Being very Catholic and hearing God's call to populate the earth, my great, great, great, let's just call her my greatest grandmother had 11 children. Only one boy, only one, survived childhood to marry and pass on the family name. I don't mean to be morbid as I share my family's trials and tribulations. I guess what I'm saying is count your blessings and cherish your children. The Little Flower teaches us to not only pray under fire, to be a Christian in the foxhole, but also when you're at the top of your game, to pray then too. St. Thérèse of Lisieux implores us to converse with God day and night, come rain or shine, to bare our souls and reach out to each other with God's grace.

Andy went back to the altar. The Eucharist was consecrated, communion was passed out, and the priest with a ringing voice shouted, "Go in peace and serve the Lord!" Father Andy didn't linger at the front door as he always did on Sunday. He needed to stop at the rectory to pick up Pope so he would have the reassuring presence of his dog at the meeting. Perhaps Gabby would feel more relaxed with a frisky, affectionate animal there. Certainly, afterwards, the boy would expect the dog to be there for the drive back to Santa Fe.

The priest and his dog pulled into the school parking lot and parked his Camry next to Maria's little Ford Focus, the only cars in the lot. They found the principal in her office. The dog greeted her with an enquiring nose and wagging tail. Every now and then Maria accompanied the priest on an afternoon run up in the national forest. She liked the dog and raised no objection to his presence now.

"The girl should be here shortly, Andy. How do you want to handle this? Gabby expects to see me alone, not with a menagerie."

The friar shared his thoughts: "I know this incest business is very delicate and the girl may not want to discuss it with a man. Of course a priest may be different. But would you talk to her first?"

The nun sighed and nodded her head. "Yeah, I can do that. That's the best for the girl."

"But one thing," the priest advised, "don't bring up Peddie's involvement right off, his eyewitness account. Hold that in reserve. After all, we don't need the boy if we have the girl confirm the story. Regardless of what happens though, we—I'm assuming you want to go along, Maria—will go up to Ray's cabin to bring the boy back. I know the way there and I'd love to have you along."

"Of course, I'm going! I'm in for the long haul, Andy. And does Ray know we're coming out there this morning?"

"Well, not quite the hour of day or which day exactly but he knows that I was coming back to pick up the boy. I couldn't be sure how long it would take to arrange this meeting with the girl. He doesn't have a regular phone up there, just a cell phone that makes for a lousy connection. It doesn't matter anyway, since I don't have his number."

The nun rolled her eyes at this last bit of information. "I have in front of me, 'Father Prepared Down to the Last Detail'. No way to reach Ray so we're kinda deaf and dumb here. I'm sorry, Andy, I don't mean to be mean. I know what pressure you're under."

The priest shook his head sheepishly as he realized the possibility of an empty nest awaiting them. But if Ray's intention was to flee with the boy, Andy doubted that having his cell number handy would make a difference.

Maria's expression changed from peevish to pensive. "I guess I'm a little concerned about how to broach the subject of incest. If she was still in school with me, I could tell her that she seems listless and troubled, what's up? But she's over at the high school now. I don't know."

The priest had a ready answer. "But her brother is missing! For all she knows he's in deep trouble. You can use that as a starting point. You know, checking up on her, how's she holding up, how's the family doing, so on and so forth. Use Peddie that way. It may lead naturally to the sexual abuse."

The nun nodded tentatively. "I guess that's the way to go. I like the girl and I think the feeling is mutual. She's probably just waiting for the right person and the right hint. It must be breaking her heart along with Peddie disappearing."

Andy nodded more positively. "You'll know what to say when the time comes, Maria. I have faith in you. The girl will feel better I'm sure. You're only as sick as your secrets."

"And what happens if the girl is in denial?" Maria asked anxiously. "Do you want to talk with her then—alone? Maybe you can work some magic. I'm being serious now. What do you think, Andy?"

"I owe it to Peddie to try every avenue. But I don't have any magic formula here. I've counseled rape and incest victims over the years but none was in serious denial. They knew a crime had been committed against their bodies and souls too, really. Some I was able to help; others seemed beyond human help at least.

One poor girl committed suicide and I was called too late for the Last Rites. I told the mother that God would excuse the suicide and her daughter would be waiting for her in heaven. Another girl was raped again by the same cousin before the police arrested him without bail this time. So we're in uncharted territory here, dangerous maybe."

Andy looked quickly around the office as an idea occurred to him. He was seeing if there was a place to hide as silly as that sounds. Could we improvise the classic interrogation room from <u>Law</u> <u>and</u> <u>Order</u>, wired for sound and containing a wall of one-way glass? Pointing to a closet in the corner, he explained to Maria what he was after.

"Are you crazy?!" the nun exclaimed. "I won't allow that! It would be a betrayal of trust big time. I'm already luring her into an ambush and you want to bushwhack her confidences. No! Absolutely not! Out the door when she comes, buddy!"

Maria was almost hyperventilating. The priest was more secretly amused than alarmed. He resisted the temptation to coyly say: "So what I'm hearing is no, am I right?" for that wise guy response would really flip her out. She was so beautiful when she was royally pissed, her cheeks flushed, her grayish-blue eyes flaring, her long fingers tapping the desk for emphasis. Andy couldn't resist another stab at her spleen.

"But you know what she will say if she says anything at all. It might help my questioning if I know the nature of her denials in round one," Andy said calmly.

"This is not a prize fight, Father, with round after bloody round! This is a wounded child coming to us. We must tend to her needs first."

The priest knew there was no more time for this. He saw that Maria's eyes were now focused over his shoulder. The priest knew who was there. He craned his neck around and managed a weak hello to Gabby. Funny how tables are turned so easily. Did the girl eavesdrop on their argument over eavesdropping? How much had she heard; what did she now suspect? The priest really wanted someplace to hide now. He looked over with barely disguised disgust at his dog curled up in the corner, asleep at the switch. Usually the dog provided fair warning of an intrusion.

Father Andy scrambled for a viable explanation of his presence. He could spit out something about school budgets, or literacy standards, but either would sound pretty lame if the girl had overheard the heated discussion between priest and nun. As usual Sister Maria reduced adult calculations to the ninth grade level.

"Hello, Gabby girl, good to see you! Father Andy and I are finished now. Come on in. Get in here, honey!"

The nun sprang off her chair and rushed around her desk to give the girl a warm embrace. The priest was taken aback by Maria's seamless transition from argument to welcome. Her body language told Gabby that she was in a safe place where no harm could come. The priest got up from his chair and motioned for the girl to sit, sit, mumbling that it was all warmed up for her. A yawning, stretching Pope came over to sniff the visitor and see if she came bearing gifts. Saying a fast goodbye, Andy exited the office with a glare over his shoulder to make sure the dog was following. He left the inner office door open so as not to give Gabby a clue that the chat was of a private nature. He did close the school office door with a bit of a slam so Maria would know there was no lurking about.

Now what? Well, the first stop was to go to the washroom. He went to the boy's and relieved himself in the short urinal. Pope followed him in and immediately found the smells fascinating, scurrying from stall to stall, jumping up on one of the urinals. He didn't want to leave when the priest called. Andy, agitated by events unfolding beyond his control, went over and grabbed the dog's collar to drag him out into the hall. The frightened dog retaliated by peeing on the floor.

The priest didn't clean up the mess. It was just a trickle in response to his master turning on him. What the heck, Andy figured, that's what we pay the janitor for. By way of apology to the dog, he stroked Pope behind his ears and coaxed him with a biscuit to come outdoors into the fresh air. The priest sat on one of the park benches outside the main entrance to the school. Pope flopped under the bench with a sigh. There they waited for the meeting to break up. And waited. It probably wasn't long in reality but the priest was tired and impatient. He had had a Holy Week for the ages already. He had his fill of ominous premonitions, long hikes in the back country, dirty secrets, and restless nights. Today promised new time-consuming challenges. A long siesta was desperately needed if he was going to lead his flock through the night. The most faithful of his parishioners were counting on him. Some came along in hopes of a miracle cure. The wheelchair-bound particularly tugged at the heart, struggling to keep up, asking the Almighty to give life to their limbs again. If their priest faltered along the way, they may take it as a sign that liberation from pain wasn't in the sacred dirt at the shrine. Instead, they faced more drab years of wasting away with only a pan sharing their bed.

The priest squirmed. What was keeping them? You can certainly count on women to stretch out the drama. He would have cut to the chase right away. Give the girl a handkerchief and forget about it. Andy wondered if a call to Sam

Fujema of Channel 4 was in order. His camera crew could be waiting to greet the rescuers returning with the lost boy. Despite Sam's stunt with the palms on Sunday, Father Andy retained a fondness for the reporter. This was the first time the priest had a scoop to offer him. The Church and the Franciscan Order would benefit from the good publicity; let's face it, the priest's career would receive a boost too. It would be Father Andy Leary and Sister Maria Anne Coligio together in the limelight, forever linked to the saving of Peddie Martinez.

The return could be the centerpiece of the Holy Thursday Mass tonight. Usually the mood was somber as it was still Lent and the eve of Christ's passion on the Cross. The Last Supper took place in ancient Jerusalem and that was certainly a bittersweet affair. Judas' kiss of betrayal at the Garden of Gethsemane followed and the seizing of Jesus for crimes against orthodoxy. The vestments at the Mass were purple and the altar was devoid of flowers. Even the traditional washing of the priests' feet with fragrant oils by a teen in the role of Mary Magdalene was played with a straight face.

Father Andy's announcement of Peddie's safe return would certainly be a crowd pleaser. Many in the congregation had gone beyond prayer and yellow ribbons to actually participate in the fruitless searches. The priest could easily fashion a winning homily. It would be heavily sanitized, for Gabby's involvement was not meant for the ears of children. And Ray's terminal illness was his to hold or reveal. The priest would give the GP-rated version for the devil was in the details.

Andy smiled at the old saw that an idle mind is the devil's workshop. His was quite the opposite, active, even hyper, God hard at work. But the rosy scenario streaking through his synapses was replaced by a rude desire to be nosy. The parochial school was not air-conditioned as school year weather on the high plains was rarely hot and humid. So teachers and administrators opened windows as needed. The priest recalled that Maria's first floor office windows were cracked open to let in some fresh air. Pope could always use a short walk. What harm could there be in taking him around the outside of the school? Perhaps the priest could catch a word or two as he ducked past Maria's windows. Andy knew he shouldn't but figured he could. So he would.

He tried to appear casual as he paused outside one of the open windows. Pope came up from nosing around and sat with his tail wagging. Though he wasn't a big barker, the priest feared a yelp may cause the women to look out. He dare not loiter long. The women were in there, sharing.

Maria's voice was as expressive as her physical gestures. "We didn't ask to be born, Gabby, and weren't offered a choice of parents. But regardless of our circumstances, as long as we're breathing, we have a chance for happiness and a good life. Love is the key, girl, love that's selfless and kind. Gentle and generous too. I'm torn up by what's happened to you. Can I give you a hug, honey? There, there, everything will be okay. I'll give you a ride. You told Freddie not to wait for you, right?"

Hearing the girl sobbing, Andy walked quickly back to his bench. So finally he knew what was to come as the girl revealed all. They could safely retrieve Peddie and take both children to the sheriff. Father Andy sat down again, pooped and breathless, and tried to compose himself before Maria and the girl emerged.

He didn't have to wait long. But it was Sister Maria alone.

"Andy, I didn't know where to find you! I was checking to see if your car was still here. It was damn awkward in there. At any rate, the girl doesn't admit to the incest and—"

The priest interrupted, figuring he hadn't heard her right. "Does, that's what you said, right? Does?"

"No, Andy, <u>doesn't</u> admit, <u>doesn't</u>! We knew that was a possibility all along. Don't get me wrong; she's terribly broken up by the alcoholism in her family and misses her kid brother badly. But when I hinted that sex can be the consequence of drinking, she acted confused at first, like she hadn't a clue. But then she got it, and said no, nothing like that is happening, are you crazy! It got quite heavy in there. So where do we go from there? Good luck if you want to talk with the girl."

The nun appeared agitated by her encounter with the girl. The priest was equally upset, with confusion and distrust churning his gut. He couldn't tell her that he caught the emotional climax to the women's give-and-take. It seemed crystal clear to me, I mean, didn't I hear Maria say, "I'm sorry about what's happened to you. Let's hug." Were they only talking about the overall depressing effect of the father's alcoholism? Not about sexual abuse at all? The priest suspected he wasn't getting the whole story. They had been in there a long time and scheming was always possible. It wouldn't be the first time women had conspired to pull the wool over the unwitting man's eyes.

But what motive would Maria have to lie? She did say the overriding concern was to do no harm to the children. Did Maria calculate that a very public legal proceeding was <u>not</u> the way to go? That tongues would wag and stigmatize the girl? Did the nun really think we can zip our lips and still stop the stealing of a child's innocence? After all, the incest happens under cover of darkness, behind closed doors. How can an outsider ever be sure it has stopped as long as that bastard still resides under that roof? We couldn't send the boy back into that tinderbox, what, to spy on his father. The priest needed to dig out the truth, at least hear the denial for himself.

"I better talk with her, yeah. Stay here with the dog, Maria. I'll be right back."

The priest strode into the school with stern purpose, a pissed-off messenger from a punishing God. Andy wondered if he had enough hell fire and brimstone in his character to pull it off. He found the girl still sitting in Maria's office, pale and puffy faced, with crumpled tissue in her hands. The Franciscan went behind the desk and sat in the principal's chair.

"Gabby, Sister Maria told me of the problems in your family. But there is a way out and that's by telling the truth, no matter how painful. The truth can set you free."

The girl seemed to shrink before his eyes. She was all of fourteen years old and appeared intent on a return to the womb. Gabby was punkish in appearance, having a small nose ring and spiky hair currently metallic blue. She had exaggerated eye shadow on and her tears caused the black stuff to streak down her cheeks. Gabby had tattoos on both arms. One tattoo looked like a band of thorns or barbed wire; the other was of a topsy-turvy blue flower. Having grown up in plainer times, the priest didn't understand the attraction of self-mutilation. Father Andy only had a cross around his neck and a class ring from seminary days. Perhaps if he had gone off to sea instead, his skin would tell more of a tale.

Gabby wasn't very tall, maybe 5'2" or so. She had the impish attractiveness of the young Audrey Hepburn; drop the punk affectations, allow a few more years of wide-eyed innocence and you'd have the charming Audrey of Breakfast at Tiffany's and Sabrina. The priest doubted that the girl had more than a nodding acquaintance with the great actress. Gabby must have her role models but the priest didn't have a clue where modern kids got their fashion sense. Baggy saggy pants and underwear showing particularly baffled the Franciscan. The girl was actually wearing a vintage lacy white sleeveless blouse along with the ubiquitous jeans of modern youth. Her waistline was straining her jeans a bit. Andy wondered if her body development leaned more towards her beer belly father than her petite mother. Unless—the priest shivered with the sudden fear that the girl may be pregnant. Perhaps that was the reason for the consoling hug by the nun. That the unholy union, the sinful encounters, was producing a baby bastard to come. God help us if that was the hard truth. That truth would not set anybody free.

That may explain the nun's reticence. With the strictures the Church placed on abortion for any reason, perhaps Maria wanted to save the priest from a moral dilemma. Andy suddenly lost his taste for ferreting out the solution to the mystery. As a priest though, he felt the need to go back to basics.

"You know, Gabby, this is Holy Week, the most momentous week in the year for a Christian. Christ went from the adulation of the crowd welcoming Him to Jerusalem on Palm Sunday to the Last Supper of peace and loyal companionship tonight. Can you imagine His feeling of betrayal later that night in the garden, when Judas turned Him in? Certainly Christ knew what was coming but in human terms, how would you feel if a loved one turned on you, betrayed you? It must have been a terrible way to die, nailed to a Cross. A terrible way to die."

The priest paused a moment to give Gabby a chance to make the connection. She stayed mum and the priest went on. "But Jesus' life tells us never to give up hope. He said, I am the Resurrection and the Life of the world to come, he who believes in Me shall be healed. She who believes shall be healed, Gabby. Sister Maria and I love you and only wish you the best. But you must come clean about what's happening in your family. No one will judge you. You want to talk about it, my girl?"

The girl looked up with hell no in her eyes.

"Nothing's going on, Father, nothing dirty at least. I don't know where Sister Maria came up with the idea that dad and me, I mean, that's stupid! He drinks too much and gets stupid and watches that sci-fi channel all night. It's weird going out into the dark living room and then seeing the light of the TV, him sleeping in his recliner, and some slimy creature attacking a scared family. It gives me the creeps. I listen to music when I fall asleep. I want sweet dreams."

The priest saw the way the man was when a special guest was visiting. He could just imagine how he was when he could kick back with family.

"When I was over Monday I saw how sick your father is. When people drink like that they do things, ugly things, that they wouldn't be caught dead doing sober. They may not even remember what they did the previous night. They may need help more than punishment. If your dad has problems with blackouts and ugly behavior, maybe we can help him see the error of his ways."

Gabby glared at the priest. "My father is an alcoholic, okay. That's not something I can do anything about. I've made comments, screamed at him even, but nothing has changed for the better. If I was mom, I'd kick his ass out the door. She carries this love forever after thing too far. Peddie running away has pushed both of them into neverland. But that doesn't mean I have to go there with them. I'm tired of talking about this, okay. Can I go now?"

The priest, on the edge of his seat with the expectation of an emotional breakthrough, leaned back in defeat. "Of course you're free to go, Gabby. One thing though, you believe Peddie ran away, right, wasn't grabbed by somebody? That's what you believe, right?"

The girl shrugged her shoulders and was suddenly dry-eyed. "If you lived in that house, Father, you'd run away too."

Andy's curiosity wasn't completely satisfied but he had to leave well enough alone now. "Sister Maria will drive you home, Gabby. Sorry about the intrusive questions. When you're older you'll understand."

"I understand now, Father. Yeah, now, yeah," the girl said in a rather winsome way.

The girl definitely had her charms. Her flat denial of incest raised a reasonable doubt in the priest's mind about Peddie's assertions. Could the boy be lying about what he saw? What would be his motive? Could he have imagined the whole thing? By all accounts, something was bothering him that day in school. He showed up at Ray's doorstep with a whale of a tale. Was it the truth? One of the kids, Peddie or Gabby, must be lying. Oh well, let the secular authorities sort it out now. The priest had only to shepherd the prodigal son home.

Father Andy got up from behind the desk to escort the girl to a waiting Maria. Gabby looked as though she could use another hug. Andy resisted the temptation. She was underage and they were alone. An innocent hug can be blown out of proportion. This is the age we live in.

The priest had experience with the physical getting out of hand. Back in late 1994 in Las Vegas, Nevada, he was serving as associate pastor of a large parish. A thirteen year old girl came into his office for counseling over a boyfriend issue. The issue was sexual in nature, his desire, her reluctance. She became quite explicit about the boy's ardent, clumsy attempts to get inside her clothes. Andy knew in retrospect that he allowed her to carry on too long. He should have cut her off with some general advice and a referral to the parochial school counselor. The priest knew Mrs. Willaway was a very concerned, sensitive person of wide experience who as needed gave advice that would burn the ears of the Holy Father.

But Father Andy made a grave mistake. He empathized—with the boy. He remembered his own fumbling attempts as a teen to prove that he was God's gift to women. That was back in the early eighties, high school days, before he offered himself up to God. He was getting aroused with the memory as this young girl related her trying experience. To this day he had no idea if she knew the effect her words had on an unneutered hetero monk. She had on her school uniform and her plaid skirt was hitched up a bit in her animation. The body language was too provocative for the priest to sit still.

He jumped up with every intention of escorting the young vixen out of his office. She didn't rise to go as expected. Thankfully she shut up about her boyfriend. Looking up at the looming friar, her eyes suddenly reflected fear and uncertainty. In response Andy sought to calm her fears. He impulsively reached down and touched her cheek. In his mind there was nothing sexual about the gesture, for sex was impossible for a Catholic cleric. But then he reached down lower to stroke the skin of her partially exposed thigh. That's when the girl jumped up and brushed by the priest, out the door screaming. Andy could hear the church secretary's expression of surprise and the pastor's office door opening. Father Leary stood still in his office, frozen in time, realizing that he was truly and supremely fucked.

If the same incident happened today, in the atmosphere of zero tolerance, his career as a priest would likely be over. Back then the Las Vegas diocesan lawyers were able to arrange a fast out of court settlement and the incident was hushed up. Father Leary was quietly and quickly transferred to New Mexico and found a home at Santo Thérèse. He was ordered to go to bi-weekly counseling for a couple years at the Jemez retreat center. That's where and when he struck up his beautiful friendship with Father Ansalmo, that wise old head. In the end exile to the Land of Enchantment wasn't much in the way of penance.

But Father Andy was ambitious, wanting his own parish and perhaps a cathedral someday. It now looked as though the parish was a cinch but advancement above and beyond may take a splash of holy water on his record. Bringing back the boy with fanfare might do the trick. He wasn't about to screw things up by hugging Gabby. Let the women do the hugging.

CHAPTER 15

▼

What keeps our weird fantasies in line are a tag team of fear and respect. Perhaps pity comes into play too. Have you ever walked your dog in the dark and suddenly you're bathed in an accusing glare, as the proximity light above the neighbor's garage door goes on? A yard dog usually starts barking, then two or three, and your own dog gets agitated. The peace and quiet of the neighborhood is destroyed. Yet another false alarm. Is true evil really put off by noisy dogs or nosy neighbors? It depends upon how committed the trespassers are, how driven, how deaf and dumb.

How committed am I to pick a child and entice him away from the skirts of his mother? In many ways the fantasy is better than the fact. Certainly it's safer. I have a constitutional right to a dirty mind. Once I act, I am in jeopardy. Let's face it; paranoid parents have guns these days. Fathers bored by ordinary work and petty problems are just waiting for the heroic moment to grab the gun gathering dust in the closet.

*   *   *   *

After dropping the girl off at home, Sister Maria returned to the school for the drive up to Ray's cabin. They quickly decided to go in the priest's Camry as it was roomier than her Focus. The dog hopped into the back seat. The priest and nun talked a bit on the drive up.

"Did the girl say anything more on the ride home?" Andy asked.

"No, not what we wanted to hear. I would have made a U-turn to the sheriff's headquarters and Gabby would be able to sleep undisturbed tonight."

"So you don't believe the girl's denials! One thing I sensed though is that she wasn't scared stiff of her father. That she was more disgusted than anything else."

"Yes, some of that came across, Andy. It must be a terrible thing for a child to grow up in an alcoholic household. I didn't get a feel for how he acts when he's sober, if he's ever sober, but often it's a Jekyll-Hyde sort of thing. That can be so confusing for a kid. A child needs his father to be a rock; alcohol and drugs make that rock very slippery. When a girl Gabby's age goes home, the corrupt world should be shutout for a few more years. We all have to lose our innocence some-day, but it shouldn't happen inside your childhood home. The memories should be happy ones. I really don't know if incest occurs in that house, Andy. Perhaps the boy was having a nightmare or saw something in the dark and imagined what the shadows were doing. On the other hand, the girl could be ashamed or embar-rassed and wants to hide the truth. I guess I'm eager to see the boy and hear what he has to say."

It occurred to the priest that in their conversations Peddie didn't elaborate on what he saw. Neither did I probe for details, search for contradictions; I mean, how do you grill a ten year old on such an awful subject? My reticence to ques-tion in depth may have led to premature conclusions. On the ride back to Santa Fe gentle but firm questioning of Peddie was in order.

Regardless of the truth about incest, one fact was indisputable—Raul Mar-tinez was an alcoholic, the in your face kind. Maria was right about the devastat-ing consequences for 99 out of 100 households afflicted by this cunning and baffling disease. But speaking for one boy growing up, it wasn't so terrible. Dad was a sweet man after all, funny and wise, whether tipsy or stone cold sober. Yet Andy remembered ugly domestic scenes fueled by the hard stuff, words between husband and wife, stinging behind the bedroom door, as mother demanded an end to insensibility. Even in anger, mother tried to be decorous in her discourse. Dad in turn was often coarse. Just accept me for who I fucking am, the man pleaded. Just become again the man I married, the wife begged. No blows from either party; no bruises in the morning. The children heard the arguments though and took sides. Andy instinctively came down on the side of his father. It was a matter of liking rather than logic or health sense.

Once the kids hit their terrible teens, clashes with the old man happened, par-ticularly when he had his Irish up. Andy's older brother, Albert, seemed to want to shield mother and confront father on his many failings. He also wanted to bor-row the family car a lot. Father and first born didn't get along and the animosity extended to dad's dying day. Andy's two sisters, Circe and Penelope, tried to stay out of the line of fire and live their lives as best they could. The baby of the family, Circe, demonstrated the most compassion towards both her parents though her peacemaking efforts never really took. The priest often wondered why his parents didn't divorce. Dad was a devout Catholic so his strong faith applied super glue to his wedding band. Mother espoused faith in herself above all. In theory she seemed a great candidate for a liberating divorce but a child never really knows what occurs behind his parent's bedroom door.

Circe and Andy were there with dad as he lay dying of cirrhosis in the hospice. It was a very profound time. The priest heard the old man's last confession and administered the Last Rites. The second son and only priest kissing the sacred stole before putting it around his own neck, arranging it so the cross was still visible, anointing dad's cracked lips and bloodshot eyes—I had to bend down to hear the confession from the man who made me, a raspy whisper of sin and regret that I could barely make out. Andy didn't need to hear the whole story anyway; dad would bend the ear of God for all eternity.

The priest glanced over at the woman he loved, the woman he couldn't have. Over the years their conduct towards each other had been proper and professional, so painstakingly proper. Yet they knew a lot about each other. They had shared their personal histories. But Andy kept secret the incident in Las Vegas. He recognized that the impulsive groping was a sin made particularly mortal by the offender being a trusted priest, the victim still a kid barely in her teens. He received God's forgiveness shortly after the incident. It took him much longer to forgive himself.

Was the nun telling the whole truth now? Was the hint of early pregnancy confirmed in her private talk with Gabby? He needed to find out the truth. The search started in the confessional before moving to the great outdoors. The boy had been found and soon the entire world would know it. The real Gabby though was still in the shadows even after the awkward tag team of interrogation. Father Andy was committed to finish what he started.

"Maria, I couldn't help but notice that the girl's stomach pooches out some. She's not pregnant, is she? Did she say anything about that to you?"

"Oh, Andy, I don't think so, God, I hope not. She's probably like a lot of kids these days who have to watch their weight. But stranger things have happened than a daughter getting impregnated by her father. It's a horrid thought I know. What would you advise her to do, Father? Carry the child to term?"

The nun emphasized the title "Father" in her question. The priest caught her drift: the conflict between Andy the man versus Father Leary the ordained priest, boxed in by dogma. If Gabby was indeed pregnant, what compelling argument could a priest make for bearing a loveless baby? The girl was all of fourteen; would forcing her to deliver her father's child embody cruel and unusual punishment of a minor? The easy way out was abortion; the more difficult option was for Gaby to give birth and put the baby up for adoption. Father Andy fervently hoped that this moral quandary was merely academic. He realized that he could earn his spurs as a priest if he upholds the Catholic pro-life position. But being an outrider for God would provide scant comfort to a girl in the family way.

"I don't see how I could tell her that, Maria. I would duck, to be frank. I know that's cowardly on my part, but what would you have me do, line up an abortionist for her? Innocent life has a right to see the light of day. Who knows if that baby might become the next Mozart, the next Mother Teresa. I know, I know, he might grow up to become another Hitler too. But isn't that what happens when you give birth? A roll of the dice."

Andy glanced over at Maria and saw that her normally fair skin was flush with rising emotion. The friar usually loved a spirited exchange with her. But somehow today, this argument about new life was sounding as old as sin itself.

"But the fetus is in the woman's womb, Andy!" Maria said with vehemence. "It's not a candidate to be called Sam or Sally until many months into the pregnancy. You know Roe v. Wade tried to sort that timing out. Before viability, it's her body; it's her call! The Church is dead wrong on this. Those men in the Vatican have no right to force a woman to become a mother, particularly since they aren't too cool on family planning. Love should be the impulse at conception; love should be in the delivery room when the baby is slapped silly into the world. A whole lot of love and patience is required to raise a child right and a woman has to be into it. It shouldn't happen because of an accident of biology and attraction."

"But the way I see it the unborn child has rights too, even one from an unholy union," the priest said wearily. "Who's to say that the soul doesn't exist from conception on; certainly the spirit of the father and mother unite at that moment, why not God? Certainly no person of faith consigns a fetus to the dumpster. The Church does distinguish between the baptized and unbaptized but the soul finds a happy home regardless."

"But you just made my point, Andy. The woman who decides to terminate an unwelcome pregnancy is not condemning the fetus to nothingness. Why men who don't have to live with the consequences—the morning sickness, the excruciating pain of childbirth, the postpartum depression—want to cavalierly condemn a woman for the most painful decision of her life. Well, I'm sorry!"

The priest wanted them to agree to disagree and enjoy the scenery. He did want to get in the last word and said what popped into his head: "And let's not throw the baby out with the bathwater, Sister." He said it with smug conviction though he never had the foggiest idea of what the phrase meant.

Andy and Maria fell silent for awhile. It was another beautiful day in New Mexico, clear skies and mild temperatures. Nature captivated them as always. They were on a mission of mercy. They had left the world of hurt and entered the state of harmony. But then the priest remembered how bumpy Ray's private road was. He wondered how his Camry would respond. Probably it would need a wheel alignment afterwards. And that costs money.

CHAPTER 16

▼

The plan was sound except for another snag: Ray and the boy were not at the cabin. The Ford Explorer was gone. The priest feared that he had been had. But then he saw a piece of paper taped to the door of the cabin. He motioned to the door and they both walked quickly up the steps.

It was indeed a note from Ray, gracefully handwritten.

> Dear Father Andy or you beautiful boys in blue—
> Just joking, Padre, I know I trust you to keep your word just as you can trust mine. So you're probably wondering if the boy and I are on our way to Cancun. No, no, just a day trip to Albuquerque, cabin fever you know. I'm hoping you're back with good (bad?) news about Gabby so my Peddie can go home safe. Don't worry!—He goes home regardless. We should be back late afternoon. You can wait if you want, go fishing, kick back. Mi casa, su casa. If you can't wait, here's a cool idea. I know you're leading the pilgrimage to Chimayó tomorrow. How about I bring Peddie over to the Santuario around noon? The pilgrims will have a real miracle to celebrate.
>
> If you want to go another way, explain in note & leave it on door or on table. Door always open for you. See you when I see you. Have a Holy Thursday and Good Friday.
>
> Love,
> Ray
>
> P.S. Love from me too. Everything will be okay. Peddie.

The priest passed the note to Maria. After reading it, she glanced down at Andy and commented dryly: "It sure sounds like you two guys are bosom buddies." The priest responded, "Very funny," and shrugged his shoulders. He wasn't necessarily surprised by this latest bump in the road; nothing came fast and easy this Holy Week though events were undoubtedly unfolding at Godspeed. The lost boy showing up at high noon at Chimayó would indeed be a sign of faith rewarded. The archbishop was going to be there along with a heavy media presence. Christ died for our sins during those three hours. The mood was usually somber and the boy's appearance would clash with that. But miracles happen when they happen. In this case of course, mere men were trying to orchestrate the glory be's.

The priest had never witnessed a miracle himself. In Rome during his one year of study at the Vatican, the newly minted Franciscan monk had met a few religious who claimed to have experienced a miracle. Most involved making torn flesh whole, healing diseases that doctors had given up on. One charming little Italian nun related a personal miracle: saved from being run over by a car running a red light. The car levitated over her. She didn't even have to duck.

Whether flights of fancy or the flutter of angel's wings, Father Andy was impressed by the glow emanating from these witnesses. They believed wholeheartedly in the wondrous nature of the happening. Any and all internal debate was resolved. **God does exist** and is with us through thick and thin. The Franciscan felt sorry for atheists who categorically deny the existence of God and believe in random coincidence rather than spiritual serendipity. Agnostics were a different breed entirely, the priest empathized with wandering souls, for doubt about God's existence came with the territory of cruelty beyond belief.

Andy and Maria had to improvise on the spot. They discussed options while Pope romped again around the meadow. Just kicking back till their return was viable up to a point. Retrieve the boy today and save the girl grief tonight. But if the wait extended to sunset, then both the priest and nun would miss the Holy Thursday Mass as well as the start of the pilgrimage. That was unacceptable. A priest must lead the Little Flower pilgrims and Father Gurule would be a poor substitute with his feet deadened by diabetes. Father Andy felt again the burden of conflicting demands.

In practical terms their own physical needs must be tended to. It was now late morning and they faced a long drive back to Santa Fe. Both the priest and nun had loose logistical ends to take care of before the pilgrimage. Andy felt he was operating on fumes. He was hungry again despite a decent breakfast. If he was alone, he'd pass the time rummaging the cupboards and drinking a couple beers.

'Mi casa, su casa' implied that any food and drink was fair game. But Andy was with the woman he always wanted to impress, and gluttony is not a courting virtue.

Without a nap the priest may turn grouchy in the wee hours of the morning. If the note said 'Be back noonish', they could wait and drive the boy back. But Andy realized that it wasn't going to be hugs and hosannas at the sheriff's headquarters. The religious were going to have to stick around for a rigorous q. & a. All of this debriefing may chew up the rest of the day. No, no, he owed it to the pilgrims to lead them with grace through the long night. He didn't have the heart to tell them: "Sorry, brothers and sisters, I'm too tired. God be with you but without me."

Maria suggested another way to go. Return to flat land and call the cops on the cell phone. The sheriff could certainly send a unit over to wait. But the priest painted a disturbing picture: a surprised Ray spread-eagled on the ground and tossed cuffed into the cage in the squad car, the boy screaming at his friend treated so. The friar could tell the police to go gentle, be fair, but it is not in their nature to take chances. A betrayed Ray may mouth off at the beautiful boys in blue and, yes, they may turn ugly as sin. The boy could be traumatized into a resentful silence and that wouldn't help his sister at all. Maria agreed that all that was possible and perhaps waiting until tomorrow was the course to follow.

The priest wondered if the issue would be decided in Albuquerque. Ray was out and about with a boy whose face was plastered on front pages around the state and flashed on the TV news since Thursday when the story broke. Andy wondered where Ray would take the boy. To a movie matinee and a visit to Baskin-Robbins afterwards? It was a sun-shiny day so maybe the boy would have shades and baseball cap on. But someone may recognize the boy and then the priest would be denied the glory of orchestrating a miraculous homecoming.

Maria and Andy decided to wait but only for awhile. He suggested a walk down to the river to pass the time. The round trip would take less than an hour and then if no Peddie, back to Santa Fe and wait for his appearance tomorrow at the santuario. The stroll was through a beautiful patch of woods to a river white with run-off. For a tingling moment Andy flashed on the image of the nun throwing her clothes off and wading naked into the bracing waters. But the priest knew that people of the cloth didn't shed their habits lightly.

Sister Maria and Father Andy had taken an occasional day hike alone together before. They always enjoyed each other's company. The scents and sounds of nature thrilled them almost as much as the dog. They talked on the way over to the river.

"Ray and Peddie invited me down for a swim the other night. It was really dark and cloudy; Tuesday it rained hard up here during the afternoon and a little drizzle at night. Boy, that water is cold. But we didn't care. I felt so free."

The nun cackled. "I'm assuming you boys were in your birthday suits. My, my, I wish I had been there to applaud!"

"Now Maria, it was all in fun, good clean fun. At play in the fields of the Lord I guess."

The priest was alluding to the Peter Mathiessen novel and movie about the tribulations of evangelical Protestants in the Amazon. The movie had one provocative scene with Daryl Hannah taking a nude dip and being spied upon by one of the conflicted ministers. Clergy lust didn't lead to happily ever after or even much pagan fun.

"That was a movie, wasn't it, Andy? Well, I saw that and you're not going to get me to bathe naked in the river Jordan, buddy. I know what you're thinking!"

"Now what am I thinking, girl? Give me a clue."

The priest was enjoying this repartee tremendously. He and Maria would very occasionally talk like this, teasing talk, but it was usually cut short by conscience and duties around church and school. Today they were in nature, away from prying eyes and perked up ears.

"You're thinking of me as a woman, Andy, admit it now, fool! You've always looked at me as a woman. Admit it!"

"All right, you got me cold. You're a woman. Congratulations!"

"And you're a man, Andy Leary, all man if I may be so bold."

"And you're a woman, all woman, the only woman for me, if I may…"

The priest didn't complete the thought because the feeling behind it suddenly overwhelmed him. He felt a profound sadness as his vocation came into conflict of himself as a man, all man.

"Oh my, Andy, you're not kidding, are you? I had no idea," the nun said with a nervous edge. "But that's not quite true, no, it isn't. A woman knows when a man feels that way, looks at her that way. You had your eyes on me for years. Come on, out with it now."

Her voice turned soft when she said, "Come on, out with it." I wasn't sure I could trust my ears, trust myself. I felt suddenly terribly exposed. Andy desired to be out with it all night long and save remorse for the morning after.

They had reached the swollen river and Andy motioned for them to go upstream. "Maria, I've been nuts about you since the first time we met, okay. I can't help myself. Listen, listen—I know this can't happen, this can't work. God has chosen a different path for us. I guess I just get lonely along the way."

There! I said it damnit, out with it all. I felt noble and resigned, like a movie hero sacrificing himself for the woman he loved. Meet you in heaven later, my love, where we will gambol together forever and ever.

But as with all fateful partings, there was time for a final embrace before the woman is dragged away to safety, leaving the hero to kiss his last bullet. Only here by the river in early spring it was the first kiss between the priest and the nun, the first embrace of a romantic nature.

She reached out, touching his arm and running her fingers down to his hand, then holding fast. The priest wondered if Adam felt the same thrill, as God's finger awakened him to human life, innocent and happy until he tasted the fruit of good and evil. Andy saw the bittersweet apple being offered, and he was so damn hungry.

They stopped and looked at each other with shimmering eyes. Andy's impulse was to play the primal man, taking the female by right and by will. Maria leaned over and kissed him while he was brooding. He wanted more and more and more…

"We need to talk, fella," Maria said in a sweet, sad tone. "I have something important to share with you. I've made a decision. You will be the first to know, Andy."

She squeezed his hand and he swung their locked hands towards the pool of calm water. There was no wild rush and leap into the waters, yelping along with the Pope. Just kids again, playing with the mutt, without a care in the world. But both of them couldn't escape adulthood, a religious life no less, with sacred obligations as well as mature inhibitions. Andy reminded himself that the soul was the only real thing, the body so fleeting.

They settled on a large rock on the bank. Maria sat in the lotus position while Andy brought his knees up to his chest, grasping his shins, his monk's robe creating a protective tent. Dappled sunlight filtered through the trees bordering the river. The dog drank noisily before coming back to settle down next to his priest.

"You know, Maria, I'm being very foolish here. Desire has gotten the better of me but I've felt happy, tremendously blessed being your friend and colleague over the years. Working with you for so long side by side, truly it's been a pleasure. I'm not worthy I know. I feel that."

The nun reached over to sharply rap him on his knees. "Now stop that 'Lord, I'm not worthy' nonsense, Andy Leary, right now! You're perfectly worthy to receive little old me, or the big bad Host, for that matter. I know I'm making light of all we hold dear but I've always cringed at that part of Mass: 'Lord, I am not worthy to receive You, only say the Word and I shall be healed.' It's like

Groucho Marx on that old game show. <u>You</u> <u>Bet</u> <u>Your</u> <u>Life</u>, wasn't it? Say the secret word and the birdie will come down, win a bundle. Seriously, Andy, our Lord gives us life and intrinsic value. It's just not right to put ourselves down."

The priest avoided a pat response. He wanted to be thoughtful and wise, a man of substance rather than one ruled by his emotions. "You say, Maria, there's a danger in putting myself down. I know that but I can see equal danger in inflating myself, you know, self-will run riot sort of stuff. I can't deny the existence of evil and go along with the notion of don't worry, just be happy. My reading of history shows that everything man does is not okay. Quite the contrary, I'm sorry to say."

Maria smiled and made a sweeping gesture with her arm. Andy's eyes naturally followed, taking in the expansive beauty. He loved the vista; it was what it was, though he had the passing thought that Mother Nature didn't trump the majesty of God, or the depravity of man.

"I know you, Andy, my dear friend; you want to put this into an historical context. But I guess I'm looking at you and me in the here and now. We are in the fields of our Lord after all. Look around you, Andy, these aren't killing fields. Look at you and me. Nothing evil here."

"But I'm bothered by myself, Maria. These thoughts about you I can't even describe—I shouldn't look at you that way. You don't deserve that."

"Nonsense, you're only human, fool! You seem determined to forget that. I gotta believe that God judges us on what we do, not what we think. There are too many hours in the day not to think crazy thoughts. We should forgive and forget our wicked visions and act with love towards each other."

The priest was thrown into a state of confusion. The nun was offering him a way out. Amaze me, my darling Sister, solve the riddle of my life. The roots of his long-standing beliefs were being called into question. As much as he wanted to be seduced by a kinder, gentler philosophy, the priest was skeptical that anyone living in the real world can abolish anxiety and still the beating heart. Tame the beast too. Perhaps that works if you're a cloistered monk in a remote monastery and only open up your mouth for vespers.

Sitting on this rock in this beautiful place with the lovely lady he has loved for so long, the man had only his friar's robe protecting him from mortal desire. Look like a priest, talk like a priest, wa-la! Behold the priest. Andy wanted to believe in mind over matter. Think dirty, act like a cad. Think clean as a whistle and the woman of your dreams will put her lips together and blow. Andy recalled an interesting snippet from the winter Olympics of a top skier preparing for his run down the slopes. Just before strapping on his skis, he visualized with a twisting hand a perfect run down the slope. The priest wanted to project such a flaw-less path through life but always seemed to have his limbs out of whack.

"I don't know, Maria, love seems awfully complicated to me. I love God but what does that mean? 98% of Americans believe in God too. What does that mean? It means diddly in our everyday life. So many are dead spiritually. I fear for my own soul. This body wears me down! It's not a good fit."

The dog got up, stretched, and crossed over to place his head in Maria's lap. She stroked him behind the ears and his sleepy eyes glazed up at her. The nun was in her element, touching something real and alive rather than dwelling in the abstract. She looked up at the priest but her hands remained on the dog.

"But you're not giving us poor souls enough credit, Andy. We live in a very materialistic society but I see people left and right seeking a spiritual experience. Many find it in the organized religion we peddle; others seek spirituality in crys-tals or peyote or some life force in nature. We should all be pilgrims and it seems as though we don't need to be told that. Something inside drives us to seek answers to our spiritual hunger."

"But we are Catholics, Sister, and not just lay people either. We are the profes-sionals and should believe our faith is the best way to go. I know that's not true for everybody but we have to pretend, don't we, encourage comparison shopping but tell the doubters that we have the best deal in town. It's our sacred duty."

The nun nodded tentatively. Her manner, pretty chipper up to this point, suddenly turned downbeat. The priest recognized the sea change.

"I told you that I've made a decision, Andy. I'm leaving the Order. I'll be leav-ing Santa Fe too. I guess I'm giving you my notice. I'll see the school year through but will be out of here by July at the latest. I'm going back home."

Andy was blindsided by this revelation. Though he was aware of Maria's increasing discontent with the patriarchal and conservative nature of the Roman Catholic Church, he didn't sense that she was unhappy with her role in the local church. Indeed, as principal of the parochial school, she wielded significant power. The Church was highly centralized and very hierarchical but while the Vatican tried to dictate many aspects of dogma and practice, local church women both lay and ordained certainly had their say. But in the higher councils only the princes of the Church were allowed in.

"But why, Maria, why?" he asked in a more desperate tone than he wanted showing. "I thought you were happy at Santo Thérèse. Everybody likes you and the children love you."

"You embarrass me, Andy, and I'm going to miss the people here, particularly the children. But I've been contemplating this move for quite awhile. You see, to put it to you straight, I want a baby, a baby of my own. I feel my biological clock is running out. It would be bad form for me as a nun to give birth. Jody and I talked about having a family and always figured we'd be smart and plan our pregnancies and have a couple perfect babies down the road. Then he went and got himself killed. I'm 37, Andy, not a minute to waste. I've got to find myself a good man who's available and rarin' to go."

The priest wanted to be a gracious loser but felt like throttling the lucky beau to be. "You won't have to search far and wide, Maria. You have a lot to offer, attractive, bright, very much so. You'll find somebody right quick."

The nun smiled at his gallantry. "Actually, I've laid the groundwork already. I know a guy there, a guy I dated in high school. Bill and I have kept in touch over the years, exchanging cards at Christmas, occasional phone chats. He married right out of college and had a couple kids. But the marriage turned sour and the divorce was finalized a couple years ago. He claims he's game again. I take him at his word. Bill was a good guy back in high school and I don't think he's changed."

"Is this Bill a practicing Catholic, Maria? A divorced man?"

"No, he was raised a Catholic but is now recovering. He attends an Episcopalian church. We'll probably go there, get married there if marriage is in the cards. I don't just want a civil service. I want the blessing of an ordained minister. I want the walk down the aisle, music, singing, the rice, the honeymoon in Hawaii."

So Maria was going Protestant on him. Andy recognized her dilemma: wanting to marry a divorced man as well as having all the trappings of a religious wedding. The modern Catholic Church was bending over backwards to accommodate the sad reality of divorce. The priest was curious about the circumstances of the man's first marriage. Was Bill married in the Church? Though unlikely with two kids, was his marriage annulled? Annulment cleaned the slate so the man could marry again with the Church's blessing. The common rationale for annulment was that the marriage was unconsummated; unless Bill's babies came from virgin birth, it was a stretch. The Church never made the process easy, no quickie divorces. Marriage was serious business. A life sentence without parole so to speak.

"I'm sure you'll get all that and more, Maria."

"Dirty diapers you mean."

"I was thinking domestic bliss."

"Bliss lasts for awhile and then the nitty-gritty sets in."

"Whatever happens, Maria, keep me up to date. Do me a favor though. Don't tell Gurule that you're taking up with the Episcopalians. It would do the old man in."

That admonition made Maria laugh. She knew all about Gurule's parochialism.

"Don't worry, Andy, I'll keep mum. I would like you to come to the wedding. It's going to happen. Where there's a will there's a way."

"God willing, Sister."

"Whatever."

"I promise to come to the wedding. I love you, you know, Maria. I value your friendship. You'll make a great mother."

The priest meant every word he said. The bubble of lust had been pricked for good. It wasn't a question of marrying purity of thought with the best of intentions. The struggle was truly over. He was committed to remaining a Franciscan friar and putting his sexual self on ice. The woman of his wet dreams was leaving, leaving behind the more durable bond of friendship.

Maria and Andy fell quiet for awhile. The priest knew that they should be getting back. Peddie and Ray may be back early; if not, tomorrow at Chimayó would be just fine. As the boy scribbled in the P.S., 'everything will be okay.'

Maria unfolded from the lotus position and got up and stretched along with the dog. She asked the priest how frigid the waters and he replied, "Titanic—fair warning."

She took off her hiking boots and socks. She reached down and rolled her jeans up to mid-calf. She went over to water's edge and gingerly dipped her toe in.

"Burr, that's cold! How did you guys stand it?"

The priest laughed at her dramatics. "Well, we said a prayer and consumed a six-pack of beer. Peddie and the Pope didn't have the beer but seemed to have no qualms about jumping in first. When I was his age, I didn't need liquid courage. Fun was the only thing that mattered."

The nun waded in to her knees. She turned and playfully splashed some water at the priest and his dog. Neither jumped to get out of the way. To Andy it felt like holy water, truly a blessing, anointing his flesh and refreshing his soul.

CHAPTER 17

▼

RAY'S OUTING WITH THE BOY AND LAST NIGHT ON THE TOWN

Ray and Peddie enjoyed themselves tremendously despite the stress in keeping the boy incognito. Ray suggested at first a movie matinee but Peddie frowned at that. The alternative idea—going to the Rio Grande Zoological Park in Albuquerque—received thumbs up from the boy. So they took the long drive into the Duke City. The park combined a zoo with an aquarium and botanical gardens. It was located down next the Rio Grande in a beautiful bosque. The two visitors spent a wonderful morning hour looking at the languid creatures. The boy was more animated than the animals in captivity. Peddie hadn't been there for a couple years and Ray hadn't visited for ages. Neither man nor beast gave the boy a second look.

They ate lunch at the aquarium restaurant where a variety of salt water fish—dolphins and sharks easily recognizable, other too exotic to identify—swam in a large tank that surrounded the tables. Ray knew very little about ocean fish. When Peddie asked him which were which, he answered confidently, "Grouper," "Tuna," and "Red Snapper" though he really hadn't a clue. Ray always found it interesting that predators that normally clashed in the wild swam peacefully in captivity. Being fed on a daily basis dulled the survival instinct he figured. Too bad their world was so small as they swam in circles with people gawking. No wonder their mating instincts were upset.

Peddie asked Ray if he should wear his sunglasses during lunch. Ray said no, figuring wearing shades inside would draw curious stares. Let's take our chances, he told the boy. The waitress took their order without a pause of recognition. Despite the tension inherent during the meal, Ray was able to enjoy his chef's salad, eating slowly, carefully chewing. A degrading rush to the public bathroom was avoided. No cannabis appetizer was required either. Out in the zoo again after lunch, both of them wore sunglasses and baseball caps as they wandered from cage to cage to moated exhibits. Ray remembered as a youth coming to this zoo and buying marshmallows to throw at the polar bears. Eventually more enlightened zookeepers put a stop to it as tooth decay and gum disease plagued the bears. Children wanting to feed animals had to settle for healthy morsels at the petting zoo.

Their only close call came as they were leaving the parking lot. A city police car was pulling in as they were pulling out. Ray impulsively speeded up as the cop car slowed down. The officer stared at the Explorer but didn't turn on his siren to stop the SUV. Ray wasn't squealing away after all. But he kept his wide eyes on the rear view mirror to make sure the police car wasn't making a U-turn.

These harrowing moments made Ray think long and hard about tomorrow. He had in his adult life several encounters with police that had soured his view of law enforcement. A couple moving violations were handled professionally; a number of roustings in and outside a gay bar in Santa Fe were not. Gay bashing, pure and simple or rather, down and dirty. Ray had been shaken by these incidents, the assume the position commands, spread those cheeks, the nightstick rap, crude comments, a night in jail before dismissal of charges. Though the last time such a morals crackdown occurred was over a decade ago, the humiliating memory lingered and just passing a policeman sent a chill down his spine.

Since those years of petty harassment Santa Fe had changed so much that openly gay cops of both genders served on the force. Indeed, old Santa Fe— heavily Hispanic, conservative Catholic, where you could count the suspected queers on one hand—had evolved into a liberal mecca, with a significant openly gay population. The growing transgender group was there to be counted too. Most of the gay couples moving in had money to spend, and spreading it around greased the way to grudging acceptance by the locals. The language had softened over the years: queers and fags became gay, redskins and injuns became (always were) Native Americans, and wetbacks became undocumented immigrants. But language alone doesn't tell the whole story.

Ray worried that the bad old days would return on Good Friday 2002. He trusted the priest to vouch for his good intentions but Ray expected rough treatment. He saw himself frisked and put in shackles and led away to blind justice. A gay HIV-positive man with a runaway boy—people will jump to conclusions. Even if the incest came to light, he was likely to be tarred and feathered as a sexual predator taking advantage of a troubled boy. With his health deteriorating, his last days on the planet would be spent pacing in his cell, puking out his guts in the exposed toilet, before finally collapsing on the bunk to breathe in his last vomit.

It had taken him many years to fully accept his sexual orientation. Growing up a maricón in old Santa Fe was not a pleasant experience. Being macho was the norm and young Ray tried to fit in. He dated girls and told dirty jokes after. He played pickup baseball games with great promise though he wouldn't submit to the draconian discipline of the gringo coach at Santa Fe High. He did okay in his studies but not so well as to invite scorn. But once into puberty Ray soon realized how different he was from his amigos.

He came of age during the turbulent late 1960's. It was a time of great social upheaval. Activists such as the Berrigan brother and the Chicago Seven led the fight against the quagmire in Vietnam; Martin Luther King fought for civil rights, with the Black Panthers representing the violent separatist fringe; Cesar Chavez led the Chicano movement, with the Farm Workers union symbolizing the search for the American dream using Gandhi-like tactics. Complicating these idealistic desires was an equally intense quest for personal liberation through sex and drugs and rock and roll. Mind expanding drugs, recreational sex when you want it, music to move body and soul to. A whole world to save besides.

Ray first felt the stirrings of same sex yearnings in the group shower after gym class. He dared not stare; he just stole glimpses and started to fantasize. He was terrified that desire would rear its ugly head for all his bros to see. Exposing him for who he couldn't be. He wanted to be one of the guys, a guy with women on his mind.

There was no sex with boys in high school. Through an act of will and out of paralyzing fear Ray forced himself to have sex with girls. It was always awkward for his heart wasn't into it. He always had to get high to do it at all. He was a callous lover boy. High school graduation couldn't come soon enough for the conflicted teenager.

His parents couldn't afford to send their only boy to a private or out of state college so he went to the University of New Mexico in Albuquerque. The first year he commuted the 120 mile round trip to and from the campus, driving a low rider that he lavished attention on. He stayed very busy that year, carrying a full course schedule as well as working part-time at a food store. He stayed as celibate as a monk and lost track of his high school friends. The young man wasn't happy but kept his mind occupied while his heart grew increasingly desperate.

Going into his second year at university he had saved enough money to move to Albuquerque. He rented a small studio apartment close to the campus. He finally had a place to call his own. Ray knew now was the time to come out. There was a gay advocacy organization on campus, Out and About. Ray joined up. He was finally in his element.

His first sexual encounter with a man was spur of the moment. His fellow student was no stranger to gay sex. Ray's high school experiences with girls helped him adapt. But the chance encounter was hurried and cramped, in a bathroom stall between classes, and unsatisfying as an expression of love. Ray's fantasy was of a candlelight dinner and a long, teasing, intensely personal conversation before the fingers entwine across the table. Ray wanted to be romanced along with being ravaged. His first gay liaison was desire alone with no tenderness together.

After his trying year of abstinence Ray felt unleashed and raring to go. He initially tried to avoid his first male lover, Gary, but both were active in Out and About so molten glances were exchanged at strategy meetings. Ray didn't know who was toying with whom, and sex void of sweet feelings didn't interest him. But it happened over and over regardless. The two men began to talk at length, sharing personal histories and hopes for the future. Gary was studying to go on to law school and become a corporate attorney. Ray was an amateur sketch artist and wondered if there was a self-supporting career there. Words of love began slipping into their conversations. They decided to move in together, into Ray's cramped studio apartment. A measure of domestic tranquility settled into the men's life together.

Ray made some fast friends amongst the activist crowd. He and Gary went out to party frequently. Ray was enchanted by his friends' bubbly conservations, thoughtful observations, really funny stuff. There was no reluctance to wear your emotions on your sleeve. It was so different from high school; the talk then was stilted as Ray couldn't share his secret self. Guilt made him button up tight, a guilt nurtured by his strict Catholic upbringing. Gradually he was coming out of that constricted state of mind and began to blossom. But he returned to the closet on visits home. Gary stayed behind in Albuquerque that sophomore year except for one memorable holiday weekend. Ray introduced Gary as his roommate, and the guest slept alone on the pull-out couch. Saturday morning the boys left after breakfast, citing the need to study for finals. Instead they headed to the empty family cabin in the Jemez, to gambol through the woods, skinny-dip in the river, and hike to the hot springs to soak.

The only discord came from a recurring argument about whether they should flaunt their love and life together, in the spirit of their advocacy organization. During spring break they went to Gary's family home in Denver. Gary's father was a lawyer; his mother sold real estate; his younger sister, still in high school, was there and his older married brother came over to visit several times. Gary's sexual orientation was no secret in that family. Ray was accepted and even celebrated as Gary's lover. Ray felt like a stranger in paradise; why couldn't he accept the family's embrace of the boys' love? He felt like blaming something and somebody—the reactionary Church, his hidebound parents, the homophobic society in general. Gary's parents put the two of them in their son's old bedroom. Gary wanted to make love but Ray balked, fearing telltale noise and stained sheets. Gary was disgusted by Ray's attitude and turned his back on his gutless lover.

Their domestic routine began to wear on the young couple. They moved out of the studio into a one bedroom but still lacked enough breathing space. Romance waned as the rub of living in close quarters became everyday friction. Gary became more domineering and Ray accused the wannabe lawyer of practicing prosecutorial techniques in what should be home sweet home. Gary began staying out all night while Ray stewed at home. One day that summer after Ray left for work, Gary moved out in a hurry, leaving the furniture as consolation.

Shortly thereafter a dispirited Ray dropped out of school and moved back to Santa Fe, living initially with his parents. He was sour on the gay lifestyle and wary of leaving himself open to be hurt again. Ray just wanted to fit in, to run hot, straight, and normal. In despair, he married.

The girl was a member of his old parish, St. Anne's, and Ray had known Susan since childhood. They played together in the neighborhood and were fond of each other. The children found a lot to talk about. Luckily they didn't date in high school when Ray was going through his callous period. Upon return from his interrupted college career, he soon ran across Susan who was unattached. They found more to talk about though Ray didn't share the real reasons for his dropping out. There was no Out and About honesty as Gary became 'Sherry' in the story of lost love. Ray was careful to blame himself more than 'Sherry' as he calculated that Susan would appreciate his manly acceptance of responsibility. He also pretended to be baffled by the reasons for the breakup as he figured Susan would love to offer a woman's perspective on matters of the heart. She did offer, eagerly, and Ray took it all in with a bemused heart. Soon he realized that he still liked Susan a lot though she was the one in love. Marriage without mutual love would seem a risky proposition but Ray had tried soaring love and flamed out.

He and Susan had friendship and respect going for them and the sex during their honeymoon was more than adequate.

But after a few months of wedded bliss Susan sensed that it was more performance art than real romance. A long, dreary series of counseling sessions took place as Susan said she was determined to "nip things in the bud." Their emotional ties and sexual techniques were examined tooth and nail. Flowers on the spur of the moment and special 'date' nights were recommended. Putting the romance and well-honed sex back into the marriage helped for awhile but the afterglow and simple hugging that women in love value just wasn't there. Perhaps the worst sign of a dying marriage was the drying up of civil discourse. Long, uneasy silences replaced small talk. But then something happened to give the couple plenty to talk large about. Susan became pregnant.

Being practicing Catholics neither had utilized any birth control methods besides Ray's disinterest. Abortion was not an option for a couple still married to the Church. So a truce was called for the sake of the baby to come. As her belly expanded with new life, the couple found more things in common. They could laugh together about a pickles and ice cream run at midnight. Ray was thrilled as he dipped his ear to her stomach and listened to the kick of the baby. Ray even went to Lamaze classes with Susan and was clutching her damp hand during contractions at delivery. Their son Benito was born and they became a true family together.

The new baby became the focus of their love and attention. Ray loved being a father and didn't resent the interrupted sleep and changing diapers. He took pride in being a good provider, working as a sales agent at the local State Farm office while taking night classes to complete an associates degree. Soon they scraped together enough money to buy a fixer-upper. A good life together and love ever after seemed possible.

Desire became domesticated for awhile. They made love infrequently but it was more satisfying as both called it making love. Ray became capable of tender moments and thoughtful gifts. Susan's attention was focused on the baby Benito. She didn't go back to work for several years, and then only part-time. That created a festering resentment in Ray, as he was generating the income without controlling the purse strings. He even took seasonal Christmas work in retail to supplement his insurance commissions. It seemed as though he was selling day and night. Stress grew. The old house always needed work. Ray found himself falling asleep on the recliner; he caught himself dreaming of miraculous escapes.

An escape hatch opened during a home visit to pitch life insurance to a couple. Vern and Louise, Louise and Vern—it's so important in sales to repeat and remember the names. The wife left abruptly before the sales presentation was over. "Back in a couple," Louise blithely said. Her exit left Ray and the husband alone, looking at each other. Ray continued to explain the features and benefits of whole life versus term but he sensed that Vern's attention was elsewhere. All his rational sales talk sounded foreign as though the subtitles didn't jibe with what was spoken. But Ray didn't fully grasp what was going on until he looked over and saw the prospect's pants unzipped and a fully erect cock pointed his way. Ray stopped talking about the importance of protecting your family's future.

It had been almost ten years since Ray had received such an invitation. But it was like riding a bicycle, the motions becoming familiar again, the emotions too. They did the deed right there in the living room, clothes tossed every which way, passion on a Persian rug. Ray cried out in grateful climax, the physical release from years of faking it. The two men laid there entwined in each other's arms, in sated repose, letting the sweat dry on each other's skin. Ray ran his fingers through Vern's chest hairs, kissed and licked his ears, did the flutter thing with his eyelashes, always a turn-on. Apparently it was mutual, for he could feel the man's penis stiffening again against his thigh. Ray responded, getting up on all fours to caress with his lips and tongue the man's balls, then his hard, glorious cock. Vern laid there moaning, delirious. Ray loved giving pleasure in this way, tasting the spurting cum, swallowing it. Being entirely in the now, blameless, with no thought of anyone but the person you're lying with. Wanting to induce euphoria, willing to receive it. Oh glory, oh god! At peace with yourself wrapped in the arms of another.

During a pause, concern about the wife's "Back in a couple" came over Ray. He asked the man about her (imminent?) return. Vern laughed. "What she meant was tomorrow. She's gone off to visit her girlfriend. They never rush a liaison." The combination of girlfriend and liaison suggested that the get-together was not to watch a three-hankie movie. Ray said, "You don't mean..." and the man confirmed, "You got it. Louise swings both ways." Oh my! Ray thought; such an ordinary house from the outside, such weirdness within. But Ray realized that he was in no position to judge, lying naked on the rug.

Vern explained further. "Right now Louise has fallen hard for this woman. You see, we not only have an open marriage but right now our relationship is not complicated by sex—with each other at least. We are free to hug each other in all innocence while being free to love who we want. We actually titillate each other with our tales of conquest. We pop popcorn and sit down to tell all. It's great fun really. Educational too!"

Ray felt suddenly violated, mere fodder for x-rated story-telling. It was time to go. As he was hurriedly dressing, he let loose a parting shot: "It strikes me as rather cold, what you folks do." Vern retorted: "Did I harm you in any way tonight, Ray? Louise and I have found that our affairs bring an element of excitement and risk into our lovers' lives. It's a service we gladly provide. But don't fret; this 'toying' with people's feelings will run its course. We too have hopes and dreams about love till death do us part. Louise is staying the night with this woman, let's see now, more times than I have fingers and toes. Dear me, they are becoming an item. Our marriage of convenience will end soon I fear. We will go our separate ways. I think we will remain friends. That's what happens when you don't take sex seriously."

Ray, briefcase in hand, made for the door. Vern grabbed his arm.

"Ray, Ray, before you go, one parting gift. Let me sign that policy and you can come over tomorrow evening to get Louise's signature. We want the insurance, really! By the way, does it have a double indemnity clause? Just kidding, buckaroo! Seriously, we want the coverage."

The used and abused man wanted to say no and leave with a modicum of human dignity but Ray the agent had a job to do. He turned around and had the man sign on the dotted line. They exchanged a perfectly proper handshake which amused the client tremendously.

*   *   *   *

The next evening Ray returned and got the wife's signature. Louise smiled broadly and Ray could just imagine the rowdy tale told over popcorn. Other chapters would follow but Ray was determined not to become a recurring character. He left Vern and Louise waving at the doorstep and that was that. He never found out what happened to the happy couple but no policy cancellation passed his desk. But Ray didn't feel satisfied with a solitary one night stand. He went on a sexual bender with other men, going to watering holes, lovers' lanes, even cruising a certain hiking path notorious for spontaneous couplings. For awhile he wasn't picky; any willing man would do. Though Ray tried to give credible excuses for his frequent absences from work and home, a wife knows and a boss suspects. At first Susan fumed but soon enough, arguments flared. She thought other women were involved. Ray had never told her of his sexual predilection. It was funny in a way when she ragged him: "Who is she, you bastard? I can smell her on you!" What she smelled was Brut. Ray managed to hold on to his job but not his wife. Susan sued for divorce and sole custody of young Benito. Ray didn't contest.

He had visitation rights and never missed the scheduled pick up/drop off hour, or a due date for the monthly support check. Once living on his own and free to come and go, his sexual overdrive petered out. In an extreme swing in the other direction he went back to church—Roman Catholic as always—and far from token involvement too. He plunged into volunteer activities at a different parish—Santo Thérèse—from the one that Susan frequented. While he would have loved to see Benito at Sunday Mass, he knew any encounter outside of his narrow window of visitation would be awkward for the mother and upset the spiritual serenity they both desired during that sacred hour. He did question why his reconciliation with religion, particularly with one that patronized gays and condemned their acts of love. He could have joined a non-judgmental religion such as the Unitarians that encouraged sexual diversity and embraced all as God's children. Ray could have found his fellows there and a healthier variety than the jokers who hung out on the hiking path and behind the yucca. But something about the faith of his youth—the beautiful rituals and vestments, the inspired singing, the odor of incense, the sprinkling of holy water—attracted him in a profound and visceral way. He set aside the Church's homophobia, just as Catholic women set aside when necessary the prohibitions on effective birth control and even abortion.

At a Santo Thérèse singles gathering Ray finally found a good guy to date and soon settle down with. The inherent fear and awkwardness in meeting a stranger with intimate intentions was intensified by two gay guys trolling in a sea of opposites attracting. His name was Peter Werke, a most interesting fellow, newspaper columnist, and a talented poet to boot. Their first date was going to a poetry slam where Pete more than held his own in the overheated creative atmosphere.

After six months of seeing each other regularly the two men moved in together and a year after that they bought a house. Very soon Susan saw through the roommate façade. Ray feared that she would rush back to court to rescind overnight visitation based on offenses against conventional morality. Instead she shook him down for more support money and Ray shelled it out. Soon she effectively rescinded regular visitation by moving with Benito north to Minnesota. There she worked on the impressionable twelve year old, turning the boy against his absent father. Ray initially visited twice a year but the weekend visits became strained. Father and son entering the touchy teenage years found themselves at odds and without much good to say to each other. When Benito turned sixteen

Ray told him explicitly that he was gay and had come to terms with it over the years. Benito's response: "I knew that already. Mom told me you were queer."

Ray was relieved when his monthly financial obligation ended with Benito's graduation from college. Dad wasn't invited to the ceremony. Benito married soon thereafter and Ray received the news in an anonymous letter with a newspaper clipping of the happy couple in Minneapolis. Dad found out that he was a grandfather from a strained five minute phone call from Susan. Benito and his wife were the type to send out a family photo with a Christmas card. Ray made the list and rewarded the thawing of relations by including a fat check with his card. One year in the spirit of mirth Ray decided to send a happy holiday's card with a photo of he and Pete dressed in drag. He slipped in a $ 1000 check to assuage any hard feelings. The following Christmas Benito sent a card without the photo.

Ray and Pete had many happy years together living in a home large enough for the men to have their own rooms: a home office/library for Pete and a studio with good light for Ray. Ray finally told his aged parents explicitly that he was gay and Pete his partner for life. They professed to be shocked, shocked though Pete was no stranger to them, accompanying Ray on frequent visits. His mom was more accepting than his father as she played hostess while dad found diversions in the computer room. Even before the frank disclosure, at Yazzie family gatherings Ray's mom introduced Pete as her son's 'special friend.'

So the two men were faithful to each other and their careers blossomed. Pete continued his widely read column for the New Mexican and took his insights and jollity to TV as host of a public affairs program. Pete the poet had a couple books published by university presses and several of his poems made the pages of the New Yorker. While royalties were measly, the public recognition was considerable. Ray also traveled with Pete to a number of nation poetry slams and the poet from Santa Fe, with his pithy, provocative, funny style, won several of them. The venues were usually bars and the free-flowing liquor fueled the creativity of the contestants as well as the cheering and jeering of the raucous crowd. It was the oral tradition reborn, though Homer was probably turning over in his grave at the over the top balladry. Women of color celebrated a rainbow perspective on the body politic; Native American poets alluded to Wounded Knee and AIM activism; gay poets emoted about coming out of the closet for good. After the stimulating performances, Ray and Pete celebrated with champagne and candlelight. A time or two, another couple joined in the afterglow.

Back in Santa Fe Ray opened his own independent insurance agency. The word got around town in gay and lesbian circles: see Ray, he's gay. Being a native son and a joiner, he kept and occasionally expanded his business amongst the old line families of Santa Fe. He was making money hand over fist. The partners moved into a larger house with great views on the affluent north side. They developed a social circle that included movie stars. Though they had their tiffs just like any other couple, the two men always worked things out before bedtime. They were looking forward to spending their twilight years together. But as it goes, darkness came sooner than expected.

During a routine health check-up in 1996 Ray was diagnosed with HIV. Pete went in immediately for testing and found he was infected too. The two men went home together to face each other in a new light. Neither had a blood transfusion recently and intravenous drug use was not an issue. So it came down to unprotected sex. Ray knew how the virus invaded their happy home. He owed his partner for life the truth.

Pete was out of town the whole week covering the Democratic National Convention in Chicago. Ray was busy at the agency but had time on his hands after work. One night with nothing good on TV, he decided to go out to a gay bar that once was his haunt. He intended on having a couple beers and chatting up a few old friends. Indeed, some long buddies were there and the joshing and catching up was wonderful. Ray lingered and was on his fourth beer when Gary, his first lover and old colleague from his activism days, came into the bar. They hadn't seen each other for some twenty-five years. Both men had aged gracefully and were within 10 pounds of their college weight. Gary had more silver in his hair and it was certainly groomed better than the hairy times of Out and About. The one time lovers couldn't very well ignore each other and the sting of betrayal had faded over time.

They went off to a booth together. Gary was visiting Santa Fe from New York City with plans to buy what would be his third home with permanent relocation upon retirement an option. His professional life as a corporate attorney was satisfying and practicing in the Big Apple put him at the center of international business. But Gary didn't want to retire in Manhattan. Another beer was drunk and the conversation turned suggestive. One thing led to another. They bought condoms at Walgreen's before going over to La Fonda where Gary was staying. Safe sex was on their minds but not on their lips. Being soggy drunk, Ray's initial erection collapsed before the rubber was secured. It was laid on the nightstand while the two men engaged in extended foreplay. Soon anal intercourse was possible. Only afterwards did it register that neither condom had been used.

Upon waking with his old lover snoring away, Ray had regrets but only faint fear of HIV. Gary looked to be in the pink of health and God couldn't be so cruel as to punish such an isolated case of unprotected sex. He said a token prayer after kissing Gary goodbye. But then the medical verdict came in and Ray had to face the Götterdämmerung music.

With the help of the wonder drugs, Ray and Pete survived together in relative harmony for several more years. But then Pete caught pneumonia and he didn't have it in him to fight any longer. He died at home with Ray holding him. After the funeral Ray couldn't sell the death house fast enough. He moved into the much smaller house in Nava Adé. With Pete's life insurance pay out Ray was able to close his agency and retire early. He didn't want to deal with people anymore on death and life issues.

CHAPTER 18

▼

Ray and Peddie returned to the cabin late afternoon. They read the priest's simple response:

> Okay to seeing you both at Chimayó. Everything will be okay. Tell Peddie the Pope will be there.

Love—
Father Andy

Ray glanced over at the boy. "It's time to go home tomorrow. School's back in session next week."

Peddie shrugged his shoulders but Ray knew that indifference was the last thing the boy felt. The boy began to cry and the man hugged him.

"Just tell the truth, Peddie, and things will work one way or another. I'll be there for you, boy, don't you worry your pretty little head."

The boy looked up with shiny eyes at his mentor. "And you'll help with my homework, huh, Ray? Like you did last year?" Ray smiled and did the herky-jerky routine that delighted the boy during their tutoring sessions. Whenever the boy was stumped, Ray would look at the work sheet with a scrunched up face, shake his head and shoulders like a wet dog, and then put a finger in his ear and twisted it as though cranking up the old gray matter. Then he would offer a teasing clue, and the boy would mimic the routine—scrunch, shake, rattle and roll out the answer. The mentor and pupil would give each other the high-five.

Peddie laughed as he remembered how much fun learning could be. But then something ominous occurred to the boy. "They won't put you in jail, will they, Ray?"

Ray wanted to ease the boy's concern. Perhaps slapstick would chase the blues away. He went into a perp walk, pretending his hands and feet were shackled on the way to his cell. Peddie caught on and broadly mimicked the movements. Gallows humor and riotous laughter echoed across the meadow and into the trees. But lingering in Ray was a premonition of impending doom. The chill made him dream of miraculous escapes. He decided to fall prey to desire one last time.

He knew he shouldn't leave the boy alone. He flirted with the idea of dropping Peddie at the rectory for safekeeping. But that would impose upon the priests and upset the stage for the high drama on Good Friday. Ray wanted his shining moment at El Santuario de Chimayó. He saw himself making a sign of the Cross on his forehead, lips, and chest with the sacred dirt as the pilgrims sang hosannas. Hopefully, the acclamations of the faithful would convert the heathens in uniform. It was best, Ray figured, not to get ahead of reality. His paranoia would surely magnify his terror and create monsters out of human beings. This was America after all, not some rinky-dink police state. No, no, the boy would be okay until dawn. Ray would be there to wake him up.

Peddie didn't fuss when Ray explained. He suggested that the boy continue reading the latest Harry Potter book and be ready to tell him all about it tomorrow. Ray left after dinner, looking in the rear view mirror at the boy waving goodbye. He felt bad but figured that his own needs could come first for a few precious hours. After all, he faced a trying day tomorrow.

Ray doubted that he would score tonight. He was out of practice as well as being visibly run-down. To be a responsible lover he would have to find someone as desperately ill as he was. The sores on his torso would be a turn-off. Gay guys recognized the signs of advanced AIDS. They usually responded with compassion but rarely were they fucked-up enough to want to jump in the sack.

Ray was on edge on the ride in. A jumble of recollections and reflections overwhelmed his mind. He felt powerless over who, what, when, and how long they overstayed their welcome. Pete was at the center of his memories, always welcome, funny, fine Pete, sprouting off inspired verse, the goofy grin turning into a glower over life's tragic twists and turns. Then the on-stage Pete was transfigured into the private man in bed, delirious with love. Pete usually slept in while Ray was the early bird. Ray would slip out of bed and make coffee for himself. He would bring the mug back to bed, part the window curtains, sit back on the pillows, and watch the shaft of morning light cross their two bodies. He felt so tender, gazing at his sleeping lover. Wanting the feeling of peace to last forever.

Gary intruded in the dream, pushing Pete out of bed. Gary was quite a piece of work; such an attractive façade hiding virulent disease. Ray recalled the vigorous university student, so sure of himself, so certain of his sexual nature, ready to celebrate his sexuality and carry all before it. And the arguments that spanned day and night, the pre-law student pushing his points, Ray soon tiring of defending doubt and recognizing ambiguity, wanting to escape the body politic and retire to a place where sex doesn't matter.

A passing car's brights blinded Ray for a moment. After a reflexive curse at the discourteous driver, he let memory have its way with him again. His son Benito took his turn. At first it was the baby who Ray cradled, and then the young boy confused by the separation of mother and father, finally the obnoxious teen growing up into a prig of a man. But then the baby boy crawled back into focus, lifted into the bed to be cuddled by mommy and daddy. The first words, the crying jags and the giggles, the wobbly baby steps. Treasured memories of fatherhood, and then they grow up.

Peddie chased Benito away. Ray was so grateful for the change. Flashbacks of tutoring the boy, the obvious joy of learning, hero worship even. The comfort of the boy's presence; Peddie's warm body next to him in bed. Ray wasn't sure anymore who was protecting whom from the travails. The boy was certainly saving the adult from utter despair, reminding him that there was life beyond disease and death. My disease and my death, I own it, Ray mused, what self-centered nonsense, as though the world ends when I die.

Father Andy rushed in to offer his blessing. The friar's voice in the confessional, murmuring the sacred words of divine forgiveness: "I forgive you in the name of the Father, and the Son, and the Holy Spirit. Amen." The skeptic in Ray, the pagan at heart, crowed that the ritual was a crock. But as he hurried out of the church after penance, he felt liberated from mortal fear—for one blessed night at least. The father confessor made all the difference in the world. Ray had admired the little Franciscan for many years. He loved to listen to Father Andy's homilies, the weaving of personal experience into the rich tapestry of the Gospels. He laughed at the flashes of humor. Ray had a Catholic friend who was conflicted by his sexual orientation and Ray suggested he talk to Father Andy. The priest told him to be true to his innermost feelings and that God loves him regardless. Ray's friend left relieved of the Catholic guilt that was eating him alive. So when Peddie came calling it was natural for Ray to seek the padre's help.

Ray arrived at the Bar None Different that had been his haunt in his younger years. Before fidelity to Pete, Ray got lucky often at the Bar None. The bar and dance club was located close to Santa Fe's historic plaza. The parking lot even on a Thursday night was as packed as he remembered it from nights of yore.

The inside of the club hadn't really changed much either. The booths and tables were spread out with their focus on the spacious dance floor. Drinks were served at a long Western saloon type bar whose surface was slick enough to slide the lager the 60 feet length if the bartender wanted to show off. In the booths were a throwback design to the 1950's, the small jukeboxes where you flip pages to view the selections, pop a quarter in, and hear a muffled song. But these juke-boxes were ornamental only and no music came from that quarter. Locals enter-taining out-of-towners would urge the gullible to make a selection and the boxes would eat the change and spit out a streaming message: THANK YOU FOR THE CHANGE—REMEMBER YOUR WAITER LOVES PAPER MONEY.

The real jukebox was just off the dance floor and a thing of wonder. There your quarter paid off big; the music of the ages rocked the whole place. The club did feature live music on weekends but the jukebox's eclectic selections filled in nicely during the week. Couples wanting to dance weeknights faced a daunting challenge as a big band tune was followed by gospel followed by country western followed by Broadway classics followed by hard rock and so on. Not only gay and lesbian couples came to the Bar None Different; straight couples looking for a cosmopolitan night out came too. The dance floor had one of those kitschy globes spinning above, producing dizzying rainbow colors that reminded many of their high school proms. For the gay and lesbian couples that memory was bitter-sweet, a rite of passage into the adult world of faking it.

The long bar had five tenders serving up drinks. Glass shelves displayed many fine and elegant liqueurs but most of the action centered on the more pedestrian bottles under the counter. It had been quite awhile since Ray had stopped in, the bar's New Year's Eve bash 1999, ushering in the New Millennium. Pete and he enjoyed themselves tremendously, dancing to the point of dizziness, drinking to the point of wobbly. Neither man was up to driving so they decided to flag down a cab. They walked to one corner, looked left right up down, all the time laugh-ing uproariously at the silliness of expecting to flag down a hack by looking up and down. Then they had an argument about whether a true American would use a term like hack. Rhymes with sack, Pete said. After a thoughtful pause, Ray agreed. So it's perfectly acceptable to use hack? Pete asked. No, no, I only agree it rhymes with sack. So I can't use hack? Of course you can, this is America.

The conversation was going nowhere and the men were still on the street corner. And it was cold that New Year's night in Santa Fe. Snow started to fall. Santa Fe is a small city and cabs are usually radio-controlled rather than out free lancing. Finally a friend from the Bar None happened to be passing. He stopped to pick up the giggling, freezing men and give them a ride home. But Pete's compromised immune system couldn't stand up to the chill. A hacking cough developed into pneumonia. Pete was dead within two weeks.

Ray's spirit broke after that. Tutoring Peddie revived his will to live and to follow the pill-popping regimen. He and the boy had spring break together on the sly but that would all end on Good Friday. Tomorrow Ray would have to fend for himself in a weakened state, behind bars with callous men.

Ray sidled up to the bar and a bartender friend from the old days came over. He said hello to Sid and received an arched eyebrow and emphatic, "Well, howdy, stranger! How's it hanging, Yazzie?" Sid knew very well how it was hanging, he knew of the disease, and had attended Pete's funeral. Ray asked for a beer and Sid said enthusiastically, "Wait, wait, don't tell me. I know, I know—let me say Cerveza! Am I right or am I right?" Ray couldn't help but smile. "Congratulations, Sid! You're right on the mark." Sid reached over the bar and shook Ray's hand like there was no tomorrow. "It's a trade secret—how I remember. You don't look Mexican to me or anything like that. It's not like a Czech-looking guy must like Pilsner, or a German is a Beck's guy. Hey, listen to the help rattling on when a guy just wants to wet his whistle. Let me get you that cold one. Heineken's, right?" Sid laughed, his shoulders shaking as he turned and bent down to pull out a bottle of Cerveza.

Sid was always dramatic and fun. He reminded Ray of a young Teddy Roosevelt, or at least the Teddy Roosevelt depicted in film. Animated like a cartoon character on speed, socially gauche, impulsively brave—Sid had been known to dress up like Rough Rider Teddy on Halloween and go bully into the night. He lived in happy union with a flutist from the Desert Chamber Music group.

"So how it's going really, Ray? Haven't seen you around, like, in ages?" Sid asked, plopping the beer and glass down with a flourish.

"You know full well how it goes. It goes like shit. I have my bad days and then I have my middling days."

Sid wiped the smile off his face. "I know, I know, you count the days left along with your T-cell count. It's rough business. Harry and I pray every day that we won't have to go out like that. That we die of natural causes."

Ray frowned and Sid recognized his faux pas. "Not that HIV isn't natural, it's natural as all get-out, it's as natural as day and night. I mean you know what I mean. Je-e-esus Ray!"

Ray decided to rescue his old friend. "Sid, it's okay, really. I wouldn't know what to say if I was in your shoes either. Forget about it. Boy, this beer really hits the spot. Thanks!"

Sid brightened and then caught 'another round' gesture from two guys down the bar. He rushed off to mix their drinks, gracefully pirouetting around two servers in his path. Ray smiled at his friend's gyrations. Then he turned on his swivel stool to see who else of his old circle was around. The dance floor was crowded as couple swirled slowly to a Diana Krall song. There were a number of people he recognized and several Ray wouldn't mind chatting up. But Ray had been in a shell for over two years and felt shy all of a sudden. Unsure of his bearings, not feeling on top of the world—Ray wanted someone to come over to him.

The back booths were in shadow and Ray wondered what delicious, teasing talk was occurring, what hand holding, what groping under the table. He noticed one shadowy figure detach from a booth and make its way towards the glittery dance floor. It became a man, and that man was Gary. The man who had killed Pete, using Ray as the stealth bludgeon.

Gary was making a beeline for the restrooms but he noticed Ray staring and gave him a shooting sign with his right hand. It was always like that—Gary the pistol and Ray with the target over his heart. Ray shook his head, trying to shake some sense into the little gray cells. This man destroyed his life, denied him the man he truly loved, gave him a wasting disease with no cure. What's the attraction? Despite the virus, Gary still appeared to be in good shape; indeed, was more physically attractive than during university years. Back then Gary wore his hair long and unkempt and was too busy with the revolution to bathe regularly. Ray, who stayed scented and bourgeois even during his radical days, would during moments of tender affection call his paramour his 'hairy beast.' Now both men were in their fifties and Gary was the one looking no worst for wear. The plague years had been so kind to the dirty rat and that was so fucking unfair.

After their fateful night in 1996 of unprotected sex, Ray was urged by his doctor, under penalty of public health law, to notify his sex partners of the HIV infection. There were only two to tell: Pete in a night that dissolved into tears, and Gary in a long distance call to Manhattan that ended in shouted recriminations. Gary accused Ray of infecting him just as Ray knew it had to be the other way around. The erstwhile lovers hung up in acrimony and hadn't talked since.

Ray sagged in his bar stool. Seeing Gary brought to mind sex, and Ray realized his chances of scoring tonight were slim or none. He wasn't about to engage in reckless sex. There was a small subculture of HIV-positive men who didn't care and exercised no caution. Ray had no compulsion to slowly kill with terminal lust. Yet he wanted to be loved tonight, even if only with the words. Sex can wait until tomorrow night, when he makes the acquaintance with the guys in jail. Ray wondered if behind bars the rules of attraction are different. Even in the muted lighting at the bar of free men, Ray knew he wasn't God's gift right now. Though he liked to pose as elegantly dissipated, a well-born duke in exile perhaps, Ray saw that the mirror behind the bar told a different story.

Some joker put a quarter in the real jukebox to hear the great Peggy Lee wax bittersweet in *Is That All There Is?* The plaintive lyrics said it all for all those who have loved and lost.

> Is that all there is
> Is that all there is
> Is that all there is,
> My friend, then
> Let's keep dancing
> Let's break out the booze
> And have a ball,
> If that's all
> There is.

It was more a solitary drinking song than a dance tune; no other paean to ennui said it so well in so few words. Ray figured he might as well gulp his beer rather than take temperate sips. But then the vision of the sleeping boy came to mind. He promised to be there to wake him up on Good Friday. Driving drunk on mountain roads at night could leave that promise unfulfilled. Ray was drinking his second beer, slumped still on his stool, wincing at the reflections of happy couples dancing in the mirror. He looked down into the beer foam and found himself saying the Lord's Prayer over and over in a whisper. Ray felt a tap on his shoulder. Startled, he swiveled a bit and looked wide-eyed into the face of Gary.

Gary kept his hand on Ray's shoulder and bent over to give him an awkward hug. Then he drew back but kept a hand on Ray's shoulders. The man handling didn't offend Ray. He actually welcomed the touching as he badly needed his physical self to be embraced. Anything, anybody to show that he wasn't an untouchable. Ray wasn't imagining himself as an incorruptible G-man fighting the Capone mob, but rather an Indian of the lowest cast, doomed to a hardscrabble existence; dying alone from a wasting disease.

"Long time no see, Ray. I remember that our last conversation didn't go well. I'd like to take another shot at that. I hate loose ends and loud arguments, don't you?"

Ray replied weakly, "Yeah, I hate loose ends too."

Gary slipped his hand down Ray's back and whispered in his ear. "Then let's talk, man. I'll shoo the boy away. We have a lot of catching up to do, don't we?"

Ray could only respond in a hoarse voice: "Yes," and allow Gary to steer him over to a booth against the back wall. There was indeed a boy there, nursing a beer, a young man still in or barely out of his teens.

Gary dismissed him with movie-speak: "Hasta la vista, baby," sounding like the Terminator. Baby face pouted but the boy got up and left. Ray sat on the vinyl seat and looked over at his first great love. As always, Gary's Spanish was mangled. In college Ray would gently try to correct him, tutor him on the fly, but Gary had no ear for any foreign language except the Latin he needed for his legal work. Gary pronounced 'Armijo' as though it was Army Joe, creating a new action figure, rather than pronouncing the 'j' as 'h' and putting the stress on the second syllable. 'Sopaipillas' became sofa pillows in Gary's argot though Ray figured that Gary was pulling his leg on that one.

Gary had always been the dominant partner. That was just in the nature of relationships, gay or straight, one person on top, the other giving way. Most often Ray was the calm one though, reserved rather than reckless, but his sweet reason was always trumped by Gary's fuck it impulse. That was the way their first encounter went, in the bathroom stall between classes, the smell of sweat and semen mingling with piss and excrement. Ray entered that bathroom an innocent 19 year old in many ways and emerged much older, much wiser to the sorted ways of the world, absolutely disgusted with himself, yet feeling so elated at the same time.

"Now, this is sure way better than screaming at each other," Gary soothingly said, though he had to raise his voice to be heard over the driving rock tune now emitting from the jukebox. Ray always figured that was by design, cranking up the volume, forcing people to lean together, to lock lips.

Ray took a gulp of his beer to clear his voice of the hoarseness. "I'm tired of screaming too, Gary. How have you been? Are you just visiting or have you made the big move?"

"No, I'm here now for good, six months, since a little after 9/11. Those twin towers tumbling down convinced me to take the old Santa Fe Trail. I had a position lined up already and a bid on a house before the attack and everything was accelerated after the attack. Man, I was in my office 60 stories up a few blocks away when the first plane hit. The only thing I missed was the asbestos dust because I stayed in my office all day looking out at the chaos. I even saw a couple poor jokers throw themselves out of the north tower windows. Splat! There's nothing like seeing that to make you want to work on the ground floor or move west to a town where two stories is about the limit. So bottom line, I've got a great house in Tesuque and a bright future in the city different. I'm lying about the future of course—I gave up a lucrative partnership in Manhattan to become an associate again at the Cowles firm downtown. Practicing civil litigation again, doing okay but nothing like New York salaries and bonuses. I'm holding my own otherwise."

Ray read the last reference as meaning health-wise, the struggle with HIV/ AIDS. In telling about his intense experience with 9/11, Ray felt Gary was reaching out to him. Perhaps reconciliation was possible.

"I could be doing better myself, Gary. I lost my partner a couple years ago and haven't been the same since. I gave up my agency. Pete's life insurance made that possible. I guess I believe in insurance."

"Well, yeah, that makes perfect sense. That was your business and you sell what you believe, don't cha?"

Ray asked if a lawyer believes in justice.

"Justice? You mean the work I do. I do believe in the rule of law but it's as much the law of the jungle when you come down to it. What happens is a clash of wits and will that often have little to do with the underlying truth of the matter. I don't deal with the criminal justice side but the perfect example of buying a verdict was the O.J. Simpson trial. That was certainly must-see TV and exposed the dark side of American justice. I mean the truth was so obvious; motive and opportunity was there in spades; history of spousal abuse, trace evidence, DNA matches. But the dream team raised unreasonable doubt and jury nullification took place.

"I was particularly impressed by the ethical gymnastics that Barry Scheck must have gone through to get Simpson off. I mean this guy is the prime mover behind the Innocence Project where they unearth evidence from old cases, mostly DNA evidence, to get guys off death row if not actually pardoned. Scheck always argues in those cases that DNA is absolutely conclusive in proof of innocence. So what did he argue in the O.J. trial? Nope, don't trust that DNA, it was tainted, collected by incompetents who were racists besides. Out to frame a football hero, I'm sure. Where's the intellectual consistency in that? Where's justice for the victims? Two people sliced and diced, and their murderer free to fuck up the surviving children's lives. Incredible miscarriage of justice! But great entertainment, I grant you."

Gary's capsule comment was fascinating to Ray. He really leaned into the man to catch every word. The lawyer's cynical view of his profession, forcefully presented, was typical Gary. As a young man he was always ready for a rhetorical fight, using colorful and precise language, wanting to win regardless of the stakes involved.

"But surely," Ray commented, "juries get it right most of the time. An awful lot of bad guys get convicted and are behind bars. Even O.J. had to pay the piper with that civil verdict."

"Yeah, the families got a small measure of revenge there. But you've got to remember, Ray my darling, that judgments are one thing, collecting quite another. His football pension, for example, is off-limits and he moved to Florida to make sure his house wouldn't be sold to pay off this blood debt. I doubt if Simpson has missed a single fucking round of golf because of this so-called judgment. Probably the only ones who got the money were the lawyers. I take some comfort from that."

Gary often turned profane when his blood boiled. Ray preferred soft words of love while Gary engaged in the universal language of screw. The men's mouths were only inches apart as Gary ended his rant. They kissed. Gary's hand held the back of Ray's head as they kissed. As always in the heat of passion, Gary was pushing too hard as if he wanted to swallow his lover whole. As always, Ray wondered if he could suck the venom from the man's heart. Gary's lust carried all before it. He reminded Ray of a schoolmate from parochial school days. Denny's emotions overwhelmed him during play at recess and after school. A simple game of tag left bruises on your skin.

Ray broke free of the suffocating embrace. Taking a deep breath, he wondered if he had lost his head with crazy nostalgia for the thrills of the first great love. When they were young men together, fumbling with notions of romantic love and the reality of domestic discord—the mind has a pronounced tendency to filter out the pain and heartache in the distant past, leaving only the heroic embrace, the tender feelings, and the passion of the night. But along with nostalgia comes practical needs; facing arrest tomorrow, Ray wanted some raunchy fun tonight. If tenderness was thrown in for good measure, all the better. He could dream of Pete's wonderful character and easy-going nature but Pete had been gone now for two years. Ray had experienced no physical love since and this was the best offer he was likely to get tonight. He was damaged goods after all. For both men the damage had already been done.

In silent assent they got up to dance. It was a very danceable Dooble Brothers song. The two men stayed on the floor for a half hour or so, frenzy followed by slow dancing, then losing yourself again in pulsating movement, then a country western song that invited you to swing your partner. It was a crazy mishmash that somehow worked until the dance floor was cleared by Sondheim's *Send in the Clowns*. No one could dance to that! Ray was spent anyway; he no longer had the endurance of youth. He moped his brow as Gary grabbed his free hand. Gary said, "Well, shall we?" to which Ray could only respond: "Yes, God yes!"

Out in the fresh air they decided to caravan it to Gary's house. Ray followed Gary's massive Hummer north from Santa Fe proper to the charming village of Tesuque. His new home was truly great and beautiful. In daylight there must be quite a view. Gary mixed drinks at his wet bar off the spacious living room. The beers consumed at the bar combined with the margaritas put both men in the mood. Ray asked the way to the guest bathroom so he could freshen up. Gary laughed and said the master bathroom could handle them both. He led his old lover to the well-appointed bathroom that seemed to be the size of Ray's bedroom in his small house in Nava Adé. The two men disrobed without ceremony, took long pisses into the bowl, and jumped into the shower. Ray felt extremely self-conscious. Gary was slender while he was gaunt; Gary's skin was flawless while Ray's was spotted with sores. The damn virus was so fickle in its rampage.

Gary's erection demanded attention. Ray went down on him under the pulsating hot spray from the shower head. But in satisfying his partner, Ray felt his own tentative erection going, going, gone. He could have tried to hurry Gary's climax but Ray hated making love that way. There should be no hurry. Gary's hands—both of them—were again on the back of his head; the groaning man taking the Lord's name in vain. Having sex in the shower left Ray feeling as clean as a wolf whistle.

Gary looked down at Ray's deflated cock and commented, "Oh, dear me! We must do something about that." They dried off and padded over to the king size bed. Ray was dismayed by the ceiling mirror over the bed; somehow, vanity views right now were not erotic. Gary tried every which way to arouse Ray's penis but the inspired efforts weren't paying off. The men unclasped and laid back on the pillows to regroup. Gary reached over to his nightstand's drawer and took out a pack of cigarettes, lighter, and two ashtrays. He offered Ray a cigarette and ashtray and both men lit up. Ray hadn't had a regular cigarette for one long year. He took a grateful drag. The smoke took the edge off. But he desperately wanted an orgasm. But it wasn't only the spasm he was after. He wanted proof positive that he was still alive. That God wasn't through with him yet.

To arouse himself, Ray decided to use Peddie—shamelessly. Not fantasizing about ravaging the dear boy, no, none of that, though he was beautiful, no, yes, but no, just talking about the strange happenings of the week. Telling Gary of his history with the boy, the academic tutoring evolving into a personal connection, finding out about the tumultuous home life. In revealing all, he hoped the confidences would rub off on his cock. Ray had the inside dope on what happened to the boy in the news. Those in the know have all the power.

When Ray mentioned the mountain cabin, Gary asked if it was the same one they snuck away to on weekends so many years ago during college. Ray said yes, yes, remembering those halcyon days. It seemed so innocent now, the two boys gamboling through the woods, soaking in the hot springs, fishing and swimming in the Jemez, making love with the moonlight through the bedroom window. Ray didn't want the memory to be benign though. He wanted to jazz it up.

Ray told his old friend and lover everything. When he brought up Father Andy's role, Gary asked bluntly why get a fucking priest involved. Ray explained the complications of incest and the hope that the Franciscan could help stop that. Gary seemed to experience more glee in hearing than Ray felt in telling. Ray didn't find anything about incest to smirk about. As he wrapped up the strange goings on in the Martinez home and what was to come tomorrow at Chimayó, he did feel closer to Gary though. Sharing secrets leads to trusting. Trusting in close company leads to intimacy. The two men had a long and complicated history. They had no future together but the night was still young.

The secret sharing sputtered out but the two men were still paying rapt attention to each other's body language. Gary leaned over and murmured in his lover's ear: "I know what you need, Ray-o. There's a pill for everything these days." Gary jumped out of bed and left the bedroom. He returned promptly with a glass of water and ducked into the master bathroom. With a cheerful hum he returned to bed with a blue pill in his hand. "Must be Viagra," Ray surmised. Gary confirmed, "You got that right, honey. Ever try it?" Ray shook his head, never needing it before. He eagerly took the pill and washed it down with a gulp of water. He leaned back on the pillows and looked up into the mirror and waited for the magic to occur. Gary told him it takes about 15-20 minutes. Gary reached for the remote and turned on the massive TV in the bedroom armoire. He told Ray, "Let's see if there is anything on about the boy." He flipped channels and lingered on CNN and Fox. Ray was tired of wild speculation about the boy's fate; he knew that Peddie was safe and sound and probably sleeping with Harry Potter on his mind. Ray really wanted to ask Gary if he subscribed to adult programming. He held his tongue not out of shyness but because he feared disappointment, softer porn than he desired, straight sex with lesbo action mixed in. Men wanting men usually had to settle for one of the XXX videos displayed in the store's back room. Perhaps Gary had such old fashioned porn ready to go. They could blow out the candle and copulate with one eye on the steamy screen.

Ray decided he was being silly. The pill alone should be quite enough. He flashed on the absurd image of Errol Flynn as the swashbuckling Captain Blood. Peter Blood wouldn't be caught dead taking Viagra. His romance with the radiant Olivia DeHavilland was all natural. Men were men back in those days. The film didn't suggest any buggering in the forecastle but heroic humping must have been the norm. Men were men then. Men are such whiners now. They cry themselves to sleep. They take a pill to make love.

Suddenly all Ray wanted to do was to fall asleep, a blessed sleep through a chaste night. But this was all screwy. He should be becoming aroused, not drowsy. He looked over at Gary who was looking back with a knowing smile. Those in the know have all the power. Why am I so tired? Ray thought. My lover has a come hither expression and a willing body. Surely Viagra time is up; where's the magic? Ray wasn't asking for much. Just one night away from mortal fear. He looked up again at himself in the mirror and saw that Gary was looking up too. Was his smile now mocking? Ray heard rollicking laughter that wasn't coming from the talking heads on cable news. No one on the tube was even smiling. Something's not right, Ray realized, as he nodded off at a lax moment when he should have been more alive than ever.

CHAPTER 19

▼

Father Andy and Sister Maria returned to Santa Fe mid-afternoon and went to their respective residences to rest. Before the nap Andy sat awhile in his recliner sipping his Jameson's. He had a lot to chew over. So much had happened since Palm Sunday. The priest anticipated a long Good Friday. Peddie and Ray will appear at El Santuario de Chimayó and the debriefing/interrogation will happen. What must be done before dark is for the mother and her children to be placed in protective custody or Raul Martinez removed from the home. The priest couldn't rest tomorrow after walking all night until Gabby's safety was assured. Andy put out of his mind the possibility of the girl being molested again tonight. Surely such incidents are sporadic with the mother and older brother residing there. The priest prayed that God wouldn't throw him any curves that he couldn't handle. Andy looked wistfully at his bed and wondered if an untroubled siesta was possible.

The revelation from Sister Maria that she was leaving was a real shocker. The Franciscan never figured anything would really happen between them; nothing, that is, of a shameful nature. A man of the cloth settles for beautiful friendships. But teasing speculations kept the man in him alive. He was under no illusion that middle age would chase desire away. Andy had years to go before blessed sleep came from counting sheep rather than female rumps.

He downed the last of the whiskey and threw off his robe and underclothes to crawl into bed. Andy set the alarm for 5 p.m., a couple hours rest before the run-up to the all nighter. At least he wasn't going to bed famished. They had stopped by a popular taco stand in Española and the priest unceremoniously wolfed down three soft shell chicken and bean tacos. Pope jumped up on the bed to sleep with his master. They both sighed deeply before falling off to sleep.

*   *   *   *

The alarm jarred the priest awake. He turned over and buried his face in the pillow as Pope nuzzled and licked. Andy said a fast muffled prayer, a prayer for superhuman strength. He rolled out of bed and padded into the bathroom to shower. Gird for battle immaculate from the start. He often felt that way after a long hot shower: Andy the world beater. As the needles of water applied acupuncture to his every complaint, he broke out in song. And what diva but the divine Sarah!

> When I'm alone
> I dream of the horizon
> And words fail me
> There is no light…
>
> Time to say goodbye

The sentiment may be bittersweet but the priest sang joyously. He didn't remember all the lyrics of course; he repeated "Time to say goodbye" several times. Andy was reminded of traditional Irish wakes he attended over the years, the laughter in the face of death. As he toweled off with vigor, Andy saw that his undaunted courage rubbed off on his dog. The Pope was smiling and squirming to go. There was scat to smell along the way. The priest as always found his dog teaching him life lessons. Don't turn your nose up on any signs of life.

But what preparation for battle was complete without a hearty meal. Mrs. Alvarez always prepared something special for the Holy Week pilgrimage as she knew Father Andy faced a long, long night. Two plates were plastic wrapped in the fridge. Andy automatically took the one crammed to the edges, leaving the one with the petite mound to the pastor. Mrs. Alvarez took Gurule's criticism to heart and called his bluff by giving him pygmy portions.

It was Red Snapper Vera Cruz, a favorite of Father Andy's. The pastor came into the kitchen as Andy's plate spun in the microwave. The two priests exchanged greetings. Gurule took his plate from the fridge and looked sadly at the contents. "It's Vera Cruz, isn't it? Vera Cruz."

As they sat down to eat, Andy shared Sister Maria's decision to leave Santo Thérèse and Santa Fe. Gurule didn't seem surprised at all.

"Actually, Andy, I was expecting our good sister to move on to greener pastures. She wants a family, no? I've seen how she is with children and heard her say over and over how blessed parents are. So maybe, just maybe, Andy, she goes with God's blessing. She's a woman of resource and will be fine as she pursues her biological destiny. After all, it's a very unnatural life we Catholic religious live. I'm actually more concerned with you. You've been out and about on mysterious business, my friend. What's going on?"

So here was another invitation to tell the truth, the whole truth. Andy decided to tack away from Peddie. He felt compelled to come clean about his feelings for Maria.

"I guess I'm more broken up by Maria's leaving than I ever thought I'd be. She's a great gal I agree. I'll miss her badly."

Words were one thing but Andy's eyes reflected the true devastation. Gurule put his fork down and reached across the table to pat Andy's forearm.

"I know, Andy, actually I've known for a long time. Your pining over our dear sister was pretty obvious to anybody with eyes in their head. I guess we have to experience something first hand to really understand. You see, my boy, Sister Muni and I went through much the same thing years ago, when we were young together. Our sacred vows couldn't overcome our attraction to each other."

This was news to Andy. He knew that Gurule and Muni had worked together to establish and nurture the Little Flower parish. He never imagined that they had worked together hand-in-hand. It was as though observing your aged parents, crotchety with each other, and trying to imagine them as young lovers together, blissful, beguiled. Gurule had maintained a photographic record of the parish's founding, growing pains, and signal achievements. Andy had occasion to leaf through the album several times. He hadn't noticed anything untoward in the proud expressions of the young priest and nun as they dedicated the school's cornerstone or stood in front of the new parish center. In retrospect, the founding pastor and nun were looking at each other with a glow far from otherworldly.

The two priests suddenly felt a revived appreciation of each other's common humanity. Gurule looked down at his morsel of fish and groused: "That woman's husband must have died of gastric distress. But I know you like her cooking so maybe it's just me."

Gurule scrapped a few spots of spice off the fish and took another bite. "I know, Andy, that you're probably wondering if Muni and I did the dirty. Well, let me tell you, when you're young and building something great and good together, working together day and night, no, things happen, beautiful sins. But both of us had to make a choice between a life in Christ or a temporal life together. We ultimately chose the spirit rather than the flesh. But it was a real struggle for years, believe me, the temptations."

Andy reached for his napkin and dried his eyes. He often advised distraught parishioners that a good cry was therapeutic. Now he was accepting his own advice.

"Father, I don't want to be silly about this but I'm going to miss her so," Andy said, feeling utterly exposed.

Gurule patted his arm again. "But I take it, Andy, that you're sticking with our band of brothers."

Andy nodded with resignation and Gurule responded: "I thought as much. You're a believer, Andy, God bless you, and God loves you without reservation. It's a noble calling, lonely at times, a lonely perch, but the wicked world and our souls are the better for it."

A glance at his watch told Andy that the time for commiseration was over as duty called. The Holy Thursday evening service was a somber one, with the priests and altar draped in purple cloth. This was the night of the Last Supper and Jesus' betrayal by Judas at the Garden of Gethsemane. Christian clergy across the world were presiding over the remembrance. At Santo Thérèse the tradition included the washing of the priests' feet just as Mary Magdalene washed Christ's feet. The apostles disapproved as they considered her a fallen woman. Jesus saw the good in her.

A few feminist church women expressed discomfort over the years with having a teenage girl play a compromised woman. One lady muttered at a parish council meeting: "It reeks of a massage parlor." Andy heard the grumble and both he and Gurule patiently explained the significance of the historic encounter. Gurule cleverly closed the discussion by asking the adult women for a volunteer to play Mary. Nobody raised their hand. A teenager from St. Michael's was chosen again by default.

The service was very well attended. A school bus and several wheel chair accessible vans waited outside the church to transport the pilgrims up to the north side veteran's cemetery for the jump start to the long march. Father Andy never knew in advance the exact number of marchers as faith is sorely tested by a bad weather. But the forecast tonight during this early spring was for clear skies and temperatures in the 40's. The vans stayed with the marchers through the night, ready to give the footsore as well as the disabled a lift. The school bus was driven to Chimayó Friday afternoon to give the group a ride back to the Santo Thérèse lot.

Seeing the pilgrims on their way was a ceremony in itself. The full choir was present, singing a dirge. What faced the pilgrims tonight was nowhere as grim as what Christ the man faced—the crown of thorns, the whipping, the Crucifixion the next day. They could only imagine the suffering on the Cross, nails in your palms, breathing your last with vinegar on your lips. Jesus did have a crucial advantage over us mere mortals. He knew without doubt that a resurrection of body and soul awaited Him. He was going home in triumph. God keeps the rest of us in suspense.

The pilgrims faced achy muscles and sleep deprivation. Several times over the years Father Andy had to lay down the Little Flower law that believers not carry walking with Jesus too far. A few of these Penitentes showed up in loincloth with whip marks on their back. They had fashioned their own life size cross out of hard wood. They wanted to truly suffer for mankind's sins. Though Father Andy recognized these men's sincerity and that their sacrifice would draw the secular press' attention to Christ's real suffering, the modern Church encouraged internal bleeding only.

Andy departed from the Franciscan brown to wear a white monk's robe lent him each year by a Dominican friend. The white served as a beacon in the dark. Andy wore traditional sandals that he saved for this overnight rite of passage only. The priest sometimes wished for thick socks and hiking boots as his feet were always blistered and even bloodied by the end of the Passion. But the friar scored points with his most ardent followers. Some of the men brought their own blood-spotted sandals along. On the school bus ride back to Santa Fe the men would compare ragged feet as fussing women applied salve to their glorified wounds. The priest couldn't walk without wincing for days afterwards.

The women marchers wore sensible shoes and the wheelchair-bound often bought new shoes in case of a miraculous rising. Those broken in body were all profiles of hope and courage but even amongst them were a pecking order based on class. The old style wheelchairs were used by the poor of the parish. They actually had a good shot of completing the pilgrimage under their own power. Often their upper body strength was awesome just as the blind person's sense of smell is sharpened in compensation. The priest pondered the idea of warring senses, of distractions as the healthy body had too many things going on at once. Paralysis can make you appreciate what little you have left.

Father Andy wasn't sure how a physical disability plays on the human spirit. If God truly liberated one or two at El Santuario tomorrow, would they come down with the demons of the mind that wear down the able bodied? Everybody loves a paraplegic while the fit are fair game. But the priest certainly knew from resigned conversations and confessions that many of these poor souls had the worst of both worlds, tangled wings as well as dread over nothing and everything.

The poor were lifted out of cramped cars and old pick-ups, with the folded up wheelchair in the trunk or on the rusting bed. Affluent parishioners had customized vans with lifts for their fully motorized scooter. The scooters through the night sometimes ran afoul of potholes and rough shoulders. A couple years ago a new one broke down and the parishioner had to fight tooth and nail to get the manufacturer to honor its warranty. But after many collective prayers and the threat of an organized boycott by the diocese at large, as well as individual lawsuit, the manufacturer gave in and replaced the scooter free of charge. They rewrote the product warranty to specifically exclude pilgrimages.

On the short drive up to the cemetery the priest sat in the front of the bus with Sister Maria next to him and his dog plopped on his lap. He was all cried out and small talk with the woman was possible. Pilgrims on the packed bus were either quiet or engaged in murmured conversations. Many had their rosaries out and were fingering through the beads.

Cemeteries at night are spooky places. This was one of many national resting places set-aside for fallen veterans, some dying on distant battlefields, others dying years later from natural causes or the lingering consequences of war wounds. A few gravestones dated back to the Civil War. Not far down the road was the site of a small but significant battle from that war, Glorieta Pass, where a force of Union militia and regulars stopped cold Confederate westward expansion. Now Glorieta was known as a site of a Baptist retreat center that attracted pacifists and religious groups of all denominations. Nearby Civil War battle re-enactors worshiped in their own way.

The cemetery was dark except for a couple security spotlights on the outside of the meditation chapel. Most of the pilgrims brought their own lights, old fashion oil lanterns as well as strong flashlights. Life and limb were major concerns as the faithful had to walk along a busy highway for many miles before branching off onto a country road. Besides safety though, man-made beauty resulted from the string of moving lights along the highway. The lights bore witness to eternal faith as distracted drivers rushed by to try their luck at the Indian casinos.

Father Andy knew that a number of the pilgrims had loved ones buried in the cemetery. The priest was going to use their names shamelessly to kick-start the march.

We are gathered for another Easter week of demonstrating our faith, of walking the walk instead of just talking the talk. No doubt we will also talk, if only to keep ourselves awake, and pray through the night, to keep our souls in tune with God. God's plan for us need not be a great mystery. The simpler the better, it seems to me. Be a good father, be a good mother, be a faithful friend, be the best son or daughter you can be, give an honest day's work and give to Uncle Sam what is due Uncle Sam. Derive great joy from sacrifice, from caring about others rather than dwelling in your own petty little world.

We are gathered at the final resting place for the bravest of the brave. Several members of our Little Flower parish lie here. Sam Montoya survived the Bataan Death March, came back to Santa Fe to raise a family and see grandkids born, finally succumbing to some war wounds that never healed properly. Sam's son Tony and grandson Sammy joins us tonight. Joey Tapia rests here, a mere boy off to war, becoming a man under fire in the Gulf, a brave soldier cruelly cut down on the last day. Joey's brother Frankie and sister Ariana both are marching with us tonight. Joyce Tremsol was recently interred here. Joyce rose to become a Colonel in the Air Force, who died tragically in childbirth. Her last breath was in giving life. In dying we are born again and her daughter Sandra is a living testament to her love and her faith. Harry Tremsol is with us tonight and little Sandra is safe at home. No doubt Sandra will be a good pilgrim herself a few years down the road.

We all march in the name of Christ tonight. It is a beautiful night and angel eyes twinkle down at us. Let us walk in peace, to love and serve our Lord.

Two altar boys and one altar girl led the way out of the cemetery. These were teenage veterans due to retire from the ranks of altar servers. The Chimayó pilgrimage and Easter Sunday Mass represented their graduation ceremonies so to speak. One teenager—a bulky boy—carried the life-sized hollow plastic Crucifix that normally graced the altar platform at Santo Thérèse. In the early days of the parish a solid wood carving of Christ on the Cross was used but it was far too heavy to be carried any distance by either altar boy or lay man. The other altar boy carried a lantern on a long pole that provided a swinging beacon for the marchers. The altar girl carried the Santo Thérése parish banner. With pride and piety the pilgrims made their way out of the cemetery.

The pilgrims couldn't bunch up much on the narrow shoulder of the highway. The slowest ship in the convoy rule applied so power walking was discouraged. Other Catholic parishes from all points on the compass had contingents out tonight. There was an annual lighthearted bet amongst the priests of Santa Fe about which parish would get the most pilgrims fastest to the shrine on Good Friday. Only $ 10 was at stake so the real goal was to arrive physically safe and spiritually sound.

The marchers talked a little and even attempted to sing some hymns led by a few choir members along for that purpose. The main problem was lack of hymnals; reading music & lyrics walking in the dead of night was impossible. The choir members and marchers could sing certain hymns a cappella and by heart but then there was a problem of selection. Holy Thursday and Good Friday were somber occasions. People remembered songs of joy better than songs of sadness. So after a few ragged sing-alongs the sounds were reduced to murmuring conversations and the whiz of passing vehicles.

The Franciscan walked with his dog on a leash just behind the altar boys and girl leading the way. It was unlikely that Pope would dart out in traffic but Andy didn't want to chance it. The dog was out of rhythm as his body clock said sleep was called for, not an all night walkabout. Sister Maria stayed for awhile at the side of the priest before drifting back to encourage her fellow pilgrims. The nun was dressed conservatively in a simple black shirt, black tights, and white blouse under a black wool coat. Except for the glimpse of white, Maria faded into the darkness. But the priest felt her presence all night long. An old pop song came absurdly to mind: "Going to the chapel and we're going to get married; going to the chapel of love." That was the only part he remembered, the refrain. He mouthed the lyrics silently over and over as he gazed sideways at his nun. She was illuminated faintly by the moon and stars and the swaying pole lantern, then sharply by the brights of passing cars. Andy knew that if any of the pilgrims saw his lips moving, they'd figure he was praying to the Lord. The priest was sad because he was going to be the odd man out at the chapel. It would be impossible to speak his piece. While abundant love would be in the chapel, one vital strain would be denied him.

The police cars out in force reminded the priest of the arrest to come tomorrow at the shrine. He wondered if the cops would pay any attention to his defense of Ray's sheltering of a troubled boy. He wasn't optimistic as Peddie's disappearance disrupted police routine and sent good citizens on wild goose chases. Excuses and explanations even given by a Franciscan friar would likely be discounted in favor of showing no mercy to a suspected child molester. People no longer took as gospel a priest's word on that subject.

The sheriff's deputies, pueblo police, and state police were ticketing speeders, watching out for drunk drivers or fallen Catholics who may have the compulsion to run over clergy. The police would also be trying to help stragglers and prevent short cutters from going overland and losing their way. Every year a few young and impatient quick steppers would be found lost and bewildered in the pinon hills surrounding Chimayó.

The priest took great pride in shepherding his flock each year. He hadn't lost one yet; no pilgrim died on him; even the dying lived through this night. There was a special bond that developed amongst the veteran pilgrims. This would be Maria's last Holy Week pilgrimage, at least wearing Catholic colors. Now with lust declared officially dead and buried, perhaps they would be blessed with a lasting friendship across state lines. But that requires hard work as well as good intentions. Andy could just imagine how time consuming husband hunting and capturing can be, as well as the baby to come. Knowing Maria's love of children, he wouldn't be surprised if she tried to squeeze in more than one. And she probably would resurrect and take public her career in education in St. Louis.

Father Andy was jealous of Maria leaving the religious life, going carnal on him as well as Protestant. He realized he was more envious of the carnality than the begetting. In his heart of hearts, despite appearances to the contrary, Andy knew he wanted to keep children at a safe distance. He had his comforts and routines at the rectory with his faithful dog; growing children stole time away. Look at the havoc one little boy was wreaking on the priest's Holy Week. But Andy had to concede that he felt more alive in the last few days than he had in years.

As the night deepened the priest dropped back into the ranks to buck up their spirits. Andy tried to get everybody to look beyond their aches and pains to the beauty of the night. Under a starry sky it's so misguided to dwell upon yourself.

CHAPTER 20

▼

Where do we get our courage from? Sober courage is such a crock. Through-out history the forlorn hope storming the breach were stoked with liquor and mad with the promise of rape and pillage. Nothing glorious about the assault; nothing to write home to mother. Philosophy of life doesn't matter when crunch time comes. We are reduced to sensation alone, desire at its most base, the desire to live, to breathe, to fuck. You know, I'm funny that way; I indulge in profanity in private conversation but try to converse in my head in prim and proper English. Sometimes I fail and whisper "fuck I don't care" but I find the exercise in self-restraint stimulating.

We fool ourselves all the time. We are just drooling for the chance to be bad boys. A few drinks, a couple pills—all bets are off, baby! The effect is heightened if you have nothing to live for; indeed, if you are dying. I've lost my moorings and a shit storm is coming. I want to clean up my act but it doesn't matter any-more. Will I look good going down? Vanity is the last thing we let go of.

*　　　*　　　*　　　*

Ray woke up in an unsatiated state. For one thing he was spread-eagled and naked on the bed with no comforter, not even a sheet for modesty's sake, looking up at his sorry self in the ceiling mirror. Nakedness frozen in time had its attrac-tions but Ray hardly felt like a nude reclining. He was bound tightly to the bed-posts. This was not an instance of two playful, trusting lovers introducing a delicious twist to stimulate desire. Ray woke with a morning erection that he could neither reach nor point in a direction that made earthly sense. Disoriented and frantic, smelling smoke and fearing fire, he lifted his head to see if he was alone. No, Gary was there, the source of the smoke, puffing on a cigarette, sitting in a comfy chair at the foot of the bed. He was wearing a white terry cloth robe and plopped in his lap was an ashtray filled to the brim with butts. He blew perfect smoke rings out that shimmied and warped as they rose. He looked delighted that Ray awoke from his beauty sleep. Gary's broad smile jogged Ray's memory of the night before. What Ray thought was so inviting was now chilling to the bone.

Ray knew this was no game. Why couldn't sex be simple and safe for just one night? There always seemed to be a steep price to pay whether you phone for it or pick it up under the red light. Gary was no stranger though. There was a history between them and some of it was quite sweet. But HIV transmission tends to sour the memory. Ray thought suddenly of the boy waking up alone in the wilderness cabin. Peddie could certainly fend for himself for a few hours or some days for that matter. Father Andy would figure out soon enough that the Chimayó miracle wasn't going to happen. But Ray had promised to be there for the boy. That promise was in jeopardy.

Ray wondered if an appeal to reason would work with Gary. Here Yazzie was, buck-ass naked, and he wanted to use wit and logic to win over his captor. He dipped into his memory for experiences that may be relevant. As a young man Ray had gone skinny-dipping in mixed company a number of times. He always found the group experience memorable more for its innocence than any eroticism. One fine summer day outside Taos Ray was hugely amused at a free for all hot springs on the banks of the Rio Grande River. Two friends from those days, Rob and Jennie, struck up a spirited conversation while standing dripping naked next to the pool. Ray was soaking in the soothing waters while gazing in wonder at his two gesticulating friends. Their discussion concerned New Mexico political matters, about an environmental measure wending its way through the Roundhouse legislative process. Jennie wanted a stronger, purer bill while Rob argued for half a loaf. Ray didn't long remember the particular points made, or even if the watered down bill was signed into law. Reason and results lost meaning in the face of naked truth.

The question of 'Shame on who' was at the bottom of his dispute with Gary. When Ray called long distance to Manhattan with the dreaded news, a shouting match ensued that sounded like angry juveniles in the schoolyard. Both men realized that life as they knew it had ended. Ray blamed Gary and vice versa. A death sentence had been levied, with a few years of medical reprieve. After a long struggle Ray had forgiven Gary though the pardon was obviously one-sided. At the Bar None Different the two men avoided the subject like the plague in hope that love-making would heal the wounded heart.

"You slept like a baby," Gary said sarcastically. "I watched you all night, my love. There's a pill for everything these days, a pill to stay awake and a pill to put you under. I took pity and sat here quiet as a ghost and didn't disturb your blest sleep. Ain't it grand to have someone watch over you?"

"So you drugged me, Gary! That was totally uncalled for. Come on, man, untie me. Let's talk about this!"

Gary took a deep drag on his cigarette, mashed the stub in the ashtray, and immediately lit up another one. He blew a fresh cloud of smoke Ray's way.

"Yeah, I gave you a pill, slipped you a Mickey, I guess you can say. They call it date rape but that's so crude. Don't worry—I didn't violate your sorry ass. I want to taste young flesh. I want something innocent for a change. I find as I get older I dream more and more of young boys. And this is America, Ray, where our dreams come true. True, true come—fucking a! That boy of yours sounds beautiful. You're really selfish keeping him all to yourself."

Ray felt a shudder go through his body. His erection died from fright. He had to talk his way out of this, to get Gary to feel pity or fear punishment.

"But Gary, whatever complaint you have with me should stay with us alone. I've told you what that poor boy is facing, the terrible family situation. Have a heart, man! The boy has nothing to do with you and me."

Even sitting Gary appeared on edge. He looked wired for an explosion, with hollowed out eyes that looked as though they would never blink again.

"In one way you're right; in another way you're wrong. In one way you're good; in another way you're bad. Go figure. But your precious boy comes into play whether you like it or not, fuckhead. You took away my youth, Ray, so I'll take away yours. Tit for tat. It's only fair. Ennie, meanie, minnie moe, catch your boyo by the toe. Or by his little dick! Why the fuck not? I don't care; what have I got to lose? Fuck it!"

Ray despaired. The facts didn't seem to matter. Their first rude encounter so many years ago was Gary stealing Ray's youth by any objective standard. As for the HIV infection, Ray's faithfulness to Pete and no intravenous drug use argued against the notion that the poison came from their household. You don't catch it from a public toilet seat or an asexual hug from an afflicted friend. Both he and Pete had friends living and dying with the disease. In gay circles you have to be a hermit not to know somebody with AIDS. No, no, NO! Gary was the promiscuous one, playing Russian roulette with random partners, feckless love. It was obvious to Ray that his erstwhile lover was operating on fumes. Ray could make an educated guess on the potent drug that Gary had taken last night. Speed doesn't last forever. Maybe he could talk the strung out man down. Sorta like those hostage dramas on TV, where the police negotiator talks a little and listens a lot and allows the pizza to be delivered and the talk never lets up. Wear the captor down; catch him off-guard. It was the only feasible strategy to follow. Ray had no back-up though; no SWAT team in the wings. He could scream bloody murder but Gary's lot was spacious, allowing lots of privacy for intimate torture. He could imagine Gary's hands cutting off his cries for help.

"You have a lot to lose, Gary. Count your blessings! You look great; you're healthier than I am; you have a professional career; you have this beautiful house and many fine things. I'm sure you have good friends. We were friends once too."

"Friends and lovers, right! I do have things, you're right about that, fuckhead, but I don't get a kick out of my toys anymore. Unless you count my drugs, yes, fucking yes, rush, rush, RUSH! I see the people at the firm noticing, staring at my back, and they want to say something but don't have the guts. My 'career' is on the skids, Ray. I'll never be a managing partner again. So don't use that argument on me! I can just see my last court appearance. 'Judge, I have to ask for a continuance because I'm dying here.' What a joke! I know you're going to tell me they'll toss me in jail for boy toy abuse. Oh, please! I just don't care! Fucking shit, we all get what we deserve. You'll be here developing bed sores while I'm getting my rocks off."

"But the priest knows!" Ray shouted. "He'll be going there to pick up the boy. You'll find an empty nest. Give it up, Gary! The boy will be long gone by the time you arrive."

"Not the way I figure the timeline. Remember, Ray, you spilled your guts last night. That priest expects the boy to be delivered at noon. I don't see him panicking right away and I know he has to stick around to sprinkle holy water around or whatever they fucking do at that shrine. I bet he'll wait till 3 or so to go to the cabin. He's the one who'll find an empty nest."

Ray wondered if prayer was the only arrow left in his quiver. In his Catholic youth he occasionally prayed for specific favors. In his troubled teenage years he prayed for God to straighten out his sexual orientation. God left him alone with that one. As an adult Ray figured that the Lord expected him to fend for himself. But the man was desperate enough now to try anything. He prayed fast and hard that Peddie would have the good sense to run away when a crazed stranger shows up. He prayed that the priest get a premonition or nudge from the higher power to go to the cabin early. He prayed that if a confrontation took place up there, that the Franciscan would be able to subdue a faithless man consumed by lust and driven by drugs. Or if a Cross in the face doesn't work, perhaps his sweet dog would turn into Cujo.

Ray could feel some give in the knots around his wrist. If Gary leaves him alive, conscious as well, there was some hope of escape. Gary looked in obvious disdain at Ray moving his lips in whispered prayer. After the personal pleas, Ray switched to the Lord's Prayer and raised his voice slightly so Gary could hear the words. Ray knew that Gary was not raised in a religious household in Denver; it wasn't a pagan upbringing or atheist or anything hostile like that to faith but there was definitely no church on Sunday. But the sentiments of the Lord's Prayer were so universal that Ray figured it wouldn't hurt for Gary to hear the words. At the very least they provided comfort to a man in need of inspiration.

Gary rushed out of the room in a flurry of white. Ray looked up in the mirror and wondered what to do next. Gary would probably be back shortly and he knew he couldn't slip either hand free without an extended struggle. If Gary saw a glimmer of hope in Ray's eyes, he very well may check the knots and tighten them so much that Ray's hands and feet would become pale white from lack of blood. So Ray stopped praying and laid still in apparent defeat. Sure enough, Ray came back shortly and beeped-beeped like the roadrunner over to the bed. Gary hadn't bothered to tie his robe. Ray noticed blotches of ash on the white cotton. It was a wonder that he hadn't set himself on fire waiting for his captive lover to wake up.

Ray looked up at his tormentor looking down. Seeing the frenzy in Gary's eyes, Ray started to pray the Lord's Prayer again, his voice rising now into a crescendo. He was terrified that Gary would grab one of the pillows and muffle forever the taunting prayer. Maybe the mere repetition of phrases like 'Thy will be done' and 'Forgive us our trespasses' and 'Deliver us from evil' would have as salutary an effect on Gary as the divine Sarah's singing had on Ray. For men reaching their time to say goodbye, providence bears repeating more than explaining. Then Gary raised his hand as though to strike down vocal faith. Ray was relieved to see that in that hand wasn't a knife but rather a roll of duct tape. One didn't die from duct tape.

Gary leaned down to urgently whisper in Ray's ear. "Say a prayer for me too."

Then Gary straightened again and unrolled with a rending noise a long piece of tape and tried to tear it off with his teeth. The thick tape wouldn't tear. With a frustrated growl Gary beeped-beeped out of the bedroom again and returned with heavy duty scissors. He didn't cut right away though. Instead he lifted the scissors and cut a circle into the air above, a weird circle, imagine an escape hatch to heaven. Then he brought the scissors down and stretched the stripe of duct tape off the edge of the nightstand to make for an easy cut. Cut made, he left the tape roll and scissors on the nightstand and rather gracefully leapt onto the bed and straddled the prone man. He placed the tape over Ray's open mouth and the Lord's Prayer became internalized. Gary brought his face down so the two men were nose to nose. Ray looked into his old lover's eyes and saw only pinpricks of hate. He could smell how sour their love had become.

"I'm off now on the yellow brick road, Ray-o! Hold down the fort for me, okay. Sweet dreams, fuckhead!"

Gary bounced off the bed, threw off his robe, and rushed into the walk-in closet. Seemingly seconds later he emerged fully dressed and was gone for good. For bad rather, in a lather—Ray laughed at the rhyme though the duct tape did a pretty good job of stifling the sound. The spirit of Pete the poet had come down to break the tension. The thought of giving up occurred to Ray. But the image of Peddie looking out the window of the cabin, feeling abandoned by his hero—the innocent boy would not let him go to his eternal rest. Ray said a final prayer before action: "Relieve me of the bondage of self. That I may do Thy will." Giving up wasn't God's will. A precious boy's life was at stake and for his sake alone, surrender was not an option. But Ray also had a less noble reason for wanting to escape the surly bonds of fate. He had to take a piss, and badly. He didn't want to wet the bed like an incontinent senior or a frightened little boy. He had always been fastidious in his personal hygiene. He often noticed that tales of derring-do left untold a certain human reality. Captain Blood never leapt onto the pirate ship or exchanged ardent sentiments with Olivia with his fly unbuttoned or pee drips on his pants.

The knot in the rope holding his right wrist to the bed post was the loosest so Ray concentrated his efforts there. By twisting and compressing his hand, the knot loosened further. He focused all his waning strength on that arm. His mood wildly gyrated from supreme confidence to utter despair as the knuckles remained stubborn. He squeezed his hand as tight as possible. Success! His right hand came free and after squeezing it a few times to get the kinks out, he was able to untie the rest of his restraints. He jumped from the bed and ran to the bathroom, wincing from the cramps in his feet and calves, letting out a grateful sigh as he took a long pee. Then he dropped to his knees and threw up into the bowl as nausea stoked by terror and euphoria caught up with him. He got up off his knees, feeling faint, jumped into the shower and turned on the hot water. He washed himself fast but thoroughly, allowing some of the soap suds from the bar and shampoo into his mouth, spitting out the stink of the vomit. He turned off the water and dried himself with as much vigor he could summon. He looked in the medicine cabinet and found mouthwash and gargled. He noticed that Gary had left his prescribed AIDS meds lined up on the shelf. Ray knew each and every one of them, side effects and the like. He opened a couple bottles and popped pills that would increase his energy, not make him yearn for bedtime.

By this time Gary had about a twenty minute head start. After hurriedly dressing, Ray was now ready to pursue. He was counting on Gary even on crystal meth having the good sense not to speed up to the Jemez, drawing the attention of the cops. Ray on the other hand could push the petal to the metal and leave to chance being pulled over. Perhaps lead the police in hot pursuit to the cabin. He knew he could simply pick up the phone for help to be on the way, perhaps a roadblock set-up. But Ray didn't trust the police to be on time or do things right. He knew from experience that they tended to be loud, clumsy, and cruel. Even if they found the unmarked private road entrance, they would roll down it with screeching sirens, music to the boy's ears perhaps but providing warning to Gary. The crazed man could flee into the vast wilderness with the boy. Or perhaps he could drive a short way up the road, turn off into a clearing (his Hummer could roll over any underbrush in the way), wait for the Keystone cops to whiz by, and then be on his way back to the main road out of Jemez Springs.

No, Ray would go after the man himself, but also enlist the aid of the priest and his dog along the way. The timing and geography should work in their favor. Several years ago Ray had taken the pilgrimage to Chimayó and knew the route the marchers take, and approximately where the Little Flower contingent should be around 9 o'clock in the morning. No major detour on the way to the Jemez cabin was called for. Then the three of them could ride like the wind after the unsuspecting Gary. Gary would be surprised as he always underestimated the resources of Ray. Bed sores indeed! He'd bring the bastard down before he could harm anybody else. In retrospect, Ray knew that he had been incredibly stupid blabbing about the boy. But he didn't realize the harm until it was too late. Ray needed to make a living amends to Peddie—fast. If Peddie ran away from death come calling, Ray knew every inch of the surrounding woods. He and the priest's Pope could track the running boy and the evil breathing down his neck.

Ray hoped it wouldn't come down to violence but decided to play it safe. On the way out he poked around the kitchen drawers and found a long knife that may come in handy. Ray had no idea if Gary was armed or not. The lawyer may have a weapon in his Hummer; the cabin could supply a couple butcher knives and a large ax. Ray couldn't see the boy defending himself with knife or ax but who knows what grandiose notions Harry Potter might give him. Ray lacked formal training in hand-to-hand combat as he missed the waning days of Vietnam with a high draft number. His last fistfight was during the difficult high school days. He was tough back then as he didn't take any shit. But now, weakened by AIDS, he was ready to go down fighting but came into the ring with more will than ways.

Would the little Franciscan monk be of any help? The priest did have his Cross to ward off evil spirits, his faithful dog to sic after the bad guy. So it would be three against one, with Christ as the wild card. Ray hoped that the hopped up Gary wouldn't have the strength of ten.

Ray jumped into his Explorer and sped out of Tesuque village. He drove over to 84/285, the Taos Highway, heading north to catch up to the pilgrims. Ray hoped to find the Santo Thérèse group before they left the main highway to go northeast to the Chimayó shrine. He drove as fast as he could though slowing to the speed limit out of habit when he spotted a couple squad cars monitoring the marchers. In the Pojoaque Pueblo area he finally saw the first pilgrims straggling along. He didn't recognize anybody. He turned off onto the two lane SR 503 and slowed down as more organized groups overflowed the shoulders. He finally saw Catholic clergy along with the lay pilgrims. He knew the Franciscan and his dog would be a highly visible presence. If there was one thing Ray knew about Father Andy, it was that he never camouflaged his faith.

CHAPTER 21

▼

The stars and half moon complimented the Little Flower pilgrims' flashlight beams and glows from the oil lanterns. The life size plastic Crucifix, the lantern on a pole, and the parish banner still led the way as several of the parishioners happily spelled the altar boys and girl, sharing their sacred burdens. The pilgrims were eager to get a taste of the suffering Jesus went through. Just a taste, for no one truly sought to die for other people's sins. They walked to save themselves from their own.

Some of the vehicles passing by beeped their horns. A couple pulled to a stop to disgorge sinners with a wee hour conversion. One fellow asked for Father Andy's blessing and then hopped back into his pickup and took off. Most of the wheelchair pilgrims and some of the able bodied (including the priest's Pope) had to take a break as the wee hour trek sapped their strength. The priest used his cell phone to call up the vans slowly following the group. The warm vans were filled with comfort foods and thermoses of coffee and hot chocolate. Sister Maria had arranged for three masseuse friends to be on call in the vans. The friar always had the impression that those who kneaded muscle tissue for a living tended to be more New Age than biblical in their beliefs. He asked Maria if his impression was at all true. She laughed and gave the spiritual lowdown on her friends. One of the women evolved from a conventional religious upbringing into an animistic faith in nature. Another—Blossom—grew up in what Maria called a "hippie commune" and eagerly embraced every passing fad in diet and exercise. Maria said she made a point of getting together with Blossom several times a year for a long chat as the masseuse always had a new twist on harmonic living to espouse. The third woman grew up Catholic and never strayed from her childhood faith. Maria said Cecilia felt she was massaging the soul along with strained muscles and flesh.

Thoughtful conversations about faith and consequences occurred all along the long line of pilgrims. Small talk was avoided like the plague. Nobody seemed to be taking the occasion lightly and everybody yearned to wear the world as a loose garment. This was one night that the priest felt like a true shepherd. He loved them all and in the darkness found their quirks of character and temperament more charming than off-putting. Andy figured the soft lighting in a bar had the same effect. Perhaps the fraternal feelings generated during a pilgrimage seemed less fuzzy the morning after.

Dawn broke as the Cities of Gold casino came into view. A long collective break for breakfast was part of the plan. The priest had arranged this unlikely location the last six years for several reasons: 1) the timing was perfect, as the casino was easily reached by dawn; 2) the buffet dining room was big enough to accommodate both the hungry pilgrims as well as die-hard gamblers; and 3) the breakfast buffet was on the house as a contribution by the pueblo council. Most of the pueblos Indians of New Mexico were long time Roman Catholics due to the historical influences of the Jesuit and Franciscan missionaries who accompanied the conquistadors. Pojoaque and the other pueblos had their own contingents on the road to El Santuario.

The casino was open twenty-four hours a day and there were numerous cars of early bird or all night gamblers in the lot. Some may have come only for the cheap breakfast. The main group of pilgrims waited impatiently inside the entrance for the stragglers to catch up. Ten minutes was the limit Father Andy permitted before hunger overcame etiquette. The priest led his flock through the main gaming room dinging with slot machines. The procession led by the altar boy carrying the Crucifix created quite a stir but had a calming effect on the slots. Christians amongst the players crossed themselves before returning to popping coins or laying down bets. The Santo Thérèse group entered the dining room and settled at the reserved tables pushed together by the kind casino staff. The altar boy gently leaned the Crucifix against the wall next to the condiments.

The priest gave his traditional fast blessing with the lighthearted appeal to gluttony at the end:

> Bless us O Lord
> For these our gifts
> From Thy bounty

Through Christ our Lord,
Amen.
Whoever eats the fastest
Gets the mostest.

A ripple of amusement swept through the pilgrims as they got up to go down the buffet line. An hour and a half break and all you can eat meant no hurry and plenty of time for seconds. Father Andy waited so he would be the last in line, figuring such restraint would show well. He filled his tray with a cheese omelet cooked to order, poached salmon, orange juice and black coffee. For the Pope he piled link sausage into a cereal bowl and asked for water in another bowl. The priest was jealous of his dog's freedom to pig out on meat while the pious pilgrims respected the fish only Friday tradition. Before eating, Andy chopped up the sausage into more digestible portions. Pope gobbled up the meat, slurped up the water, and settled down under the table for a nap. His routines had been upset mightily and the priest could sense his displeasure.

The pilgrims ate their fill and rested their legs for the final three—four hour stretch to the shrine. They figured on leaving the casino by 8 a.m. sharp so they didn't have to rush to arrive by noon. The general manager of the casino came over to say hello. Just as in previous years he apologized to the priest that gaming continued even on high holy days. He joked that pagans needed a place to go too. Father Andy always responded the same way, with a faux stern rejoinder: "They can just go to hell!" which drew guffaws along the table.

Of course even true believers were lured by the temptation of earthly gain. Several wandered out onto the game room to try their luck. If anyone won a fast fortune they didn't boast about it when they came back. They slunk into their chairs. Back in the fold they soon regained their spirit. Kindred souls as well as fellow sinners love company.

Father Andy and Sister Maria started to get everybody together for the final push. Thermoses were filled with coffee and the altar boy retrieved the Crucifix. He led the way through the gaming room into the light of day. It would be clear skies the rest of the way. Heavy coats and the oil lanterns were stashed into the vans. The Little Flower group reached the SR 503 turnoff and started up the scenic country road that ran through Nambé and then a few miles beyond to Chimayó and the old adobe church. There was no shoulder on this two lane road so the pilgrims marched on the pavement. The few vehicles moved slowly past the many marchers.

The Santo Thérèse group was just reaching Nambé when a Ford Explorer pulled to a stop next to the vanguard. Father Andy was curious and initially pleased to see Ray jump out. But where was Peddie? Ray motioned for Andy to come over to the SUV.

"Peddie is in trouble. Come with me quickly," Ray said, trying to keep panic out of his voice.

"What trouble? You were supposed to bring the boy along."

"He's back at the cabin. I'll explain on the ride up. Please let's go now!"

The priest saw he had no choice and wasn't necessarily surprised. Nothing ran smoothly on this mission of mercy during Holy Week. The mention of trouble made the priest want a trusted ally along for the ride. That ally must be a person in the know—Maria.

"Sister Maria is coming along, Ray. No argument! This is not open to discussion."

Andy turned away from Ray's open mouth and went back to his bunched-up flock. Curious faces looked to him for an explanation. He went over to Maria and whispered urgently in her ear: "Royal screw-up! We have to go pick-up the boy. No time to waste."

She nodded but looked over at the faithful. Who was to lead the pilgrims on the final leg? Sister Maria took it upon herself to choose and walked over to her friends the Alarid's. Gloria was a trusted colleague, her vice principal, and would lead with grace and without question. Gloria recognized Ray from his tutoring and asked Maria what's up. Maria saw no reason to lie.

"Good news, Gloria! The Martinez boy has been located and Father Andy and I are going to pick him up. We'll meet you at the shrine later."

Tomas Alarid impulsively reached out and grasped the nun's free hand as the two women hugged. Maria turned to go as Gloria gathered the crowd around her. Gloria proclaimed, "Peddie's been found alive! He'll be at the Santuario later. Glory to God! Glory to God!"

The surprised pilgrims broke out into a cheer and many made a sign of the Cross. Father Andy held the front door open for the nun and then joined Pope in the back seat. Ray did an awkward turnaround on the narrow road. They sped west, towards the Jemez.

The priest took a few moments composing himself before asking Ray to explain. Just before opening up his mouth to ask, Maria piped in.

"Father Andy filled me in on what's happening with Peddie, Ray. I know you're trying to help. What's gone wrong today? Is the boy safe?"

Ray was trying to calm down, for he feared the embarrassment of dry heaves. He wished he had a joint to help him mellow out as he drove like a bat out of hell. He quickly decided to tell all.

"I told the wrong guy about the boy and where he's at. I thought the guy was a friend but that turned out to be terribly wrong. Gary's gone after the boy."

The priest filled in the gaps and jumped to assumptions. The wrong guy must be gay, and probably HIV-positive. This Gary character wasn't going out of his way to save the boy. Andy needed to know how dangerous the man was.

"Who is this guy, Ray? Come on, level with us. Is he HIV-positive? Is he after the boy for sex?"

Ray looked into the rear view mirror at the agitated priest leaning against the back of the seat. The nun looked over her shoulder at Andy and shook her head in disbelief.

"The answer is yes, a sad yes to both questions, Father. I'm so sorry this happened. I didn't realize how sick and hateful Gary had become. His name is Gary Yalman; he's a lawyer, recently moved here from New York. He's the guy I talked to you about, Father, Gary from college, first love Gary. I didn't think, I just didn't think. You see there's drugs involved, crystal meth I think. I'm not sure if he's going to come to his senses. He's on his way up to the cabin right now. He's probably going to beat us up there."

Sister Maria asked the critical question. "Is this man armed? Does he have a weapon?"

"I don't know, Sister, that's why I brought this along."

Ray reached under his seat and held up the butcher knife he lifted from Gary's kitchen. The priest groaned, second-guessing his decisions this week. He should have said at the get-go, screw my vows, the boy's safety comes first. Better expulsion from the priesthood than a ruined or dead boy on his conscience. He was furious with Ray for leaving Peddie alone. And why did he have to share secrets on the eve of a glorious homecoming? Personal indiscretion and religious dogma has now led to a desperate ride to the rescue. But what manner of road warriors were they? A white clad friar, pudgy and short, whose last physical fight was in grade school; a nun lithe and athletic to be sure but with no training in mortal combat; an AIDS-ridden weakened by his disease; and a fifty pound dog sleeping right now and better at chasing rabbits than tracking human kind. Only Ray was well rested. If this Gary has a gun, holding up the Cross or brandishing a knife would offer a pathetic defense.

"Ray, Ray, now put that knife down!" the priest said emphatically. "We aren't taking any more chances. We call the police now! You're going to have to give them directions. I'm going to call 911 now."

They were now past the US 84/285 intersection, pivoting west at the Cities of Gold, and left the straggling pilgrims behind. They were on the major road up the hill to Los Alamos and the Jemez wilderness beyond. Ray looked into the rear view mirror again and nodded.

"I know I screwed up, Father. You have a cell phone?"

The priest took out the cell phone that was stashed in the all purpose pocket in the loose sleeve of his robe. He dialed 911.

"Hello, what is the nature of your emergency?" It was a woman's voice, matter of fact, sounding a tad bored, as though expecting another false alarm.

"This is Father Andy Leary from Santo Thérèse in Santa Fe. I know where the missing boy, Pedro Martinez, is and he's in danger from a man called, called Gary, Gary…"

He put the phone down and asked Ray the last name again. Yalman, Gary Yalman. The priest got back to the 911 operator.

"The guy's name is Gary Yalman. Listen, the boy is alone in a cabin up a private road near Jemez Springs. You have to send help. We're on our way there now."

The lady's voice showed more interest now. "You said Peddie is there? The Martinez boy is there? Jemez Springs, right?"

"Yes, yes, a cabin close to the springs. This Yalman guy is on drugs and out to harm the boy. He's ahead of us we think and will get there before us. We need help at the cabin. Let me find out what he's driving. Wait a minute…"

He turned again to Ray. A big Hummer, only saw it in the headlights, maybe red, Ray responded with a shrug. The priest got back on the cell.

"The guy is driving one of those Hummers, probably color red. But let me give you over to the owner of the cabin. Ray can give you directions. You see, I've only been there twice. Here's Ray."

He passed the phone over, leaned back, and began stroking his dog. Pope barely opened his eyes before drifting off again. At the speed they were going, the cabin was only a half-hour or so away. Has Gary arrived already? Is the boy in his vehicle and they're on the way out to points unknown? Is Gary chasing Peddie down or violating him in the cabin right now? The possibilities were horrid. One could hope that the man couldn't imagine Ray escaping so fast and being in pursuit so soon. Ray was spelling out his last name—Yazzie—for the operator. He gave directions to his obscure road, quarter mile past mile marker 23, and repeated them again. He then handed the phone back to the priest.

"She wants to know the number, your cell phone number, Father."

The Franciscan was frustrated by the simple request; I don't know the damn number, I never call myself. He glanced at Maria for help but she shrugged her shoulders.

"Listen, ma'am, I confess I don't know this number. I use this phone infrequently. Listen—is there a unit on the way? We'll be there shortly."

The operator's voice sounded cautious now. The priest could see her writing out, Crank? on her notepad. "Well, Father Leary, right? That's Sandoval County over there. Many state and local units are tied up with the pilgrimage. You know all about that, right, Father?"

"Yes, yes, I know about the pilgrimage. I was there with my people and now I'm here, okay?"

"The county sheriff has been notified and will respond. Please wait at the entrance to that private road so you can guide the officers to the cabin. Is that an A-O.K. on that, Father?"

Andy muttered, "A-O.K., 10-4, whatever," and then heard the click as the 911 lady hung up. The priest didn't know their routine and response time but figured they would send out one squad car at least. They couldn't afford to take a chance.

Father Andy looked at Maria and put his hands up in a 'we'll see' gesture. They had reached Los Alamos and went through the small town in record time. The priest figured that if they ran across the city police or lab security, they could flag the squad down. Or since every traffic law on the books was being violated, the cops may pull them over. A priest in a friar's robe would be taken seriously and the police persuaded to caravan on the double up to the cabin. But the police weren't around when you needed them.

They were now back in nature whizzing by heavily forested areas with scattered clearings where the labs located their outlying work buildings. Then they came down a rise and around the bend and saw again the Valdes Caldera preserve, the vast valley looking so tranquil, the grazing animals so happy to be the object of binoculars and not gun sights. The priest vividly remembered passing this way before, once praying anxiously that he find a live boy at the springs, the second with Sister Maria that finally brought to the surface Andy's desperate desire. Now Father Andy was at full circle, praying that he find the boy safe and sound at the wilderness cabin. He assumed Sister Maria was doing the same.

That what they were really made for—prayer. Violence of biblical proportions was not part of their ministerial brief. Wrath was reserved for almighty God, not mere mortals. But the priest doubted that God was going to strike down this Yalman down. No doubt He had the power. But on this earthly sphere God expected the faithful to do the fighting. There was no easy way out.

Father Andy wondered if they should game plan various scenarios. A movie came to mind, The Dirty Dozen, where the convict soldiers and the hard-bitten Lee Marvin singsonged their tactical war plans in rhyming couplets on the plane ride into Nazi-occupied France. The priest smiled slightly at the thought of this motley crew creating a rhyming or reasonable sequence of surprise attack. Most likely the sheriff's deputies will be at the turn-off or arriving shortly. The priest knew he should pray for that conclusion but lurking in his mind was the recurring image of monk as a hero sleuth. Pounding a cross into the heart of the vampire. Shielding the boy from tainted blood.

The rescuers dwelled on fantasies and fears the final few miles. They reached the rutted road and no black and white was visible, no sirens heard. Should they wait as directed? Ray decided that issue for all by not stopping or even slowing down. Bounce, bounce, bounce on the washer board surface. Pope jumped up, rudely awakened, and hung out the window with his nose on alert. Would the dog be called upon to track or attack? The priest's heart began to pound as he envisioned a gun being pointed at the boy…either boy.

The cabin was almost four miles off NM 4, the Jemez main road. Ray did slow to a crawl the last 100 yards or so. There was no police car pulled up there. But the Hummer was there, Gary's pet, blue. No one was in it; no one was in sight. Were the predator and his prey in the cabin, or was there a chase in the woods going on? Ray stopped quietly behind the SUV. They got out without slamming the Explorer's doors, and gratefully without a yelp from the dog. They approached the cabin door fearing what lay beyond.

CHAPTER 22

▼

They crept up the wood stairs onto the weathered plank porch, wincing at every creak. The side windows were open and the lacey curtains fluttered in the breeze. There was no sound of living or dying behind those curtains—no screams or moans, thank God, just silence. The priest didn't feel any eyes upon him, eyes red and malevolent, a hand twitching on the butt of the ax. Murder-suicide was the worst case for the boy, though the safest situation for the rescuers. The best hope was that the boy was out there running for his life or going to ground. He looked over at Ray and saw that the man had the butcher knife at the ready. Where have my moral qualms, my due respect for church doctrine, brought us to? The brink of bloody violence, that's where. He wondered if they should break down the door or peek through the windows first. Sister Maria took the initiative and slowly turned the knob.

Maria pushed and the old door swung open with their fear amplifying the creaks into a cacophony. The dog knew no fear or at least smelled no danger. Pope rushed in with the wannabe saviors at his heels. The main room was as Ray had left it, no signs of struggle, nothing disturbed. He went quickly to the bedroom door that was open a crack and confirmed that nobody was there. Andy's terror dissipated but he now knew that the great outdoors contained all the fear in the world.

"They must be out there," the Franciscan said. "Let's hope the boy is giving him a run for his money. There must be a zillion places to hide. We wait for the police, yes?"

Ray responded angrily. "We wait for the police, no! The boy is in danger and the damn cops are running late. We have to go after him. We have to find Peddie!"

With a disgusted mutter Andy went to the door and motioned to the great expanse. "But where do we go, man? Where do we look? We have 360 on the compass. Come to think of it, I don't even have a compass. Which direction, Ray?"

The nun, quietly observing the two men ragging on each other, spoke up in the gentle but firm tone she uses on the playground.

"You're both right, if that's any comfort. We can't sit and wait but it won't help to go off half-cocked either. Come on, Ray, you know these woods. Where would Peddie go, what trail would he follow?"

"The river! He knows how to get to the river and we saw some fishermen down there the other day. If he finds no one there, and he can't shake Gary, he may run to the hot springs. We went there three times since we came out here. Peddie should be able to follow that trail and if Gary loses sight of him, well, I don't think Gary's much of an outdoorsman."

The priest interjected. "Yes, yes, and there may be people soaking at the springs too. People who can protect the boy, fight off one man."

Ray went into the kitchen area and pulled out a drawer. His pointing finger counted as the priest and nun heard his whisper: "One, two, three, there!" Then he rushed to the small pantry and found there what he was counting on. He returned to the religious at the doorstep now carrying a small ax to compliment the knife.

"I think all my knives are still there, and this is my only ax. So unless he grabbed a knife from his own house, or has a gun, we should be okay. Let's go, Father, let's get after him."

Maria spoke up again. "One of us has to stay here or drive back to the road to wait for the police. They have to get the lowdown on what's happening."

Andy saw the logic in dividing their forces and was too antsy to be the one to wait. "You're right, Sister, and I want you to wait. Ray and I will do the chasing, right? I don't know what makes more sense, sitting tight or driving over to Jemez for help. But it strikes me that this Gary may circle around or he may be out there now, waiting for us to clear out. That Hummer out there..."

Suddenly the priest realized what needed to be done. He knew nothing about disabling engines but not even a Hummer could go far on rims alone. Andy looked at Ray and demanded, "Give me that!" Ray meekly offered the priest the choice of ax or knife. Andy grabbed the ax. He hustled over to the Hummer.

Several hacks per tire were sufficient. The priest enjoyed the frenzied hacking and seeing the Hummer tilt with three of its tires deflated. Andy realized that he was getting overwrought. He felt like raising the ax above his head like a primeval warrior and letting out a war whoop. With a quivering hand the chagrined priest gave the ax back.

Andy wasn't sure if holding on to his cell phone made more sense than turning it over to Maria. In the high and low pursuit he may reach a sweet spot where a call to the cops was possible. On the other hand, Maria in the Explorer should be able to use it on the short run out to the highway or into town to find the errant cops. He handed the phone over to the nun.

"You may find this handy, Maria. Ray and I know these woods pretty well so we won't get lost out there. Tell the police to send help towards the McCauley Springs I guess. If we're right, that's where we're likely to end up."

Ray motioned with the ax in the direction of the river. "We have to go now, Father. Let's go—please!"

"I know, Ray, but let's give the dog a chance to help. Is there a piece of clothing that Peddie has been wearing?"

The Pope wasn't trained for tracking but was as game as his master. McCauley Springs were several miles away over rough cut trail. If Peddie is hiding somewhere off trail, the dog may be able to follow the scent. Ray understood and went into the cabin. The priest looked out upon the vast wilderness. Very little was undiscovered territory as backpackers had been hiking known trails and breaking new ones over the years. Father Andy wasn't a novice in back country hiking. He knew how to rough it. But the threat of the weather turning or wild animals attacking paled compared with the danger that Gary posed. He was out there, a feral man.

Father Andy wondered if the man had been raised Catholic, whether the sight of a white robed friar would lead him to prostrate himself and beg forgiveness. Given what Ray had said about crystal meth mixing with lust incarnate, the priest doubted that Gary was going to go down easy. Force may be required. A measured use of force, justified in the eyes of God to save innocent life.

Ray came out of the cabin with a bottle of spring water, the Sony Walkman around his neck, and gym shorts in hand. Andy looked curiously at the Walkman and Ray explained, "Hearing Sarah may offer the boy some comfort." The priest thought of the downside, giving Gary warning of their pursuit, but he said nothing as he hadn't a clue if a siren song would scare the man away or pacify the beast. Ray gave the shorts to the priest. Andy knelt on one knee before Pope and put the shorts up to his nose. He hoped that Peddie's scent was still strong. The dog and the boy seemed to bond the other day and that may help too.

As always the priest was amazed by how a dog was stimulated by smells that human beings dismiss as gross. Also Andy noticed that Pope sensed on the wind either sounds or scent that the priest couldn't smell or hear. Father Andy prayed that today would be no different. He stroked the dog behind the ears and then pointed in the general direction of the hot springs.

"Go find Peddie, boy! Peddie!"

The dog took off and the priest got up to follow. As he double-timed it past Maria, he had the impulse to hug her for good luck but settled for his hand grazing hers. As he and Ray reached the edge of the meadow and were about to plunge into the woods, Andy looked back half-expecting Maria to be wistfully waving. Instead, she was jumping into the Explorer to tear back to the main road.

Ray deftly followed the running dog but the priest soon fell behind. His ritual sandals were fine for the magisterial pace of the pilgrimage but flimsy for a chase over rough ground. He could feel the chaffing and knew the leather would soon bite through the flesh. Andy was suddenly grateful Sarah Brightman was along as her lilting voice kept him pointed in the right direction:

> When I'm alone
> I dream of the horizon
> And words fail me
> There is no light
> In a room where there is no sun
> And there is no sun if you're not here
> With me, with me
> From every window
> Unfurl my heart
> The heart that you have won
> Into me you've poured your light
> The light found by the side of the road
>
> Time to say goodbye
> Places that I've never seen or
> Experienced with you
> Now I shall
> I'll sail with you
> Upon ships across the seas
> Seas that exist no more
> I'll revive them with you

The song stirred deep emotions in both of the men rushing to save the boy. For Ray, the 'you' was both Pete and Peddie. He missed terribly his long time companion and still felt guilt over the circumstances of his passing. If only he had stayed in that fateful night, gotten drunk at home or whacked off or called Pete long distance and talked and talked, he would be settled in happy domesticity this day instead of running half-crazed after the fully crazed. Was it time to say goodbye to the boy? Did he screw up that selfless love too? For that's what he wanted to feel for the boy, something selfless for a change, a shining moment. And how faithful was he to the ideal? He abandoned the boy in search of wanton desire, a one night stand, morning wake up to evil. Peddie deserved better than to be running for his life at age 10.

Father Andy also turned from physical discomfort to concern for the innocent boy somewhere up ahead. The priest had never experienced real terror in child-hood and too felt responsible for failing the boy. But he knew this was no time to dwell on regret. Later, later—a Catholic priest always makes time for guilt. Andy's emotional connection to the boy was far more tenuous than Ray's. They didn't have the same history. But Peddie was one of his children, an angelic pres-ence amongst his flock. Father Andy took his role as shepherd as a sacred com-mitment.

The irritation of his sandal's leather played again on the friar's mind. Perhaps barefoot was better but his soles were hardly trail ready. No, he would stay hell-bent-for-leather awhile longer. The Sarah song brought to mind the woman he left behind. The priest realized that the Maria of his dreams was fading away as she shed her religious trappings in favor of a secular life. His colleague Maria had always been there for him, a true friend and trusted sister in the service of Christ. Andy realized the folly of wanting more. Either embrace God or a woman; as a priest you must choose. The problem lies with the fact that this woman is more lissome and easier to embrace. The Little Flower provided the answer if he would but pay attention. Pray, pray, pray hard, for prayer is a surge of the heart, a cry of recognition, a whisper of love, embodying both trial and joy. From those trials, the priest realized, comes liberation from fear. In this frantic search for Peddie the priest was finding himself.

The sound of a distant siren distracted Andy, making him turn his head while still running, and he stumbled over a broken branch. He cursed as he fell and scrambled fast to his feet, his white robe soiled, and gazed towards the out of sight cabin. The police were finally on their way. The cops were clumsy and loud but at least they had nightsticks and big guns. If Gary was packing, the cavalry couldn't arrive soon enough. The priest wasn't sure if the county sheriff would be able to navigate their way to the springs using Ray's cabin as the starting point. They may have to backtrack to the campground and take the well marked trail from there. Delay, delay, delay! That route would take about two hours by foot. Perhaps ATV's or fast horses could be called upon. Maybe a helicopter was available.

The sound of the diva was now way ahead as Ray and the dog were out of sight. Father Andy didn't like the idea of Pope cornering a dangerous man without him being there. He decided off with the sandals so he could run faster. If he kept his eyes on each footfall, he could avoid broken branches and prickers. He kept his sandals in hand, partly out of nostalgia, but also figuring he could whack Gary with them. Fresh blood was already on them.

The fear of his dog running into trouble gave Andy a second wind. Soon Ray was in sight again, still far ahead, and Andy caught a glimpse of his dog. Pope wasn't barking, which was good, as he saved his bark for when prey were cornered, usually up the tree or down the hole. The priest ran faster. He hadn't run like this in years. He was sweating freely and brought up the loose sleeves of his robe several times to mope his brow and prevent the salt from stinging his eyes. He doubted that he could keep up this pace much longer. He had been walking all night and now God was asking His disciple to run all day. But then he heard his Pope start to bark. The music stopped abruptly. The priest's heart began to pound as hard as his bare feet.

The pools of hot water making up McCauley Springs were located up a small rise. From the direction the priest was coming, the faint trail dropped into a trough and rose abruptly, making for slow going the last twenty-five yards or so. With the music off, the dog's barking became louder and persistent. It sounded as though Pope had cornered the man. The priest thought he caught the faint sound of raised voices on the wind. He couldn't see a damn thing yet. The mid-day sun through the branches was bright and his eyes stung with sweat. He reached the rising path and didn't pause to gather himself. His white robe, fine for walking on the level, now proved a hindrance running uphill. Andy tripped and only kept his nose out of the dirt by catching his falling body with outstretched hands. The sandals were cast by the wayside now. The priest struggled to his bruised and bloody feet again, feeling faint headed, and grabbed exposed roots of the scrub trees for balance and a leg up. The Franciscan began to curse again in frustration but then caught himself. He changed seamlessly to chanting prayer: "God's will be done, God's will be done, God's will be done." He wasn't sure if God was providing the final kick but he finally made it to the top, every fiber of his being aching from the supreme effort. He looked through burning eyes at what was happening.

Gary was holding Peddie close to his body, arms wrapped around the boy's neck, the two standing with their backs to the largest pool of steaming water. Both were fully clothed and no weapon was visible, thank God. Ray was standing a few yards away, his arms outstretched, the butcher knife and ax butt down in a gesture of appeasement, while Pope was leaping back and forth, his fur ruffled and ears on alert, growling now that he saw his master had shown up. The dog knew something was up, instinctively keeping Gary at bay, but not knowing how to separate the innocent from evil. The eyes of all the characters told the story. Gary's were red and unfocused, flitting from the growling dog to the pleading Ray, pleads backed by the threat of hacks and slashes, then looking down at the delicious boy squirming in his grasp, and now seeing a monk in a dirty white robe rushing up to join the argument. Peddie's eyes were red too, from crying, his terror obvious with a fiend's arm around his neck. Ray's eyes were crystal clear in comparison as if he knew his destiny was on hand, a living amends to make through gentle persuasion or brute force. The priest's smarting eyes were darting almost as much as Gary's, Andy trying to estimate the situation, what action to take, what words to use, what prayer to say! "God's will..." was okay as far as it goes but what exactly does He suggest I do here and now.

Ray turned and was grateful to see that Father Andy had arrived. His emotional appeal to Gary wasn't working; indeed, the man seemed to be getting more agitated with each heartfelt word. Now with a human ally present, even though the good father seemed to be on his last legs, together they should be able to rush Gary before he strangles the boy or snaps his neck. Odds are the boy would survive. But Ray wanted a certainty rather than a probability. He owed the boy that. And there was the question of unspoken coordination between the priest and himself. I mean, I can't tell Gary, "Hey man, I need to consult with Father Andy here on how to tackle you. Just hold tight, okay?" No, more persuasion had to be tried, words with a spiritual slant, framed by a professional. If a miracle was required, better a priest to beseech God. Ray hadn't a clue if any remnants of Gary's soul existed beyond the frenzied skin. Can a soul coexist with speed and lust? Ray knew that Gary had been raised in a non-religious household. Gary's parents related some funny and wistful stories on Ray's only visit years ago to their Denver home; stories about Gary being raised in a commune during their 1950's beatnik days. Ray doubted that Gary was a believer in the sweet hereafter. But then Ray suddenly remembered the man's urgent whisper in his ear: "Say a prayer for me too." Gary's voice had sounded resigned rather than sarcastic. Perhaps the man still knew right from wrong and could be persuaded to refrain from mortal sin.

Father Andy figured from body language that Ray had been pleading for the boy's life. He knew it wasn't two strangers confronting each other. But whatever logic was used, whatever appeal to pity or for old time's sake, the man was still holding the boy against his will. Father Andy had dealt with drug abusers on many occasions in his ministry but usually it was in a halfway house or rehab setting. The patients were usually weaning away from their drug of choice rather than embracing it still. If Ray was correct, the crystal meth was still rising in the blood. The priest suddenly wished that he had a flask of Jameson's. Andy didn't want to go to war without liquid courage on his breath.

"Gary, I'm Father Leary from the Little Flower Parish in Santa Fe," Andy said by way of introduction, happy that his voice sounded stronger than he felt. "I know you're probably not happy to see me and I'm sorry we have to make each other's acquaintance under these circumstances. I don't know the law of man in these circumstances but I do know the law of God. He's a very forgiving God and I bet if you stop now, the civil authorities will be understanding and appreciative too. But Ray told me that you're a lawyer so you know the score. I don't think you really want to hurt that boy. He's just a boy, Gary, why don't you let him come with us? We walk in one direction; you walk the other. How about it?"

Andy thought his words might be registering; at least the man appeared to be listening. His grip on the boy wasn't lessening though. Peddie wasn't wiggling any longer as though he instinctively recognized that Father Andy had a chance to talk the crazy man out of hurting him. When Gary pulled up to the cabin Peddie rushed out expecting it to be Ray and instead finding an edgy stranger. Peddie didn't trust the reassuring words. ("Ray sent me up here to pick you up. He's over at the shrine waiting for us. His car broke down; that's why he sent me. Have you ever driven in a Hummer? It's real cool. Come with me now.") The boy began backing away warily as Gary walked slowly towards him. The man's eyes were off in never-never land, red-rimmed, and he carried a lit cigarette in his hand. He put the cigarette in his mouth, freeing up both hands. Peddie turned and took off. He heard the man curse and the boy looked back expecting pursuit. But the man was looking over at the Hummer, then back at the fleeing boy. His hesitation gave Peddie some breathing space as he reached the temporary safety of the tree line. Just before the boy plunged out of sight the man took up the chase on foot.

Peddie knew he needed to find help fast. The river was the first place to look for it. No one was there; perhaps up river towards the main road was the way to go. But Peddie knew people might be at the hot springs too. He and Ray had run across some in the waters. Ray told him that good people who love the outdoors go to soak there. Peddie knew the way and it was almost a secret way. The crazy man wouldn't be able to figure it out. But then the boy heard a noise behind him and turned and saw the never-never man not twenty yards away and coming up fast. Peddie took off again—the secret way.

He hoped to lose the man in the woods. The man stumbled and fell several times but kept coming; most of all kept the boy in sight. After the scramble up the hill Peddie was spent. No good people were at the springs. He turned to bravely face the bad man.

Gary said nothing to the priest. Father Andy couldn't stand the silence. Silence may imply consent in lawyers' circles but they were far from the halls of justice. He looked over at Ray who motioned subtly with his hand. The priest assumed that Ray was trying to tell him that we were running out of time for words. But Father Andy wanted to hear from the lawyer first before jumping him.

"What does it profit you to harm the boy, Gary? Where's the justice in picking on the innocent?" the priest asked, trying to goad the man in thinking like a lawyer again. "I'm sure you've run across in your practice people who hate with a passion. Do you really want to join them in their little bickering corner of the world? Do you really want to go out like that? Be as bad as that. Come on, Gary, you don't want to live out your days in a cage. Let us help you. Give the boy a break and give yourself a chance to live."

Gary's face flushed as though all his blood was rising to the surface. He had initially looked bewildered as his plans to ravage Ray's boy were coming to naught. Now he was just angry, so very angry.

"What else did that fuckhead tell you about me? Did he tell you that I caught the bug from him? That we made something we called love and the bastard we produced was AIDS. He should have warned me, the asshole, full disclosure. We go back years, priest, and as college kids we had quite a thing going. Loved each other and everything that goes with love. To be fucked this way by a lover and friend. It just isn't fair!"

No, the priest agreed without saying so, it wasn't fair. Pronouncements of love should not be a death sentence. A beautiful thing, going naked into the arms of a loved one. The consequences should be death-defying.

"I'm sorry it came to that, Gary, but we have to live through our troubles without taking it out on the innocent." The priest raised his voice to Old Testament proportions. "For God's sake, man, let the boy go. You're a child of God just as Peddie is. For the sake of your soul, let that boy go!"

He knew he must speak with absolute authority, with nary a false note. The words must ring with eternal truth. The priest flashed back on that conversation he had with Ray about Hemingway and John Donne. That sad quotation—'Ask not for whom the bell tolls, it tolls for thee'—came into the calculating mind of the Franciscan. Father Andy was sifting through what might work to keep the man talking. No doubt Gary felt sorry for himself, the aggrieved party. How do you move a man from self-pity to pity for a little boy?

Whatever—the words seemed to be having a positive effect. Gary loosened his grip on Peddie's neck. The boy responded by biting his wrist. Gary yelped in pain and jerked the wounded wrist away from Peddie's mouth. With the back of his good hand he hit the boy's face and Peddie fell down to the ground. Ray rushed forward to shield the boy from the enraged man. Gary, exposed now, holding his wrist to staunch the bleeding, reacted too slowly to the dog leaping at him. He lost his footing on the bank and, with Pope's teeth still locked on his upper thigh, fell with a splash into the shallow pool. With the shock of sudden immersion in hot water the dog let go. The man gained his footing before the dog. Gary grabbed Pope by his fur and hit the dog with his fist. Then he heaved the whimpering dog out of the pool and turned to scramble out the far side.

Father Andy was at first immobilized by the quick fire action. Then he saw in horror his dog struck and flung from the pool. That did it! The time for human reason and biblical injunction was over.

"You son of a bitch!" the priest roared.

Andy leaped into the water and onto Gary's back. Under the weight he went down on his knees in the water and the two men grappled. The priest, totally enraged, plummeted Gary with his fists. Gary tried to fight back but seemed to lack a fighting spirit. But as the priest finally came to his senses and unclenched his fists, the man slapped him across the face hard.

More insulted than hurt, the priest screamed again. "You son of a bitch, son of a bitch!"

Father Andy went after the bleeding Gary again, grabbing him by the neck and pushing him under the water. "Had enough, had enough, had enough!" Bringing the man up for air only to be kneed in the groin. The low blow was cushioned by the water and their closeness but hurt regardless. The priest took him down again and this time didn't bring him up until he was limp. Father Andy was in another world entirely, in a little bickering corner of it, where emotions rule the roost. Where you live to fight another day, but the other fella doesn't.

Andy felt a hand on his shoulder and turned to face the new threat. It was Ray. "Settle down, Father. It's over, finally over. Let it go!"

Father Andy came out of it. He looked down with sudden horror at Gary floating face down in the pool, his blood spreading in the water. What have I done? The priest looked past Ray to Peddie sitting dazed on the bank, holding the dog licking his bruises, the boy with a trickle of blood on his chin. Now whose blood was that? Was it Gary's, from the bite on the wrist? Andy felt a deep stab of fear. What's done is done, God's transcendent will or man's overwhelming desire. The ones the priest cared about had survived this Good Friday. The Passion of Christ's Crucifixion was over for another year. But the priest had done God's business the hard way. The Franciscan wondered if the stains could ever come out of his white robe. It was a borrowed robe after all, and would have to be returned to the Dominicans in original condition. Tomorrow he could go back to his order's brown. Perhaps the feeling would be as if he was reborn. The priest looked down at the reddening water and lunged for dry land, to escape drowning in his victim's blood.

*   *   *   *

The police helicopter arrived first. The chopper couldn't land as the closest meadows weren't spacious enough. So the exhausted survivors waited for help by land. Peddie, knocked senseless by Gary's blow, was lying with his hurting head resting against Ray's leg. The priest had bruises and an ache in his groin but no permanent injury. His poor feet would need several days of inactivity to heal. He did hobble back to the heartbreak rise to retrieve his ritual sandals. Pope had settled down next to the friar for a snooze, seemingly not damaged by rough treatment. Ray was worn to a frazzle but otherwise okay. He actually slept well last night under the spell of Gary's little blue pill. The terror at the thought of losing Peddie and the frantic tracking through back country had taken its toll on his compromised immune system. Germs on the make sensed open pores in the skin.

The men and the boy were all talked out and just needed peace and quiet for awhile. Nature was cooperating; quiet except for the rustling of leaves in the wind, an occasional squawk of birds, a squirrel scampering by the sleeping dog that barely fluttered an eyelid. One bird landed on Gary's floating body and began peaking away. The priest knew that they should shoo it away and pull the body from the water but Andy was in a dreamy state of indifference. He didn't have the energy to show respect for the dead.

It wasn't long before men on horseback showed up. One wore a uniform and the other two looked like cowboys. The priest figured that the latter were posse members, volunteers in rural New Mexico countries skilled at search and rescue, tracking desperadoes too. The riders took in the scene from on high their horses: the boy everybody in God's creation was looking for; a monk in a muddy, bloody robe; a dog stretching with a wary eye on the neighing horses; and a thin, tall man, a long knife and ax on his one side, the boy on the other. Beyond the living a body floated face down in a pool with steam rising and a carrion bird atop.

The deputy got off his horse and casually kept his hand on his holster as he approached Ray. He asked the thin man to turn over the knife and ax butts first. Ray complied. The deputy asked him to stand for a frisking. Ray submitted though his body language protested. He was ordered to sit down again and make no trouble. The friar was not frisked. Father Andy wondered if the deputy was Catholic, and feared violating the person of a monk. If I had murder on my mind, I would wreak havoc in sheep's clothing. The Franciscan looked over at the floating body. He knew he should be confessing that I did it, I did it, dear God I did it! Ray had nothing to do with it, leave your filthy hands off him! It was self-defense, pure and simple, and the boy's life was at stake. His dog's life he would leave out of the equation. The deputy may not be a dog lover. Awhile ago the priest read an interview of a famous songstress being asked about the creative origins of her signature love song. She admitted that she wrote it with her precious dog in mind. The men in her life played second fiddle.

The deputy looked the boy over, noting the dazed expression and heavy bruise on his forehead. He spoke into his radio, summoning the chopper to return and drop a stretcher to airlift Peddie to a hospital. The priest finally stirred, taking the deputy aside to pass along the message to have the boy checked for HIV infection as well as concussion. Andy motioned over to the body in the spring. The deputy repeated, "Infected, huh," and nodded with a grim expression.

The two men and the dog would have to hike over to the Jemez campground where the Sandoval County sheriff and Sister Maria waited. One posse member would stay to preserve the crime scene. The horses were too tuckered to handle two riders atop. The deputy, out of respect and noting the priest's distressed feet, told Andy to ride his horse while he walked beside. A similar invitation wasn't extended to Ray. The thin man would have to walk. So after the helicopter whisked Peddie away, the men left the springs behind.

Deputy Lara asked the priest if he wanted to talk about it, about the events leading up to the deadly confrontation. The priest decided there was nothing to hide, and told it all, the incest included. Given the facts, Andy asked Lara if Ray was likely to be arrested. The deputy said the decision was not up to him. Then the priest asked if he was going to be arrested for drowning Gary. Lara said the story as related certainly indicated justified homicide. But the sheriff and district attorney will go over the facts and decide the disposition. As for the alleged sexual abuse by the father, that was a no-brainer. The accused is removed from the house immediately or the children placed in protective custody, pending investigation. The deputy told the priest: "I probably shouldn't be telling you this, Father, but child abuse is one crime where you are guilty until proven innocent."

Father Andy wondered aloud if he was going to be sleeping in his bed tonight. Lara didn't see why not but said, "Now don't take that as gospel, Father," chuckling a bit at his quip. It took a moment for the humor to register but then the priest laughed, too hard, too loud. The deputy told him to hush now as he was spooking the horses.

CHAPTER 23

▼

As the priest feared, Ray was handcuffed and read his rights when they arrived at the parking lot. Father Andy and Sister Maria protested but the Sandoval County sheriff told them that by their own admission, the suspect had spirited the boy away and stashed him in a remote cabin. Whether it was shelter from a troubled family situation, or abduction for immoral ends, would be subject to further investigation. The dead body complicated the situation to no end. While the priest copped to the killing, it had to be determined if the motivation was self defense and protection of the boy or maybe there was more there than meets the eye. Father Andy angrily responded, "Well, arrest me then. I'm ready to go!" The priest offered up his wrists for cuffing. The sheriff smiled and came up with a clever turn of phrase: "No, Father, I guess I can release you on God's recognizance. But don't go getting the idea that your church can offer you sanctuary. That notion went out with the Middle Ages."

Ray looked back at the religious just before one of the deputies pushed him head first into the caged back seat of a cruiser. His face had a mocking smile that the priest read as told you so. The fag gets his ass hauled away while the man of God is given every benefit of the doubt. Father Andy had the impulse to shout out that he would pray for him but sensed that Ray wasn't in the mood. Ray needed hard-nosed legal representation as well as God's intercession. Andy wondered if Ray had a lawyer he could call upon.

The Sandoval County sheriff, Max Ramirez, huddled with the priest and nun, asking about the allegation of incest. He had already heard a little from Sister Maria but wanted to hear more from the priest. A law enforcement professional with many years of hard-bitten experience, Ramirez betrayed no shock over the story. He had had his fill of human folly and low life; rarely does a cop see the good in people. He told the two that given the present danger to the Martinez girl, he would have one of his deputies drive them back to Santa Fe right away so the story could be repeated to Sheriff Baca. The concussed boy had been airlifted to St. Vincent's Hospital in the capital city. Since the allegation originated with Peddie, the investigation of incest moved back to the scene of the crime. Ramirez shrugged his shoulders and said that matter was out of his jurisdiction.

On the ride to Santa Fe in the back of a squad car Andy gave to Maria a sanitized version of the chase and fight to the death. His guilt didn't prevent him from glorifying his role in the righteous violence. In this version of events the harm to the boy was the instigating factor rather than Andy's visceral response to his dog being struck and tossed. The slap in the face, the kick in the groin—given the provocation, would God expect His disciple to turn the other cheek. If the priest had let the rabid man run, a poor hiker may have fallen victim. Maria listened with great interest. But she kinda took the glory out of the gore by asking: "Did you really have to kill him?"

Andy knew the nun had touched upon the crux of the matter. To say that the drug-addled, HIV-riddened man was asking for it or needed to be put down for the public health was for God to know, not for His disciple to assume. If he had let the unarmed man go, the police was likely to catch Gary when and if he came out of the wilderness. Andy didn't know if he could do justice to the primal feeling he experienced in the heat of battle, explain so soon that troubling reality to the woman of his dreams. Perhaps with time would come perspective. But the priest sensed he would be haunted till his own death by Maria's question: "Did you really have to kill him?"

They were dropped off at Santa Fe County police headquarters. Sheriff Baca was expecting them. He took all three, dog included, into his office for a frank talk. After hearing the priest out, with Maria occasionally interjecting, Baca shook his head sadly and said to Andy: "So bottom-line on Sunday during the search you had your suspicions and told me nothing. On Tuesday you knew for sure where the boy was and you didn't call me up. On Thursday you go back to that cabin and find the boy missing and you just go on your merry way. And today a man dies at your hands, a bad man by your account, and the boy came within a whisker of being raped and maybe killed. And now you tell me his sister was in danger of sexual attack by her own father each of these long days and nights. Shame on you, Padre, shame, shame!"

The priest had no ready response but for contrition. The confidentiality of the sacrament of penance and reconciliation was a weak defense when measured against the known and unknown consequences of delay. The known was a ten year old boy being terrorized and knocked about, his sick attacker beaten to a pulp and drowned; the unknown was whether Gabby had been abused the last few nights. Even now, the boy's bite on Gary's wrist may mean that Gary kills after dying. And as for ongoing harm to Gabby, even if Raul had kept his dirty hands to himself this Holy Week, the priest could just imagine the probable trauma from sleeping up the hall from her molester. Every noise in the night could be Raul creeping towards her door. The priest felt sudden bitterness towards the Church and its inflexible rules. In a world demanding and often deserving situational ethics, the Roman Catholic Church stood unbending, saying to its faithful both lay and ordained, do it my way or hit the highway to hell. If worse comes to worst, Father Andy knew his conscience would rag him without mercy. Perhaps for dogmatic purity he would receive his just reward in heaven. Maybe God would grace him with an explanation of how greasing the way to a cruel fate on earth leads to a kind afterlife.

Sheriff Baca's fit of anger seemed to pass and he asked the two religious if they wanted to come along to witness Raul's arrest. The priest said yes, yes; the nun nodded okay. Father Andy asked how Peddie was doing at the hospital and Baca said he would check. He made the call in their presence and got the doctor treating him on the line. He listened more than talked, and did share the plan for the imminent arrest of the suspect dad. The sheriff listened some more, apparently to a second physician too. Baca ended the conversation by saying, "If you think that's best for the boy, doc, we'll be right over. Bueno."

Baca hung up and looked at Andy and Maria. "A surprise request from Peddie's doctor, actually the shrink they consulted. Physically I guess he's okay, maybe a mild concussion, some bruises around his neck. No indications of HIV infection by the way but the doctors say it's a little early for that to show up. At any rate, the shrink says the boy has shrunk into himself—these docs sometimes have a sense of humor, believe me—and maybe it would help him to see his father taken into custody. That might help the boy to feel safe. Anyway, his mom and siblings don't know he's back yet and a reunion might help the boy come alive again. Peddie will be going back to the hospital for observation overnight. So we take the doctor's advice, no?"

The sheriff, Andy, Maria and the Pope drove over to St. Vincent's in Baca's 'moving command center', a supercharged SUV. Following in caravan were deputies in two conventional squad cars with the caged back seats.

The sheriff elaborated on what was said on the other end of the line. "The doc hadn't heard yet about the incest from the boy or much of anything else. You heard me tell him that I would have to question Peddie sooner rather than later. We do need some confirmation before a successful prosecution. The boy needs to tell on tape what happened, and the girl has to be willing to testify. But don't worry—we can hold the drunk without bail for awhile and arrange for a home away from home for the mother and kids if some slick lawyer springs him. I know, Father, that I was thinking on Sunday that Amelia was involved in some way in Raul's killing of the boy. I'm so happy I was wrong. The mother will be overjoyed to see her long lost son. No telling though how she'll react when I blindside her with the nature of the charge against her husband. We trade a good one for a bad one. How's that, Father, a good one for a bad one?"

The priest was thrilled that the sheriff was confiding in him again. Andy had some serious doubts about the plan the psychiatrist had cooked up and the sheriff embraced. The burly Raul may be both drunk and belligerent; he seemed the type to have guns around the house. Though three deputies and one sheriff should be able to handle him, Andy could see the man barricading himself in the house with his daughter as hostage. His mangy dogs would give warning of the caravan coming up to the house. The dogs may even threaten the intruders. Andy didn't like the image of police guns being fired at poor animals defending their turf. The Franciscan in the back seat of the command SUV stroked Pope's fur and whispered to him that everything would be okay; he could stay in the vehicle and they would be home soon. The sun was going down and it was time to go home for well deserved rest.

All of them, with the Pope on leash, piled out on the SUV and went into the hospital reception area. Despite the sheriff's presence and the friar's robe, the stern receptionist wouldn't allow the dog to go up the elevator to the ward where Peddie was being treated. Father Andy was incensed, as he often brought Pope on his regular morning visits to Catholic patients. The dog had all his shots after all and provided the seriously sick with a furry and fun diversion. Andy argued, "Evelyn lets us up there all the time," referring to the friendly morning receptionist. But shift change had occurred and the evening gatekeeper wasn't about to bend the rules.

Baca pulled the priest over to a chair to calm him down. They all sat waiting for the boy to be brought down. Andy tried to pray his fear and impatience away. After about fifteen minutes, Peddie was brought down, accompanied by a doctor and nurse. The boy was walking slowly as though in a daze. But then he saw who was waiting. Andy let the dog off leash, and Pope leaped up on the boy, almost knocking him over. The boy giggled and vigorously stroked the dog. Peddie was wearing the same clothes—jeans, T-shirt, athletic shoes—as he had on at the springs. The priest noted several blood stains on his shirt. The nurse carried a jacket in her hand and helped the boy into it. It was man-sized and covered the boy neck to knee. Peddie looked in good spirits now even though he sported a blackened eye. As they turned to go, the priest glared over at the receptionist, motioning to the happy boy. See, see, bitch, the boy comes down glum and leaves with a smile on his face. The priest was feeling very profane these days.

The doctor said he and the nurse would ride in a separate vehicle and that the boy should come with them. Baca overruled him. "Maybe on the way back, doc, but going out there the boy rides with me and the dog." So three police vehicles and one civilian SUV pulled out of the hospital parking lot to make the short drive to the Martinez compound.

The priest and the boy rode in the back seat, with Pope fidgeting between them. Sister Maria rode in the front seat with Baca. Good Friday was winding down with the colors of a spectacular sunset, filling the priest as always with wonder at God's creation. Peddie asked the sheriff if he wouldn't mind turning on the siren and after a moment's hesitation the sheriff complied. The boy yelped in delight as the Pope turned agitated at the loud, sudden noise. The radio cackled and Baca answered the call: "Baca here…No, no, Rudy, keep your siren off. I just did it as a favor for the boy. Let's do the quiet routine to the location." He put the radio back, turned off the siren, and chuckled. "They follow their leader like sheep, no."

Baca glanced over at the boy.

"So Peddie, what's happening here is we're going to take your dad away from the house so your sister will feel safe. That's what you want, no, your daddy out of the house."

Peddie said in a distracted voice. "Yes, that's what we want. Is the dog okay, Father? He looks okay."

The boy reached over to hug the dog.

"Sure, my boy, the Pope bounces back as good as new. He went after that guy after he hit you. I don't know if you saw that."

"I saw something, Father, but it was all kind of fuzzy."

"How's your head by the way? I know it's a hard head." The priest smiled. "You got quite a shiner there. That's what we called a black eye when I was a kid—a shiner."

Sister Maria piped in. "Yeah, back in the stone ages, when dinosaurs ruled the earth."

The sheriff joined the good-nature joshing. "And then the missionaries came clothed in white robes, to convert the pagan world and get the dinosaurs to say their prayers before chowing down or going beddy-bye. That Father Andy there, boy, I bet you didn't know he was back there teaching those dinosaurs a thing or two."

Peddie perked up and laughed.

"I saw dinosaurs once! Freddie took me to see dinosaurs down in Albuquerque. They weren't really dinosaurs. They didn't bite off heads. Freddie told me not to be scared but I wasn't scared at all. Monsters have to be real to be scary. Freddie taught me that but he forgot he told me."

The adults laughed in delight. The priest marveled at the resiliency of children. Peddie was only a few hours distant from running for his life and now they were driving to a possibly violent confrontation with his abusive father. As the dinosaur story indicated and other anecdotes about the family, eighteen year old Freddie was father in fact to his kid brother. Doing the things you'd expect a doting father to do. Freddie was mature beyond his years. Raul was lost in space.

The caravan quietly pulled into the Martinez compound off Richards. There was still faint light from the setting sun. Raul's Bug Out truck was there and the priest saw the dogs coming out of their den in the rusted out old truck. Andy winced at the sound of the barking. The priest wondered if the confrontation would begin in the yard instead of the house proper. But the cops didn't have to subdue the dogs; Peddie knew how to handle them. The boy jumped out of the SUV and went fearlessly up to the three dogs. They stopped barking; the pit bull stopped snarling; they greeted the lost boy with leaps of joy and licky fits. Despite their pacification, the priest shut the door on Pope's desire to join in the love fest. Property rights supersede free love. Freddie, Gabby and Amelia came to the door to see what the ruckus was about. Seeing Peddie with the dogs, they rushed out to greet the boy. It was quite a joyous family reunion. But the priest noticed that Baca's eyes were glued to the open door to the house. His deputies joined him and the lawmen went into a huddle. They broke in less than a minute and the sheriff went over to the family cuddle.

He gently pulled Mrs. Martinez aside, out of earshot of her children. He began explaining the crude facts of family life. Father Andy and Sister Maria stood respectively to the side, alternatively smiling at the kids celebrating, and then frowning at the sheriff and mother urgently conversing. Suddenly Amelia cried out, "No, no!" in an anguished voice and jumped back from Baca as though from the strike of a rattler. Baca reached out to her in a conciliatory gesture but she was having none of it. She turned and ran for the house. The sheriff and two of his men followed fast. The priest, nun, and psychiatrist went after them. After a pause the children joined the rush, eluding the remaining deputy's attempt to restrain them.

Father Andy took in the scene in the crowded living room. Yes, the TV was on and a glance at the tube told him another sci-fi show was playing, this one instantly recognizable as the venerable <u>Star</u> <u>Trek</u>, with Dr. Spock discussing otherworldly issues with Captain Kirk. Raul, in jeans and T-shirt, was again reclining in the sectional, looking more befuddled than dangerous, wasted again if the Coors cans were any indication. Impulsively he pointed the remote at the TV and turned up the volume. Spock and Kirk's voices went to warp sound. The sheriff walked over to Raul and grabbed the remote out of his hands and turned the TV off. Raul responded by throwing the beer can at him, hitting the sheriff on the shoulder, some beer sloshing onto his uniform and the tile floor. Baca looked down at Raul in disgust. Raul looked up at the law and stuck his tongue out. Then he noticed Peddie peaking out from behind Freddie.

"Peddie, my son, you're finally back. A sight for sore eyes, my boy."

Raul brought his heavy legs down, clicking shut the bottom of the recliner and wobbling to his feet. He couldn't maintain the vertical and fell back onto the seat. Sheriff Baca's face soured before turning officially stern.

"Raul Martinez, you're under arrest for suspicion of sexually abusing a minor family member. You have the right to remain silent; anything you say can be used against you; you have the right to legal representation; if you cannot afford an attorney, one will be appointed by the court. Do you understand what I am saying?"

Raul looked stunned. He didn't seem to understand anything. He sat there, clutching another beer, bloodshot eyes flitting left and right, seemingly pleading for salvation or anything close. Amelia was standing close to her husband but was slowly edging away. The normally quiet, morose woman almost screamed out the question:

"Did you do this awful thing, Raul? Did you touch our Gabby?"

Raul looked up at his wife and shook his head. He was getting it now. He sputtered out, "I didn't do anything wrong, Amelia baby. I meant nothing..."

The mother cried out in pain, "Oh, Raul!" and turned in tears and rushed out of the room towards the back bedrooms. The sheriff motioned for his deputies to lift the suspect off the recliner and out of the house. Raul was almost a dead weight at this point, muttering incoherently. The sheriff grabbed the priest's arm and said urgently:

"Father, Father, help me out here! Get the children out into the yard. Please clear this room so we can get this guy out safely."

The priest, with Sister Maria and the doctor assisting, began shepherding the kids out into fresh air. The psychiatrist walked over to the nurse who had remained outside with the last deputy and began talking with his colleague, motioning over to Peddie. The Martinez children were staring with wide eyes at the lawmen half-dragging their father towards one of the cruisers with a cage. The dogs began making a racket again. Then over the barking could be heard a loud screech. It was coming from Amelia, rushing out of the house, whipping a baseball bat in the air. Sheriff Baca, leading the deputies burdened by Raul, turned to assess the nature of the threat. Amelia swung the bat at her husband, hitting him in the tender groin. The man cried out in excruciating pain and dropped like a stone as the deputies let go to grab the enraged mother. Baca knelt to put a restraining hand on Raul's shoulder but the man was down for the count. The doctor and nurse went over to comfort Peddie and shelter him from the terrible scene. Freddie held his sister tight. Sister Maria reached out and grabbed the arm of the priest. Father Andy, with the pressure of her clinging hand, felt a surge of desire. Oh God, will it never let me go!

The police easily disarmed Amelia as all her revenge was exhausted with the one low blow. Baca held her as the deputies dragged the moaning man over to the cruiser. They unceremoniously threw him into the back seat and Baca told the two to take off. One of the deputies asked, "To the hospital or to the jail?" and Baca said jail first and have the nurse on call look him over. The sheriff turned back to calm the mother and called the doctor and nurse over to help. Father Andy looked at the police car pulling out and then over at the kids watching. Something odd happened in the face of tragedy. Freddie gave the high five to his little brother and then joined Gabby in a group hug. Peddie almost disappeared from view, squashed between brother and sister. People respond to stress in strange ways; rarely are feelings and actions in sync. But children are resilient and have a wonderful capacity to put the memory of pain aside and live in the moment. People find what pleasure they can in this crazy mixed-up world. Feeling a sudden chill though the evening air was balmy, the priest brought his hand up to lightly brush Maria's cheek as she smiled sadly and shook her head no, no.

*   *   *   *

Amelia Martinez was given a pass by the police, not charged with any crime. But the psychiatrist easily persuaded her to come back to the hospital to spend the night with her little boy. Both could sleep soundly under sedation. After a brief stop at the station house, the priest and nun were driven over to their respective residences for desperately needed sleep. At the rectory Father Gurule asked him what happened. Several pilgrims called up very concerned that Father Andy and Sister Maria had not returned with Peddie to the Chimayó shrine. The priest told his pastor briefly that the boy was safe but asked if filling in the details could wait for breakfast together tomorrow. Gurule looked over his obviously exhausted associate, noting the red splashes on his dirtied robe, and said okay to a long talk tomorrow. The old priest clapped Andy on the arm before turning to go back to his room. Gurule suddenly had an inspiration: "Andy, how would you like your eggs tomorrow?" The Franciscan summoned the energy to chuckle. "Easy over, Father, and thank you."

Before blessed sleep Andy took the Pope out for a short walk. Even when hobbled by bruised feet, the priest needed to pay attention to his dog. Andy tried to quiet his racing mind as they gingerly made the circuit around the block. His utter physical exhaustion helped ease the psychic pressure. When they returned to the rectory the priest stripped off his robe and underclothes, took a long hot shower, dried himself, put his bathrobe on, and went over to the dresser and took out the Jameson's. He poured out a generous portion and sat in his recliner for a bit. Andy glanced over at his pilgrimage robe draped on a chair and mused about the possibilities. That dirty robe was just made for TV. Back at the station house an unidentified photographer (from the New Mexican?) snapped a couple shots as the priest was getting into the squad car for the ride home. Bloodstained clothes had provided good visuals throughout history, assassination chic so to speak. Jackie Kennedy wore her bloody dress the rest of that fateful day in Dallas and later in Washington; Jesse Jackson in Chicago said Martin Luther King's blood anointed his clothes after the Memphis murder. Perhaps he should call Sam Fujema of Channel 4 tomorrow for an exclusive. Get on top of the story, spin it in his favor, the heroic friar rescuing the innocent boy and smiting evil. Maybe tomorrow he could rush to take temporal advantage.

Before slipping under the covers the priest figured a short prayer wouldn't hurt. But it wasn't formal prayer that came to mind. Rather a phrase from the Gospel According to John, 11/35: "Jesus wept." The grieving of the women he cared about drove the man-God to tears and to breath new life into Lazarus. What a warring nature that Jesus had to contend with! In the face of inconsolable mourning, He said loftily to the women: "I am the resurrection and the life: he that believeth in me, though he were dead, yet shall he live." He had the power to mend what was broken; He approached life with unblemished hands and an immaculate heart. But as a man did human desire ever surge at the sight of a woman weeping, a woman reaching out for physical reassurance? God's Franciscan friar in 2002 A.D. finally put his Good Friday to bed with his beloved dog next to him. Pope licked himself clean before dropping off himself.

CHAPTER 24

▼

Ray was taken to the Sandoval County lockup in Bernalillo for processing. He was routinely fingerprinted and went through the humiliating body search. Given the short term nature of stays in this facility, there was no prison smock given to him. His valuables—wallet, UNM class ring, the partner ring that he and Pete had exchanged so many years ago, and the Walkman with his prized Sarah CD—were taken away along with his belt. The cavernous Ray held up his pants with one hand as he was escorted to the holding pen. There were a number of men there to welcome him. One of them wanted the lowdown: "Hey. Ramos, what did this sucker do? Was he a bad boy on Good Friday?"

The deputy waited until Ray was safely behind bars before answering. He muttered but it was crystal clear to the guys milling near the bars.

"This is the queer asshole that took that boy over in Santa Fe last week."

Ramos then left the men to their own devices. Ray could feel the sullen hostility. These were men given to impulse; most appeared to be coming down from something. The DUI cases were fairly obvious, sleeping it off on the floor or massaging their throbbing temples. Given enough time together everybody's offenses against society became known. Of course some blamed the racist society or the coarse culture for their crimes; many proclaimed their innocence. There were thirteen men crowded into the holding cell. Most were charged with relatively minor offenses—petty theft, public intoxication, isolated weenie wagging—but a few faced hard time if convicted of assault and battery, rape, domestic disturbances with injury involved. But even bad men can't stomach certain crimes; at the top of their short list is sexual abuse of a child. Ray was the only one in custody charged with improper conduct with a child. His was a special case, 'short eyes' in prison parlance, with a circle of hell reserved for their sorry asses. If a preview of that hell can be arranged, the inmates did so, with relish.

Prisoners with time on their hands often kept up on current events better than the law-abiding population distracted by jobs and family. Most of the men in the cell read with interest the crime notes in the <u>New Mexican</u> and Albuquerque <u>Journal</u>. Of course Peddie's disappearance was front page news. His safe return and the strange circumstances surrounding the family had not yet hit the newsstands or as breaking news on local channels. Deputy Ramos didn't enlighten the inmates with the news that the boy was found alive.

Ray looked around at glaring eyes and sensed that staring them down was fruitless. Equally futile was crying out, "I did nothing wrong!" as proclamations of innocence were frequent in jail and discounted as pulp fiction. Ray knew that a cell was his fate when he decided to offer shelter for the boy. This was the price for not calling the police immediately and turning Peddie over. Of course if he just stuck to the plan, and not taken a detour to the Bar None, perhaps he would have been released and not have to spend the weekend or beyond with men very different from you and me.

Deputy Ramos told Ray as he escorted him to the holding cell that the sheriff would be talking to him later. Ray formally asked for legal representation. Ramos said that was the sheriff's call. A testy Ray said no! It was the constitution's call. He could see the deputy take offense. But Ray didn't care about hurt feelings; he was sick and tired of official ignorance or callous disregard of the law. He wasn't going to be pushed around. Gay bashing used to be popular sport in New Mexico. It had fallen out of favor in certain quarters. But Ray was locked up in a mostly rural county where posses still exist and mouthing off by a queer was frowned upon. Ray wasn't going to take it anymore. But he knew well not to use a cell of pissed-off men as a soapbox. A sudden thought humored him; if you guys really got to know me, what's not to love? He dare not laugh. A chuckle behind bars can be misunderstood. Several of the guys couldn't stop pacing and trash-talking, crisscrossing in front of him. Rat imagined himself on a leaky life raft in a roiling sea, surrounded by fins in the water.

An hour or so later Ramos came to retrieve him. He was escorted out of the large room that was dominated by the holding tank. Ray noticed surveillance cameras in two corners high on the wall pointed at the tank. So that's how they kept tabs, the jail keepers out of sight but observing the wild life remotely. Ray wondered if his little bickering corner of the cell was in the frame. If the crisscross became a lunging attack, would a homophobe like Ramos come rushing to his aid? That would be a true Holy Week miracle. Maybe Ray could convince the sheriff that solitary confinement would be the way to prevent contagious blood from messing up his fine facility.

Sheriff Ramirez was waiting in his office. He was a lanky Hispanic somewhere in his fifties. He took obvious pride in his appearance, slicked-back silvery hair and a droopy but well trimmed mustache. The sheriff gave Ray the once-over before surprising him by offering his hand.

"We haven't been formally introduced. My name is Max Ramirez and I'm the law in this county. And you are?"

"I'm Ray Yazzie from Santa Fe. I'm the cat's meow in that county."

The sheriff laughed. "Cat's meow, my dandy. That's very funny. I suppose you can call me the top dog of Sandoval, no. Well, enough happy talk for now. My mad dog Ramos told me you want to call your lawyer. I don't have a problem with that. You want a dime, Mr. Yazzie from Santa Fe County. Just kidding! Use my phone and no need to call collect. I'll give you some privacy but don't go messing in my drawers, man. I'll be outside that window. One thing though, please tell me when the esquire will be showing up. The sooner he comes, the sooner we can clear up this mess. I should be hearing from Baca soon about his investigation in Santa Fe. That Martinez boy will be questioned sooner rather than later. Maybe it will be good news for you. Okay, buddy?"

"My name's Ray, not buddy, Maxie?"

The sheriff didn't laugh this time. "Ray, yes, Ray as in gay. I'll remember that. And Yazzie as a last name! I wonder about the origins of that; did your ancestors start out crazy or what? Make your call, Mister Ray Yazzie. Don't worry—it's not a party line!"

Ramirez got up and left the office, closing the door behind him. But true to his word, the sheriff stayed outside the large window that looked out onto the squad room. Ray had squirreled away his lawyer's business card when he took Peddie up to the cabin. Figured he might need it. His lawyer, Shelton Grimes, was in to take the call. Ray had known the capital city attorney socially for many years and had to use his professional services on occasion. Grimes was gay himself and had become radicalized as a young attorney by the petty harassment he witnessed. He represented many gay men over the years on a wide variety of civil and criminal matters. Recently the lawyer had been taking a more visible role in Santa Fe Democrat politics. Shel told Ray the last time they talked that he was contemplating a run for the city council. The lesbians had one of their own on the council already; the time was ripe for the men to have their champion too.

Ray was brief with Shel, saying only that he was in the Bernalillo lock-up and the charge concerned the disappearance of Peddie Martinez. After a pause the lawyer said he would drive down immediately. Before hanging up Ray told Grimes about the palpable hostility he was feeling from his cellmates as well as the officers outside the bars. The lawyer told him that Ramirez was okay by reputation so just sit tight and keep a low profile. Be there within the hour.

Time passed slowly in the tank before Ramos came again and told him his lawyer had shown up. Ray was worn out by the trials of the day and the need to stay on high alert. It was now almost 5 p.m. and he hadn't eaten since last night's dinner with Peddie. The issue of food was going to be on the table with his lawyer. He felt hungry enough not to worry about the lack of a marijuana appetizer. He wondered if jail food would make him sick.

Shel Grimes waited in an empty visiting room. Ramos stayed in the room but sat next to the door, far enough away for the lawyer and his client to huddle with some privacy. As always, Grimes was dressed nattily in bow tie and poplin suit, with a finely fluffed handkerchief in his breast pocket. Whenever Ray saw him, he always thought southern lawyer, that Grimes should be arguing a case in a sweltering Mississippi courtroom where all the ladies cooled themselves with hand fans. The old fashion look was mitigated by Shel's long hair in a ponytail.

Ray gave chapter and verse to his lawyer about the events since Peddie showed up at his doorstep. In talking about his experience with Sandoval law enforcement, he included the gay slurs and provocative comments made by the deputy sitting right over there. Grimes made copious notes in a small notebook. After a half-hour of talking Ray was pretty well played out.

"You've got quite a story there, Ray, one for the ages. I'm assuming the boy and this priest will back you up." (Ray nodded.) "Well, then I think your prospects are good for a reasonable bail. As for criminal charges, we'll have to see what the district attorney comes up with. We certainly have a sympathetic story to tell a jury and I think I can make this Gary Yalman the fall guy. You know, I ran across the guy once in court and I had a bad feeling about him. He seemed too hyper and heartless. Now you tell me that he was on crystal meth. That explains a lot. No, I think Gary will do nicely as the personification of evil. People love to hate lawyers gone bad. I think I can beat any charge of child kidnapping but endangerment might be a more difficult issue. Worst case is a plea deal to a year or two max. That's the case as I see it now but there's something more profound beyond that, a far greater cause."

"Far greater cause?" Ray echoed faintly.

"Yes, yes, Ray, don't you see? Your actions in protecting this child and ultimately his sister from parental abuse can be presented in a very positive light. As you know adoption rules for gay couples have been loosening in this country. Your caretaking of a child at great personal risk shows what the larger gay community is capable of. Our brethren are tarred and feathered by the religious right as child seducers and abusers on the make. Gary might become the poster child for this bigotry. But then there's you and your gallant efforts. The media is going to have a field day with this duality, the gay angel of mercy versus the devil incarnate. The fact that the devil was slain by a Franciscan monk adds real juice to the story. We just have to hope that the public will admire the angel more than detest the devil."

Ray followed Grimes' scenario all right and could see himself floated as a gay angel. But in a few minutes he had to go back to a cell where common humanity was lacking as well as angelic virtue. Before he could bring up the fact that he was scared shitless, the lawyer mused some more.

"The drug issue explains a lot too. Everybody figures that drug abuse can lead to a violent episode. Of course the responsible use of social drugs should not be sullied by one bad apple. I mean, why should booze be legal and marijuana not? Does that make sense? Why don't we just tax the hell out of our vices and wipe out the national debt? But that's not my fight. I want to advance the cause of human rights in terms of sexual orientation."

Ray could see Ramos stirring in the background. He had to get his lawyer away from the big picture. He asked Shel about bail and an isolation cell until it's granted. Grimes' gaze came back from far horizons to the here and now.

"Oh yes, my friend, bail will be granted. The only problem is one of timing. A holiday weekend is not the best time to get a bail hearing in this county. Judges up here don't work weekends except for emergencies. It's not like a big city where there's enough crime to keep the courts going 24/7. So Monday morning sharp we get the arraignment going and spring you before the day is out. In the meantime I will talk with Ramirez and get you out of that holding tank. Promise!"

"What about some food, Shel? I'm hungry."

"They haven't fed you yet? And you've been here, what, three, four hours now. Outrageous!"

Ray felt the need to be explicit. "Right now, Shel, I'm going back to a cell with a bunch of guys who haven't bathed in ages. They have very bad manners, believe me. And thanks to that jerk over there, they think I abducted Peddie and had my way with him. They don't even know the boy is alive. I need to get out of there—now!"

His voice was raised enough to get Ramos' attention. The deputy smiled and wagged his finger, then pointed at his watch. Ray looked again at his attorney in despair. Saying the Lord's Prayer with particular emphasis on the words, "Deliver us from evil," would probably be more potent than talking further about legal realities.

"Like I said, Ray, I'll talk with Sheriff Ramirez about the cell situation and the food issue. I'll tell him about the open prejudice that deputy is showing. If one hair on your head is harmed, I'll raise such a stink that the feds will come in to investigate civil rights violations."

That's fine and good, but I'll be too dead to see justice done. Ray was too far gone to plead any longer. He motioned to Ramos and got unsteadily to his feet. Grimes stayed seated, somewhat nonplussed, as he sensed his client's unhappiness with the game plan. It was the only game in town, the only rational course of action the attorney could come up with. Ramos led Ray out of the room. The prisoner didn't look back or say goodbye to his lawyer.

Back in the cell Ray found his corner occupied by one of the most menacing crisscrossers, now taking his rest on the floor, legs provocatively spread-eagled in front of him. Ray wasn't about to ask him to move over. He couldn't find another corner to back into as they were occupied by men similarly postured as though airing out their privates. The rest of the jokers sat against the bars, some with modestly crossed legs, others leaning with their chins on clenched knees. The only room to sit was in the middle of the cell surrounded by accusing glares. So Ray sat down and figured trying to stare down, what, thirteen men who hated his guts wasn't going to work. He thought again of pleading his case, telling what is, after all, a rather intriguing tale. He wondered if he had any fight left in him. He just needed a decent meal and a good night's sleep to regain his fighting spirit. But maybe for the present a few well chosen words in defense of his honor would suffice.

Ray was about to speak up when Ramos came back and unlocked the cell door. He motioned to the man in the ring. Ray got up with alacrity. He felt the glee of a man who escaped the hangman's noose. He even had the absurd impulse to hug Ramos but the deputy would ward him off with rubber gloves and billy club. Yes, rubber gloves; Ramos probably figured every fag he ran across had the AIDS virus. The strip search he was subjected to after booking told the story, the sores and scrawny frame that come with the advance of the disease. Ramos led him out of the holding room and into an adjoining corridor with individual cells. The deputy opened one at the very end and Ray shuffled in. The cell had one bunk and a flush toilet. As Ramos locked up, he asked if the prisoner wanted a tray of food brought in. He got no response as Ray dropped on the bed and fell fast asleep.

*   *   *   *

Ray didn't wake up until a deputy rattled his cage early Saturday morning. Yazzie spent all day in isolation. They brought food for him but he barely touched it. He had nothing to read and no deck of cards to play solitaire. Actually, though, the lack of diversions was okay for the day as Ray laid back listening to the faint music coming from a radio at the guard station up the corridor. The station was playing Golden Oldies and Ray let his memory shimmy and shake back through time. It was as though he was growing up again with a looping soundtrack. Everything was in a bit of a jumble; he could hardly phone in requests. All the insecurities of childhood came back, overblown ones in retrospect as he survived them all, but then several songs took him to puberty time. What occurred then had a lasting legacy; a troubled rite of passage as he tried to squeeze through the straight and narrow. The throbbing teen music compelled him to move his muscles, even dance a short bit. Ray remembered how much freedom he felt as he didn't have to discipline his herky-jerky limbs to the demands of touch dancing. Everybody in those days was encouraged to do their own thing on the dance floor. Oh sure, slow dancing happened occasionally, with creeping hands and thighs rubbing each other the right way. Ray danced with girls in those days. Slow dancing was torture. Ray remembered dancing, wanting so much to share in the ecstasy of the glowing attraction between boys and girls, clumsy, ardent, profane, innocent, as many feelings erupting as the colors of nature.

The songs he associated with his college years in the late 1960's came on. A time of personal liberation, out and about with his bad self, laughing at conventional morality—he remembered the sex alright but mostly the lively conversations, vivid language, great stories, uninhibited talk, talk, talk. Ray loved every precious word. Sure, his group indulged in petty feuds and catty gossip. But, looking back, it was so much fun. Slightly delirious with so little food in him, Ray lifted his head half-expecting his old friends to be there. He fell back on the thin mattress, seeing that he was truly in isolation, having to settle for memories alone, to pass the time.

The Golden Oldies station stopped with the end of the 1980's and jumped back to the 1950's. Ray didn't regress as he didn't want to stop the recap of his emotional life. It was 1985 when he met Pete at the church singles gathering.

First it was infatuation; then it was spending more nights together than apart; then it was scrutinizing home economics and deciding to pool their resources; at last it was 'marriage' though the state didn't sanction it and the church didn't bless it. But the right feelings were there and the commitment too. Faithfulness for so many years; unfaithful for one night; mortal sin doesn't pay. You have to live and die with the consequences. But despite his legal jeopardy, he didn't want to beat himself up for being human. If I had to do it all over again, I'd just make different mistakes.

No, Ray wanted to think only the best of the human beings he had met and felt something for. His late mother's face floated in his feverish mind, embracing her only child and later the grown man, wishing for loving grandchildren living near but settling for a far distant and cold Benito, mom never celebrating her only son's lifestyle but treating Pete with civility and even maternal warmth on occasion. Father Andy stopped by to visit his delirious friend. Ray was very fond of the Franciscan. The friar's stern words to Gary at the springs distracted him enough to give the boy and dog biting room. Ray, having gone on the overnight pilgrimage once in the mid-nineties (Father Andy's first year in Santa Fe, his first march to El Santuario), knew well how the walk alone is an endurance contest. Add a desperate run over rough ground, dressed in a heavy robe and sandals no less, and a fight to the death at the end of it, well, Father Andy proved to be stout in the best sense. And Peddie—how was the dear boy? He seemed a little whacked out by Gary's blow. Ray too saw the trickle of blood, Gary's tainted blood maybe. But the boy wasn't a vampire and didn't swallow, did he? Ray felt a surge of affection for all his people. He was finally dwelling in selfless love. By taking wants out of the equation; by checking his ego at the door. It wasn't so hard when it was a cell door.

He rediscovered the long form of prayer too this long day and night, on Holy Saturday. These were not the rote prayers from his Catholic school days, prayers mumbled without deep reflection or heartfelt emotion. Instead the prayers were intensely personal. His jailers could put him in isolation, but not from his God.

*   *   *   *

On Easter morning Ramos came to wake Ray personally. He was openly abusive. "Fag man, up and at 'em. We serve a full Sunday breakfast for child abusers. You can have your dick served between two buns, with ketchup or mustard, or sauerkraut, huh, or a dick on a stick is very slick too. You got a fucking poet here, man. Get your ass out of bed."

Ray had slept poorly through the night and was in no mood. The radio up the corridor, while never blaring, stayed on all night, Golden Oldies all night long. Ray saw some humor in his situation. During the previous day, Holy Saturday, he felt himself reaching for a true communion with God through fasting and praying. But in the face of profane realities, how do you make the epiphany last? If only they had changed the station on the radio, to a religious one, playing centuries of spiritual music, from the Gregorian Chant to Jesus Christ Superstar. But being behind bars meant the loss of freedom to change the station, to control the volume. He did have the freedom to tune out the deputy's bigotry, to not rise to the bait. But Shel Grimes was right about one thing: the cause of human rights is rarely advanced by suffering in silence.

"Ramos, you don't know your ass from a hole in the wall. Peddie Martinez was never abused by me. We left the guy you want floating face down in the springs. And as far as my dick is concerned, you can eat it for breakfast, lunch or dinner. It's really good for dessert too. I don't have to take any shit from you."

After a long day and night flat on his back, this spirited defense of body and soul was thrilling to Ray. He flashed on the defiance he showed jeering classmates in high school. They were only guessing but turned out to be right on. Ray didn't win every fistfight back then but always came home exultant even if bruised. For it was his primal self he was defending, his God-given sexual self. As teenagers neither he nor his tormentors understood sex except in a crude way. All of them threw themselves wholeheartedly into the fray. Ray gave heterosexuality a try, okay, but it didn't come natural. His only hope of lasting happiness lay in the embrace of men. He had found a good one in Pete. Their partnership perished because of a whim on a lonely night. No human relationships stay on an even keel given the heavy weather that life together stirs up. We just have to ride out the storm. And try not to act like drunken sailors once we hit port.

Ramos didn't verbally respond or raise his nightstick. The deputy's eyes just glared in rage. Ray felt condemned in those eyes. Ramos didn't want to hear any evidence to the contrary. Shel Grimes better come back fast to spring his client or Ray may be transformed from role model to martyr.

Ramos spit out that prisoners were entitled to one shower a day. Yesterday Ray was so out of it that the deputies didn't enforce the exercise period or hygienic routine. Today Ray welcomed the chance to wash off the grime of the chase. The jailer unlocked the cell and motioned to the prisoner to go first. Ray looked at the nightstick and wondered if Ramos would jab or poke or pretend that an attack provoked him to beat the prisoner senseless. They walked past the radio at the unmanned guard station. Ray almost laughed at the serendipity of the vintage song that was playing. On impulse he reached down and turned up the volume. Ramos said, "Hey, hey" and jabbed the nightstick in his back, but surprisingly restrained, irritating more than causing sharp pain. Ray didn't remember the group but the song was the universal anthem for people trapped in little boxes, dead end jobs, loveless couplings. The lyrics represented the classic desire for miraculous escapes:

> We gotta get out of this place
> If it's the last thing we ever do
> We gotta get out of this place
> If it's the last thing we ever do
> We've got a better life
> For me and you

Ray was led into a changing room with hooks up on the wall. He was happy to see that it wasn't going to be a shower with the guys from the holding cell. Apparently solitary confinement meant solitary everything. Ramos said, "I'll give you 10 minutes, fag, to make up for missing yesterday's delightful soak with the boys. Don't have to worry about dropping the soap today! It's Easter Sunday after all; make your peace with your God."

At least Ramos left the shower room with his dirty mouth and mocking eyes. Ray was relieved that the man wouldn't see him naked. He wasn't much to look at anymore. He wasn't really asking for a fountain of youth; just someone to say a kind word, offer a cup of cool, clear water. Ray undressed and entered the shower area. It was a similar layout to what Ray recalled from high school gym class: an open area with eight shower heads. He remembered the secret excitement he felt by the naked bodies so near. In that one way high school is a rich experience if you are gay. Ray turned on the water and was grateful that it came out piping hot. There was bar soap in the wall dish but no shampoo. He couldn't work up much of a lather but the water alone was cleansing. After the shower he felt his appetite may return. Ray wondered what was on the breakfast menu.

On the far side of the shower room was a door. Behind that door was a small utility closet containing mops and cleaning supplies. The door was normally locked except for supervised cleaning periods. The door opened now, from the inside, and a prisoner emerged, one of the crisscrossers who trash-talked the worst and whose limbs seemed on time-release jolts of electricity. He was wearing rubber gloves and carrying one of the mops. Ray was visible through the steam, his head under the delicious needles of hot water, face to the wall. The prisoner didn't waste time. He swung the mop head against the back of Ray's head, smashing it against the hard tile wall. Ray went down with a groan, bleeding from the forehead, knocked almost senseless. Ray wanted to get up, fight like he used to, but his mind didn't seem to control his limbs anymore. He felt his attacker put a foot hard on his lower back, and then felt the mop pole being rudely inserted into his anus. The guy started giggling as he leaned over to push the pole deeper. There's nothing like dying to concentrate the mind. But there was no life passing at warp speed before my eyes. Been there, done that. That was Ray's last revelation before darkness fell, the last sound, lewd laughing at his expense, feeling the pole roughly removed and the shitty wood whacking skin and bones.

CHAPTER 25

▼

Father Andy received the news through a phone call to the rectory from Sheriff Ramirez. It was the second time they had talked during the weekend. On Saturday Andy had called the Bernalillo jail facility to see how Ray was doing and when visiting hours were. Sheriff Ramirez was in and the priest talked directly with him. The sheriff told him that his man had been in his cell seemingly sleeping most of the day and eating sparingly. He had his lawyer visit on Friday and was likely to go before a county judge on Monday for a plea and bail hearing. Call back tomorrow and likely the prisoner could be made available. Father Andy told the sheriff that he would like to bring the sacrament of communion Sunday afternoon to Ray and any other Catholic prisoner. Ramirez said fine; visiting hours on Sunday ends at 5 p.m. The priest told Ramirez to tell Ray that he would come down around 4. The sheriff ended the conversation by saying he may come in for a little chat with the priest.

Instead of the afternoon visit of course, the phone rang at the rectory very early Easter Sunday morning.

"Father Leary, Sheriff Ramirez here. I'm afraid I've got some bad news for you. Your man was attacked this morning and has been airlifted to St. Vincent's. He's in pretty bad shape. I don't think he's going to make it."

The priest was gathering himself for a long morning of services celebrating Christ's Resurrection. This is all wrong; Easter Sunday was supposed to be about putting death on hold.

"He was in your custody, wasn't he, Sheriff? How could this have happened?"

"That's under investigation, Father. We have some rough characters in here this weekend. We'll find out what happened. We have a deputy up at the hospital in case Yazzie's able to tell us something. Anyhoo, I figured you should be the first to know, you being a priest and all, and this guy's a friend, I guess. He was a buddy of yours, right, Father?"

"Yes, yes, he was, is my friend. Does his lawyer know this happened?"

"I haven't been able to reach him, it being Sunday and all. I left a message on his voicemail."

"Who has Ray retained?"

"The guy's name is, let me see here, Shelton Grimes. He practices in your town."

"What's his number? Does he have a cell phone listed on his card?"

"Oh yeah, I see it here. I didn't notice it before. That number is (505) 690-0770. I guess I could call him but, you know, these lawyers can smell a wrongful death suit a mile away. He'll be by. If you want to call him to see his client over at the hospital, feel free."

The priest didn't really know this sheriff or the jail he ran but he had the creepy feeling that it was a sloppy operation by accident or design. He wondered if Ray could bear witness to official corruption or gross negligence. It was time to hear the man's confession for the second time this Holy Week. It sounded as though he did his penance in advance.

"Sheriff, I gotta get going!"

He hung up even as the sheriff was trying to get in a last word. Probably Ramirez wanted to schedule a q & a to hear further the priest's version of the week's events. Andy looked at the phone for a few moments, expecting the sheriff to ring back. But then he said, screw the demands of the corrupt law; a priest's place is at the bedside of a dying parishioner.

The Franciscan rushed into his bedroom to get his Last Rites kit. He jumped into his Camry to hurry over to the hospital. Luckily Gurule was scheduled to handle the 7:30 no frills Mass; Andy's first duty was for the High Mass at 9:30 where the choir actually started their glorious singing at 9:15. He had to be back for that. It was ludicrous, of course, fitting the dying into a busy schedule but a priest on Easter owed it to the people in the pews to be there on time. The color purple was put in mothballs in favor of the rainbow colors of the happy liturgical season. The deep sorrow and sacrifice of Lent was over.

Ray was in intensive care. The sheriff's deputy was on guard over at the nurses' station but this prisoner wasn't about to escape. Ray had an intravenous needle in his arm, tubes down his nose, and oxygen mask over his mouth. His eyes were wide open. A young doctor with a nurse hovering was attending to the patient. The priest was about to take the doctor aside to ask about Ray's prognosis. Looking at all the life support, Andy figured the news was grim and that Ray shouldn't hear it. But the priest received the prognosis without words, just a sad shake of the doctor's head, a professional judgment, turning the doomed over to a spiritual specialist to tend to the eternal soul. The E/R doc then quietly withdrew to apply his skills to those who didn't require a miracle. Father Andy kissed his stole in the ritual fashion, opened his little vial of consecrated oil, and squeezed Ray's hand as he leaned over to speak into his ear.

"Ray, Ray, I'm so sorry to see you in this state. Can you hear me? Can you speak at all?"

Andy felt a slight pressure in response and Ray's eyes were certainly expressive. Both men's palms were wet with perspiration. The priest's palms often perspired, a sign of erupting nerves, a secret sign as he shied away from clammy handshakes that would expose the emotional truth. Now was not the time for vanity, as Ray's lifeline had almost run its course. There was barely time for the grace of God. Would there be an opportunity for a deathbed confession of who killed me?

Ray looked down at his breathing mask and Andy understood. The priest lifted the mask and a torrent of words was unleashed. But Andy would have to be able to read tortured lips as no intelligible sound emerged. Almost every visible part of the man was bruised; his voice box didn't escape punishment. No doubt the whole story of the assault was being revealed, every gory detail. Who did this to you, man; official collusion? I could be the conduit to your lawyer to see justice done. The priest kept holding Ray's hand but shook his head sadly, eyes tearing, his friend speaking volumes with nothing understood. Ray finally had nothing more to say as he no doubt felt his soul packing up to leave for a place of no comment and no need to know. His lips stopped moving. But then he made one last supreme effort and the priest leaned over to catch the last gasp to make sense of it all. Andy thought he heard, "No matter" or "No más" but perhaps it was his imagination. The priest put on the oxygen mask again but sensed the pure air was going into a void. He quickly applied the oils to Ray's forehead, mouth, and ear lobes. Then he said the essential:

"I forgive you in the name of the Father, and the Son, and the Holy Spirit. Amen to life, Ray. Amen to life, my dear friend."

Ray's eyes lost all expression and the priest heard the death rattle and sigh. His friend was gone. The priest reached up to his eye lids and gently shut them. They were no longer windows to the soul anyway.

*   *   *   *

Father Andy got to the church in time. He changed into his fanciest vestments and joined the swelling crowd in the gathering space outside the sanctuary doors. The faithful—both the constant ones as well as the devout for the holy day—showed up early for the High Masses at Easter as they wanted to find a seat rather than have to stand during the whole service. The long ritual included the life-affirming rite of baptism. Easter celebrated the triumph of life over death, eternal life for those who lead worthy lives. Or to those who confess their sins on their deathbed. The priest often wondered if the Church offered an easy way out for remorseful chronic sinners. Sin by the gross every day of your life; just keep that last appointment with clergy before the grim reaper comes calling. What if Hitler had called, say, a Lutheran minister to the bunker? 'Forgive me, Father, for I have sinned. I ordered the killing of millions of Jews, homosexuals, Communists, some Aryans too if found defective in mind and morals. I now see the error of my ways.' What penance would be appropriate? Several million Lord's Prayers? But no, the living matters, day by day; not just what is muttered upon dying. The priest shared enough of Ray's life to know that the man did battle royal with his demons both real and imagined. At war over the nature of his being. Finally at peace with the good Lord explaining it all to him.

Father Andy was standing amongst his flock, waiting with Gurule who made a point of being at each service on Easter and Christmas. There with the priests of the Little Flower was the altar girl and boys from the pilgrimage, on their last official day of service. One boy was carrying the large Crucifix from the pilgrimage, to be placed back onto its hook behind the altar. Everybody was waiting a few minutes for the traditional procession to start. Father Andy knew that when the door to the sanctuary was opened, the choir and musicians would let loose.

On hand as secular witnesses was a mini-cam crew from Channel 4, led by Father Andy's favorite reporter, Sam Fujema. Sam was in the gathering space at Father Andy's invite, with the tacit approval of the pastor. Andy promised Sam a sit down after the service to give him an exclusive on Peddie's disappearance and the desperate chase to save him. The story along with the video of the High Mass would be a godsend of good news for the Church. Andy also gave him a tease that may turn into a must-see news segment; Peddie and his family would likely be at Mass today. Back at home Saturday afternoon, Amelia Martinez told the priest over the phone that she would try to bring the kids to Mass, her normal 9:30 Sunday Mass. The conversation was short but telling. The priest asked how Peddie was doing and how was she doing? Amelia said fine, fine, and actually sounded fine saying it. The doom and gloom tone so typical of her over the years was absent from her voice. Andy enquired gently about Gabby. The mother said she wasn't moping about and was out somewhere with Freddie and Peddie. The priest was mildly amused when she asked who did the flower arrangement on the altar this year. Andy answered that a woman who works for Fred's Flowers— Luisa Oliso—agreed to fill in—on a temporary basis. Amelia said I'm sure she'll do fine in such a skeptical tone that the priest almost laughed.

Suddenly a murmur started in the back of the crowd, then shouts of joy. A spontaneous chant of "Peddie, Peddie, Peddie" began as the faithful parted, revealing the brave boy coming through. Peddie was accompanied by his mother, brother and sister, making their way to where the priest stood. The boy ran the last few feet and threw himself at the priest in a hug of thanks. The worshipers laughed and many crossed themselves and shouted, "Praise the Lord!" Father Andy was media savvy enough to know that this embrace by Peddie before the cameras would play well in the archbishop's eyes. As the true story gets out, second-guessing was inevitable. But doubters would be faced with evidence of tangible love of the boy for his parish priest.

*   *   *   *

The killing of Gary and the arrest of Raul Martinez on the sexual molestation charge hit the local news late Friday. There was even national coverage on Saturday, mostly because of the novelty of a priest involved in the killing of a suspected child molester. All the reports assumed that Father Andy had no choice at the springs. The news programs ran a recent photo of Gary, his New Mexico driver's license photo. This one didn't look any better than yours. The reporters also found out that the deceased was a long time attorney. A bad lawyer getting his was a popular slant that a number of reporters mentioned. On Saturday a picture of Raul surfaced, Raul in his Bug-Out uniform. In contrast the photo of Andy from Friday evening in his soiled white robe made him appear more saintly and heroic than he felt.

Ray wasn't initially mentioned in Friday's breaking news flash but by Saturday his name surfaced and the fact that he had been arrested on child endangerment charges made the reporters dig deeper. By Saturday night Sam Fujema broke the news of the connection between Ray and Gary going back years to the love and friendship they shared in college. The possibility of collusion between the two in the taking of the boy was broached on one of those Fox News crime shows. The reality of Peddie running away from home on his own, rather than snatched away by evil men, had not been reported on yet. Andy felt a heavy responsibility to set the record straight.

Sheriff Baca called Andy on Saturday to set up a time for a formal interview. The priest put him off till Monday, citing Easter obligations, and the sheriff didn't press him. They set up a time Monday morning at 9 and the sheriff casually said, bring a lawyer along if you'd like. Andy replied that that wouldn't be necessary. He had nothing to hide.

The Franciscan asked Baca if Gabby had given confirmation of the abuse. The sheriff hesitated before answering:

"Well, Father, I know you've been involved with this mess from the get-go. I guess I can share with you that no, the girl hasn't confirmed that yet. The boy says he saw it; the girl says it didn't happen. Gabby is the alleged victim and if she sticks to her story, we haven't much of a case. Maybe she's scared about testifying. Maybe she wants dear old dad to go away but not serve any time. Raul denies the abuse too, says he was drunk Friday evening and didn't know what he was saying."

Since Andy had the sheriff talking, he wanted to find out everything. Gabby's distended stomach begged for explanation.

"Was the girl examined? That's standard procedure in rape and incest cases, isn't it?"

"Yes, yes, sure is. The girl's no virgin and…remember this is like confession again, Father, no tattle-tale on this, right, Father?" Baca paused and Andy mumbled reassurance. "The doctor tells me that the poor child is with child, a couple months along. Sad situation, no."

"Oh no! Sister Maria and I feared that, feared the worst. Has anybody talked with her about this? Given her counseling or whatever?"

"Oh yes, the doctor did but she's mum about how the girl responded. Privacy considerations she said. I pointed out to her that a crime against the girl was alleged. This doctor said that the girl told us already that her father wasn't involved. Well then who was involved, doc? She said the girl didn't tell her. We may have to shoot for a paternity test but with the girl a minor and denying the crime, it's tough. Of course we have at least a statutory rape charge against Mr. Anonymous. I've already asked the mother for permission to go ahead. She's says no too! So we're stymied here, Father. Say a prayer for me, okay."

"I sure will, Sheriff, and will ask for the collective prayers of the congregation also. But what do you think will happen now? We certainly can't have that drunk back home knowing that his son snitched on him. Look, I've talked with the boy, and he saw what he saw. Incest can be a deeply shameful thing; maybe that's why the girl isn't talking. But that man is a gross danger to his family. You know how he is. Give me some hope that Peddie's not going to be beaten up and that Raul won't become the proud daddy and grandfather on the same day."

"I did interrogate Raul at length, "Baca responded. "He waived his right to an attorney for now at least so we had a free-wheeling conversation. That baseball bat in his balls really sobered him up. I don't think he's going to weasel his way back into the good graces of his family anytime soon. He's talking rehab, joining AA, cleaning up his act, no. Today he's got the heebie-jeebies with no booze to take the edge off. I even offered him a pint if he would just tell the truth. I could see he was tempted but he went back to not guilty, Baca, you got the wrong man. Of course he's going to stay behind bars for awhile while the DA figures out how to proceed with the case. But even if the charges are dropped, I think he vamoose out of town. His wife thinks he did it; she said he was always up late and now she knows some of what he was doing besides watching TV. His reputation is shot around town. Too many people have seen him drunk and disorderly for too long not to believe that he may have raped his daughter in a blackout, whatever. I think he's headed for skid row somewhere, maybe on Mars, unless he sobers up through AA or religion. Stranger things have happened."

Then the priest put in a good word for Ray.

"I called your counterpart in Sandoval to check up on my friend Ray. He supposedly was sleeping and unavailable. That Ramirez didn't…"

Baca interrupted. "He probably has him in solitary, that's standard procedure, isolating him from the general population. Not a whole lot to do all day but maybe read and sleep. Listen, I've got a call out now to Max. I'll see what I can do for your boy."

"Thanks, Sheriff. Doesn't Ray have to be transferred over to your jurisdiction? Couldn't that happen today?"

"Hold on, buckaroo, extradition doesn't happen overnight. Sandoval County has more of a problem than we do to get an arraignment done over a weekend. I would imagine Monday morning his lawyer will be in court there to spring him on a modest bail. I'll mention to Ramirez that the boy didn't appear abused by anybody but that guy you took care of back at the springs. Didn't know a priest could do that kind of damage. You must of been eating your Wheaties."

"Okay, okay, Sheriff. You know, I'm sorry I couldn't be more open with you but we priests have to protect the sacrament, you know, the bonds of confidentiality. Now everything is out in the open and I'm free to talk."

"So that's it—confession started you on your date with destiny. In this case a priest is the first in the know. I'm jealous as hell; I always find out too late to prevent the crime."

After saying goodbye to his second sheriff of the day, Andy mellowed out the rest of Saturday. For one thing he needed to give his battered feet a break if he wanted to move with grace on Easter Sunday. So he laid low with his dog, drank a bit of Jameson's, and took a long siesta. Archbishop Beckworth called but Gurule ran interference, saying their Franciscan friend was indisposed. Andy was very grateful as he needed some time alone to sort things out.

*   *   *   *

The priest lifted the boy off his feet and whirled him around to the delight of the congregation. The altar girl took Peddie's foot on her chin, a glancing blow, but enough for Andy to guide the boy back to earth. Peddie cried out, "I love you, Father!" bringing a new round of sighs and smiles from the faithful. The friar stooped to give the boy another hug and then stood up to greet the rest of the family. Amelia Martinez seemed in marvelous spirits today, slightly dazed by the TV camera lights but with a rare smile on her face. Both Gabby and Freddie were gazing fondly at their mother, then defiantly at the priest. Father Andy knew a message was being conveyed: See, Father, see, we now have a mother worthy of the name, happy now after so many years of a dour marriage. The priest reached out and hugged the slight woman. Then he shook Freddie's hand despite the moisture on his own. In his enthusiasm he almost hugged Gabby but then thought better of it. He just patted her arm briefly.

Sister Maria was out there somewhere, on the fringes of the crowd. She and Andy talked on Saturday, Maria asking his advice on when her resignation should be announced. They agreed that the joy of Easter Sunday, with the added wonder of Peddie's safe return, shouldn't be ruined by the sad and shocking news. The announcement (leaving out the marrying desire and parenting wish) would be saved for an ordinary Sunday. The school year had almost two months to play out plus the summer for Father Andy and the school board to find a replacement. Probably a qualified nun from a diminishing pool would be hard to find. He knew the imperious Claire would be impossible to work with and Sister Muni was much too old and doddering. Perhaps now was the time to turn the reins over to a lay educator such as the amazing Gloria Alarid.

The doors to the sanctuary were opened and the procession began with the choir singing joyously, the quartet of musicians playing beautifully. The Martinez family was escorted by one of the Mass volunteer ushers down to the front pew. Usually this pew was open to first-come but no one rushed to beat the family to it, the family that had been through so much together. Father Andy was suddenly distracted by the phrase, so much together. The boil had been lanced; the pus oozed out; healing was now possible. Naturally the drama of the illegitimate baby-to-be needed to be played out. A medical solution that may or may not be moral or fair to the fetus would probably be found. This whole sorted business started for the priest a week ago in this sacred space, a man smiling with secret knowledge, smiling when everybody else was worried sick. The boy was in safe hands now, with a chance to grow up right. The AIDS scare was still there but God couldn't be so cruel as to cut down a child just beginning to blossom. No, it wouldn't come to that. The boy would survive. Father Andy had told no one yet, least of all the happy boy, of the cruel passing of their mutual friend. The boy would find out soon enough. Freddie was still there to serve as surrogate father. A strong male presence, someone to point the way to adulthood, to explain away the nightmares of a child's imagination.

The baptisms during the early part of the service were always a cause to celebrate. Baptism gave each of the newborns a clean slate, wiping original sin from their nascent souls, and they would be held blameless for sin until confirmed into the age of right and wrong. Peddie at age ten was a couple years past the Catholic rite of passage into the fine world of sin and salvation. The priest could hardly wait for the boy's next visit to the confessional. Will the boy feel any remorse over putting his hero, his mentor, into harm's way? Being airlifted out, the dazed child was spared the sight of Ray being taken away in handcuffs. Hopefully the boy will remember his friend in happy repose soaking in the hot springs or floating in the cold river before the race to the death began. Every time Peddie listens to Sarah singing *Time To Say Goodbye,* the song will come to life because of its bittersweet connection to death.

Father Andy had prepared a little something for his homily, just a few inspiring thoughts as the service was long enough already. He decided to say what was in his heart. As he left his ceremonial chair, he saw that the Martinez family were holding hands in the exposed front pew. Peddie on one side, grasping his mother's hand, Amelia clutching her daughter's, Gabby clinging to Freddie's hand. The priest wondered if any of their palms were sweating.

> Brothers and sisters in Christ, welcome to this house of God, our Little Flower Catholic community. We are celebrating a great mystery and joyous occasion, the rising of Christ from His tomb, a body as any

body in death, rising from that corruption to a perfect state of grace. He was going home after a short stay away. But Jesus Christ fit a lot of living in his 33 years on this planet. Miracles galore, sermons on the mount and in the town squares too, walking on water and rising above the fray, challenging the orthodoxy of the day and getting crucified for His trouble. But to me the most eloquent testimony to Christ's transcendent humanity occurred in the Gospel According to John. Lazarus was dead and the women were wailing. They wanted him back, the good man he was. Martha's crying moved Jesus but Mary Magdalene's tears pushed him over the edge. The description in John is hauntingly simple—Jesus wept. Jesus wept, for He loved them all. And then after weeping He raised Lazarus to live once more.

Our great joy today centers on the resurrection in Jerusalem so many centuries ago, at the beginning of salvation time, when Christ died for our sins. Our happiness today is deepened by the local resurrection of our boy Peddie Martinez. Peddie is here with his family. Boy, don't be shy now. Stand up and take a bow!

Peddie looked at his mother first and she nodded. The boy shrugged to his feet and the crowd could almost hear the aw shucks. The faithful began to clap and most stood in ovation. The boy's shy posture faded fast as he raised his hands over his head, clenched and shook them, in a gesture perhaps copied from end zone celebrations. Amelia had to pull him down on the bench before he made a complete spectacle of himself. A wave of gentle laughter suffused the congregation.

It's certainly hard to keep a good boy down. Welcome back, Peddie, from your extended family here at Santó Thérèse. Though we can laugh about it now, what we went through was serious and heartbreaking. I know our good friend, Ray Yazzie, a valued member of our parish, helped you along the way, helped to bring you home safe.

Father Andy paused here, trying to regain his composure before he continued. He felt a surge of emotion and knew he was close to crying inconsolably. As far as the boy knew, all the people in the church knew, there was no cause for anything but tears of joy. The Franciscan was cursed with secret knowledge and it gave him no sense of power at all.

Pardon my hesitation and, yes, my tears. It's been a trying week. A short vacation may be in order. Peddie here didn't have much of an Easter break. Hey boy, how 'bout you and I play hooky tomorrow and go fishing?

Peddie laughed and yelled out, "Ray too! Ray too!" The priest quickly continued:

And the Pope will come along too. By the way, folks, if you are visiting today for the first time, I'm referring to my dog Pope, not the Holy Father, who's in Rome today doing his sacred duty. I'm getting way off track but no matter. You know, sometimes I wonder if Jesus really wept because He knew that it was His destiny to soon leave this vale of tears, where every feeling is possible. He was going home to a place of eternal happiness, everlasting peace, hearing an aimless melody perhaps, nary a false note but only one note after all, with no end in sight. Don't misunderstand me, my brothers and sisters, heaven is certainly far from a mixed blessing. I guess what I'm saying is cherish human life, every precious moment of it.

The priest knew he was probably sounding over the top as sweat broke out on his brow and upper lip. He looked over at the Martinez family clinging to each other for dear life.

I'll end with a personal observation but no final judgment. They say the sins of the father are visited upon the son. Let's watch that we act with love for each other, proper, precious love, for it is out of such love that Jesus wept.

Father Andy glanced again at Peddie and his family as he returned to his ceremonial seat. The priest settled into a sort of fugue state, determined by an act of will to put regret behind him, to fix things once and for all. But then he cursed, you bloody fool! It is God's will, not mine, be done. How easily we forget.

978-0-595-67711-5
0-595-67711-8

Printed in the United States
62202LVS00004B/22-27